Aditi Mediratta st... for the *India Today* daily, *Today*. ...
to fictionalized reel crime, her first release as an associate ...
was *Once Upon a Time in Mumbai*. This was followed by *The Dirty Picture*, *Once Upon a Time in Mumbai 2*, *Azhar* and *Baadshaho*. After graduating from Prague Film School in 2017, she wrote and directed short films like *Elevated* and *Kaboom*. She has also written the scripts for two experimental shorts, *Rajkumari Woke* and the much acclaimed *The Girl in the Pink Frock*. She has co-authored a book, *The Stranger in Me*, which was published by Om Books in 2019. She is working on a biopic on the life of an iconic film star from the 1970s.

Michaela Talwar is a trained journalist and multidisciplinary artist. She is the co-founder and creative director at Harkat Studios, a boutique arts studio and alternative performance space in Versova, Mumbai. As part of her work at Harkat, she is an arts enabler who has produced, curated and facilitated over 400 theatre shows, film festivals and exhibitions in various forms over the past six years. She also leads the creation of marketing video content for various film studios and OTT platforms like Netflix and Amazon where she produces viral videos, ads and title sequences, and sometimes designs posters for indie films. She has co-produced several short films, including *And Sometimes, She Loved Me Too, (Love)*, the *Ek Minute* series, and directed various short form content such as *Intellectual Masturbation* and *Rajkumari Woke*. In 2015 she published *Empowerment through Audiovisual Storytelling in Rural India*. A polyglot, she originally hails from Germany and has lived in many cities and countries, but nothing shaped her quite as much as Mumbai has.

NAKED
a novel

Aditi Mediratta
and
Michaela Talwar

Om Books International

First published in 2023 by

Om Books International

Corporate & Editorial Office
A-12, Sector 64, Noida 201 301
Uttar Pradesh, India
Phone: +91 120 477 4100
Email: editorial@ombooks.com
Website: www.ombooksinternational.com

Sales Office
107, Ansari Road, Darya Ganj,
New Delhi 110 002, India
Phone: +91 11 4000 9000
Email: sales@ombooks.com
Website: www.ombooks.com

ISBN: 978-81-960433-5-3

Printed in India

10 9 8 7 6 5 4 3 2 1

To the voices ... see, I was listening

Prologue: *Is this real or something you remember?*

Somewhere in Assam. The light falls gently, caressing, like only light at this time of the day can, the row of small houses on the almost darkened street. A child is playing alone. A man cycles slowly. Wherever it is that he is going, it can wait. He takes the time to enjoy the gentle breeze on his face. In the corner, a pair of lovers take advantage of the shadows to exchange a quick kiss.

It's either dawn or dusk. It's difficult to tell. And perhaps irrelevant.

A hut. Aita's. Made of bamboo and a roof of tin covered with dried palm leaves, a little front yard with a vegetable bed laid out with dried mud and some rose bushes, protected by a low fence. The wooden door with its faded pink colour is framed by a neem and tulsi tree on either side. Through a clean window, the soft rays of light enter, lighting up what they choose to and leaving the rest in the shadows.

Where the light decides to fall, there are splashes of colour: A big multicoloured dreamcatcher, faded yantras drawn with chalk on the blue wall, two bright cushions on a comfortable-looking armchair, the cupboard painted with bright motifs. A copper plate with bundles of herbs on it next to the old kitchen stove directs a small beam of light towards the charred wall where it finally loses its power, coming to rest in the black.

The light refuses to decide. It plays with the shadows and teases Chinky's face as she moves, making it by turns pretty or plain, ethereal or stodgy. Her expression remains consistently tragic. Chinky is sitting on the edge of a wooden bed with a brightly coloured bedsheet and looking into the old but still vibrant face of her grandmother, eighty-year-old Aita, as she lies on the bed ready to leave her human body.

The light is helpless, it cannot play games with Aita. Her face remains invariably bright, emitting a strange glow. She looks much more at peace than her granddaughter who is stroking her hand and staring intently at her face.

Aita winces as Chinky squeezes her hand too hard. Chinky apologizes and loosens the grip on the hand, just a little.

"Don't stare so hard at my face, child." Aita smiles. "It's going to change anyway."

Chinky's eyes widen a little as she stares down harder at Aita, perhaps expecting her face to start melting and rearranging until it matches the features and textures of her youth. "Not right now." Aita chuckles, as if reading her granddaughter's mind. "I meant in your memory. When my real face is gone from here and exists only in your mind. You will sometimes see more wrinkles, sometimes less. Sometimes you will make me more beautiful than I ever was. Memory is after all the least reliable way to remember something, isn't it?"

Despite promising herself that she would not cry, Chinky's eyes fill with tears: "You are not going to be here tomorrow, are you?"

Her grandmother shakes her head. "Not in this body, no."

Chinky runs her little hand over her grandmother's face, strokes her grey hair. "But you will still be watching over me."

It is more a question than a statement and Aita answers as gently as she can: "But why will I do that, child? I will no longer be your grandmother once I leave this body. No, I'm going to leave you to live your life and I'm going to live too in whatever form the afterlife takes."

"But what if I can't manage without you?"

"Then you will have to learn. If the universe wanted you to depend on me, it would have kept me in this body longer." Now she is the one holding Chinky's hand and pressing it gently. Staring up at her face, as if she is trying to imprint it in her mind as well. Aita's breathing is shallow, her body is tired, it wants her to stop, to leave; their relationship with each other after all these years is now tenacious at best, but Aita gathers her strength, bends it once again to her will, her granddaughter needs to hear this. "Alright, just once," she whispers to Chinky.

Chinky looks at her, questioningly.

"If at any time you are too overwhelmed by life, come and talk to me. Go to the place where you feel at peace the most and call me. You know how to. I will be there ... but just one time only."

Aita kisses Chinky's hand, gently reaches out and wipes away a tear, her finger lingering just a little on her granddaughter's cheek. "You are enough, child. Everything you need to live is in you. You don't need anyone else, not even me."

Aita's hand drops to her side. It refuses to move anymore. "Now go out," she tells Chinky, smiling wistfully, lovingly. "After eighty years together, this body and I need to be alone for our final parting." It takes effort but Aita lifts her arms to envelop Chinky in one last hug.

Chinky gets up reluctantly.

"I have liked being your grandmother. Maybe we will meet again." Then she shuts her eyes, there is no need to open them anymore.

Before leaving, Chinky picks up the amulet lying next to her grandmother on the bedside table. With one last look at Aita, Chinky leaves, shutting the door behind her.

Outside, the sky darkens, it starts raining heavily. Maybe night has fallen or maybe the new day has been obliterated by the darkness of the clouds. In their cover, Aita's soul leaves her body. The bamboo windchime hanging on her door sways and rings out a musical goodbye, the departing soul looks down once at a small figure huddled in the dark. Then it's gone.

It is raining heavily as a body washes up on the beach in Versova, Mumbai.

Unharmed, it is an oddly perfect effigy of youth nestled amongst the broken POP limbs of the recently drowned elephant god.

The sea makes no difference between her and these former deities; it pushes out all things that no longer have a soul.

It is Chinky, completely naked. Clutched in her hand is an amulet. Open and empty.

1

8.30 a.m.

Sub-inspector Gaikwad shakes his finger in agony. This is the second time in one day that he has pinched his skin in the buckle of his belt. Adding to the pain is the squawking of the news coming from the latest complete waste-of-money purchase his wife had insisted upon during the last Diwali sale: a 30,000-rupee, 50-inch, smart TV hanging on the formerly white, now off-white, wall.

The TV always annoys Gaikwad. It practically takes up the whole wall and makes the rest of the living room look even smaller and shabbier. The only saving grace is that it hides an ever-growing fungus stain. It also serves as a cue for his wife Meenakshi to nag about getting a new couch. As if the one they have had for the last ten years is no longer comfortable enough to watch the same old daily soaps now playing in a new frame. What a stupid thing to have blown his bonus on! (Not that he had had a choice. Meenakshi had already ordered it online – cash on delivery.)

And now, Meenakshi is barely focusing on the lunch she is supposed to be packing for him in the kitchen. Instead, she keeps rushing out to gawk at the news. Even though the anchor is just about to repeat the same thing for the sixth time: "In a sensational discovery, the naked body that washed up on Versova beach last evening has now been confirmed as Chinky's, the popular online love and relationship advisor, with two million followers on YouTube alone."

The visuals alternate between a blurred image of Chinky's dead body, lying horizontally on the beach, and an equally blurred image of Chinky's upright body, saying something that is muted – which gives the anchor a chance to repeat for the seventh time: "*In a sensational discovery…*"

The reason for the blurring? Both times, the bodies are equally naked.

"This is so sad," Meenakshi exclaims for the third time. The anchor has already gone into his eighth repetition. Gaikwad sighs, the smartness of this household is decreasing with every smart device added to its furnishing.

"What has the city come to? This is just terrible. That poor, poor girl and her poor family…" While Meenakshi sounds 'worried', her expression is positively gleeful. She is enjoying this early-morning tragedy as she slowly sips her tea.

"This is what the city has come to," grunts Gaikwad, holding out his hand for the tiffin. "Everybody is so addicted to drama that a young girl kills herself just so that you all can get your fix."

Meenakshi stops sipping her tea and purses her lips, as she usually does right before making her first move on the minefield of early-morning drama: "Are you saying it makes me happy when people die? Or are your investigative skills telling you that people are getting murdered because their killers are trying to boost TV ratings?"

"Has there been any official statement that she was murdered?" He can barely hide his consternation as he picks up his police cap from the counter. "She drowned. People drown. Especially when they get into the sea during the monsoon without knowing how to swim. Please don't go around spreading irresponsible gossip. You are a policeman's wife. Speak with care."

"Really?"

She gestures expansively towards the TV where two naked versions of Chinky are sharing a blurred split screen. "Tell me, Mr Policeman, do people normally take off all their clothes before accidentally drowning in the sea? Is this Goa or Mumbai? Did you see many naked people at Juhu beach last Sunday or were all the women properly covered up? Wow, if you need *me* to point that out, maybe the wrong person quit their job and became a policeman's 'wife.'"

Lately, she's been bringing this up again and again as if it was a real argument. Obviously, he was not going to be sitting at home while his wife went out to work. That was not how 'it works'.

Meenakshi was a traffic cop when their marriage had been arranged by their parents. For a while, he had allowed her to go out and do her duty, but when their son Rohit was born, it was kind of understood that the time to 'play cop' was over for her.

"You know we couldn't both be in the police." Then trying to placate her, he adds, "Would you have liked our child to grow up an orphan?"

Meenakshi does not react. She has heard this argument too many times already to waste energy reacting to it. Instead, she looks pointedly at his gut, spilling out over his trousers.

"How many criminals have you run after lately, shooting your gun at them? Bang, bang, oh no, he shot me!" She does a really bad imitation of somebody pulling ugly faces as she fires an imaginary gun. She gets hit, dramatically holding onto the kitchen slab, bending backwards, only to retrieve the rolling pin, wiggling it into Gaikwad's face. "Or maybe you are scared that you will get a heart attack from all the chai and pakoras you keep having during your 'breaks'?" She pushes the rolling pin against his chest, still not shifting her gaze off Gaikwad's midriff.

Gaikwad can't hold it in any longer. "I have to go." He releases his breath and his stomach with a loud hissing sound, edging towards the door, trying to end the argument he is not going to win. "I have some people to meet about this case."

"Meet people, interview them!" snorts Meenakshi. "Are you a policeman interrogating suspects or a call centre employer verifying credit cards? If I still had my job, I would hang them upside down and beat a confession out of them."

"You were a traffic cop..." Gaikwad reminds her. He is getting annoyed now, his day has not even started and he can already feel his acid reflux acting up again. "You were cutting challans for people. You don't know what the hell you are talking about. Just give me my damn tiffin and stop complaining about your 'career'. Your salary wasn't even that high. I already give you the same money for expenses, don't I?"

He burps a little as he finishes speaking. Fucking heartburn early morning.

"Who gives a damn about salaries?" she scoffs. "Do you know how much a traffic cop makes in bribes? Especially during festivals? Just from drunk drivers? You don't even make money on address verifications of passports anymore." She scoffs again.

A loud cheer rings out from outside, followed by bells and trumpets. Another idol is ready to leave a devotee's home to find a new one at the already polluted beach. Meenakshi takes it as a sign. "See! Even the gods agree with me." She leans out of the window. "Yes, yes, Bappa, take my prayers to heaven with you, ask them to give my husband some sense."

She folds her hands, the very picture of virtue and piety.

Gaikwad gives up. She has already delayed him, and with the festival traffic he couldn't afford to waste any more time. Anyway, it's not about the money. It's about who wears the pants around here and she is clearly wearing a sari, though tied in typical Maharashtrian pant-style, tucked between her legs.

"I will be home late today," he tells her firmly as he takes the tiffin from her hand and steps out. "Just keep the dinner warmed up for me and do some dusting today, there's too much dust on everything."

He starts his bike.

Through the window he can see the TV band in red, flashing, "…WANTS TO KNOW, WHO KILLED *CHINKY* AND WHY?"

2

8.40 p.m.

"Was that you, sir?"

Gaikwad isn't embarrassed by the sounds his body produces, so why does his subordinate have to mention it?

"Yes, Sahil. It's dinnertime and we are still sitting here." The anger acids are rising. "Thanks to you."

"Me, sir? But, sir, it can hardly be my fault that all these people have taken so much time. And that the tree fell on your bike, sir. I mean, you had parked it there."

His stomach responds with another factory-like growl. Gaikwad closes his eyes, the pain emanating from his upper right abdomen is becoming palpable. He clenches his teeth.

"Take a deep breath, sir."

"Damn it, Sahil, which mechanic will still be open once this is all over? I should send you out. Right now. Without a raincoat!"

"Sir, you are getting worked up. Please breathe."

"Obviously I am going to breathe. Everybody breathes, even an idiot or an infant. Really, you act like nobody knew how to live before the Internet started telling them all these 'secrets'. As if people used to hold their breaths for days before some new-age, self-styled Internet guru told them to breathe and made millions out of stating the obvious."

"Sir, it's protruding again."

"What!"

"Your vein … just like last time … when you hyperventilate, remember? Please calm down. Here," Sahil fishes something from his uniform pocket. "Have some candy."

"Don't be such a drama queen." Closing his eyes slowly and firmly, Gaikwad rubs his abdomen, moving his hand in grand strokes over his belly.

Sahil gives up.

"Sir, maybe if we show some evidence, things will proceed quicker?" he whispers.

"This hardly counts as evidence; not like we found the murder weapon," Gaikwad mutters, more to himself. "What is this beeping?"

Is hunger playing tricks with his hearing now? He puts his right index finger into his ear, the sound becomes less. Can't be internal, he concludes and opens his eyes.

"Sorry, sir, I have forgotten the code once again…"

With an apologetic clearing of his throat towards the blonde man sitting opposite, Gaikwad pushes his chair back, and Sahil to the side. He punches in the code for the lock of the little green-grey metal safe and takes out a plastic bag with only one item in it.

"Was it this necklace?" He slides the plastic bag across the interrogation table. Still leaning back against his chair, Vincent examines the silver amulet shining under the halogen light. "I don't know. I never saw it."

"But you just told us this whole story of how she picked it up from her grandmother's bedside table when she was dying!"

"Yeah. But I didn't see it happen, did I? How could I, man? I'm just telling you what she told me."

Vincent leans across the table, looking straight into Gaikwad's eyes. There is a glint of menace. Then, he lowers his gaze towards the shiny pieces of cold metal which may have once lain on Chinky's warm skin. He always loved when she wore silver. The chunky kind. It created the perfect contrast. To her slender limbs, her dusky complexion, the warmth of her body, the softness of her soul. Though he had never bought her any jewellery. He probably should have. It's a thing a man in his position in her life should do. But then, there are so many things one 'should' do. Should wear nice clothes, should be polite, should earn money, should buy stuff, should love each other, should shave clean – stay clean – should stay in touch, should respect law and order. He scuffs, his eyes meet Gaikwad's. *Seriously?* Though he could have probably stayed in touch. He did. In a way. She didn't. Well, she didn't know that he was there, that he always knew. Anyway. Once you start with it, it never ends.

"But yeah, it looks close to what I imagined."

Gaikwad sighs, hands the bag to Sahil. "Back to forensics. And bring chai. And samosas." Then looks at Vincent. "You want?"

Vincent waves his hand. No.

"Why, do you suppose," asks Gaikwad, "was she holding on to this amulet?"

"Why do people hold on to things? Fear of losing them obviously." Vincent's eyes darken as he says these words, his lips untwist a little from their perpetual smirk, for a second he almost looks vulnerable.

Gaikwad stares at Vincent's face wondering if he has found a chink in his 'tough guy' armour. But Vincent must have seen

Gaikwad shift in his seat. The lips curl back in position, the eyes as cold and inscrutable as before.

"And the sea can be rough, no, during the monsoons? Makes sense to hold onto things when you step in. Look what happened to her clothes."

"Are you trying to be funny, Mr Vincent?"

"Please, I assure you, the last thing I am is 'funny'." Vincent looks at Sahil. "Why do you keep nodding your head when I speak, like I'm saying something really profound and intelligent."

Sahil looks flustered, he stops mid-nod. He looks at Gaikwad for directions. Vincent notices.

"Sahil, will you get the samosas or would you like me to get up from my chair and get them myself?"

"No, sir, sorry, sir. I'm getting them right away, sir." He looks towards Vincent. "I also nod a lot when Gaikwad sir is speaking, it doesn't mean he is saying something profound, it is just respect."

Gaikwad throws a look at Sahil, the constable scurries away from there.

"I think I hurt his feelings, hope that's not going to make me suspect number one and solve your case for you?" Vincent leans back and looks defiantly at Gaikwad. The old wooden office chair creaks.

Gaikwad looks at the clock. This one looks like he is going to be a hard nut to crack.

Not like the two before him. They had been much more cooperative and they had really liked to talk. Especially the first one. The flatmate, Miss Iti, who wasn't the flatmate anymore. Well, technically Miss Iti and Mr Abhishek had both been flatmates and technically neither was anymore, since Chinky's body is lying in the morgue now *with a very different set of 'flatmates'.*

Gaikwad mentally checks himself, what is this distasteful brand of humour he is amusing himself with? He must be really tired or maybe it's the effect of the man sitting in front of him. He looks like he would enjoy cracking jokes about dead people while attending their funeral.

Yes, it had certainly been the easiest with Miss Iti. His patience was the only thing that had been tested. How nice it would be if impatience was the only problem for him right now.

A beep. Meenakshi has sent a picture, but it won't load. He looks again at the wall clock. Ten a.m. seems so far away...

3

9.25 a.m.

Iti looks at her watch, distracted momentarily by the way it catches the light and sparkles, the pinks and blues winking then disappearing again. She almost smiles, it's so pretty — especially in the light of her squalid surroundings. She pictures herself, elegant in a discreet, white, long summer dress. Perched delicately on the edge of the wooden chair, with its vintage patina peeling off, her little beige shoe tapping the floor, signalling impatience. She wonders idly if the police personnel scurrying around her are aware that her rather plain-looking shoe actually cost more than their entire month's salary. She looks at it again, wondering why she bought it. Why blow up so much money on something so boring? She doesn't like it anymore, so ugly and brown, just like the chair she is sitting on, just like the tea they have placed in front of her, just like the uniforms everybody is wearing. What monochrome reality is she trapped in?

Fighting off a familiar sinking feeling in her stomach, she looks again at her watch. But even the light outside has diffused – it is not enough to make the watch sparkle again. Iti sighs loudly, as if trying to expel the dark clouds gathering in her mind and outside.

Where has all the colour gone? Unbidden, a picture comes to her mind. A beautiful girl with black hair and pink lips. Big, red earrings dangling about her pale, almost white face. The whole effect, iridescent, almost ethereal.

A wave of sadness engulfs Iti even as the image fills her with warmth and dispels the heaviness in her stomach. *Chinky*, breathes Iti, silently, closing her eyes and concentrating on Chinky's face. She feels herself relaxing.

A soft cough and Chinky vanishes. Iti sits up straight, eyes wide open. There is a big brown belly standing in front of her. Iti blinks, trying to find some colour highlight to focus on. There is none, even the air around the man to whom the belly belongs is as brown as muddy sludge.

"Iti Ma'am?" He holds out a hand and introduces himself. "Sub-inspector Gaikwad." Not even his name is interesting. Iti looks discreetly, yet pointedly at her watch.

He is late. She sees Gaikwad's face twist into a slight grimace. "Sorry, for the delay … traffic…"

Of course, traffic, the blandest and most predictable excuse in Mumbai.

Gaikwad looks at her untouched tea as he walks across the desk and seats himself opposite her.

"Would you prefer green tea? I have some. Part of the new health regime for the police." He opens his drawer and holds out a box for her inspection.

Iti nods gratefully, she wouldn't mind looking at a little bit of green. Relieved at having her approval, Gaikwad quickly asks for a cup of hot water from the boy in a dhaba waiter's uniform standing outside the office door like a guard.

"What about you?"

"Not first thing at the station. Maybe later." He orders a normal chai for himself.

A moment of awkward silence, broken abruptly and clumsily by Gaikwad. He grunts trying to wiggle open the wooden drawer underneath the desk. The monsoon moisture shrinks the wood and makes doors and drawers a pain to open. Even his wooden chair seems to have become smaller. His hips are practically stuck to the armrests. That's why, once he sits, he tries not to move. Which by the afternoon usually causes his ass to hurt. He looks longingly at the wedge yoga pillow kept on the windowsill ... But, no time to get up now, he needs to get going. He will ask Sahil to hand it to him later ... Finally, the drawer gives in. He takes out a brown paper folder. It lands with a loud thud between Gaikwad and Iti, making the table shake on its uneven legs. He opens the file, pulls out a picture, and shoves it in front of Iti's face: "Is that you with the deceased?"

Iti winces, the word – *deceased* – and the picture, both seem equally offensive. For a moment, she ignores Chinky and looks at herself. It must have been taken a decade ago ... She should really make her Facebook albums private. Her face is so round, her cheeks so chubby – what was it that Surat called them? Gulab Jamun ... Too much gulabi in this photograph, that is for sure. What is she even wearing? She lets out an audible sigh, feeling sorry for the girl who used to think that a pink sleeveless kurta worn over capri pants was the height of fashion and that anything hot pink was sexy.

"It's an old picture," she clarifies.

"But it's you, right?"

Iti shrugs. "Is it really me or just a girl on the way to becoming me?" She almost smiles – this was such a Chinky-like thing to say.

Gaikwad barges into the little moment Iti is having with herself.

"Can you identify yourself as the person with the deceased?"

Iti looks at Chinky's picture. Is it really Chinky or just a girl on her way to becoming 'the deceased'? "It's Chinky," she tells Gaikwad, "not 'the deceased', not yet."

Gaikwad is about to say something but changes his mind. "How did you know the … Chinky Madam?"

A smile flits on Iti's face. "Who says I knew Chinky?"

Gaikwad looks confused. "Isn't that you with her in the picture?"

Does standing next to a person mean that you know them?

"Thank you." Iti's hot water has arrived. Silently, Gaikwad hands her a teabag. Iti dips it in the water, watching it turn golden. The tightness in her chest has loosened, just a little. She looks at Gaikwad. He is staring at her, waiting for her to finish.

She smiles at him. "I'm sorry. I should probably answer the question you think you have asked? How was I acquainted with Chinky? Where did I meet her, etc.?"

Gaikwad nods.

"She was my flatmate. My first friend in Mumbai. The first thing I loved about the city and the reason I knew right away that I was never going to leave."

"So, you are not from Mumbai?"

"I was not born here, no. That happened in Agra."

"Is that where you grew up?"

"Hardly at all. That's where I was raised. But I only grew up in Mumbai. In Agra, I was still a child…"

Iti's thoughts trail off as images of Agra flash through her mind – crowded, narrow, dusty, and colourful. She lets herself linger, feeling almost homesick.

Gaikwad clears his throat but nothing yanks her back to the beige reality of the interrogation room. No, Agra is not home. Home is Mumbai. *Even with Chinky gone?*

"How did you come to be in Mumbai, from Agra?"

A little more focused, Iti lets her mind slip down the narrow alleys and bazaars of Agra to where Surat is. Where she is, or at least some version of her, that is holding her breath as Surat bends down and kisses her on the lips. The first kiss is quick and furtive. Her heart is beating so fast, not so much from the excitement of the kiss but more from the fear of being caught. Surat had agreed to join her for some window shopping in the bazaar, her favourite pastime, and his too. Although for different reasons – in the crowdedness of the market an occasional touch, a brush of the hand, a protective arm around her back, if even for a second, goes unobserved. Between the chaos and heat of chikankari shops and jalebiwalas, they had found themselves in a cool shaded alley, usually occupied by shopkeepers stepping out for a cigarette. The kiss is ok. It's not unpleasant. But it doesn't really inspire her to risk another one, out here in the open. Any moment one of her father's former acquaintances could sneak up on them, or worse, tell Surat's parents. Surat looks disappointed as she pulls back, but he doesn't stop her either. That annoys her. Why is he being careful? Aren't guys supposed to not be able to use their heads once the blood has rushed to other places? At least that's what it says in all the books she has read.

"Ma'am?"

Gaikwad's voice snaps her out of her reverie but that feeling of annoyance with Surat time-travels and comes back with her.

Where does he get off blaming it all on her when, clearly, he started it?

"Sorry, what did you ask me?"

"I asked how you came to be in Mumbai and meet Chinky Madam?"

"Yes, I was going to tell you that. Was hunting for the right memory. Sorry I went back a little far. Happens, doesn't it, when you go back to a place you haven't been to for a while? The thing you have gone to look for is right there, but you get distracted by all the other things. Time just sort of jumbles everything together, doesn't it?"

She can see that because she is *'ladies'*, Gaikwad is keeping his annoyance in check.

His phone beeps. It's Meenakshi. *'I hope you remember what day it is today…'* He doesn't. He checks his calendar. The phone beeps again. It's a ring emoji.

"Ma'am, I have other people to meet about this case, so if you could…" Gaikwad's tea arrives. He doesn't even wait for it to be set down. He grabs it directly from the server's hand and takes a big, grateful sip. He burns his tongue. This day is littered with small pains. *All that's missing is a paper cut.* He takes another sip, just to spite his luck. Aah, that's better. Nothing like a cup of hot tea to make the day better.

Iti can feel him relaxing. He is not as tense as he was a few seconds earlier. Perhaps he wouldn't mind a little story if she keeps it short?

"My father used to own a small ladies boutique in Agra. He was an excellent tailor, at least for Agra. I studied fashion design in a private college, so I could work with him after graduation. But he died while I was still in college. My mom sold off the boutique so she could pay my fee and I could complete my graduation, but I would no longer have a place to work in after graduation."

Iti shrugs. "Isn't this kind of like that short story we read in school, 'The Gift of the Magi'? I don't remember it exactly, but wasn't there some selling of things and somebody buying a hat for somebody who no longer had a ... actually, I don't remember what she no longer had but she didn't need a hat for it anymore. Or maybe it was a pin."

Gaikwad looks up at her. His small glass of cutting chai is almost half empty.

Iti quickly stops digressing.

"I got a job after college. A small shop run by a husband and wife who thought they were designers. I didn't much like working for them. The hours were long, I was just cutting patterns, not mine, theirs. They used to mark them out with chalk and I had to cut, exactly. There was no creativity involved, I was so bored. So, when Surat asked me to marry him, I accepted. My mother was happy, she always liked Surat. She never said anything but I know she knew that we were not 'just friends'. Well, he was my fiancé now and I guess she was relieved. She could openly acknowledge our relationship. And then out of nowhere, a film came for a shoot in Agra. It was so exciting. That's all we talked about for days. We were all taking detours on our way to work, so we could just get a glimpse of real shooting. We just saw some people running around or the backs of the crowds who were more determined and had got there before us and were now standing there, completely still and silent, like a wall. Not letting anybody else see what they were looking at. Maybe they got to see some actors. I don't know. They sure tried. Funny thing, the actors were not even famous and they never really got to be either. In fact, I saw the lead actress at a coffee shop just last week and I spent more time checking out her handbag than her face. She had one of those fake LVs, they are very popular all over Lokhandwala, certainly more popular than she is nowadays."

Iti snorts, but Gaikwad is looking far from amused. She gets back to her story.

"But whatever, this was Agra and they were actors and we wanted to see them. And then I found out, they were looking for a costume assistant, just for two days, over the weekend. So, I applied. I just wanted to break through that wall of people and get in the middle of the action. Maybe get an autograph. But I never did. There was no shooting those two days, just a mad and frantic hunt for local costumes..."

2009

Iti can see it now. It is almost like watching a film. In her head, a wide shot of a busy Agra road, a small scooter with two figures is zipping through the traffic jam.

She looks close to how she looked in the picture that she has just been so dismissive about. Capris and sleeveless, one anklet (it gives her a certain edge, doesn't it?), her dupatta wrapped like a Parisian scarf, fluttering in the face of the person sitting behind her. The assistant director is holding on for dear life. What was his name? She cannot remember. Call him Vineet? That seems like a forgettable name. So many ADs are called Vineet.

"Do you think you could maybe slow down a little?" Vineet exclaims as Iti hits another pothole and he bounces from his seat.

"This is slow, I have to go slow because I forgot my licence at home. Ha ha, you should see me when I have my licence, then we can really get around fast."

Vineet prays silently that she loses her licence.

"Get out of the way!" she yells at a man.

Vineet recites the Hanuman Chalisa feverously, ready to die with his eyes closed.

He still has them closed when Iti's scooty has come to a halt outside a bustling clothes market. "We can't take the scooter inside, it's too crowded," Iti apologizes.

Vineet is happy to assure her that it is no problem at all. He gets off, his legs still feeling a little bit wobbly as Iti takes him around the market.

Dotting the street on both sides are shops selling all kinds of clothes, from kurtas to denim, from chikankari to dresses. Iti navigates it expertly, politely turning down the hawkers calling out to them urging them to visit their shop.

"Not today bhaiya, sorry."

She knows exactly where to go for whatever he needs.

"You are good at this." Vineet is impressed.

"Of course, I grew up in Agra. I know it like the back of my hand. Especially the best places to find clothes. I have studied fashion design, too, you know. I was seventh in my class." She looks up at him, waiting for him to congratulate her. "There were fifty students," she adds when he fails to.

Vineet is busy rummaging through a pile of clothes. He is picking them out and putting them on two separate piles. Over one pile, he continuously mutters, "NG."

"What's NG? Is that the name of the heroine?"

"No, it means 'no good.'" He picks up a sheer black top with a deep neckline.

"This one looks good, but too daring for somebody from Agra, you think?"

Iti touches it, a little annoyed at the Agra remark.

"It's here in a shop in Agra, isn't it? So obviously somebody is wearing it."

"Would you wear it?"

Iti takes the top from him and slips it on over her head. "Here."

It looks a little silly on top of her kurta.

Vineet grins at her. "Is that how you would style it?"

Iti looks at herself in the mirror. "Just put a small lining inside, it wouldn't be so transparent. I can do that for you."

"Ok, sold and maybe after the shoot, I can give it to you as thanks. Since we are not paying you anyway."

Iti looks thoughtful. "Then give me something the heroine wears for a longer time, so people can just look at me and tell I'm wearing something from the film. That would be cool."

Vineet laughs.

"You know you should come to Mumbai. Work there in films, I think you would be great at it."

"Really, you think so?"

"Absolutely."

"Wow, that's a great idea. And so nice of you. Thanks."

She smiles brightly at him.

Vineet gets a call. He excuses himself as Iti continues rummaging through the clothes, her eyes dreamy, a smile playing on her lips.

Vineet is agitated by the time he is done with the call. "Listen, I have to leave. Emergency on set. You finish shopping. Get five sets of clothes for daywear, two for college. Take this top. A couple of dresses and oh, something for yourself." He hands her a wad of cash. "Will this cover it?"

It looks like a lot of money. "Easily."

"Great. Just get these to the set and give them to Pankaj, he will meet you near the jalebiwala."

He gives her a quick side hug and rushes out of there.

Iti never sees him again.

But that seed he has planted in her head grows into a giant tree really fast and takes up all the space in her mind until every other thought and version of her life is pushed out. No other plan makes any sense. She must go to Mumbai. Agra is not big enough for her.

"Since when is Mumbai your dream? You have never even talked about visiting it. Not once. Can you even find it on a map? Tell me, Surat, I am just her mother, maybe she doesn't tell me everything. But she is stuck on the phone all day with you, so you must know. Have you ever heard about this great Mumbai dream of hers?"

Surat takes a step back as Iti and her mother both stare at him. Until now he was busy observing, preparing chai for the three of them, almost touching his nose to the brim of the pot where tulsi and cinnamon were increasingly darkening the ginger-infused water.

He looks at Iti like a schoolboy who got caught without his homework, clueless about what he was supposed to say. Well, Iti had actually told him exactly what to say, word for word and he had agreed. He might have pointed out that despite having known Iti for almost all his life, he had never heard of this 'lifelong' dream of hers until 5 p.m. yesterday, but it didn't matter what he remembered or not from the hundreds – probably thousands – of conversations that they have had over the years. His job was to be by her side, no matter what. She would do the same, naturally. So why is he now so dumbstruck? Almost as if he is rooting for her mother to win this argument?

Surat's silence goes on too long for Iti's taste – he has either forgotten the 'script' or is about to go off it and it's time for her to interject and improvise. "Do you just want me to be your wife and never have any ambition of my own? Is that what you want, too? That I stay in Agra and sacrifice all that I have worked so hard for?"

"You worked on that film for two days and they did not even pay you." Iti's mother dares to voice what Surat would feel too disloyal to even think.

Surat looks gratefully at Iti's mother, a fact that escapes neither of the women. Well, he may agree with her mother, but he does not have the security of having given birth to Iti – she can leave him. And he knows that.

"It's not about how long you have had the dream; it's how much it means to you. And it's not just about the money. That junior director told me that I have real talent and I must come to Mumbai and work with him. Tell her, Surat. Tell her, you are my fiancé and you want me to go and I must listen to you since we are engaged now…"

Iti looks triumphantly at her mother who snorts. "Please, we both know how much you listen to Surat."

9.45 a.m.

"Ma'am, could you please just come to Mumbai now and tell me how you met Chinky?"

Iti sighs; clearly Gaikwad never tried to be an actor and settled for being a cop. He has no sense of storytelling and certainly none for drama. Chinky would not have approved of him being the one to hear her story and investigate the events that led up to her death. Or maybe she would have. It'll help him grow. She decides to help him.

"I could but I don't think that is the only question you have for me and to answer the ones that come later, I need to do this thing which is called setting up. If you don't understand what happens now, you will be confused about what happens later."

Gaikwad's only response to that is a loud clearing of his throat and an expression signalling his fast-eroding patience.

Iti concedes defeat – for now. "Ok, so long story short, Surat convinced my mother to let me come to Mumbai."

Iti sighs. "You know my mother is so progressive, she never even stopped me from having a boyfriend. Any restrictions I might have had growing up were more to do with my safety than what society would say. So even though I played it like that, I have to say I was inwardly a little offended that it took my boyfriend's approval, instead of my desire, to convince her that I could move to Mumbai. I didn't question it at that time of course, I was getting my way after all. But it bothered me for years, till I finally asked her. She said it was because she wanted to be sure Surat would not blame 'her' later. Well, I guess she knew me better than I knew myself."

She takes a sip from her green tea.

"How did I feel about leaving him? I know you haven't asked but I just feel like the question kind of asks itself at this point. But don't worry, the answer is really short. I have no memory of any feeling except a sense of huge anticipation and excitement from the second I landed in Mumbai."

"Where is Surat now?"

Iti stares at Gaikwad, looking a little gratified.

"Very nice of you to want to know. But don't worry, we are not done with him. He comes again in the story. But you have to wait for that part."

Gaikwad gestures impatiently.

"What was his connection with Chinky? Why are you talking so much about him? Do you suspect that he and Chinky had something…"

Iti looks at Gaikwad, her face a study of confusion and amazement. And then she laughs, "I underestimated you, you do have an imagination, but you are obsessing over your investigation. Forget for a second that Chinky is dead and you are here to find her 'killer'. I am telling you a story and like in a story there are several characters but not all of them are guilty."

"Madam, are you saying you are guilty?"

Iti's eyes cloud over but she shakes her head and manages to smile, a little weakly, at Gaikwad. "Of which crime? There were so many."

Finally, Gaikwad can feel the tingling in his belly! Is she about to talk herself into a prison cell, he has heard of such garrulous criminals whose lawyers are paid huge sums of money just to get them to shut up. In fact in the US they even have the police tell them to keep quiet. What an asinine thing to do; is it your job to catch the guilty or caution them about their 'loose lip'. Fortunately, the police are more evolved and realistic about these things in India. He is certainly not going to stop her from confessing to the murder of Chinky. He needs it on record. If he gets her to confess even more crimes, he might be able to put it in as additional documentation for his promotion!

He tries to calm himself, taking a small breath and putting on a grave look says, "The 'one' that resulted in the victim's death."

"What makes you think there was just one? And what makes you assume her death was a crime? But if you listen to me, I will name everybody who played a part in whatever led to her death and you can decide who is guilty."

Gaikwad is silent for a second, then he nods. "Ok, go on." This is going in the right direction. For sure this jabber mouth of a woman will present a few more crimes to him which he can add to his record.

Iti takes a deep breath. "Where was I? Oh yes, at Chhatrapati Shivaji Terminus, on my way to see Chinky for the first time, though of course, I had no idea at that point that she even existed. Strange how the events that shape your story the most sometimes just start as a side story, nothing to do with the life you have planned for yourself. But what can you do? Sometimes the story just writes itself and all you can do is go along..."

2009

Iti's expression is blissful as she steps out of Victoria Terminal. The platform is as crowded, dirty and full of people as any platform in Agra, but something still feels different, maybe it's the sense of urgency and purpose with which everybody is moving. Or maybe that's just how she remembers it in retrospect, after spending all these years hearing about the great Mumbai spirit. Maybe that's coloured her memories of what was perhaps a completely uneventful arrival and perhaps a completely different station. Or maybe she was the one with the sense of urgency and purpose.

She's here, she is finally here, now what?

Iti pulls out her phone and makes the obligatory call to her mother to tell her that yes, she has reached safely, yes this is Mumbai only, no she did not get down at the wrong station, yes, she is sure...

"Ok, bye. I have to call Vineet. Of course he is expecting me. Like I have told you a hundred times, he has promised he will arrange everything as soon as I reach. Tell Surat I'll call him up at night."

Iti hangs up before her mother makes up questions faster than she can make up lies.

Truth be told, Vineet had not answered her calls or replied to the excited text she had sent to him, informing him that she had taken his advice and was coming to Mumbai next week. Of course she could have called him again, but his silence had been strange. Maybe he was locked inside a charged-up set for days on end without a ray of sunlight and too busy with helping create the next *Filmfare* award winner to find a plug point for his phone. The butterflies in Iti's belly flutter fiercely and affirmatively at the thought of this kind of life. But then, to find him she would have to visit all the film studios of the city, one by one … She has done her research – there's Mehboob with its little courtyard, and of course the legendary YRF, Filmistan and Film City which is hidden in an ancient, rumoured to be haunted, forest right in the middle of Mumbai. But how would she get to all these places? And there must be hundreds of rooms in each studio… The task seems a bit daunting.

Thankfully, this time Vineet answers on the fifth ring. Iti exhales in relief, barely able to contain her excitement: "Heyyyy, Vineet it's me, Iti from Agra. I'm finally here. Where should I come?"

Five hours later, Iti finds herself complaining to Saif the broker who is taking her to a PG in Versova. Iti is so upset, she is barely noticing the lane they are walking down. If she had been looking, she would have appreciated that they have already passed two cafes, one STD booth, a cybercafe and a dry-cleaning shop, all less than a 100 metres apart.

"Can you believe this man? He told me to come to Mumbai. Practically assured me that I had a job waiting and now when I call, he says, 'Iti who?' What does he mean by 'Iti who?' We just met, not even a month ago. And Iti is not that common a name. It's not like Pooja or Priyanka. I don't even know any other Iti besides me and I'm sure he doesn't either. So obviously if it's Iti, it is Iti *me*. What a jerk."

She exhales loudly. Saif the broker grunts, he is not even pretending to listen to her. But he looks up when she stops ranting and suddenly smiles at him. Iti has a nice smile. Sometimes it takes people by surprise and makes them smile back.

"Well, at least he gave me your number. I really did not want to stay in a hotel for the night. I mean I would have if it had come to it but I have never stayed alone in a hotel before. Is it safe in Mumbai for a girl to stay alone in a hotel?"

"Depends what hotel."

They have arrived at their destination. An apartment building on the 'wrong side' of J.P. Road. Saif has a quick word with the guard as Iti finally looks up and takes stock of her surroundings.

"This is a really shabby-looking building. Why can't we see something on the other side of the road? That's where the ocean is. What's the use of living so close to the sea but keep a road in-between?"

"Do you have a husband?"

"No."

"Everything I have for bachelors is on this side."

Iti sighs, but she lets Saif take her inside the apartment complex, across a lawn that is more dust than grass, to the most dilapidated wing in the entire building, finally up a dingy staircase. In her mind she is already wondering if she should maybe have a quick wedding with Surat so they could get a house across the street. With a sea view. Why would she live in a city with an ocean if not to see, smell, hear and feel it?

She is from Agra, she is used to dirty paan-stained stairwells, but this abnormally narrow staircase feels decidedly claustrophobic. She has to walk three steps behind Saif to not have his behind poke right into her face. And if someone would walk down the staircase at the same time, they would have a solid standoff. Who would have to trace their steps back onto the landing? Are there any rules of courtesy? Saif stops abruptly. She has to turn her face and take a step back to the right to avoid touching the grimy wall. Under his armpit, Iti can see the door to the apartment – her new home?

A plump woman in a battered nightgown answers the doorbell. Iti peeks inside and gets a glimpse of two plush-looking purple sofas with fluffy velvet cushions on them and a wall that looks newly whitewashed. That is not too bad. She smiles at the woman. The woman doesn't smile back, she doesn't even say hello, just steps aside and lets Iti come in. Saif waits outside.

That doesn't sit too well with Iti. What's going on? What if this is some kind of kidnapping racket? She checks the landlady's hands for chloroformed hankies. The hands are empty, but what about the pockets? The nightie has two. She darts one more look in Saif's direction.

"Why isn't he coming in?"

"It's a girl's PG. It's not allowed," says the woman in a monotone.

"Not allowed by whom?"

"By me."

Iti looks at the stony face. The mouth set in a thin line is more used to issuing edicts and instructions than engaging in reasonable debates or conversations. It would be pointless to argue for Saif to come with her.

"You stay right here!" Iti instructs him as she follows the landlady inside.

The landlady slams the door shut on his face.

The living room looks even more expensive from the inside. The wall above the sofa is surfaced with leather tiles with little mirrors stuck where the tiles meet. And the grilled windows are half-covered by purple silk curtains. The living-room table looks like it's made of marble, the glass top supported by four gold-coloured swans. On the wall opposite the sofa, a giant LCD screen is playing a TV serial in such saturated colours that Iti almost feels the urge to get inside the TV and tell the actress to please change into a sari that matches the decor of the room. How does someone living in *this* building afford all of this? Is she pretending to be poor on the outside to hide nefarious illegal activity? Do the neighbours know what's going on inside this house? Are they all in on it? What has she got herself into?

"I just sent my mother your address," says Iti pointedly as she follows the landlady out of the living room, to a narrow passage with a white door at the end. "She knows I am here, with you."

"Parents have to inform at least a month in advance before visiting." That monotonous voice betrays no emotion at all.

Is that a good sign? Iti is not sure. The landlady pushes open the dirty white door to reveal a shabby room.

Iti looks around. Whatever money this woman is making, it clearly finished by the time she was done with decorating the living room.

This room doesn't look like it has seen a new coat of paint in at least a decade. In fact the bleached-out pink wall paint is coming off in several places. Is that fungus in one of the corners? Actually, following it with her eyes, it seems to not only be in the corner but spreading across the wall and ceiling, the colour gradient from mossy green to pastel green to grey and finally fading just above the very doorway in which Iti is standing, her neck twisted upwards. The wooden patina is chipping off the door. She looks back straight to assess the room. The grills outside the window are completely rusted, though somebody has made the effort to put up a tattered string of prayer flags like they have in the Himalayas.

How old is this room? It looks older than the rest of the building. Hell it looks older than her.

The landlady is rattling off a list of instructions.

"No lights on after ten. No boyfriends coming into the building. No cooking in my kitchen. Also no non-veg eating allowed from outside. No showering for more than five minutes."

Iti interrupts her, "You want me to pay 3,500 for just *this* room? It's smaller and uglier than my toilet at home."

"No, not for the room. Just for this bed. There are two other girls staying here. And 3,500 was last year, the new rate this year is 4,500."

Iti now notices a slender, fair girl with big red hoop earrings and bright pink lipstick. Chinky is sitting on top of one of the beds. Meditating.

She stares at her. Just then, Chinky opens her eyes and looks at Iti.

"I'm glad you will be living here with us. I like your face, it's interesting."

Iti blushes, suddenly shy. "Thank you. You are very beautiful too."

Chinky doesn't shift her gaze at all.

"I didn't say beautiful, I said interesting. I like your energy."

She smiles at Iti. The smile that starts at her mouth, crossing her apple cheeks until her eyes sparkle and her whole face lights up. Suddenly the room doesn't seem so shabby anymore. Its ugliness becomes essential to offset Chinky's perfectly ethereal beauty. A sliver of light comes in through the window and burns the image into Iti's mind. Everything about this moment seems visually perfect. She is mesmerized.

The landlady clears her throat.

"So are you taking it or not? I don't have all day."

Iti blinks. The light dims a little, but she is already sold.

"I'll take it, but for 4,500 I want you to include food as well."

The landlady frowns. She takes a moment. Then she nods. "Just one time. No breakfast and no dinner, only lunch, one vegetable and two rotis, that's it."

"Add daal and salad."

"Ok, but no pickle."

"Except on Sundays."

The landlady shrugs a grudging ok.

Chinky smiles approvingly at Iti. It's a nice smile, not as magical as before. But that's ok. Sometimes magic just needs to happen once to do its work, that's enough.

4

Iti is given a tiny, single bed in the corner of the room. Chinky seems to have the big bed. Well, it's fair, reasons Iti, mentally comparing the two beds. Though hers is not even half of the other one and Chinky is so tiny... But no, she will not quibble. It's fair. Chinky was here first.

"That's Valarie." Iti does not understand. She follows to where Chinky is pointing. A slightly chubby girl with a pretty face and close-cropped curls has entered. She is holding a big bag and flings it onto Chinky's bed, before turning around to look at Iti, for barely a second.

"Do you have a lot of stuff?"

"What?"

"I have a lot of stuff and I have been using 'your' side of the cupboard, because those exploitative cheapskates have just one cupboard for three people." She leans against the said steel cupboard. "How much of it are you going to need back?"

Iti points towards her luggage, it's just one bag. But before she can say anything, Chinky has slid smoothly off the bed and appeared at her side. "She is going to need all of it, Valarie."

"She barely has anything. It's not even going to fill up half the space."

"Empty spaces are more important than full ones. That's what we use for manifesting."

Valarie rolls her eyes. "Here we go again, but please tell me, Great Mistress of Hoodoo, how am I supposed to manifest anything if I no longer have space for all my things?"

"You already manifested this situation, so you could get rid of what you don't need."

"Ugh, you make up answers for everything." Valarie turns the heavy handle down. It's the kind of cupboard where Iti's grandmother would keep her expensive saris and jewellery. Indestructible — neither fungus nor moths can penetrate it; she was told it's even fireproof! But instead of neatly stacked Benarasi and a safe full of wedding jewellery, this cupboard is filled with oversized t-shirts piled on top of one another in no discernible order. Valarie pulls them all out and throws them on the floor. Having finished making the floor look exactly like the inside of the cupboard did one minute ago, she turns theatrically towards Iti. "All yours, madam. Hope you enjoy your empty space."

Iti looks pointedly towards the pile of things on the floor. "Is that 'your' side of the floor?"

Valarie gapes at her. Iti smiles, to take the sting out of her words. It seems to work. Valarie laughs. "Not as dumb as she looks. Leave it there. I'll go through it later and pick out what I need and maybe the rest will magically vanish."

She fishes out a towel from the pile on the floor and disappears into the bathroom.

"Valarie, this is no time to take a bath," the landlady yells from somewhere in the house.

"It is my first and last one this week, so I have a lot of water credit," Valarie yells back. She starts singing loudly, confidently and very much out of tune.

Chinky smiles at Iti. "Do you want me to help you with your unpacking?"

Iti nods gratefully, then asks, "What is manifesting?"

"Everything that happens," answers Chinky.

Later, with all her clothes neatly folded and stacked up on her side of the cupboard (including, on the landlady insisting, her toothbrush and toothpaste), Iti brings out her most prized possession: her set of romantic novels. They belonged to her maasi and were appropriated by her over time. She places each one of them with utmost care on the top shelf of the cupboard.

Valarie, who has finally come out of her shower, after spending more than the allotted five minutes, is perched on the bed, with her headphones on her head, singing softly to herself. Still out of tune.

From the corner of her eye she is watching Iti; her pile of things still on the floor.

Chinky picks up one of Iti's books, flips open a random page and starts to read aloud: "*She trembled at his touch* ... what is this about?"

Iti resists the urge to snatch the book back from Chinky. Instead, she only darts a worried, possessive look as Chinky is flipping through.

"It's a romance novel. They are the best ones. This one belonged to my maasi. It's about this really rich, handsome but arrogant guy and this simple and sweet, very beautiful girl who falls in love with him and..."

"And they live happily ever after," interrupts Chinky. "Strange I didn't think you were the type who liked such predictable endings." She closes the book with a loud 'clap'. "But tell me, do you have a man who makes you tremble at his touch?"

Iti looks up, surprised at the rather personal question, but also a little flattered to already be sharing such an intimate conversation with Chinky. "Well, I have a boyfriend. His name is Surat. He's very nice. He's my best friend. In fact he only convinced my mother to let me come to Mumbai ... he always supports me in everything."

Iti's phone pings. She looks at it and squeals in delight.

"Ouf, he has such a long life. It's my Surat. He just topped up the balance in my phone so I can talk to him at night. He is so sweet."

Chinky looks at the half-naked couple frozen in a water-coloured embrace in her lap. She gives the book back to Iti.

"Do you think the people who write these stories ever wish they could end them differently?"

"You mean not have a happy ending? What would be the point then?"

"To be surprised."

Before Iti can respond, Chinky speaks again.

"I liked how you bargained with the landlady. I can see that about you – you are smart. Though you have been protected. People think you are cute and small and underestimate you. But in your head you are tall and formidable, aren't you?"

"How can you see inside my head?"

"The same way I can see your head, it's there."

Iti looks excited and shoves her hand in front of Chinky. "Tell me more. Will I get a good job here?"

Chinky moves Iti's hand away from under her nose. "I'm not a palmist. I sense energy and yours is interesting."

Just then, there's rapping at the door. The landlady.

"Chinky, how many times have I told you that no boys are allowed, so why has that boy come here again to see you?"

Chinky grins happily. Her entire face transforms. From a mysterious, delicate beauty, she suddenly looks like an excited young girl.

"Because he is not a boy, he is a man."

Chinky turns to Iti. "Do you want to come with me and my boyfriend? He is really rich, he can take us to some cool places. In his car."

Valarie, whose headphones are clearly letting in more than just music, snorts, "He is also really old."

"Well, it takes time to get rich and I prefer a self-made man to somebody who has only inherited his wealth."

She smiles again at Iti.

"Come."

Iti smiles back. "Okay. Let's go."

She puts her phone back into her capri jeans pocket.

5

Iti has to admit that Valarie was right. Chinky's boyfriend *is* old. Years later of course she would realize that he wasn't geriatric, but seen from the lens of a twenty-one year old, anybody in their late thirties is just months away from being sent to an old-age home.

The 'man' Chinky introduces as Nitin does not smile or even say hello to Iti. He just nods and unlocks his car with a remote control. Iti is no expert on cars, she can't tell a Honda from a Hyundai, but she can tell a big car from a small car and this is a big car, ergo expensive. Chinky did say he was rich.

Iti slides into the backseat and scans Nitin's face in the rearview mirror, trying to decide if he's good looking. She can't tell, her eyes keep getting drawn to his receding hairline already littered with grey. It doesn't really matter what his face looks like. He is bald and old; she doesn't like him. Ten years later her assessment of men's looks would be much kinder but right now she is disappointed. She would have preferred somebody much cuter for Chinky.

Chinky gets in at the front and kisses him affectionately on the cheek. *Ugh.*

"Where do you want to go?" Nitin grunts.

"Just drive around. Let Iti meet Mumbai."

Nitin drives at a leisurely pace. *Like an old man*, thinks Iti, unkindly, but she is happy for the drive. They are not zipping past anything. Anyway, how would they? There's a traffic signal every 500 metres – it's the same at Agra but here some of the cars actually stop. Iti feels a little guilty as she remembers, she herself never stops at a signal, unless a cop is around.

The signal they have stopped at right now has a timer. So cool – like a countdown! But bad for morale that it still has ninety seconds left.

"They shouldn't tell people that they'll have to wait for so long. Even if I was going to stop, I wouldn't, after seeing that I'll be stuck for one-and-a-half minutes," grumbles Iti.

Chinky smiles at her. "And yet, in another moment you might feel that ninety seconds is not long enough."

A red blinking light fills the car. Iti turns her head to see where it's coming from. A discotheque on wheels is approaching from behind and squeezing itself into the space between Nitin's car and the one next to them. She rolls down the window, to check the rickshaw out and admire how the driver left a paper-thin gap between the two cars on each side. The rickshaw driver sees her and starts fiddling with something above his head on the roof of the rickshaw... *"ae dil hai mushkil jeena yahan..."* The strains fill the rickshaw, the space between them, the car and Iti's ears. Iti claps her hands in delight. The rickshaw driver gives her a jaunty grin – now, is she even more impressed? Iti blushes, and rolls up the window, although not fully. She leaves a small gap... *"yeh hai Bombay meri jaan..."* And suddenly as she is leaning back in her seat, looking at the ceiling of the car going from light red to deep red and back, she wishes for the signal to stay red a little longer. She looks at Chinky, expecting her to comment on it, but she is busy whispering something into Nitin's ear, he has his hand on her thigh... *"zara hatke, zara bachke, yeh hai Bombay meri jaan..."* Iti hums along the song – one of her mother's favourites.

The interior of the car returns to its normal colour. The song has ended. They have left the signal and the rickshaw zooms out of sight faster than her scooty. Awaking from her daydream (though it is actually night already!), Iti looks out of the window. The roads are like a river of cars, SUVs, rickshaws, cycles, bikes and pedestrians, kept together by buildings everywhere. Not an inch is left idle... *"kahin building, kahin tramein, kahin motor kahin mill..."* The song is stuck in her head now. Iti lets it play.

She is expecting Chinky to point out various places to her, but Chinky is mostly silent, speaking only now and then in whispers to Nitin. Nitin's replies are monosyllabic and unintelligible to Iti. But the silence allows her to take in the city at her own pace. The smell (something between garbage, sewage and sea salt), the lights, the flashes of colour, the incessant honking, the rickshaws racing with the expensive cars, *"zara hatke, zara bachke"*, the slums, the high-rises, the bungalows. Later, as she gets to know the city better, she is able to close her eyes and pick out individual places from the sepia-coloured memory of her first drive.

The petrol pump, shaped like a lotus, which she would use as a landmark many times. The construction at 7 Bungalows which would eventually become a metro line that she would use often, even when she got herself a car. That mall in Lokhandwala that would become her favourite until she discarded it for the bigger and fancier one in Lower Parel. Those little shops at Bhandu Nagar from where she would pick out her future almirah which has stayed with her ever since. Today she is seeing all her 'favourite' places for the first time.

It has not even been twenty-four hours since she set foot in Victoria Station and she is still a 'tourist'. Can you be a tourist if you have no return ticket, a place to stay and a friend already? A warm feeling surges in the pit of Iti's stomach, shielding her from the cold of the AC in the car. Outside, the city is still sweltering in the humidity of the monsoon that has announced its presence but not yet arrived completely.

In-between the high-rises, people have squeezed tiny chai tapris; the half-foot distances between one society gate and another are occupied by a cobbler here, an ittarwala there. Iti spots the Kolhapuriwala who will soon become her go-to shoe shop. The sidewalks alongside well-kept park walls have become what looks like permanent homes to temporary structures – tents made out of saris, children playing with a pot while their mothers sleep, their head covered with their pallu, their faces turned towards the wall. In and out of the park walk uncles in white trainers, aunties in salwar kameez and hunky dudes who look right out of a Bollywood movie... *"Insaan ka nahi koi naam o nishan..."*

Iti strains her eyes. "Chinky, see that guy jogging on the sidewalk, with his headphones, doesn't he look exactly like Hrithik Roshan?"

"You mean he looks the same in real life as he does in films." Chinky laughs. "Well spotted."

"No way!" objects Iti, trying to get another look at the jogger but he has already sprinted out of sight. "That was not him. It's not possible. Where were the bodyguards?"

"Oh, he comes here alone, every evening."

"Really?" Iti doesn't buy it, she has seen enough paparazzi pictures of him in *Filmfare* and he is always surrounded by a horde of bodyguards on set.

"The bodyguards are just for show on set. Actually nobody here cares about celebrities. Unless you're Amitabh of course…!"

Iti is mesmerized by how casually Chinky calls the demigod of Bollywood by his first name.

On cue, Chinky points out, to the right. There's a knot of people in front of the big bungalow with its high walls and two security guards outside. It's Amitabh Bachchan's – this is momentous! Later, it would just be the place from where Iti would often take a U-turn to get to PVR. She would also pass it on her way to Prithvi Theatre.

"Can we go to the beach?" Chinky looks at Nitin. He shrugs. Giving it a moment, he adds, "But not Juhu, too many tourists."

Iti is pleased to notice that Nitin clearly doesn't see her as a tourist.

"Let's go to Bandstand." Nitin looks at his watch. "It's 11 p.m. I hope we won't get too much evening traffic."

"Evening traffic? Aren't people supposed to be home by this time?"

Nitin cannot be bothered to answer. Chinky has more empathy for her small-town naivety. "Mumbai never sleeps, people work around the clock, so 11 p.m. is a perfectly normal time to be out."

Chinky is right. The coffee shops are filled with people, they pass a CCD with a blinking sign 'Open until 1 a.m.'

She pulls the sleeves of her kurta and looks back out of the window where a bunch of girls in hotpants on a scooty negotiate with an aunty at the red light. She observes the scene – maybe the aunty scolded them for their outfits? Another aunty joins in. Women in Mumbai are so tall, both of them are practically towering over the girls. Iti feels sorry for them. But the two aunties laugh, clap and tap one of the girls on the head. She hands them something which the first aunty puts inside the blouse of her bright yellow sari. They are now passing Nitin's car. Iti's stomach tightens. She quickly turns her head. Suddenly there's a rapping on her window. Iti jumps off her seat. A face is staring at her. She's clapping and looking at her questioningly, yellow pallu thrown over her face. Iti finds herself recoiling. She has never been comfortable around 'them'. She remembers her cousin's wedding in Agra where the hijras had turned up towards the end, demanding money, all hoarse voices and incessant clapping. That had not gone well. To her horror, Chinky has rolled her window down and is speaking with the transvestite. "Don't do that," Iti tries to whisper, "she might pull up her sari and show you her 'thing.'"

"Didi, how's it going? I haven't seen you around."

"I had gone to my village. Who is the heroine in the back?" She points towards Iti who shrinks in her seat.

"Has she come from America? As if she has never seen a hijra before." She waves her hands in front of Iti's face and laughs.

Iti wants to hide but she braves a smile. She didn't mean to be offensive to Chinky's 'friend'. Chinky puts her hand into Nitin's pocket, pulls out a fifty-rupee note and hands it to Iti, gesturing towards the 'aunty'. Iti timidly stretches her hand out of the window and gives it to her. The transvestite grins at her and puts her hand on her head. "Good girl, you will become a heroine and marry a hero, who do you want, Shah Rukh or Salman?"

"Hrithik." Iti laughs, feeling suddenly relaxed and a little scandalized with herself. She is speaking with a hijra, what would her mother say? The signal has changed. Nitin steps on the accelerator. "Bye," shouts Iti, waving. Chinky looks at her, her expression approving.

"Do you feel like having chai?"

Iti perks up. "Always."

They finally come to a halt at Bandstand, next to a guy with two massive steel vessels on either side of his cycle.

"Do you have any tea?" asks Chinky, before Iti can say anything.

He doesn't. Iti is disappointed but in a second, the cyclewala calls somebody over who has tea. Chinky buys three cups. The plastic is so hot, Iti burns her fingers. It's perfect!

Iti, feeling indebted, pulls out her wallet but Chinky stops her. "Hold on to this. You are going to need it for longer than you think." Then, casually, as if they have been best friends since kindergarten, Chinky takes Iti's hand and walks her to the promenade. Nitin pays for the chai.

The tide seems to be high, the waves are crashing against the rocks. Iti stares into the sea, letting the wind whip her shoulder-length hair all around her face. Salt mingles with the remnants of sweetness on her lips. Around her, couples are walking by.

From above, Mumbai, with its mix of slums and high-rises, might look like an ocean of concrete next to the 'real' one, with its own shoals and rifts. Some people might feel insignificant and sad knowing that they are but a tiny droplet in this vastness. But Iti, in anticipation of her bright future, as promised by Chinky, feels like she is part of something bigger.

A group of friends is speaking animatedly, and a little too loudly. A man comes by asking if they want coffee. Another man spreads a cloth on the floor, opens up a case, pulls out a banjo and starts playing. Iti takes a sip of her tea. For the second time in her life, she falls in love, but this time it happens much quicker.

"Come, let's take a picture of you in your new 'home.'" Chinky has Nitin's flip phone in her hand and smiles at Iti.

"Can he take a picture of you and me? I want to send it to Surat – he will be so impressed that I met someone who can look into the future!"

6

3 p.m.

"People simply cannot see into the future. Clairvoyance is not real and the people who think it is are just crazy."

Gaikwad looks at the wall clock. 3 p.m. He wonders if the package has arrived. The last notification on his phone came at 2.30 p.m. *On the way.*

"She also said she was a witch. And if you don't believe me, here, she even gave me a business card, see."

At the onset, the man in the perfectly ironed and starched, blindingly white shirt had not looked very promising. Gaikwad wonders what business would bring such a solid middle-class character to live with someone who ends up naked and dead on a crowded beach. Crinkling his thick eyebrows in distress, the man hands over a visiting card to Gaikwad, forcing him to lift his eyes from the screen where he has, unsuccessfully, been trying to find out how to track the package on the app. For a man, Abhishek has impeccably manicured nails. As if he had cut them just before coming. Not in his own house, but done at a parlour.

"Look at this, can you believe the things it says? *Singer, dancer, spiritual advisor, vlogger, salesgirl, barista, actor, art director, model, TV personality, reader* — reader? How is that a job? Are you working in a publishing house? No, you just read books and it's there on your visiting card. Insane, totally insane. I am surprised she did not add 'insane' to this card. It has everything else. And here, look at this. It also says *witch*. She is, I mean, she was, meeting people for the first time and handing them a card which says that she is a witch. I mean … what does that even mean?"

Abhishek picks up his cup and swallows a mouthful of air — the cup is empty.

He nervously dribbles his fingers on the empty cup.

Gaikwad points to the cup. "You have already asked for another cup. This one was finished."

Abhishek's head shoots up as if caught in the act. He chuckles nervously.

"I know what it looks like, but really I'm not insane. I am just nervous. Not because I'm guilty of anything! But because…" He gestures with his hands. "I am at a police station. It's a bit upsetting."

"Well, I'm at a police station, too, I'm not upset." Gaikwad tries a little humour to put Abhishek at ease. All his fidgeting and rocking back and forth is starting to put his own teeth on edge.

Abhishek stares at him in wide-eyed horror. "Of course, of course, sir. I certainly did not mean to deprecate your place of work. It's not a bad place at all. It's a great-looking office — very bright and airy. I wish my office looked this professional, instead of looking like a kindergarten with all those pop colours. May I take some pictures and show them to my boss?"

Gaikwad intercepts the constable who has come with Abhishek's coffee. "I think you have had quite enough caffeine."

"Just one more, sir, please. I promise this is my last. I need it to calm down from my first two coffees, I assure you – this will help."

Abhishek's hands are shaking a little, guilt tremors or caffeine-withdrawal panic, or actual caffeine withdrawal since he finished his last cup of coffee about five minutes ago? Gaikwad sighs. Just the burnt smell of this strong black soup is making his heart burn a little. How has this man already had two of these? No wonder he is all over the place. His insides must be on fire.

"First you calm down and then I will give it to you." Gaikwad takes the coffee and puts it in front of himself.

Abhishek looks at it. Gaikwad can see him, holding back his hands with visible effort to prevent them from reaching out and snatching the mug. This man has serious addiction and impulse-control issues. Would he still have controlled this impulse if Gaikwad was not a cop? Probably not. Gaikwad makes a mental note.

He smiles his most affable smile at Abhishek, it is actually his copy of Sahil's 'affable' smile. Gaikwad doesn't have an affable smile of his own.

Abhishek takes a deep breath and composes himself.

There is the sound of thunder and a loud crash.

"SHOOT OUT!"

Abhishek ducks under the table.

"Sir, a tree fell on your bike." Sahil is back.

"Oh, thank God." Abhishek climbs out from under the table.

Gaikwad glares at him, gets up quickly. "A whole tree uprooted and fell on my bike? Nobody was hurt I hope?"

"Well, it wasn't a whole tree. It was a branch. But a really big branch."

Gaikwad throws a dirty look at Sahil as he rushes out, apparently expecting his superior to follow suit.

Abhishek quietly picks up the cup of coffee and takes a long grateful sip. Then puts the cup back, moves it about a little. *Would the officer be able to tell it was moved? Was there any dust around that he has disturbed?* He makes some vague sweeping motions with his hand, trying to put the dust back. He catches himself; *he is acting utterly ludicrous.* He pauses. Willing himself to be calm, he leans back and stares at the ceiling. The rusty fan is rotating unevenly. There's a lot of dust on it too. It makes him dizzy. Again, he picks up the cup and takes another sip. *Hanged for a penny, hanged for a pound.*

Outside in the parking lot, Gaikwad removes the branch from his bike and inspects it. It's a bit dented but it will 'live'.

"Really, Sahil, you need to stop being so dramatic. You are a cop, not an actor."

Sahil clears his throat.

"Speaking of actors. Sir, can I please sit in on this interview? I am a big fan of Chinky Ma'am. She has really helped me. Her videos, her words, her way of living, of thinking – it was all so inspiring."

"Really? How?"

Sahil eagerly pulls out his phone and shows Gaikwad a video of Chinky titled 'Loving and being in love: unfortunately not the same thing'. Chinky is stark naked in the video. At least it seems so. The frame ends just a millimetre above her nipples, her long dark hair put behind her ears, her shoulders fully exposed. She is not wearing any jewellery; her collarbones and slim arms expose an almost juvenile body type. The woman speaks with an erect posture, similar to the yoga gurus who give online webinars. Gaikwad catches himself wondering if she's sitting in padmasana, naked…

"…watching this really made me understand why my wife first friendzoned and then left me."

Gaikwad shakes his head, looks at Sahil, then again at the video, back to Sahil and yells in disbelief: "Are you mental? Why are you showing me porn at the police station?"

Holding the phone, he marches back inside. Sahil rushes after him.

"The porn is in your eyes, sir. Shut them and focus on the words."

Gaikwad continues his march straight up to Abhishek, waving the video into his face. "You didn't tell me your friend was doing porn."

Abhishek is shocked.

"Porn? Oh no, that's not true. Sure she did those naked workshops but I assure you nobody in those workshops was attractive enough for it to be called a pornographic performance."

"What?"

Abhishek looks uncomfortable: "What?"

Sahil slaps his forehead. "Oh damn, I have heard about those classes. But I was unable to attend and now, it's too late. I should have listened to Chinky Ma'am, the perfect time to do something is the first time your heart mentions it. I call myself her fan and yet I didn't even take advice from the video that got over five million views." He sighs heavily.

Gaikwad puts a hand on his forehead. He sits down on his chair and looks at Abhishek. Suddenly Abhishek no longer seems like the craziest thing to have happened to him all morning.

"So, to get back, you thought she was a witch?"

Sahil sits up, looking suspiciously at Abhishek. He whispers, "Sir, in some parts of the world, in fact even in India, people used to kill witches by drowning them. I think they still do, somewhere in the Northeast, Assam or so..."

He gestures towards Abhishek.

"Sahil, if you want to sit here, you will sit quietly."

"Can I please have my coffee?"

Gaikwad picks up the mug and hands it to him, noting that it's already half-empty.

Most perpetrators expose themselves through the tiniest of mistakes ... He adds another mental note.

"Ok, so you met the deceased ... are you okay with me calling her the deceased?"

"Of course? What else are you going to call her? The resurrected? She would like that I'm sure, but, well I guess she wasn't as powerful a witch as she thought."

His mouth twists into a wry smile. *Is he disappointed or vindicated or just plain mocking?*

"So you met her, at a coffee shop you were saying?"

"Where else?" Abhishek half smiles. "Coffee shops are my preferred locale for relaxing and I was very stressed on that particular day."

Yet nothing compared to how stressed he is right now.

His stomach was hurting on that day also, but that had an element of sweetness and anticipation. Abhishek can almost feel the same sharp, bittersweet ache again, somewhere between his heart and his stomach, as he remembers...

7

2018

It is a sunny, sweltering October afternoon in Mumbai. *A strange kind of autumn*, thinks Abhishek, annoyed at the number of times he has already wiped his face, to no avail. He looks at the time on his phone. Still four hours to go before Kartik would be free. His eyes linger on the wallpaper, on the stubbled face of a handsome man, with a bun and deep dimples. Is it too creepy to have his face as his wallpaper? They are not exactly 'official' yet. Abhishek sighs, running a finger over Kartik's dimpled chin. Kartik's face is pure perfection. Opening the camera on his phone he looks at his own face, wincing in disappointment. What is it with these dark circles? *Shit, he should have popped a pill and slept.* Instead of staying up all night, staring at Kartik's pictures, rereading all his texts, alternating between agony and anticipation. At least he should have slept in the plane, but he couldn't, he could barely even keep his seatbelt fastened and sit still. He can't remember the last time he has felt this kind of restlessness. He touches his cheeks, they are shining so bright he can almost see another reflection of his shiny cheeks in them. *No, this will not do.* He cannot go to meet the love of his life looking like an attraction from an amusement park freak show.

He reaches inside his bag for his little case of compact powder – *never leave home without it* – pulls it out and opens it. Pause. He changes his mind and drops it back inside the bag. What's the use of doing it now? There's still four hours to go, it will just get sticky again and he might attract too much attention. A dude powdering his face in the middle of the day, who does that?

"Actors mostly."

Abhishek looks up in surprise. A girl is staring down at him. The first thing he notices is the excessive amount of cleavage practically shoved into his face. Framing the cleavage is a cheap, shiny-looking ruffled neckline. Above the cleavage is the face of a girl, probably from the northeast; 'chinky', the racist slur for people from that region, springs unbidden to his mind. He quashes it quickly. He notes that she is wearing too much make-up – just looking at all the layers of foundation and blush makes his pores feel clogged again.

"I'm sorry, did I ask the question out loud?"

"No, not with your words, no. But, I can hear your thoughts, I'm a sort of mind reader."

Of course you are.

Abhishek nods politely and tries to get back to his coffee but the mind-reading girl doesn't seem to be much good at reading body language. She holds out her hand. "I am Chinky."

Abhishek almost jumps out of his seat.

It's illegal to call you people by that name, I think.

The girl's mouth twists into an amused smile. "Illegal to call me by my name?

"Your parents named you Chinky?"

"No, I did. My parents died before I learnt to speak, before I could tell them my real name."

Ignoring his pointed distaste for the nonsense she is babbling, she sits down next to him and smiles.

There are so many teeth in that abnormally wide smile.

Abhishek involuntarily pushes his chair back a little, trying to move away from her, feeling a wave of self-righteousness and indignation overwhelm him – not even one hour in Mumbai and it is already getting on his nerves. For starters, why is October behaving like May? Outside it's hot and humid, inside the coffee shop everybody is so loud and animated, they don't care that it is impossible for one solitary person to just enjoy a quiet cup of coffee alone with their thoughts. And now there is a crazy woman sitting next to him. It is intolerable. The things one has to do for love.

"Ma'am, I'm sorry but I would actually like to sit alone…"

"I have an empty room for you."

What the devil!

"Ma'am, I don't know what scam this is. But I am not interested in going to any room and doing anything with you. No offence."

Chinky laughs a shrill, manic laugh. Abhishek looks around, surprised that nobody else is noticing or reacting. She could probably murder him right here and the famously indifferent Mumbaikars would not even look up from their phones and laptops.

He can feel actual goosebumps rise on his arm. Chinky laughs again.

"I'm not a prostitute, silly. Here, you can see my business card. See it doesn't say prostitute anywhere … I don't believe in sex for money. Both are enjoying it, so why should one person have to pay, right? As you can see from the address, I live in a location that is suitable for your purpose. And I have a spare room. I can rent it to you. Let me know."

She shoves her card into his hand.

Abhishek manages to keep his voice even and in control. It might be dangerous to get her angry. "Thank you, ma'am. But I am not looking to rent a room here. I am on a short trip; I shall be leaving soon."

Chinky takes his hand and holds it; she stares him deep into the eyes – a bit too long.

"That's what you should actually do, but I think you are going to decide to stay longer for him. Well don't worry, it will be alright … in the end. Now reply to him, keep it casual."

She touches him lightly on the shoulder as she walks away.

He receives a text. It is from Kartik. *Running late, I'll be home around 9 I guess. What happened? All ok?*

"Wait, what ... wait."

But she is gone. Vanished into thin air, he would have thought, if he didn't know better.

8

3.30 p.m.

Gaikwad and Sahil are listening intently.

Sahil is awed. "Wow, I have goosebumps. I knew she had sixth sense, too. See how nicely she caught it, isn't it, that you were there to meet someone?"

"She did see me staring at my phone. Probably smiling like an idiot. Then checking out my face. I do not think it was difficult to deduce that I was there to meet someone."

Gaikwad clears his throat. "So I'm thinking it was a love case for you, but then she said 'him', so what was…"

Sahil throws him a pitying look. "Sir, please, you need to get modern. Nowadays it can all be a love case. Boy girl, boy boy, girl girl…"

Comprehension and disbelief dawn on Gaikwad's face. Abhishek's defences are up. "It's not a crime, you can't arrest me for this. Anyway, I only admitted to love, I didn't talk about any deviant ... behaviour."

He looks towards Sahil for support. Sahil gives him a thumbs up.

Gaikwad holds up his hand. "I have zero interest in your personal matters. Just please don't describe anything of a sexual nature."

Sahil jumps to Abhishek's defence. "Sir, that's discriminatory, what if it was a man describing his sexual relations with a woman, would you stop him?"

"YES!"

Gaikwad turns to Abhishek. He points towards the file lying open in front of him. "So it says here, you are from Delhi."

"Yes, sir."

"And you come to Mumbai for this ... man?"

"Yes, sir."

"You said you came just for one weekend. How many weekends have passed since then?"

"Many."

"So why are you still here?"

Abhishek sighs. "Things just didn't go like I imagined they would."

"How did you imagine they would go?"

"The way they went for my parents when they met each other."

9

2002

Unfortunately for Abhishek one of his earliest memories is walking in on his mother with her lips around his father's p ... no, no, even after all these years he couldn't bear to think about it. It was scarring, but not as tormenting as the little needle pricks caused by their constant PDA which he had to endure over the years.

His parents just cannot seem to keep their hands off each other. Abhishek has spent his childhood cringing in embarrassment as his parents eschewed all sense of propriety and managed to whisper sweet nothings and 'do' nasty things to each other at the most inappropriate places, including at his grandmother's funeral. Abhishek had the singular misfortune to be in the bathroom, lying inside his grandmother's big bathtub, pretending to be a whale, happily blowing water out of his mouth, while his parents had suddenly walked in. *Shit, why did he not shut the door?*

But he had been in such a hurry at first and after he had relieved himself, he had just peeked, on the other side of the shower curtain, to look, yes, really, just to look at the 'forbidden' bathtub. His grandmother had had it as long as Abhishek could remember, which was just as long as he could remember not being allowed to use it, because it would get 'dirty'. So this bathtub that nobody was allowed to use had stood in his grandmother's bathroom all these long years, denied the very purpose of its existence, until now, when Abhishek had wandered in to answer its desperate call for 'meaning', by quickly removing his clothes, running it full of water and sinking inside.

It was all going well until, as usual, his parents had ruined it.

"Don't cry, babe," his father was whispering to his mother. "I know it's awful, but your mother had such a good life."

That was true, Abhishek's grandmother did have a good life. What can be better than lying in bed all day, with two servants fanning you, while you berate and curse them for not fanning you fast enough. Why his grandmother couldn't just switch on the AC, Abhishek could never understand.

Abhishek should have probably announced his presence right then. But he did not want to get into trouble for disrespecting his grandmother and violating her virgin bathtub, barely hours after her death. So he kept quiet. Cowering behind the semi-transparent shower curtain, hoping they would not notice his presence (in hindsight it would have been rather ironic if this would have been the one time that they realized he was 'around'), he had been quiet enough to hear his father say, "Let's try and get her back."

That had piqued Abhishek's interest. *Get her back? Like how? Like a ghost?* He had held his breath, wondering if he was about to see his grandmother standing upright for the first time (*would she be mad about the bathtub?*).

He heard his father whisper, "Let's make a little girl, maybe your mother will be reincarnated through her."

That was the day Abhishek had learnt how babies were made. He never forgot that 'lesson'.

When Abhishek was sixteen, his best friend's parents got divorced.

"Why?" he asks his friend who is crying even though his guilt-riddled father had just got him a new Blackberry which his mother tried to top by getting him a PlayStation. Abhishek doesn't even have a Nokia yet, he is too 'young' apparently.

"Who knows," the friend shrugs, "they said they just fell out of love because they were together for so long." He opens the PlayStation. "Wanna play Grand Theft Auto?" Abhishek does not, he hates these racing games. But he is intrigued by the impossibly muscular avatar his friend had chosen.

"I will just watch. How long were your parents together?"

"Eighteen years! Man, that's longer than I have been alive! It is such a waste."

The friend's avatar in what was supposed to be a racing game picks up a bat and randomly starts beating people on the head; he has gone rogue. Tears roll down his friend's cheek as the screen turns red. Abhishek smiles, his parents have been together since they were fourteen. So it might come to an end any day now!

Abhishek imagines himself curled up in bed next to his mother, both of them drinking hot chocolate as he tells her about his day and she listens, because he is the only person in her life now. Her phone is on silent so she doesn't have to see the calls of her annoying husband begging her to take him back. Abhishek has all her attention. Later they watch a movie on the new big TV that she has given him for his room because she no longer has to waste her money on extravagant gifts for her worthless soon-to-be ex-husband. He sighs happily.

In another scenario, he sits in his new car that his father has given him, because he no longer has an expensive wife to spoil. *Tears in Heaven* is playing on a brand-new music system with four speakers, as Abhishek has a man-to-man talk with his father and his father listens attentively. Later he tells Abhishek how proud he is of the man Abhishek has become. "I should have paid more attention to you when you were growing up, son, but your mother, that woman just took up all my time. I am so sorry, son. Can you forgive me?"

"Of course, and we can always start now, doing all the things we could never do before."

In his dream, Abhishek presses down on the accelerator and zips over to a bar to get some whiskey with his dad. On the way back he picks up ice cream for his mother.

Life is going to be so perfect as soon as his parents separate.

They never do. Before he knows it, Abhishek is standing in the corner alone, nursing a beer as his parents raise a toast with whiskey to each other and forty years of love and togetherness. As they extol each other and all the happiness they have brought into each other's life and all their happy memories, Abhishek wants to barf. Isn't it kind of obscene if not borderline creepy for his father to be describing in such detail, what a lissom and beautiful lass his mother was as a sixteen-year-old and how one look at her already blossoming body had set his heart, and other things, on fire? Fine, so his father was just fifteen, too, but doesn't that make it worse? Everybody knows what complete perverts fifteen-year-old boys are. This is all so objectionable. Almost as objectionable as his parents not mentioning him even once.

"Why did they even have me," he mutters to himself, but it's a rhetorical question. He has heard that story. They were so consumed by passion one night, nobody bothered to wear a condom.

Abhishek slips out of the party, feeling blue and a bit like a forgotten condom himself. He is driving around aimlessly, but *what the heck, it is Saturday night*. On an impulse and because he spots an empty parking spot, he pulls over outside of TCC, a new and popular nightclub. He doesn't care much for the Bollywood music pumping out, but he needs another drink and maybe they will play some house music later, once they run out of evergreens. Abhishek goes in. Unaware that behind these closed doors, past the hefty entry fee and the two bulky bouncers, is the love of his life just waiting to lock eyes with him. There will even be a special song playing just for them in the background. And as soon as he sees him he will just know that he is 'the one'.

That is how Abhishek's internal monologue plays every time he goes to a bar, a nightclub, a cafe, or even a hospital. He is constantly waiting for true love to appear and take him by surprise and in its big strong arms. The irony is of course completely lost on Abhishek that for a guy who claims to have such a deep distaste for everything Bollywood, his idea of love and romance is straight out of every other Technicolor Bollywood dream.

This time, albeit, cupid is around and on Abhishek's side, and the love of his life – or at least the most dramatic love story of his life – is waiting inside. How dramatic he cannot even begin to imagine ... Abhishek could really have used some of that clairvoyance thing and made a run for it now, especially since his shoelaces have come untied and he almost trips at the door. He could have seen it for what it was: a sign. But he does not. He just hopes nobody has noticed, quickly ties them back and steps in.

Two hours later, Abhishek feels like he is glued to his spot. He has been trying to leave for the last one hour, but where is the space? People are dancing like maniacs. Every time he puts a foot forward, he is petrified that somebody is going to step on it and ruin his expensive, brand-new faux leather boots in that amazing shade of subtle purple which the untrained eye could mistake for 'manly' dark brown. So far only people from the female sex could identify the correct shade and had hence probably deduced which side of the river Abhishek fished on ... But for the majority of the population, he remains a 'normal' dude from Delhi, South Ex. Sad. But safe. Abhishek looks down again to admire his lovely boots and just then some idiot spins his girlfriend on them and immediately spins her away before Abhishek can blast at him.

Feeling annoyed and frustrated, Abhishek picks up a tissue from the table, drops a bit of his vodka on it and tries to wipe away the offending, muddy footprint. He is decidedly flushed by the time he looks up to find a pair of eyes performing a leisurely scan of his body and then his face. The eyes take their time, moving up his fitted denims, the shirt that is suddenly feeling too hot against his skin, up to his chin with the little cleft. They linger for a moment on his pink lips and then meet his eyes. These eyes which are now locked with his come attached to a really handsome and rugged face, complete with a stubble and a bun. Abhishek feels like an actual butterfly flew into his mouth and is now fluttering around in his stomach when the lips part into a rakish smile and…

10

4 p.m.

"I said I did not need so much detail. Is all of your story going to be this 'graphic'?" interrupts Gaikwad.

"No, no. I am no good at telling stories. Chinky always said I was in too much of a rush to get to the 'ending'. I miss all the little details that would make the story interesting…"

"Well, you certainly didn't miss anything now."

"But that's only because I have replayed this in my head over and over so many times, and…" Abhishek shrugs.

Sahil gestures impatiently. "Sir, why would you interrupt just when it was getting good? So what happened then? Did he just come over to you and tell you how much he likes you?"

"Something like that."

11

2018

Abhishek and Kartik end up in Abhishek's car, after Kartik manages to expertly navigate them both out of the bar, as expertly as he is navigating Abhishek out of his clothes right now.

"This is really cool, usually I am the one in charge, maybe…"

Kartik silences Abhishek's nervous babble with a kiss. Just like they do in the movies. Abhishek's heart plummets all the way down to his perfect purple shoes. He kicks them off at some point and does not even notice. Somebody's hand brushes against the music system and 'Pehli baar mohabbat' starts to play. Suddenly Abhishek no longer hates this song. It is perfect and it is now 'their' song. By the time, they have got their clothes back on and pulled out of the parking lot, Abhishek finally asks Kartik his last name and also if he can have his phone number and walk him to his car.

"I don't have a car, I took a rickshaw."

That is odd. Not that Abhishek is looking for a sugar daddy, but Kartik does not look poor. Even his underwear was Björn Borg – original. But what kind of rich person does not have a car?

"You could drop me back to my hotel if you like. Show me a little bit of Delhi on the way. I'm here for just a couple of days."

Abhishek is relieved – that explains the lack of a car. Not that he cares if the man he has met 'five minutes ago' and now wants to spend the rest of his life with is possibly middle class. *But even middle class people usually have a car, he would have to be really poor to not have one.* Abhishek ignores that snippy little voice in the back of his head and smiles up at Kartik. Kartik smiles back. Damn, he's beautiful. "So where are you from?"

"Mumbai."

"Well, then you are really going to love Delhi. We have big roads and our metro construction is no longer causing traffic jams. Ha ha."

No responsive laughter from Kartik.

Half an hour later, Abhishek tries to curb his disappointment. He has just taken Kartik on a big round, all through the Chanakyapuri embassy area and Kartik has barely looked out.

"This is where all the embassies are, it's really beautiful. Look how green it is and so clean. That is the American embassy. Is it not impressive? I can drive closer if you would like to take a better look."

"Is there somewhere we can park? I feel like I want to take a better look at you."

Abhishek blushes. "Maybe not here, it is the embassy area, they might find it suspicious if we ... aaaahhhhhmmmm."

12

For the next two weeks, the cell phone is either an instrument of torture come from the bowels of hell to especially torment Abhishek or the gateway to a thousand raptures and delights, created just for him. The two alternate every few minutes. The only constant is the tenacious roller-coaster.

A typical post-meeting-Kartik-morning for Abhishek: Abhishek wakes up with his heart beating fast, in excitement and trepidation. The cell phone lies on its face on his bedside table. Abhishek caresses it gently, he is holding his breath.

Should he turn it over and look at it? He had heard it beeping at night. Was that Kartik? His heart had hammered so loud in his chest when he had heard that ping. But he had dared not check. What if it wasn't him? He would just die of disappointment. He had waited till 2 a.m. for a reply to his text. How much longer was he supposed to wait? Abhishek would have waited all night, would have kept checking his phone every five minutes for the rest of the night, but he had a presentation in the morning. He had to sleep.

He had wondered if he should maybe just switch his phone off for the night? Then he could tell himself that Kartik must be messaging. It would also make him cool, because he would not be messaging back right away. He had done that last week and in the morning there had been a message waiting for him. A long one, too, Abhishek had almost wept in relief after having spent the night, tossing and turning in agony. *But that was last week. What if today there is nothing? What if Kartik has met someone else? What if he never messages him again?* Abhishek's hands go cold. He moves them away from the phone. *What if that beep had been Ananya?* Oh, why did he not think of that, it probably was Ananya. She had messaged him to gossip in the middle of the night just last month. *Why the hell does she do that? She has a husband, why not gossip with him? Why let him think that his boyfriend is messaging and then have him be disappointed that it's just her? Why be married and play these stupid games with your single friends? Why even have friends?*

If he was married to Kartik he would certainly not be wasting his time messaging anybody else. Abhishek's stomach is in knots now. Is Kartik ever going to marry him? What if he has already broken up with him? What if there has been no reply all night? How is he going to handle that? Abhishek yells to his maid to bring him some coffee. After that he will look at his phone. Or maybe he will just check it after his presentation? Yes, that's probably a good idea. But what if Kartik has messaged, maybe he should check it now?

Five minutes before his presentation, Abhishek finds out that he has received six messages last night, but not even one from Kartik or even Ananya for that matter. He is numb as he opens his laptop and hooks it up with his projector. It is lucky he has done this presentation so many times, he can go through most of it on autopilot. He just hopes nobody notices the slight quaver in his voice or that he is rushing through most of the points. He wants this to be over, so he can send Kartik a cheery text and casually ask him what he has been up to. *Please let him not have been having sex with someone else last night.* Abhishek composes and discards about a dozen 'breezy' messages in his head as he takes his team through the social media projections for their current campaign of a health-food start-up.

Halfway through the presentation, Abhishek's phone pings again. Now he is too keyed up for autopilot mode to function effectively. All he wants to do is check his phone. It's impossible to focus on anything else. The rest of the presentation is a disaster. As soon as it ends he rushes to his phone. His boss is pissed off but at least his stomach has stopped lurching. He has received his reply. It's all good. It stays good till evening. Then he sends Kartik a cute selfie and Kartik replies, 'Will talk in the morning.' *Full stop? What does this mean? Why can't he talk at night? Who is he out with? What are they doing? And why is he saying 'talk' and not 'chat', are they going to have 'the talk'? Hello again, sleepless night, my new best friend.*

13

Obviously he cannot go on like this.

"What should I do, mom?" It is 11 p.m. Dinnertime at the Ghosh's.

"Speaking of doing ... do you know what your father did today?" asks the proud wife – a rhetorical question which she answers before Abhishek can express his consternation. "You know how Mr Gaur keeps parking his car in our spot? Well, your father told him he could not do that anymore. Isn't he amazing? The way he just stands up for himself?"

Abhishek's father beams proudly, his wife lovingly strokes his hair. "You know it's remarkable – your hair is as luxurious and thick as the day we met. It's so sad Abhishek will probably go bald before he's thirty..."

"What? Why will I go bald, when my father still has a head full of hair?"

"It's basic genetics, son. Children inherit the hair gene from their mother's father and you know Nana is all bald."

"Maybe our Abhishek will meet somebody who doesn't care about looks."

That is his opening. "Actually, Mom," Abhishek tries again, "I met some..."

"Babe, would you still love me if I would lose my hair?"

"It's strange that you ask this now. I was just thinking how sexy you would look if you shaved your head. I think it would really bring out your jawline."

His mother is stroking his father's jaw. Abhishek gets up. "I am going to Mumbai."

"Pack some warm clothes, dear."

"Why? It does not even get cold there."

"Darling, do you remember how cold it was in Darjeeling when we went there for our honeymoon?"

"Of course." His father chuckles. "But as I remember we didn't have much use for clothes to keep warm."

That is his cue to exit. Abhishek leaves the room.

Two days later he leaves the city. His parents are vaguely aware that he has gone somewhere to look for love.

14

4.15 p.m.

"That's awful!" Sahil is shocked. "They didn't even care that you were gone…"

Abhishek shrugs.

"And then you came to Mumbai?"

"Yes, we have a branch office in Mumbai. I just told my boss there was a family emergency and I had to go to Mumbai for a few days. He spoke with the people there and told me to coordinate the work from there. He could have just given me a few days' holiday, but…" Abhishek shrugs. "He is a slave driver and now with the Internet, location seems to have become irrelevant…" He trails off.

"Except for police work," Sahil jumps in. "You cannot do that over the computer!"

"Well, not until they replace you with robots."

Sahil is aghast. Gaikwad quickly interjects. "And that's how, as you have told us, you met the deceased. But how did you come to live with her?"

"I had not told Kartik that I was coming to see him. It was supposed to be a surprise. I did not even book a hotel. I guess, I assumed, he would ... anyway. So I waited at the cafe where I met Chinky. I think he thought I wanted to skype with him, because I said I was excited about seeing his face. He was really not expecting to see me outside his door."

"Not even when you asked for his address?"

"Oh, that I had taken weeks ago. I took a picture of his passport when I dropped him at the hotel. But not in a creepy way!" *Oops.* He realizes what that might sound like and adds, "He was a stranger from another city, and what if he went back and never called me again? I just wanted to have a backup plan. Just for my mental peace. I did not, of course, intend to use it. Really."

"And yet you did." Gaikwad glowers at Abhishek, his face a study in suspicion. "You took the coffee without my permission, you picked up this man's passport without his permission. Do you understand that your actions are not entirely ethical?"

Abhishek flinches visibly. His mouth purses and he folds his arms across his chest.

Gaikwad's phone pings. Sahil has texted him. *Sir, if u keep revealing ur suspicions, u r going to put d suspect on guard.* Gaikwad stares at the message, unsure how to react. Sahil makes a good point, but he will be damned if he would acknowledge that.

Still, he tries to smile ingratiatingly at Abhishek, willing his eyes to look eager. "But I understand, love makes us do foolish things. Even Sahil here, he wanted us to use our men for surveillance on his wife after she left him." He throws a spiteful look at Sahil.

Sahil opens his mouth to argue, but changes his mind and nods his head. "Sir is right. I have been there, so I certainly don't judge you."

"Me neither," says Gaikwad, "I have watched my assistant go there."

He leans forward, like he has seen Sahil do. "Well, go on, I too am eager to know what happened next. Tell us everything, don't hold back at all. This is a safe place of no judge…"

His phone pings again. *U r overdoing it sir.*

Gaikwad stops talking, continues smiling.

Abhishek looks at his audience, their faces turned eagerly towards him – all friends here, just talking about that evil thing called love. The tension in his chest eases a little.

15

2018

Abhishek's heart is hammering. Actually, his pulse rate seems to have changed since he met Kartik, this hammering being the 'new normal'. His palms are cold – his body temperature has changed too, as he stands outside Kartik's apartment, taking it in. He is still getting over the sheer ugliness of the building. It looks like one square piece of fungus against a backdrop of cement skyscrapers deserted midway in the building process. On two floors someone has strung laundry between the pillars of what was once intended to be a balcony. He wonders who would live in a place like this. The construction workers? He shudders at the thought of a dozen rowdy village men living in a fungus-infested, under-construction building with no sanitation.

The wannabe balcony is overlooking something which could pass off as a river. But for the stench. *Does this entire neighbourhood not have proper sanitation?* It literally, most definitely, is a river of shit.

Abhishek's bile rises. He covers his mouth with a handkerchief and takes a deep breath. It smells of Kartik. It had dropped out of his pocket during their little tête-à-tête in the car and Abhishek was impressed that Kartik was carrying one, assuring him further that he had met his dream man. He breathes out and looks up at the building in which this perfect gentleman supposedly resided.

At least Kartik's building has glass in the windows. Although none of the residents seem to care much about cleaning them. The skyline of similarly ugly high-rises is reflected in the smear marks of the pigeonhole-sized openings in the wall. He prays that those are bathroom windows. Although his better sense tells him that no architect, not even a Mumbai one, would build the bathroom on the wide side, facing the street. The building has a grim expression, long streams of rust running down its facade like tears or angry wrinkles. Despite the two palm trees in front of the gate, Abhishek is overcome by a sense of hopelessness. Aren't film stars supposed to be living in Bandra? This building doesn't look like even their staff would agree to live there. *Middle class*, that dreaded word again. *Lower middle class*, the voice ads. *Shake it off, shake it off. Money is not important.* And it is hardly Kartik's fault how the building looks. Maybe they have some dispute with the builder. Anyway, the door looks nice. It's a nice deep black. Very muted and tasteful. Maybe they can get a door like this, when they have their own apartment.

No, no, shake that off, too. Keep it cool. Be casual. Abhishek takes another deep breath and rings the bell. Then he holds in that deep breath. He's too keyed up to even exhale. Footsteps. Any second now he is going to see Kartik. He plasters on his sexiest smile.

The door flies open, as he says, "Heyyy surprise!" to a tiny, slim woman in denims and a loose tee, staring up at him. *What on earth? Is Kartik secretly married to a woman?*

"Yes, I am surprised, who the hell are you?"

"I'm, I'm…" *How old is she? She's tiny … is she like a sugar mommy? Is his boyfriend a kept man? In this dump?*

"Is this Kartik's house?"

"Well actually it is in my and my husband's name. But yes, he will get it someday as we don't have any other kids."

Oh, so she's not his sugar mommy, she is just his mommy.

Abhishek grins awkwardly at her. She grins back, then yells really loud for such a tiny person. "Kartik, you have a friend and he has come with flowers for your mother."

She looks at the flowers in Abhishek's hand. Abhishek quickly hands over the bouquet to her.

Kartik comes out. He looks in surprise at Abhishek and formally shakes his hand. "Hi, this is a surprise. I didn't know you were in Mumbai."

"Yes, yes, sorry I meant to call you, but, you did say if I was in Mumbai … for work, I'm here for work … I should look you up … sir?"

Kartik throws an exasperated look at Abhishek. His mother is busy arranging the flowers in a vase.

"Come, let's talk in my room."

He walks towards his room. Abhishek follows. Kartik shuts the door behind him.

Abhishek quickly takes in the room. This is Kartik's room. His bedroom. It's very orange. A bold choice of colour. A quality that he admires in Kartik. Here and there are random black designs on the wallpaper. Spontaneity – that's how he swept him off his feet. The bed is also black. *His favourite colour.* That's fine, they can get more black furniture once they move in together. It's classy. And there, with the rumpled sheets and the white pillows is where Kartik lays his head. And he knows that mirror. It was there in the last nude selfie, perfectly angled so what Abhishek got wasn't just frontal nudity but…

"What's going on? You didn't tell me you were coming to Mumbai."

"It was … quite sudden. We have an office here. My boss asked me to liaison with the office here. I'm here just for the weekend."

"So you are here for work then?"

"Of course, why else would I suddenly be here?"

Kartik seems to relax, he moves closer to Abhishek.

Just then his phone pings. Abhishek notices that Kartik is smiling as he texts somebody back.

"Too bad you are on such a short trip. I'm horribly tied up this weekend."

He gets another text.

So am I, I'm all tied up in knots inside and it's already been over six weekends.

"Well, it's not that I have to leave on Sunday. It's possible that my work would extend by a couple of days."

"Oh, ok. Well, weekdays are so busy for me. And my office is in town so it takes forever to get back. But let's see, maybe we can get together before you leave."

He gets back to his phone. Abhishek looks miserable. His heart slows almost to a halt – *so much for the new normal.*

"Kartik, will your friend be joining us for dinner?"

"No, ma, he already ate."

He smiles at Abhishek. "You don't want to waste your first night in Mumbai having my mom's cooking and listening to her chatter. Why don't you go to Carter Road, it has some excellent eateries and it's right by the sea."

"It's okay, I already ate…" *…my heart. It is sitting like undigested lead in my stomach now.* "I'll just be getting back to my hotel." *Stop me, please stop me, don't let me leave.*

"Great, where is your hotel? I'll just ask the guard to get you a rickshaw."

Kartik picks up the intercom, looks questioningly at Abhishek.

Abhishek is nonplussed. He pulls Chinky's card out of his pocket. Khar Danda.

"That's Dunda, dude! You are such a Delhi boy. How did I forget? Remember Chanakyapuri?"

Kartik winks at him.

Abhishek's heart picks up pace again. Much better.

He moves closer to Kartik.

"All the time. Do you ever…"

"Wait one sec, the guard is saying something … oh okay, your rick is here. Wow, that was quick."

He hangs up the phone, and looks almost ruefully at Abhishek: "Call me if you are still here on Monday. We will do something."

Darting one quick look at the door, Kartik pulls Abhishek in for a quick peck on the lips.

Abhishek's heart almost explodes out of his chest.

Kartik's phone pings again.

16

The rickshaw drops Abhishek outside that crazy lady's apartment building. He had handed the driver the card when he asked him where he wanted to go. And to his surprise he just nodded, did not negotiate and zoomed over the highway into the little alleyways unwaveringly until they landed right here. He did not even have to ask for the way. While Abhishek is impressed by the man's aptitude, he is not sure anymore if he wants to be here. On the dimly lit sidewalk, a long-haired clochard is agitatedly talking to an invisible friend. *Great. Even more crazy people. Why is he not surprised?* The dark fellow with the matted hair changes tracks and heads towards the direction of Abhishek's rickshaw, ready to start a conversation with a human of flesh and blood. *Panic.*

"Are there any good hotels around?"

"For what kind of food? There is one called Indian Punjabi, it's very good."

"No, no, I'm not asking for a restaurant, actually…" *Fight or flight?* No, there is simply no alternative. True love demands to be fought for. "Never mind, I'll get off here."

Abhishek pulls out his little bag and gets out of the rickshaw, pays the driver and looks at the building. To his shock it's not bad at all. The facade is clean, there's even a little lawn by the gate with some flowers in bloom. What the heck, he might as well just go up.

The door to Chinky's apartment is painted a surprisingly soothing, pastel blue. Abhishek is still debating whether to ring the bell or just turn around and leave when it flies open and Chinky just stands there, with a big welcoming smile and an equally big cup. The smell of freshly brewed coffee and something else, that reminds him of hot apple pie, instantly warms and relaxes him, as does the soft music he can hear playing inside her apartment.

"I added a little cinnamon," she says, handing him the cup and luring him inside. *What choice does he have?* He could really do with a cup of coffee right now and a little company would be nice too.

Abhishek steps in and looks around. The lights in the living room are a little dim. But not particularly alarming. All around him are little figurines of angels, elves, different gods, a centre table with a red silk cloth and a deck of tarot cards spread out all over it.

Abhishek prays silently to a couple of the figurines as they pass them and Chinky takes him to what she calls 'his room'. She pushes open the door. Abhishek looks at the rather bare room. It just has a bed with a blue bedsheet against a blue wall, the other ones are white and there's a comfortable-looking cane armchair in the corner. Next to it is a side table, with a night lamp and some kind of a book with a big stain on the cover and a French press on top. It's the same one he has in his kitchen back home.

Abhishek takes a tentative sip of the coffee she has given him. It's delicious.

Chinky smiles at him. "I hope you like your room. I would have decorated it more but I didn't want anything that disturbed your energy. Anyway you will have enough time to decorate it yourself."

Abhishek takes another sip of his coffee.

"Don't worry about decorating. I don't plan to stay very long. How would you charge me, weekly or…"

Chinky brushes it aside. "We will see when the time comes how much money I need and how much you can spare. I'm just glad your energy is compatible with this room or you could not live here."

Abhishek looks uncomfortable. He chuckles awkwardly, picks up the book lying on the bedside table and looks at it.

"I left this for you, in case you feel like reading."

"Thank you, I really don't like trashy romance novels."

Chinky smiles at him. "Strange how sometimes the things we want from life and from fiction can be so different."

The front door opens and then slams shut. Abhishek almost spills his coffee.

"Does somebody else live here too?"

"No, no, that's just my lover Satchit. Well, I'm going to go have some sex with him now. But please don't hesitate to interrupt us if you need anything."

Abhishek gapes at Chinky – *hasn't he suffered enough?*

"Thank you, I'm good."

"Well then see you in the morning."

Chinky leaves to welcome her lover. Abhishek shuts the door behind her, turns around and puts his ear on the door. *How soundproof is this? How loud are they going to be?* Well at least he will feel right at home, falling asleep to the sound of other people having sex.

Wallowing in injustice and self-pity, Abhishek goes to the window (cleaned!), opens it and looks out.

Noise, traffic, brightly lit shops. A chai tapri and a coffee shop, with people spilling out onto the pavement. Mumbai is alive and active, rumour has it that this is not going to die all night. Abhishek shuts the window. A look of disgust on his face.

He walks over to the door again. Giggles – from the other side of the door. He quickly moves away from that end of the room and sits on 'his' bed. After spending a few seconds pretending to check his clients' social media stats, he finally lets himself move on to what he actually wants to do: stalk Kartik's profile.

There are a bunch of pictures taken near the Gateway of India. But wait – the last time this picture had fifty-seven likes, who is the new fifty-eighth? Abhishek opens it. He has already checked out the profiles of all the other boys who have liked the picture, so he can spot the new one almost immediately. Who the hell is this Achal? Why did he like a picture which is weeks old? Is he a new friend or an old friend who has suddenly discovered that he would like to be more? Abhishek goes to Achal's profile. Godammit, it is private. All he can see is a tiny thumbnail of a profile picture. Abhishek squints at it, trying to decide if this Achal is cute or not. Is that a double chin? Please let it be a double chin. No wait, that's just the light. He actually seems to have a really nice jawline. Abhishek takes a screenshot and then enlarges it for a better look. His heart sinks a little, Achal is definitely cute and that tee is a little too well-fitted for him to be straight.

He goes back to Kartik's profile to see what else this Achal has liked. There is the Gateway of India photo, he hasn't liked the selfie but there he is again, liking the picture Kartik has put of a sunset ... and ... what the hell is this? There is the picture of Kartik at a party. Abhishek has seen this picture before but did not really pay attention to the people around. Now he is wondering how he could have possibly missed it. Over there, in the corner is the slightly blurred picture of somebody clearly staring at Kartik. Is it this Achal person? Abhishek zooms the picture, it does look like Achal, the hairstyle is similar. The body is good. But is it the same guy? It seems to be and he is definitely staring ... lustfully? Is that his agenda, is this where they met. Is that a phone in his hand? The same one he has been texting his boyfriend with?

A slight pressure on his bladder reminds Abhishek that he is spiralling. Getting obsessive and in his head again.

He gets up; maybe a walk to the toilet will cause a little pause in the loop. He needs to step back, take a small bathroom break and then he can come back and look at the picture again, because right now he is sure he is seeing things. In his single-minded quest to find out the truth behind the disconcerting 'like', he had neglected the tightening of his trousers around the lower part of his abdomen. With his bladder so full, his stomach is bulging out.

He opens the door next to his room, searches for the light switch, unzips his pants. *Where is the accursed light?* His fingers dab against the surprisingly smooth concrete wall. Finally they sense the plastic. He flicks it, and lets out a sigh of relief. But, instead of a toilet, he finds himself almost peeing into a bucket with a broom in it. Staring back at him are canvases, paintings, a shelf full of shoes, some nice-looking shirts on the floor ... He closes the door.

Five minutes later, Abhishek is still looking for the toilet. It is clearly not attached to his room. He searches the corridor in vain. He walks up and down the corridor. *Maybe the door is hidden – that would fit the crazy lady's sense of humour...* He traces his hand along the wall and walks very slowly, one step at a time. But there are only three doors, the one on the left leads to the really tiny kitchen. He tries the door on the right once more. Suspiciously, he lifts the shirts to check if it was maybe one of those 'hole in the ground' situations but no, the ground is all solid. Nothing, not even a crack in the wall that he could pee in.

There is nothing else to be done now, unless he wants to use the kitchen sink, which of course he does not. The shame of it would haunt him forever, and since he is already haunted by the shame of walking into people having sex, Abhishek rushes to Chinky's room and starts banging on the door. She would know where the toilet is.

Chinky opens the door. She is stark naked.

"Oh my god, you are naked!" Abhishek states the obvious.

"I know, I was having sex. It's better without the clothes…"

"Where is the toilet? I really need to go."

"Oh, it's in my room. Good thing I told you could interrupt me if you needed something…"

Abhishek rushes into the room. In the background he can see a man, Satchit presumably, quickly scrambling for the bedcover in panic.

Chinky, still casually naked and absolutely indifferent to it, opens a door and leads him into the bathroom. She also takes this opportunity to show him around. Of course completely ignoring the towel hanging by the door, which might have made this situation just marginally less uncomfortable.

"And if you need to take a shower in the morning, there's the switch for the geyser, this is the tap for hot water…"

"I'm good, could you please…"

"Yes, of course, and if you need to dry your hands…"

"I will figure."

He extends a hand as if to usher her out, then retracts it, looking distastefully at her naked shoulder.

Chinky shuts the door behind him.

Abhishek sighs in relief.

Outside, he can hear Satchit and Chinky kissing.

He groans and sits down on the toilet.

"Oooh babe, that's so hot…"

Abhishek shuts his ears, rolls his eyes. Looking at the ceiling, he hums a little tune under his breath to shut out the sounds from outside – this is going to be a long night…

17

2012

The stars are shining through the cracks in the roof. The night sky has dipped the entire room in a blue hue. Even Chinky's naked skin has a bluish touch to it. Her long black hair reflects the silver moonlight in every curl as it winds down between her breasts, along her slender waist, like a river in the night flowing towards her belly button and the delta below...

"They are sparkling like the lights of Bombay in the night," a muffled voice from the outside notes. "Or maybe not quite. They are less hyper. More static. Like diamonds in the sky."

"That's so cliche..." Vincent rolls his eyes as he lifts his lips from Chinky's pelvis. She smiles as if she didn't hear what he was saying, totally engrossed in their intimacy. She pulls his stubble, trying to kiss him.

"I mean, what gave people, artists, the right to occupy phrases and expressions until the end of time? Damn, there's another one. And another one, and another bites the dust ... Argh!"

The people outside their hut have moved on to singing 'Diamonds in the sky'.

"What the fuck is wrong with these people? It's impossible to concentrate!"

Chinky's loving gaze shuts.

She pulls herself up from underneath Vincent. "Why do you have to be so negative? Making love is sacred. It's about letting go, letting your body and mind be drawn towards the ultimate energy, towards bliss. And you just ruined the energy

– just because people outside were having a good time! You can't let yourself have a good time."

Vincent sits up on the bed, looking hurt and indignant.

"Come on, baby, why are you angry with *me?* Those assholes were screwing up my concentration. You know how my mind wanders! Somebody just needs to tell them to SHUT THE FUCK UP." With the last words, he turns towards the bamboo door, yelling at the strangers on the other side. But his voice is drowned by a big wave breaking against the shore.

"The tide is coming in..." Chinky has lifted her hot body from the crumpled sheets. She walks out of the hut, into the blue of the night. Naked.

"Where are you going?"

"To the sea. I need some pure energy. My aura feels contaminated."

Vincent stares after her. With a groan, he throws himself onto the bed. Chinky's smell is still lingering on the thin cotton. Her scent is something between lavender and pepper. Never before has he met a woman with such an intense scent. Maybe it is because she doesn't shave. Just sticking his nose in her armpits turns him on at times. Though her legs are marvellously hairless – a gift from her grandmother she said. *Don't think about her grannie, man! Think about that bush between her legs ... yes, that's better ...* Vincent groans a second time and moves his hand between his legs.

18

7.25 p.m.

"That's disgusting." Gaikwad looks extremely uncomfortable. Sahil is busy inspecting the rusty table lamp.

"Is it? You find a man satisfying himself after he has been left high and dry by a woman disgusting than raping her? Bloody hypocrites!" And he hadn't even shared his thoughts with them – obviously. The lavender-pepper memory is his alone. But he felt that it was important to share the kind of independent spirit that Chinky was. Who forgoes having sex with a man like him to go swimming instead? Sahil nods his head, as if he agrees with his unuttered thoughts.

Gaikwad raises his eyebrow. "You seem to have a lot of anger issues."

"Thank you. Everybody who lives in this world and does *not* have anger issues is a fool, I think."

"Did you often get angry with Miss Chinky?"

Vincent's face softens. "I probably should have been. But sometimes she seemed not really of this world."

"What about all her other lovers? She seemed to have been a promiscuous woman. Did that bother you?"

Vincent starts laughing. It's a hopeless laugh. He buries his head in his palms, speaking more to himself than them. "You people are so ridiculous, you don't understand anything."

19

2009

"You don't understand, Surat, I cannot just come back to Agra … Oh come on, two months is not that long! Finding a job takes time, do you know the population of Mumbai?"

Iti twists the cord of the phone in her hand, looking anxiously at the seconds ticking on the display counter hanging inside the booth. Another 20 seconds and she will have to disconnect, even her phone is out of balance and the closest shop around has a minimum 100-rupee top-up. She covers the mouthpiece with her hand and looks at the lanky owner of the shop. "Can I pay you ten rupees tomorrow and you extend my call by three minutes, please?" She smiles sweetly at him.

Chewing his gum loudly, with a conscious effort to display boredom paired with annoyance, he looks into the long notebook lying open in front of him, while typing something on his Nokia. A "beep" emitting with every letter. He is typing an essay.

Iti turns back to the phone. "So I was saying…" Iti is distracted.

The owner has finally looked up from his book, but instead of responding to her positively, he throws her a penetratingly stern look. Now he is walking over to her booth. He knocks at the glass.

"Madam … Madam! Iti – it is your name, right? Well, as you can see it says here you still have to pay twenty-five rupees from yesterday. You have used two hours on the Internet and paid for just one."

Iti again covers the phone's mouthpiece. "I barely used five extra minutes, I was attaching my resume and your connection was slow. It's not my fault. I already explained it to the person who was sitting here yesterday, I don't know why he still wrote that…"

In Iti's hand, the handset beeps, the line disconnects. Her 20 seconds are over.

"Even one more minute means you pay for the whole hour. It says so right here." He points at the white piece of paper stuck on the door that reads '25 *rupees per hour*'.

"See, nothing about minutes. It's 'by' – 'the' – 'hour.'" An exaggerated pantomime movement accompanies each word: the right hand turns outwards, the index finger lifts, the fingertip taps onto the watch attached to the left wrist.

"Well, in that case, I'm going to use the fifty-five minutes I have left."

Iti sits down at the empty computer. She pulls out a piece of paper from her bag. It is a printout of production houses listed from A-Z, with their names, phone numbers and email addresses. Iti starts to scan it at H where she had left off last....

"If I log you in, it's a new hour, you have to pay for it."

"This is robbery and if this is how you treat your regular customer, I'm not going to come back here again."

She gets up to leave, the man stops her, "Twenty-five rupees please."

Iti hesitates.

"I will get it tomorrow."

"So you will come back tomorrow?"

The man folds his arms across his chest and smirks at her. Still chewing his gum.

Iti swallows her pride, it's either that or pay him right now and go without dinner again. Anyway, who is she kidding? This is the only cybercafe on this street. If she doesn't come here, she will have to go all the way to Model Town to send her resumes and the one over there charges thirty rupees an hour.

"Yes," she mumbles, "you know I will."

"I know," says the man, "anyway I have your address." He gestures towards his notebook. "So unless you are planning to leave Mumbai and go back to Agra, I will get my money."

"I am never leaving Mumbai and I am never going back," Iti tells him firmly.

Her phone rings, she flips it open, it's Surat. *Thank goodness!* She walks out, holding the phone to her ear.

"What happened, I thought you would call back."

"There was a long line for the phone," Iti lies. *How many times can she ask him to pay for her to call him?* Anyway she has a bigger favour to ask today. "Listen, could you please put in some money for my rent? I am a little short."

Surat pauses before he asks, "Sure, how much do you need?"

A longer pause at Iti's end. "All of it."

The next five days she keeps adding up her credit at the cybercafe. It's like she's already part of the Mumbai rat race. She grows accustomed to the perpetual feeling of exhaustion. A good feeling.

20

Iti closes her eyes. Chinky is humming under her breath. The evening is softer than the day was.

The day had been harsh and hot and disappointing. She had finally got a reply to one of her emails – an interview at an advertising agency in Lokhandwala. Iti had checked her wallet. After paying the cybercafe for the Internet and for printing out the address on a pixelated map she had no more money for the rickshaw. Surat had put in the cheque last week like she had asked him to but it was taking a while to cash.

There was nothing to be done and it was only about an hour until the interview. So she had walked. It was not that far. Not by Mumbai standards at least. In Agra this much walking would have taken her almost to her paternal grandparents' house and they always went there by cycle rickshaw, never walking and certainly not at two in the afternoon, on a muggy day like this. It hadn't rained in two days, so it was a special kind of hot monsoon day in Mumbai. The kind where the dust from the road, whirled up by the constant barrage of vehicles, attaches itself to the invisible water droplets in the air only to stick to the exposed skin of the already hassled passer-by.

Iti had walked mainly on the road, amidst the traffic. The pavements, where they bothered to exist at all, were either cracked and broken or occupied by vendors selling food and their customers munching on a Bombay sandwich or licking their fingers from the sweet spiciness of a chowmein dosa. No use looking at those, they are way out of her budget. Keep walking, Iti. As she passes a tea stall, her steps falter, inadvertently slowing her down. She throws a longing look at the man selling chai and khakri biscuits. Should she get one? But her back is already drenched in sweat and her white blouse has stains under her arms. More 'heat' did not seem like a good idea right now. Maybe on the way back. Hopefully the office will have an AC and maybe they would serve her chai. Once she got there, that is.

Walking in the afternoon is not nearly as relaxing as walking at night is.

Those moments are blissful, the breeze blowing on your face, the faint smell of salt in the air, the rustling of the palm trees … definitely better than the exhausts of various rickshaws blowing hot air onto your feet as you weave your way in and out of the traffic stuck at a red light.

How she wished she had her scooty with her, but her mother had absolutely refused to even consider it. "Too dangerous, I know how bad Mumbai traffic is."

It was no use arguing with her and telling her that it was more dangerous in Agra, especially with the way she drove. Here with all this traffic jammed around her, where would she even get the space to pick up the kind of speed she needed for an accident to be actually dangerous? At worst she might topple over from boredom at a red light and twist her ankle.

She mops her brow with her sleeve, a second before realizing that she probably shouldn't have. Shit, why did she wear white? There is a big grey patch on her left arm now. Wow, her face must be really dusty. She surrenders, there's nothing she can do now – except for making it to the interview in time.

And finally she had made it. Sweaty, exhausted, looking a little worse for wear, but she was there. She was proud of herself. She was the only one who was. She had gotten exactly five minutes in the AC and a glass of water before the interviewer had stood up, shaken her hand and thanked her for coming. He had not even waited for Iti to leave before looking at his hand, left clammy and muddy by Iti's sweaty palm, and wiping it vigorously with a napkin.

The sun was already hidden by dark clouds when she had stepped out and she no longer had any reason to look crisp and clean so she had stopped for chai on the way back and then she had gone to the ATM.

And now she is finally home…

Iti lets herself relax as she lies down on the bed and tries to exhale the stress of the day. She is 'safe' for one more month. The money has come, Surat has paid her rent.

She has gained one more month to find work. She feels a little guilty that she has lied to him again – thankfully her rent has not really gone up to 5,500. But she needs these extra 1000 rupees to survive – to go out, to look for work, to call him. She hates that they now have to ration their calls. Or rather the rationing happens automatically with their phones running out of balance one after the other. Sometimes Iti goes to the booth and calls, just to say a quick bye. Sometimes Surat manages to find a cheap top-up and calls her back. But it always ends too soon. There is still so much more to tell him. But like her, he is struggling for money too. He is already sending her half of his salary and he also has to give some of the money at home. Maybe she can top-up her phone a little more this week if she eats a little less.

Her stomach rumbles, almost aching as the smell of the fish curry rice that Valarie has ordered wafts up to her nose. Her mouth is so full of saliva she cannot even open it. What the hell is wrong with Valarie? How does she not even offer to share? It's so rude. Iti places a pillow over her head, trying to block out all thoughts of food, but she is so hungry and Valarie is eating so loudly. She prays that she chokes on a bone – it would serve her right!

"Do you want to try my new nail paint? Nitin got it for me. Here, let me apply it for you."

Iti feels a depression on her mattress. Without even waiting for a response, Chinky pulls her hand out from under her pillow.

She sits up. Chinky is wearing a pleasant perfume or maybe it's the oil in her hair. Iti doesn't have a name for the fragrance yet, she finds out later that it's called lemongrass. But whatever it is, it calms her. She can no longer smell the fish. This new smell is permeating the whole space around her and soothing her senses, as much as the gentle touch of Chinky's hand as she applies the nail paint. The paint too feels soft and cool on her nails. The humid, relentless heat of the day seeps out of her body, cooling all of it.

"There, this is done. Give me the other one."

Iti looks down at her 'finished' hand. She is a biter and although her fingers are long and tapering, the chewed nails at the end have always made them feel a little 'stumpy' and ugly. But not right now. Maybe it's the pink or maybe it's the way Chinky has applied the paint – so perfect and even – for the first time, Iti has a sense of what at least a part of her would be like as a 'woman'. She knows in that second that her struggle is temporary, her future is already set. She is going to be the kind of woman who keeps her nails long and paints them in beautiful and expensive colours and only holds things that complement the beauty of her hands.

Iti stretches out her hand to touch the woman she is going to become.

"It's a lovely fuchsia," Valarie's voice breaks in from the present and the woman from the future vanishes, leaving behind Iti, broke but no longer hungry, sitting on her bed in her ugly room, which is looking oddly charming and mysterious in the dim light of the seashell lamp that Chinky has switched on.

Iti looks at her nails again.

"Fuchsia? But this is pink."

Valarie rolls her eyes.

"Some fashion designer you are. Fuchsia is also a sort of pink."

Iti immediately pulls out her notebook and writes.

"How do you spell it?"

"Read the label."

Iti does.

"It says here it's from Inglot. What's that?"

Valarie snorts.

"You idiot, that's an international brand. Wow, Chinky, that's an expensive nail polish. At least married men are generous with their gifts."

Iti jumps to Chinky's defence.

"Don't be catty, Valarie. Of course he is not married."

Chinky stretches lazily. "Oh no, that's not true. He could be, I sometimes do sense another woman's energy on him. But that could also just be another lover. She seems nice, a little emotionally distant from him, but she means him well."

Iti is surprised. Is she also disappointed? She's not sure. Maybe, just a bit. But she ignores it. She likes Chinky, this doesn't change anything. Anyway it's not her fault, it's Nitin's.

"And that doesn't bother you that he's also with another woman? He's taking advantage of you."

"No, as long as her energy doesn't feel toxic I'm ok with her presence. It is even pleasant sometimes. I guess like him she, too, is a gift from the universe. I accept and respect them both."

Valarie smirks.

"She accepts everything because she is a whore and the universe is her pimp."

Chinky laughs. She doesn't look offended at all.

Iti smiles too but she puts away the nail paint and opens her little red notebook again.

"What are the other good imported brands of nail paint?"

She scribbles furiously as Valarie shows off her knowledge. From nail paint they move on to shoes.

Iti is feeling decidedly more content and peaceful by the time Valarie announces that it's time for lights out, she has to sleep now.

That's the cue for Iti to smuggle in under the covers with her book. The night light rule had been a bit of a contentious issue between her and Valarie with Iti protesting that she liked to read at night before sleeping and Valarie protesting much louder that she had a job and needed her sleep.

"I don't have a job so I need to relax by reading."

"If I am late for my job I will get fired and I hate reading."

That had gone on until Nitin had gifted Chinky a little portable night light which could be clipped onto the pages. Chinky had graciously given it to Iti as if it had been meant for her anyway.

Iti loves it. The darkness shutting out the rest of the world while this tiny light illuminates only the pages in front of her, making her feel as if it is just her and the people in whatever story she is reading. Their intimate little world of the night.

Already excited about her nightly adventure with M&B, she prepares herself a cup of chai, as she usually does – extra milky and extra sweet, with extra comfort and extra calories. Then she slips under the sheet, balancing the cup on the mattress.

Her phone rings, Iti squeals excitedly. It's Surat, he has 'borrowed' his sister's phone after she left it lying around.

"She has a post-paid connection, so we can talk for a while – or at least until she notices that her phone is missing…"

Iti is so excited she forgets to keep her voice down. "I had another interview today. The agency was amazing, their AC is so terrific, it cools you down in five minutes and it's so close, it's walking distance from home … ouch!"

A pillow comes flying at her, thrown by a furious Valarie. "Stop yapping about your stupid interview, you've already talked about it all evening. Let! Me! SLEEP!"

The pillow hits the cup of tea, knocks it over and spills the hot liquid onto the bed and on Iti's book.

"Damn! Deepali aunty will kill me. And my book."

Tears stream down her pale cheeks.

She picks up her soggy book. The pages are stained with tea.

"It's ruined! This brown is never going to come off. It looks terrible. I don't even want to look at it anymore." Iti's lips are quivering. She's frozen.

Chinky and Valarie quickly rush to her side and pull off the bedsheet. "I'm sorry, dude, I'll pay for the cleaning. I'll tell your Deepali aunty I did it."

Iti ignores her, she picks up a t-shirt from the floor to dab the tea off her book.

Surat's distorted voice shouts from the floor: "Hello, hello … hello?"

Valarie is trying to make amends: "It's not so bad, see, you can still read the text."

"I know, but it looks so bad. I keep my books so carefully. Once, my cousin took one of my books and dog-eared the pages." She sighs helplessly. "I didn't speak with her for months." A continuous 'beep' emits from the floor. "This is so heart-breaking."

She hugs the book like a mother cuddles a hurt child.

Chinky gently touches the precious square containing Iti's little secret world of pleasures. "Don't look at it then, if it makes you sad. I will keep it for you. You can take it back when the stain doesn't bother you anymore."

Iti sniffs. She experiences a moment of separation anxiety.

"Then we also don't have to tell Deepali aunty."

Iti squints at Valarie with resentment.

"Sorry. I didn't mean it."

She goes back to her bed, not without picking up her soggy t-shirt and draping it around her bedpost to dry.

Chinky reaches out to Iti. She sniffs once more and hugs her book even tighter. Chinky takes it from her gently. Suddenly, Iti remembers her phone.

"Surat?"

But the line is disconnected. Iti looks at it sadly, she types out a 'sorry'. Another wave of sadness rolls over her. It doesn't go through, she has no more balance. She lies awake, with her open eyes staring at the ceiling, waiting for Surat to call back. But he doesn't.

Somehow, her eyes close eventually. She enters dreamland alone. It's dark and quiet. The people in the book cannot find the threshold to step from their paper world into her dreams.

When she wakes up in the morning, it is raining. Iti squeals in delight and rushes to the window. The book and the abruptly ended phone call both forgotten.

21

7.30 p.m.

They intrude on his thoughts. They all do, they always have. "What are you thinking?" "What happened in school?" "What did your father say?" "How is his new wife?" "Is your slut mother still sleeping around?" So many questions. Why aren't his thoughts allowed to just stay inside him? Why do they have to be dragged out and exposed? Like the grooves on his LP records, every time a memory is dragged out and replayed, it wears out. Why must his head be filled with only emptiness?

And now these cops.

"What does it matter?"

"It does. Just tell us how you met the ... Chinky Ma'am."

"No."

Aloof to the point of desperation, Vincent refuses to let this memory be worn out by 'Dumb and Dumber'. He made love to her, he married her, she died. Why does it matter where it started? That's not now it's arranged in his mind anyway. His thoughts are stacked like his records: the ones that made the most impact right on top and the ones he loves best at the bottom, so they can be accessed only occasionally.

Why can't they leave this, his happiest one, untouched?

He silently plays it in his head.

He had hoped to find a spot on this earth where he would not have to meet a single human soul. Where he could wipe clean his being from the politics he had been ensnared by. The only way to detangle himself was to flee. Yet another lesson that good intentions lead nowhere when they are targeted towards fellow humans. A cynical smirk flits across Vincent's face, he sands the coconut shell in his hand a little more vigorously. "You should be grateful for the place you were born into." He can hear his mother's voice.

"Grateful for an accident?"

"You are no accident, Vincent darling. You were pure intention. The Divine wanted you to be one of the first to be born out of and into this beautiful place. And only a mother knows how it took hours of agony to make that happen." Bored, he rolls his eyes. He has heard the dramatic story of his thirty-six-hour birth before. "There is no other place like it on earth!" That is true. The glassless round windows and the hand-dug stream around their house are probably one of a kind in the world, but so is his grandparent's mansion – at least from the pictures… "I am sure that your parents say the same thing about Charleville, Maman."

"The divinity had left that place long before any of us were born."

"They have a church."

"And we have the Matrimandir."

"Exactly my point."

"It's not the same thing. Not at all! I know you are feeling disheartened about the last council meeting," she touches his stubbled cheek gently, "but maybe you just need some quiet time inside and recharge your energy with some positivity."

"The people in the building right next to it have sucked all the positivity out of it. Through their ass."

His mother suppresses a lopsided smirk on her faintly tinted lips. But the gentle deepening of the laughter wrinkles around her green eyes betray her effort to appear stern. She has never been able to be strict with him. Sometimes he says something obnoxious solely to see her trying to keep a stone face. It's hilarious. But he wasn't joking right now. He meant it.

"My funny child. They just mean well. Aren't you happy that they ask for your opinion?"

"They don't *ask* for my opinion. They *demand* it, as if I had some obligation to it just because I was born here. What if I don't care? What if I have a completely different opinion?"

All his life he has felt like a bait dangling between two hungry wolves. In Auroville, there is always politics going on, one against the other. And he is stuck in the middle. But instead of just letting him hang there in zero gravity, they tug him to the ground, forcing him to stand by either this or that opinion. Why can't he just be?

"I feel crushed."

She cocks her head. Sometimes she looks like a giant crow, in her dark indigo kaftans.

"Everyone pretends to be so free spirited. But in the end, all of you are just as bad as the places you left. You think Auroville is the greatest 'nation' of them all. Why don't you just send me to war already? Put up a flag in the front yard?"

"Vincent, you are exaggerating!"

"Oh no, you know what's better? I will put up a board in their front yards. With big fat letters … WHITE PRIVILEGE."

"I am sure they will find another plot for Kofi."

Kofi was one of the 'new' residents. He had come all the way from Ghana to settle in this godforsaken village in south India and his first stop was Vincent's guest house. Vincent was amazed by his genuine belief that this place could do something good – for humanity at large. That there was actually some merit in the idea of bringing all people from opposing parts of the globe together under one roof of self-planted banyan trees.

Vincent didn't share his view, not after spending more than thirty years there. But some of his naivety had infected him. How else could he explain that he actually believed if one added a few good people, the place itself could become good?

Vincent's hand has become red from the relentless sanding. The beautiful surface of the coconut shell is slowly coming to the fore. How stupid to vouch for him instead of Marie at the allotment meeting. How did he not see that he had picked the side of an outsider amongst the outsiders?

"Can I borrow this?"

Vincent's stream of memory is interrupted. Holding one of his coconut shells in her palm, the new girl, Chinky, cocks her head in a half-smile.

"Sure."

Admittedly, he did not find a place completely devoid of people. He still has his human needs, like hot food and a place which flushes the undigested shit out of sight.

But at least non-socializing behaviour is met with the same response here. The girl has already vanished.

She seems to be spending an odd amount of time at the beach. He wonders if she came with friends because he has never seen her carry anything else than a water bottle and bandana; no towel, no book, not even a frisbee. She came with literally nothing but her hammock. Maybe her friends are hanging out somewhere else and she wanted to sleep in peace and solitude here at Paradise Beach. He can understand that. The only way to escape people's incessant need for socializing is to literally have a separate island.

It is only in the evening when Vincent sees her again, stomping like Rumpelstiltskin on the beach. A little figure with stick legs jumping up and down on one leg around a fire. He suppresses the urge to laugh out loud and decides to sit down on the warm sand to watch her performance.

The breeze is mild, the ocean surprisingly calm. Behind it, the rays of the sun setting somewhere even further west has dipped the sky in a warm subdued orange.

He just sits and watches. Until a drop of water hits him. Chinky is passing by, dripping in sea water from the bath she just took.

A sudden urge to discard his self-imposed silence overcomes him – "What were you doing there?" – quickly adding, "Not that it's any of my business."

"I was putting out a fire."

"You didn't have to. It would've gone out by itself, you know. Latest when the tide comes in."

"The tide won't reach there. That's why she's put them there."

"Who?"

"The mother."

A sudden flash of The Mother's counterfeit on his mother's altar flickers before Vincent's inner eye.

"The mother of the babies."

"Which babies?"

"The turtle babies."

Vincent scans the beach for the flat round body of a turtle, but all he can see is beige, no black spot anywhere. Maybe she is hiding in the shadow of the coconut trees.

As if reading his thoughts, Chinky answers, "She went back into the ocean long ago. It only takes her a few hours to nest, not like us humans who take so long to give birth."

"So now there are turtle babies on the beach?"

"No, they are still inside the eggs. But I'm sure they'll hatch soon. I can feel it!"

Vincent wonders how a girl with hips through which most definitely no human baby has ever made its way out can 'feel' when a turtle egg is going to hatch, but despite himself he keeps this thought inside his head.

"That's why I had asked you for the coconut shell. I thought I could move the eggs away from the place where people make fires…"

"That's a good idea."

"But then it suddenly struck me that nothing should touch the egg, or the baby might die!"

"You could just build a little fort around the eggs so no one comes near."

Chinky's almond eyes widen in awe. Excitement lights up her face! Vincent can't help but notice her astonishingly impeccable skin.

"Could you help me? I saw you have a whole mountain of them. Do you need them for something specific?"

He wants to say yes, he is making jewellery out of them. But who is he fooling, he is hardly going to make a hundred pairs of earrings and frankly, is already getting bored with it. So instead, he answers, "Sure."

He feels strangely drawn to the dusky girl with her almond eyes. Someone who has so politely recognized his wish to be alone, who has not unnecessarily introduced herself or forced him to share a beer or join him for a morning yoga session…

From his hut, he takes out a sheet and together they gather
all the coconut shells.

Suddenly, Chinky stops. "These are beautiful."

"Hmm…"

She has discovered a pile of earrings. If she asks, he is not
going to offer her to take one, like he had done with the last girl
who had visited his hut, for other, more carnal reasons. But she
doesn't. Instead she mumbles something about 'art', but he isn't
sure, the clinking of shells rumbling against each other in the
sheet drowns out her voice.

Instinctively, they divide the different nesting areas
between themselves, each quietly and concentratedly placing
one little brown shell, some with hair, some already sanded
into a shiny clean dark brown, next to the other, like little
fences. Leaving enough gaps for a baby turtle to pass through.
Vincent has no idea how big a baby turtle would be, but he
copies Chinky and trusts that she knows. Maybe she is a
biologist or something.

The sun is almost rising when they are done with the
work. Strangely, Vincent does not feel like leaving just yet.
Instead, he draws a little pattern around the 'forts' into the
sand. Knowing that no tide will come there makes him smile
a little. It has been a long time since he smiled just to himself.
It is almost as if he has found the silence he was longing for
only now, protected by an invisible circle. He looks over his
shoulder, Chinky is walking around, mumbling something
to herself.

She feels his gaze.

"I am casting a protective spell."

"Are you some kind of witch?"

She smiles in reply.

In silence, they both walk back to their little spot on the
rock overlooking the beach. As Vincent closes the bamboo door,

he strains his ears to listen to Chinky. Something buried deep inside the darkness of his heart wishes that she cast a protective spell on him too, to make him always feel this much at peace. He closes his eyes and enjoys this unknown feeling. Just for a moment. Or maybe a little longer.

Outside, a crow caws. Is it announcing the arrival of the day?

He isn't sure whether he has slept at all. But he feels weirdly rested, and excited. Vincent takes a few deep breaths, this uncalled-for excitement is usually a first foreboding of a brooding migraine.

To his surprise it is already afternoon. His favourite time at Paradise Beach, when a blanket of numb quietness covers the puffy faces of the twenty-odd 'residents' who have gone to sleep in their hammocks in order to be fresh and ready for their nightly parties. He checks out the hammock left of his door; unsurprisingly, it is empty.

He stretches, puts on one of his Buddha shirts without buttoning it and slips into his warm flip-flops.

He has just crossed the dune when he almost stumbles over Chinky. She is lying on her belly.

"Shh…"

She pulls him by his shorts, forcing him to kneel next to her. In front of them, the beach is boiling.

"Did your spell go wrong?"

"Thank you."

"For what?"

"For thinking that I am such a powerful witch." She pauses. "But mostly for helping to keep them safe. Look how happy they are."

Now he sees it. Hundreds of tiny turtles are wiggling their way into the surf. It's the most adorable thing he has ever seen in his life. The hairs on his arms rise, goosebumps, a tingling further all the way to his lumbar spine where it lingers, comfortably unsettling. She squeezes his hand; he can't remember when he took it. Or did she?

22

2018

Abhishek leans to the back, then to the front, *no, backwards was better*. He balances on his heels. No … He needs to crouch a little … *It's no use*. He exhales in exasperation. The mirror frame hanging on top of the bathroom sink has been covered with an excessive collage of shells, leaving hardly any space for the functional part of the fixture. A benevolent observer would see this as an artistic interpretation of the city – a mess of scraps and rubble – reflecting only what is necessary, devoid of all vanity. But Abhishek's mind is not known for its benevolent nature. *Is that a trail of ants?* Minuscule pieces of shell are trailing in a neat line on the cement path, off the grid, into a hole in the wall next to it. *Great, another suburb in the making at the cost of … Damn, without his daily fix, his brain just trails off the grid, too.* Abhishek wipes the sweat off his forehead, neatly combing his hair back where just the right amount of gel keeps it in its original place. He twists the strand on his left temple which has a habit of falling out of line and tucks it under the stiff top cover.

The mirror refuses to show anything but a fragment of his coiffure. But what he really needs to see is how all of him is looking in the dark blue pants, white shirt and polka-dotted tie which he has chosen to wear for the first day in his Mumbai office.

He has an idea. First checking for any unwanted stain left by Satchit, or his predecessors, he climbs up on the commode. But the mirror is not his friend today, all he can see now is his waist. Due to the early-morning bending and crouching his shirt has become a little untucked. He tugs and pulls at it to make it sit perfectly inside his pants again. Then he climbs down carefully so that his shirt remains creaseless.

Before leaving the tiny bathroom, he takes one more look into the mirror. Well, at least his face looks nice, despite the harrowing night he has had. He is lucky that way. Very little of his late nights, constant worrying and overthinking ever show up as wrinkles or dark circles on his mostly flawless skin.

"Caffeine is supposed to dry the skin, but who cares if it makes your soul glow."

Abhishek almost yelps in shock. *How does she move so soundlessly and how does she keep answering his unspoken thoughts? They are not even addressed to her.*

Chinky is smiling at him with a cup of steaming hot coffee in her coffee-coloured hands.

Abhishek inhales deeply. He could get used to the cinnamon on his coffee. Reaching to take it from her, his hands grab nothing but thin air. She has already moved with it to his room.

He has no choice but to follow the coffee she is holding. She places it on his bedside table and looks at his open laptop. Abhishek rushes to shut it.

"That doesn't look like your boyfriend." She is looking at Achal's page which Abhishek found on FB. This page is private, too, but at least the profile picture is much bigger than a thumbnail, especially when it is zoomed to pixilation.

Close enough to see the beginnings of a double chin, but also too close to decide if the eyes are a regular brown or a much more attractive, catlike hazel. Unless of course those are just contacts. Which would make them and the person they belong to dreadfully tacky.

"No, it's not, it's just..." Abhishek frowns. "How do you know what my boyfriend looks like?"

"I don't."

"But you just said..."

"And that implies that I have an opinion on what he does 'not' look like, not what he looks like. I don't think he looks like this."

Because he is not cute? *Just say he is not cute, without speaking in riddles and using woo-woo language.*

"I don't see people as cute."

Of course you don't.

"Do you see him as cute?"

That's what I've been trying to decide all night.

Abhishek grimaces as he tries to answer her like a normal, rational person, in the hope that it will inspire her to do the same with him. "Well, he has a really nice cut to his face. But that looks like a double chin, right? Or maybe it's just the light. Because if I see from here..."

He moves his face far to the left, practically contorting his upper body perpendicular to the floor.

"See from this angle, does that look like a dimple?"

Instead of replying like a normal, rational person, Chinky begins to undress.

Abhishek slams his laptop shut and holds it against his chest, in some kind of inexplicable reflex. Why is he hiding himself? He is not the one removing his clothes.

"What the hell are you doing?"

"I'm making a video about how beauty lies not just in the eyes of love but also in the eyes of jealousy and insecurity. I'm sure his lover never looked as long and obsessively at his picture as you did."

"Who is his lover? I mean I have not the faintest idea what you could possibly be talking about. And also can't you speak without being naked? First, you women complain that you are objectified and no one takes you seriously and now you need to be naked to get people to listen?"

"I can't be hiding behind my clothes and still be authentic."

Abhishek is doing a quick scan of his room. Has she hidden any cameras here? What if she is secretly taping him. What if she taped him last night when he had been looking at Kartik's pictures and … thank goodness, he is too much of a prude to do anything without a sheet on top, even if he's only doing it to himself.

Chinky is already speaking into her phone. "…and then you think that they will love somebody else because they are smarter, or prettier … Well, if you spend so much time thinking about this 'somebody else', you are certainly appreciating them more than you are appreciating yourself. It's like the two of you are in a relationship and your 'partner' is the third wheel…" She turns a little, to catch better light on her face. Abhishek deftly steps out of the way of the new frame. He shoves his laptop in his bag, picks it up and hurries out of the room. He does not want to be featured in any videos with her, certainly not naked ones.

In the doorway, he turns around. "Just because I am gay does not mean you can just expose your bare breasts right into my face without my consent!"

"You are right, being naked is about your own skin, not about other people's sexuality. I will do something about it."

Abhishek receives an alert on his phone. He peeks inside the door once more. *Nope*, whatever she is planning to do about 'it', does not involve her putting on clothes. She is still filming herself, stark naked.

"Could you please hand me my blazer? My uber is here, I've got to get to the office."

Two hours later, Abhishek's mood has gone from foul to 'downright foul'. *What the hell is wrong with this traffic?* Of course it is Mumbai, so there is plenty wrong with the traffic, everybody knows that, and Delhi traffic is no peach either, but he left his house at 8.30 a.m. and has just reached the first crossing on the main road. For the past hour now, his Uber has been maintaining a steady 5 km/h.

"Is this normal?" *Should the traffic not open at some point? At least when we pass a signal? Just to give us a little window to gain a little speed and time!*

The Uber driver shrugs, indifferent. "At least we are moving…"

Abhishek peers out of the window. The lady in the cab next to his is typing furiously on her laptop. In the two minutes he spends staring at her, she does not stop even once. The man on his left is gesturing expansively with his hands while staring into the dashboard of the red Hyundai 120 he is driving. He is clearly in the middle of a long and passionate conversation with someone via Bluetooth. Not the slightest bit of anger in his expression. The car has moved a couple of meters by the time his call ends. He takes a breather, picks up a bottle of … water? He takes a long sip from it, then starts another call. He is just as passionate about this one. His smile shows a lot of teeth and he does not even look out once to check on the traffic, he just keeps talking and 'centimetering' his car forward.

Abhishek sighs, quite apparently he is the only one perturbed by this situation. All around him, people are just getting on with their lives.

"What is the ETA?"

"Eleven sixteen."

"I was supposed to reach by ten." *I cannot believe I am going to be late on my first day!*

He inhales deeply, willing himself to be calm. *It is ok. You are just here for some days. It does not matter.*

"What time do you think I should start from Khar if I want to reach the office by ten."

"Seven thirty or forty-five if you want to beat the morning traffic."

So that's what Kartik meant by the long commute. It really is a bitch. Abhishek feels a little better. At least there's an explanation for Kartik's coldness. He was just tired. *Poor baby.*

His stomach growls, reminding him that he had skipped breakfast due to the events which unfolded in the morning. He has to concede that one cannot live on coffee alone, even if it is laced with a fragrant bark. Lord, he is beginning to feel really hungry. Maybe the office has a canteen ... that is, if he ever reaches. The ETA has now changed to 11:18 a.m.

The chronometer shows 11:32 a.m. by the time Abhishek manages to reach the building which houses his Mumbai office. It is a nice-looking edifice, with granite floors and tall glass doors, but of course he cannot waste one more second admiring it.

"Hold the door!" he yells, rushing into the elevator and almost slamming into a guy who seems to be delivering a lot of pizzas.

Finally he can see his reflection in the highly polished copper door of the elevator. His shirt is slightly creased at the waist and his tie has come a little askew. Once he straightens it, he is happy to see that he looks almost impeccable. This could also be due to what offers itself as a comparison: The pizza guy standing next to him is wearing torn denims and a shirt that looks like somebody put it inside a capillary tube and took it out.

The pizza guy catches his eye and smiles. Abhishek moves from the smile to the boxes of pizza, feeling suddenly ravenous. The sinking feeling in his stomach is hitting his brain now, turning his whole body into one big ball of hunger. The pizza carton on the top is a bit lopsided, so close, he can almost reach over and snatch a slice. Who knows when he will be able to go to the canteen. There will probably be a ton of meetings first. He shoves his hands into his pocket to stop them from following the frantic signals his desperate brain is generating. His tongue is left free to flap about in his mouth.

"Good man, this may seem like a strange request, but do you think you could sell me a pizza?"

The man looks up at him in surprise. "Sell you one of 'my' pizzas?"

"Yes, I will pay you extra. I will give you 400 for that small pizza. Tell them you lost it. That should cover more than the cost of the whole pizza which is around 300, I think. Even if they cut it from your salary, you will still make a profit. Or you could sneak away some of the garlic bread — it anyway gets lost so often in an order, does it not? Or half of it and tell those guys you have reduced your portions. It is a lot of money for one measly stick of bread. Just take it."

Abhishek shoves the money into the man's hands and stares at him. Hunger has lit up some savage part of his brain and he no longer has any control over his actions in the civilized world.

The man takes his money and hands him exactly one slice of bread.

Abhishek practically inhales it. His brain, no longer trying to keep him from 'starving to death', switches off survival mode and activates 'I-could-die-of-embarrassment' mode.

"I am so sorry, I don't know what came over me. It's just that I had an over-three-hour-long commute and no breakfast. Dear me! I cannot believe I did this, I am so embarrassed, I could just die..."

The pizza guy smiles.

The elevator dings, they get off on the same floor.

"Where were you coming from?"

"Khar."

"Why didn't you take the train?"

A couple of girls pass them as they walk along a long corridor. The pizza guy seems to be going in the same direction as Abhishek. Abhishek waits until the girls are out of earshot. *He does not want to sound like he is trying to impress the ladies.*

"As a matter of fact, I do not take buses and trains. I have a car back home in Delhi. I am just passing through Mumbai."

"I have two cars, but in this traffic, they are better off in a garage."

Abhishek looks in surprise at the guy. "Two cars? Wow! The tipping scene must be great in Mumbai."

The man throws him an amused look. They have finally reached their destination. At least Abhishek has reached his destination and is staring at the locked door, hunting for a bell. The pizza guy has either followed him or is delivering the pizzas to Abhishek's new office.

Abhishek is about to request him to keep the secret of his garlic bread fiasco between the two of them, when the pizza guy places his thumb on a little scanner by the door. The door unlocks with a click.

"That's how you do it. Come in, Mr Delhi. Oh, and I guess this is also where I tell you: I head the Mumbai office for Morpheus Communications. My name is Hassan."

He reaches out his hands and ushers Abhishek inside. "This is so cool. I always wanted to do this typical romcom thing with a cute girl. You know, I take her parking space and she gets angry, then comes in for an interview and finds out I'm her boss. Do you mind if I change your gender when I tell this story?"

Abhishek is a little dazed as he is led into a cheerful-looking office, full of people dressed almost as shabbily as the pizza guy, who is not actually a pizza guy but his boss.

"Come, let me introduce you to the team, they are going to love our little 'meet cute'. We can tell them all about it over pizza. You get one slice of garlic bread less of course, ha ha."

Abhishek smiles, although he is not amused at all.

The clock shows 3 p.m. His Mumbai office was 'hate at first sight' for Abhishek and in the three-plus hours he has spent here, it hasn't grown on him one bit. For one thing, everybody is dressed up as if they have come to audition for *Roadies* or some other teenage reality show. *Can one not look 'cool' in clothes that are intact and ironed?* The girl at the 'desk' – an old window shutter refurbished with a glass top and painted in screeching pink probably by the girl herself – next to him is wearing pyjamas; or at least Abhishek would recommend her to wear this pair of trousers only behind the closed doors of her bedroom, and that too only if she is committed to remaining alone in her bed. Furthermore, and worse, they are all looking at him as if he is the odd one for having bathed and brushed his hair for such an ordinary occasion like coming to office instead of arriving in whatever clothes he was lounging about in last evening.

He could swear he just heard someone whisper that he was dressed as if he was going for a wedding.

"Well that's typical Delhi." Whoever just said this has not even bothered to keep his voice down.

Abhishek is furious, he gets up and looks around. In the corner behind him is a gaggle of people lounging on the broad wooden swing – *a life-sized oxymoron in any 'decent' workplace, which clearly marks this one as anything but* – giggling and whispering.

"Shhh..." somebody shushes, as his head turns, looking daggers at all of them.

Sheepishly they pretend to go back to work, sticking their noses back into their laptops, as if he was not at all the subject of their afternoon gossip. Of course, he is using the term 'work' very loosely here. *God knows how much work is getting done when everybody seems to be talking and laughing so much. This is an office, not a place of 'fun'.* He suppresses the urge to shout this out loud.

He catches himself still staring, clearly making everybody uncomfortable. *Good.* They are all taking great pains to look away from him, all except one person. A smallish built, slightly effeminate boy gazes straight back at him. Abhishek averts his eyes quickly, but not before noticing the boy throwing him a smile. Abhishek knows that smile. It is not just friendly. Well, whatever. He is not interested. And neither can he work here. It is impossible to focus at this level of noise and movement. Where do all these people keep going? This is the fifth smoke break the girl in the blue crumpled dress has taken. Her original perfume of cheap 'sweet pea' has been overtaken by ever-new layers of nicotine until it reached its current pinnacle of appalling 'cold ashtray' scent. *The whole room is going to reek of something vile once she comes back inside.*

Abhishek gets up. He straightens his tie ... hesitates ... removes it ... folds it neatly, keeps it on his table. He marches straight to Hassan's cabin and knocks on the glass door.

Hassan looks up and smiles cheerfully at him. "Hey, come in. Are you hungry again?"

Abhishek shakes his head.

Hassan offers him a biscuit anyway.

"No, thank you. Actually I have a problem. I normally work alone in a cabin. It's a little hard to concentrate around all these people."

Hassan throws his hands up helplessly.

"I feel you, Mr Delhi, but unfortunately we have just one cabin here and I have to be in it, because it has my name on the door. But feel free to come in and chat with me anytime if you have any other trouble. I could do with the company."

He sits back on his chair and smiles expectantly at Abhishek.

Abhishek gives him a thin smile and leaves. He almost bumps into the boy who was staring at him.

"Oh no, were you complaining to Hassan about us being mean to you?" The boy smiles again, teasing and clearly flirting.

Abhishek shakes his head. He tries to head back to his chair.

The boy introduces himself, "I'm Riyan and I honestly really like what you are wearing. It suits you."

"Thanks."

He tries again to move past Riyan.

"How's Mr Sharma? He was a bit unwell last time I was there. Said the pollution was getting to him."

Abhishek stops. "Have you been to our Delhi office then?"

"A few times."

"I am so sorry. I seem to not remember seeing you there."

Riyan smiles and touches his shoulder gently.

"But I remember you."

He lets Abhishek pass.

The next few days are equally disheartening. You would assume that they would have got used to him looking appropriately dressed for a day at work by now, but no. They still stare as if he is the one who is 'out of place', wearing a shirt in 'office'. But at least he refuses to give in to the subtle group pressure and dress up – or should that be down – like a slob. The only thing he has let go of is the tie. But that is about as informal as he is ready to go. Anyway, he is not left with much of a choice. The only other clothes he has carried with him are far too casual for work. He has his standards.

Abhishek sighs. This is hell but he would still be happy to suffer through it if only Kartik would call. Or even text. Although, he does text – but only in replies. As if they were still in two different cities. The weekend is almost here, and Kartik has still not made any plans to meet or spend time together. He sighs again.

"Hey, what are you doing this weekend?" It's Riyan again. That boy is persistent, Abhishek will give him that. He just refuses to be ignored.

I shall be with my boyfriend, I hope.

"Not sure, why?"

"Want to come out clubbing?"

Abhishek looks again at Riyan, wondering if he would photograph well. He does have kind of a cute face. Maybe a few pictures with him at a party on social media would make Kartik understand that he is not the only fish in Mumbai's really polluted sea.

"Maybe, I will let you know."

After work, Abhishek wanders off to the Gateway of India. At least that is within walking distance from his office. He has been coming here since his first day in town. Standing by the balustrade – just like countless other tourists. But unlike the normal tourists, Abhishek has not spent even a minute looking at the Gateway or marvelling at the boats standing majestically at sea. Neither has he noticed the orange sun setting into the grey waters behind him because what he is looking for is not in that direction.

His eyes are busy scanning the road which leads people towards the Gateway. His searching eyes keep catching the attention of the gazillion couples who linger around the monument. Watching them enjoy crowding the air with their unnecessary PDA puts Abhishek in a foul mood. Especially when they approach him, requesting him to "please click our picture."

"Why?" asks Abhishek, as one more boy tries to give him his phone for a "take our photograph pleaseee…"

"Why do you think that I would have nothing better to do than take your picture?"

"Because you are just standing here all alone, doing nothing. Wouldn't you rather be the one my babe and I tell our future children about? We can tell them how you photographed our first kiss in Mumbai!" The couple proceeds to kiss, long and hard, right in front of him.

It reminds Abhishek of how long it has been since anybody has kissed him this passionately. The 'Delhi' in him instinctively decides to focus on the outrage. He smacks the boy's hand away, really hard. "Just because you are some kind of pervert trying to make pornographic videos of your girlfriend to share later with your friends and brag about your masculinity and virility, does not give you the right to try and make me a part of it. Do it yourself."

The couple disengages. They are also outraged.

"What did you say, asshole? Porn? What the fuck is wrong with you, man? This is my fiancée, why the hell will I share her video?"

"Oh, so is that honour reserved for your other girlfriends – whom you will do anything with but marry?"

The girl gasps at Abhishek's words. Her 'fiancée' prefers to use his fists, landing a perfect left hook on Abhishek's cheek.

It sends him staggering. He actually sees stars and then – even more incredible – he has a vision of Kartik, walking, no, running towards him, anxiety sketched all over his face. Abhishek shakes his head to get rid of the hallucination. *Has this idiot damaged his brain?* The mirage refuses to vanish. In fact it has even acquired a voice and is saying … things … which are not translating into words, but only gibberish.

It takes Abhishek a few seconds to realize that this is no hallucination. It *is* Kartik and he is not speaking gibberish but Marathi to the pair. They respond in equally rapid Marathi. Suddenly, all three heads turn towards him.

"Hey, what a surprise running into you here," says Abhishek, standing up straight and being very nonchalant while also quickly tucking in his shirt and straightening his hair as discreetly as he can.

The boy throws him one last dirty look, his girlfriend says something which is probably rude but of course he does not understand. Then the girl puts her arm around the boy's shoulder and takes a selfie. *She could have just done that in the first place.*

Abhishek looks at Kartik, desperately trying to dredge up some kind of explanation that has him coming off as cool.

Kartik reaches out and touches his cheek, right where he's been punched. "Ouch!"

He is in heaven. *Is this what 'bittersweet' feels like?*

"You are just 'trouble', aren't you?" Kartik gently caresses his cheek, smiling tenderly at him.

Abhishek could die of happiness. Fortunately his brain knows that this, too, is just a figure of speech.

"Come, let's put something on this beautiful face before it swells."

Abhishek is committing it all to memory, the table with its worn-out brown top, now coated with the romance of 'aging and witnessing life' – like this moment. The wall blackened with soot from the open kitchen slips into his mind and transforms into a black-and-white charcoal painting that even years later his brain insists was hanging there. From now on whenever Abhishek will see a Udupi restaurant anywhere, his heart will give a little flutter and go back to this moment, where he is right now, in the original Udupi restaurant, sitting absolutely still as Kartik applies ice on his face. *Yes, this is what complete and utter happiness feels like.*

Abhishek's memory also provides the background score: '*Pehli baar mohabbat*' playing in the background. A detail which could be true, as Bollywood is the choice of music for this particular restaurant.

As far as he remembers, the song comes to an end at the same time Kartik's phone beeps. This is also when the moment breaks. Kartik answers the phone and gets up.

"I have to go now. It's been a long day. Will you be hanging out here?"

Abhishek gets up too.

"No, no, I have to go home as well. Let's go together. My new place is quite close to yours actually, maybe I can even…"

"Oh, I'm not going home. I'll be getting off at Bandra. But sure we can take the same train."

"Train?"

Kartik has already started moving. Abhishek runs behind him.

"Sure, let's take the train. It will be fun."

Fifteen minutes later Abhishek is visibly shaken, as he tries to stand as close as possible to Kartik on a really crowded platform. The board reads 'Platform 3'. How has he reached here? When did they leave behind platforms 1 and 2? Abhishek has no clear recollection except for wading through a massive crush of people.

In fact the experience of the last five minutes has transported him to when he was nine years old. His parents had taken him for the annual book fair at Pragati Maidan. Never before had he seen so many people in one place. *I am just a little boy, I am going to get crushed,* he had thought, as his father had held fast onto his hand, pushing through the crowd. Abhishek had kept his eyes shut the entire time. He had opened them only when he had heard his father ask if he wanted to buy something from the fantasy section. They were in front of a stall which was selling books for children, except that Abhishek could not see any books, only even more people in front of him. Then somebody had jostled him from the side to get to the front and Abhishek had lost it. He had thrown a huge and very loud tantrum and demanded that he be taken home RIGHT NOW. He had not stopped bawling and yelling until his embarrassed father had picked him up and marched out of there.

Now, Abhishek can feel the same sense of panic bubbling in his stomach as the train pulls up a surge of bodies. *Can he throw a tantrum and have Kartik carry him away from the platform?* But where is Kartik? Abhishek backs away in panic. He cannot see Kartik anywhere. The train starts moving, Abhishek is left standing behind on the platform. Kartik is gone.

He is in a state by the time he reaches home.

Despite the crowds still milling about him, he had continued waiting for – he knows this so precisely because he had timed it and felt every excruciating second pass – eleven minutes, in the evidently futile hope that Kartik would realize that he had not boarded the train with him. And upon having said realization he would waste no time in boarding the very next train back to the same spot where the two had been separated.

But no such luck. The number of people seemed to be multiplying on the platform, some vomited out within the few milliseconds that a train would care to stop, the others just seemingly materialized out of thin air, but not one of this mass of scurrying humanity was Kartik. But even so, Abhishek had waited, rooted to the same spot, until the moving bodies around him lost all form and feature and could no longer be distinguished as having any mass or substance. Just lines of movement. Out of the corner of his eye, he had been aware of the time on the clock, slowly counting 60 more seconds, until the display had changed to read 2100 hours. That was when he had decided it was a good time to go home. Kartik was not coming back.

Somehow he had pushed and shoved his way out of the transit barn and its human cattle, and hailed a cab. As the vehicle had weaved and jostled through the equally baneful herd of human bodies trapped in their sauntering tin cans, albeit mercifully less than what it was in the morning, so had one thought rattled relentlessly in his mind: *Kartik did not care that I was left behind.*

It had been a relief when the taxi had finally stopped outside Chinky's building. All Abhishek wanted to do was to go inside and retreat from the evil of the outside with a cup of coffee. *Maybe he could even tell Chinky what had happened…* Although she would probably have some indecipherable and frustrating riddle for him. At the very least, she would not judge and even if she did, he did not care enough about her opinion to be bothered by it.

So it is with a sense of almost relief and gratitude to be back home … well, not quite home, but at least to a place of refuge … that Abhishek turns the key in the lock – only to smack into the protruding, hairy and naked belly of a completely unclothed man. He blinks, the naked man multiples by about 100 and the whole room is full of similarly naked men. He blinks again and the number reduces a little, but they are still everywhere. Like a wall-to-wall carpet of animated bodies on display in all their nude grotesqueness, inside the living room. What the hell is going on?

"I am not ashamed," shouts one of the naked men. "My belly might be bigger than my penis but it is not a contest."

"Size lies in the satisfaction of the beholder."

"Some women like to cuddle."

"It is not about women or what they like. How much affection do you feel when you look at yourself? Do you feel like you want to cuddle yourself?"

Chinky pops into view, fully clothed for once, although given the circumstances and the rest of the ambience, who really cares? Abhishek is still standing at the door in a state of semi-paralysis, doing what can only be described as 'dithering'. His recently traumatized soft brain tissue is unable to make a decision – should he go in and demand they stop this nonsense, or just whirl around and leave? But go where? His right foot unwillingly detaches and equally unwillingly reconnects its nerves to Abhishek's brain which has succumbed into an infinite loop of stepping over the threshold, immediately retracting, stepping forward, then back again. Fortunately, Chinky reaches him and ushers him inside, ending his temporary brain freeze.

This also causes his voice to return. "Oh my bloody fucking god, what is happening here? An orgy? Devil worship? Is it a cult? Do you all think you are aliens?"

"No, no, even though those are all exciting things, this is just a workshop. For people to feel comfortable in their skins."

"But why the hell are they all naked?"

"They are just minus clothes. They still need much more work before they can call themselves naked."

The crowd cheers. Abhishek looks at them in disbelief. A naked man touches his arm tentatively.

"I think you will feel happy if you get yourself out of these clothes."

Abhishek backs away, alarmed.

"Nobody sees my naked body except the man I love."

He storms past all of them into his room and slams the door shut. Locks it. Double checks the lock. And finally sits on the bed, holding his head in his hands. *Breathe. Inhale, exhale, go to your happy place...* But what is his happy place? ... That restaurant! Should he go back to the restaurant?

Before his thoughts can wander further, there is a knock on the door.

"Hi, may I come in?"

Abhishek sniffs. If she is carrying the cinnamon coffee he will let her in.

The smell hits him as soon as he thinks about it. *He doesn't know where his happy place is, but wherever it is, it's going to have coffee, to put the 'happy' in it.*

He reaches for the door, then stops.

"Have the naked people gone?"

"Yes."

He advances to open the door, then stops midway. "Are you wearing clothes?"

A sigh.

"Yes. No reason not to while speaking with you."

Abhishek opens the door. Chinky lets herself in. She is carrying coffee for both of them. Abhishek takes his cup, waiting for her to leave. She does not. Instead, she proceeds to sit on his bed, crosses her legs in full padmasana and looks at his face. Then she looks at his dishevelled work clothes which add to the dismal picture of distress that is Abhishek.

"You know, that gentleman was right. You *would* be happier without these clothes."

Abhishek's head jerks up from his cup of coffee. He is furious. After the day he has had, he deserves some peace.

"How many naked men do you need to see in a day? What kind of sick perversion is this? I am sorry but I am not into whatever creepy, crazy…"

Chinky is not listening to him. She has walked out, over to the closet he had once mistaken for a toilet, and is now rummaging for something inside.

Abhishek follows her, he has found his high horse and he is not about to alight from it, not without a good heartfelt rant.

"You know, in any interaction between two people there needs to be this bare minimal but extremely important thing called a 'boundary', and one usually does the other the very basic courtesy of respecting it. But if that concept is offensive to whatever bohemian thing you consider your 'vibe', I can just move out or…"

Chinky has found what she was looking for. She pulls up a stack of colourful linen shirts and pants.

"I think you will feel better in the office if you dress up in clothes which are less 'demanding.'"

Abhishek looks suspiciously at the clothes she is holding up. They do look nice.

"What do you think my clothes 'demand'?"

"Attention mainly." She grins at him. "And a lot of care from you."

Abhishek smiles despite himself. He loathes to admit it, but she is right.

He reaches for the clothes tentatively, picks up a shirt and holds it against himself.

"Why does this look like a good fit? Have you been secretly shopping for me?"

Chinky smiles, looking wistful.

"Maybe that is what I was 'actually' doing…"

She caresses one of the shirts gently. A half smile plays on her lips, her eyes locked onto something that is visible only to her. She seems to have left the room.

Abhishek finds himself suddenly concerned. He reaches a hand towards her, before he realizes what he is doing. *He needs to bring her back.*

There is a sound of a key turning in a lock.

Abhishek jumps in surprise.

Chinky returns with a quick swivel of her head.

"Are your naked people back?"

Chinky smiles. "One of the most naked, if I recognize the footsteps correctly."

23

7.45 p.m.

Vincent pushes a sketch of Adi Shakti towards Gaikwad. The policeman looks at it. "What is this?"

"You asked me who all had a key to Chinky's apartment. This is the only one who made an impression on me. Her name is Jhansi I think."

"Where is her face?"

Vincent shrugs. "Her face ... I don't think I cared about that. But this is a good representation of her soul."

He stares at his own sketch, at the flow of colour pencil strokes on the paper. Some would say that colour pencils are for kindergarten children, but people say a lot of shit. Maybe he is stuck on the emotional level of a kindergartener. So what? Didn't Picasso himself say that the biggest feat is keeping the child within the adult alive? Of course these words coming from a dead artist make them wisdom. Nobody listens to an artist who still breathes. If he'd tell this dimwit of a policeman why he prefers ... he wouldn't value it. Let alone understand. But then again he also didn't ask. Vincent's mind takes him back to the only person who ever honestly wanted to know.

24

2013

"But why exactly do you like colour pencils?"

"Because they show the process even in the final piece."

Vincent is squinting his eyes as he tries to make out the soft strokes of the first colour layer. He looks up, takes a sip of his beer and winks at her. "Plus, they do take me back to the easy times of childhood where I would just doodle away without thinking much."

"Yeah, it's nice to just do and not think. I can only do that when something is really difficult or really easy."

"Like right now."

"Like my job."

"Which one is more difficult – cutting cookies or having sex?"

Vincent does not look up from his sketch.

"You would think it's the cookies, but it's not."

Sweat is dripping from Jhansi's forehead onto the dough. Chinky removes the stencil, lifting the spikes of the star with a huge kitchen knife and balancing it onto the baking paper. She had insisted that they light the house only with fairy lights. Which does make everything look more Christmassy. But Christmas cookies were most definitely not invented in a place where one would sweat their ass off to make them. They probably came into being for the exact opposite reason: to warm the houses of the medieval merchants who had returned to their icy hometowns with bags filled with Indian spices. That's why Christmas smells a bit like India. And why Indian kitchens smell like Christmas. This one most definitely does.

A warm fuzzy feeling bubbles up in his stomach, a faint memory of happy childhood days far back in the past, and a caring mother… But it is hard to enjoy the atmosphere when all he can think of is the urge to stick his head into the freezer. His shirt is sticking to his chest – the hair, in an urge to escape the sauna and catch a breath of fresh air, poking out through the stitches of the fabric.

"Why don't you just take it off?" Smelling like the ghost of Christmas cookies, Chinky moves her oven-hot fingers along his hips, gently lifting up his shirt.

"How do you always know what I am thinking?"

"That men always think about sex is not rocket science." Jhansi graces the two lovers with a dramatic eye roll.

"As a matter of fact, I was *not* thinking about sex. It's too damn hot. That's what I was thinking."

"It seems that heat fires up your artistic spark though." Chinky takes the paper from Vincent's lap and holds it into the light. Her gaze wanders from the paper to Jhansi who is still standing at the kitchen counter, the pallu of her sari tucked in around her waist, fairy lights shining through the little strands of hair that have gone up in all directions from the humidity and heat. As she leans back to drink water from a steel cup without touching it with her lips, her Adam's apple moves up and down with each thirsty sip.

"You've captured her perfectly." Chinky plants a salty wet kiss on his lips. His lips are colder than hers.

25

8 p.m.

Gaikwad turns to Sahil. "Why don't you put this on the noticeboard, ask people if they can 'identify' this soul." The sarcasm in his voice is unmistakable.

"Chinky could have. But then if she was here you wouldn't have needed this investigation, would you?"

Sahil and Gaikwad exchange looks.

"Are you thinking that somebody broke into Chinky's house to steal something and Chinky saw them and they killed her?" asks Vincent.

"It's logical. No, sir?"

Gaikwad gives Sahil a death stare. How was one to get the suspect to talk, if he pre-empts everything?

Vincent interrupts his rising irritation. "Except that nothing about Chinky was logical, so why should her death be?"

Gaikwad sighs, maybe this is the key – reveal more information to see if he takes the bait. One has to own one's mistakes to rise above them and then strike gloriously!

"So, Miss Iti has told us that you were not very happy with the number of people who had a key to Chinky Ma'am's apartment."

"Who is Iti?"

Shit, he did not take the bait.

"Sorry Indian names are too complicated for me sometimes."

Sahil nods vigorously. "I agree. Sometimes even I can't tell the difference between Sukriti or Supriti…"

Gaikwad throws a dirty look at him. He shuts up.

"There are literally THREE letters in this name."

"That's why I don't remember it."

Gaikwad sighs. He shows Vincent a picture. The man with the parchment-coloured, haggard face squints at it.

"I might have seen her in the apartment. She probably had a key too."

Gaikwad is exasperated.

"Of course she would have had a key. She was living there, how was she to get in and out without a key?"

"Would you ask a thief the same question?" Vincent chuckles, insolently.

26

5 p.m.

"Wow, you really took long in there. Anyway – quick now, who was it that entered in the middle of the night?"

Sahil does not even wait for Abhishek to sit down in his chair. Abhishek ignores his chair and walks over to Gaikwad's. He bends down and whispers something into Gaikwad's ear.

"Hey, that's not fair, even I want to know. Sir, please, you must tell me."

"He said the toilet is not flushing. There, now you know. Now please go attend to it."

Sahil is nonplussed. Abhishek groans quietly, even more uncomfortable. Both avoid looking at each other.

Gaikwad clears his throat. Finally his subordinate gets up. "But don't start till I'm back."

"This is an investigation not a storytelling session."

With surprising authority, Sahil marches out into the anteroom where a bunch of policemen are whiling away their time between Windows 98 screensavers and piles of paper.

"Somebody forgot to flush the toilet. Panday, go get a bucket of water and sort it out."

Abhishek visibly flinches as everybody turns to look at the cop who has come in yelling and glaring at all of them.

Mortified, Abhishek tries to communicate with Gaikwad via his eyes. *Please do not tell him it was me.* He does not reciprocate.

Alright. Just act as if you do not know what's going on. You are just a guest here, not your station, not your business. Abhishek suppresses the urge to whistle to make it even more apparent how nonchalant he is. *Still, no harm in disappearing from the scene.* He searches for something to lean against, so he can hide his face from the men in the other room. *The shelf.* With his index finger he nudges the paper napkin with a half-eaten samosa to the side, rubbing the stain of ketchup with a fresh napkin, so he can place his elbow…

"DON'T."

"What?"

"That's evidence." Sahil has come to the rescue. Or maybe not.

All heads turn towards Abhishek.

"That's a sample." Abhishek does not get it. But he is also too embarrassed to react. His elbow still hovering above the shelf.

"What?"

"It's a DNA sample from a crime scene."

"Sahil! WHY IS THIS HERE?" Gaikwad makes a half-hearted effort to get up. It takes him time to lift himself out of the chair. He decides not to. The effort and anger have turned his face dark red.

"And what is wrong with you guys? Are you animals? Panday!"

Somebody scurries after the said 'Panday', a young officer with the onset of a paunch, carrying a mop and a pail of water.

Sahil cautiously removes the napkin and samosa from the edge of the shelf.

"We are out of containers, sir. The shifting, you know, sir…" Then turning to Abhishek, "You haven't touched this, right? Otherwise I'll have to take your DNA sample, just to be sure…"

"No, no!"

He knows how this works. First they take his DNA sample and next thing he knows, some day in the future, they have a big case to solve and not enough suspects and voila – they have planted his DNA somewhere as evidence and arrested him. Somebody gets a promotion for their 'quick' work and he is sent to jail for a crime he was not even aware had been committed.

"Okay, sit down."

"So you do not need my sample?"

"No, we are out of DNA collection kits."

Of course they are.

Mouthing a silent prayer of gratitude to the same shoddy police work that was about to get him an unfair life sentence just a few seconds ago, Abhishek exhales in relief.

"Could I also have another coffee please?"

"Maybe you should not until our little plumbing issue is sorted," replies Gaikwad.

Abhishek flinches again.

Sahil, who has removed his invisible jacket of sudden authority, looks at Gaikwad. "I think they will take care of it for now, so I don't have to go, do I?"

Gaikwad shrugs.

Sahil sits down, all attention on Abhishek, lays out his notebook and pencil in front of him, his eyes searching Gaikwad's. *Not a storytelling session, an investigation!*

Abhishek walks back to his chair and sinks into it. "She said her name was Jhansi, or maybe she came from Jhansi. I do not recall … Her presence had rattled me a fair bit."

27

2018

Chinky steps out of the kitchen. Abhishek dithers. On the one hand, his senses most definitely cannot take anymore assault but, on the other, the prospect of spending the night in the closet seems even more unpleasant than the one he had spent in the bathroom. For one there is no toilet here.

A shimmer of something sequined catches Abhishek's eye. He peeks out. He can make out the silhouette of a woman wearing something deep cut and so shiny that it hurts his eyes – but much less than her naked flesh would have. He exhales in relief and steps out to greet her.

The lights in Chinky's living room are dim, but the woman has angled herself perfectly to catch whatever light the lamp can spare on her face. She seems to be doing it deliberately, although Abhishek cannot really imagine why. She does not seem to have a particularly beautiful face. The jawline is a little too pronounced and as she tilts her head slightly, it looks as if she has a faint stubble on her chin.

"I'm Jhansi."

Abhishek is not sure at what point the realization hits him that this is not a woman. Is it the stubble or her voice, hoarse and raspy, clearly masculine.

The person in the shiny clothes stretches out a small, almost dainty hand. Abhishek stares at it, the sequined dress, the cleavage on display, suddenly it all makes sense.

Abhishek turns to Chinky. "I think I left the gas on in the kitchen. Could you please help me turn it off?"

Jhansi chimes in before Chinky can pass as much as an amused glance in Abhishek's direction. "Yes, Chinky, better turn off that gas before I cause a fire."

"It's risky, na? Because I'm smoking hot," she explains to Abhishek.

"I got it," mumbles Abhishek, escaping into the kitchen. Chinky follows. From the living room Abhishek can hear Jhansi putting on some music. A slow jazz number.

"Well, now that we are here, maybe you could turn the gas on for real?"

Abhishek looks sheepish. "I do not want you to think I have anything against transexuals, but…" He hesitates, unsure how to say it politely.

Chinky seems oblivious to his discomfort. Humming a strange tune, she pulls out a drawer with several oriental-looking boxes. Lingering awhile, she retrieves one purple and one plain gold-coloured one.

"I mean I get it. A person born in the wrong body feels like they were denied the choice, so they exert their power to choose, rather forcefully, with their clothes, and of course it can get a little overboard and sparkly…"

"Smell."

The purple sachet is shoved under his nose.

It smells like room freshener. Or the sachets one places in the cupboard to keep moths away…

"This is food?"

"Bees might call it 'food'. But it is also edible for us humans."

"Anyway, I was saying, clothes in themselves are not a problem, I am just concerned that these may be work clothes and the kind of work that requires this particular dress code..."

Chinky sprinkles a bunch of purple kernels and some tiny white flowers into the boiling pot.

"Can you look out of the window for a moment?"

"Why, are you expecting more 'guests'?"

"Maybe. Look up – how full is it?"

"What?"

"The moon."

"I cannot tell. It's not round, more like a lopsided egg ... hey, you are digressing!" Abhishek cannot believe that he fell for this trick! But Chinky is already leaning out of the window.

Mumbling something like "this might do" to herself, she walks to her room, opens the cupboard and rummages through one particular shelf. Abhishek follows her.

"Listen, so I gather from her appearance that she is most likely – without judging prematurely here – a professional in a trade that..."

"Got it!"

Chinky gleefully throws on a white kaftan of sorts.

"You are right, Abhishek. Every trade requires the right kind of clothing. Otherwise the 'feel' just doesn't come, does it? And especially for unique tasks that require human intimacy I believe one should not even wash them. Why remove all the beautiful layers and layers of magic created by so much sweat and labour? Here, smell!"

She shoves her sleeve under his nose.

He pushes it away. Rudely. "No, I do not want to smell whoever you had sex with in this! What I was say..."

"But I'm not talking about sex, silly! I'm talking about something much more potent – though sex can be helpful here. I'm talking about magic."

Chinky has returned to the stove. She turns off the kitchen light, takes a piece of wood from her sleeve – *how on earth did she keep it there?* – and lights it with the gas. Again humming this strange tune.

"You are not listening, I am telling you that I am not comfortable with a prostitute in the house!"

The last sentence is a lot louder than he had intended. It may be because Chinky has chosen that exact moment to stop humming or maybe it is because the jazz playing outside has shushed a while to listen to him, or perhaps he is the one who has caught the pause between the tracks, but Abhishek knows his voice has carried. All the way to the next room, where everything seems to have gone perfectly still. Abhishek holds his breath and strains to listen. But listen for what? What sound can a person make to indicate that they are offended? Nothing crashes against anything else. But nothing moves either. Why isn't the music resuming? Is it the calm before a storm? What kind of language would a transsexual prostitute have at her disposal to express her anger? Abhishek's ears burn from the words he has not even heard yet.

He looks towards Chinky for help. She indicates that the tea is ready, handing him three cups and three coasters. "Please set the table."

She herself has walked out with the pot which is smelling like somebody doused it in lavender and chamomile. A strange mélange of smells but not unpleasant. Should he follow her to the living room? Alas, he has the teacups. So unless he would like to force Chinky and her 'guest' to drink out of the spout, he probably should.

Abhishek braces himself for just about anything as he walks into the room to face Jhansi. She is standing with her back to him. As she turns around with a satisfied smile, Abhishek notices that she is holding a vinyl in her hand.

Now he sees a whole stack of them. So that's what she has been rummaging through? How has he not noticed a LP player in the house? It is right there, just next to the couch. Hard to miss but he usually prefers not to linger in this room. All the esoteric symbolism makes him uncomfortable, a reminder that he is voluntarily living with a crazy lady. Next to the LP player is an even more magnificent gramophone. Complete with a big shiny brass horn. Abhishek moves closer to examine it. It looks like a genuine antique. *Has she acquired it by accident?*

Jhansi has pulled the vinyl out of the cover. Abhishek looks at the title. It is *Pretty Woman*.

"I really like this soundtrack," he says, trying to make amends.

Jhansi quirks an eyebrow at him. "Of course, it's 'beautiful' when Julia Roberts does it but a problem when it's plain old Jhansi."

He tries to mumble an apology.

"The tea is getting cold." Chinky has poured it out into three cups.

Jhansi whirls around and does a little pirouette. She glides gracefully towards the table and sips daintily at her tea. One leg crossed neatly on top of the other.

She notices him staring and suddenly grins, showing sparkling white teeth with an admittedly charming gap between her incisors. "One of my customers likes to play dress up. Makes me pretend 'th-at I ahm thee Queen of Eengland.'"

Abhishek busies himself with his own tea. It tastes a lot less complicated than it smells, like crushed flowers and sugar crystals. It calms him almost instantly. *What has she put in it?*

Jhansi seems to echo his feelings. She sighs deeply. "Thank you, Chinky, this is just what I needed. I had such a day. My landlord evicted me again." She turns to Abhishek, including him in the conversation.

"Oh, that's terrible," Abhishek musters as much sympathy as he can in his voice, "is it because of your..." He clams up, realizing the faux pas he has just made.

"My profession?" She smiles at him. "Yes. If I knew that it would cause me so much trouble, I would have gone with my first career choice."

"Which was?"

"To be an actor of course. Isn't that what every pretty girl in Mumbai wants? But you hear all these stories about actors not getting houses. Nobody told me the same thing happens to prostitutes. I guess it's just not something people want to have conversations about. I don't know why. It's a profession, too, just like any other. And at least not as boring and predictable as nine-to-five slavery."

She grins at him again. Abhishek has a feeling that she has subtly put him in his place without uttering a single cuss word.

He looks at Chinky, she is engrossed in her tea, and not part of this conversation at all. Clearly she knows that Jhansi can take care of herself.

An uncomfortable silence permeates the room.

"So how do you know Chinky?" Abhishek asks. His tongue has almost automatically begun to form words that would fill the empty space with polite conversation. The kind that one has when seated opposite a stranger at dinner parties with no option to escape – just that this was *his* house and quite obviously he could escape to his room. But something keeps him glued to his spot. Some unreasonable kind of fear ... a feeling of ... he is unable to pinpoint it.

"Who else has a key to this house?"

28

2010

Yash Chopra.

The creator of her Technicolor childhood dreams. The one who sowed the seed of a career in Bollywood in her young heart. A dream that lay dormant. 'Badal pe paon hai' from Chak De India starts playing in her mind. She has watched it so many times. Just like those young, spirited female hockey players, she too is far away from her 'gaon', just waiting for her dreams to soar. A sudden shiver of anticipation overcomes her – her life, too, is turning into a film ... ab to bhai chal padi, apni ye nao hai ... and now she is actually here, at the place where film ideas are turned to the most Technicolor of all Technicolor realities.

At YRF.

She can feel the seed growing into a tree, just like the ones here in the courtyard. Since she has passed the security, mustering all her courage to not quiver in her voice, she feels already one inch taller. She follows his instructions towards the entrance into what looks like the main studio building. The studio which has made them all – the stars smiling from the walls at each stairwell: Sridevi, Madhuri Dixit, Kajol, Katrina, Kareena, Shah Rukh Khan. Oh my god! Shah Rukh might have walked on those very tiles which her chappals are touching at this very moment. She pauses. Maybe he slid his hands along the exact same wall where she is standing right now. Where would his hand have touched the paint? She looks at the beige wall next to the collage of Bollywood posters. Gently placing her hand on it ... Someone pushes her shoulder, almost knocking her over, running up the staircase.

"What are you doing here? Don't you have any work?" the girl with a clipboard in her hand demands to know from Iti. She is wearing her glasses on her forehead and looks very serious. She also has a walkie-talkie headset.

Iti concludes that she must be an important part of the film crew. She reaches out her hand: "Hi, I'm Iti. It is my first day today. I'm the costume assistant."

"Go to Divya ma'am's make-up room and get her yellow dupatta."

"Oh my god! Divya Gupta! Is she on set anywhere? Where is…"

"Get the dupatta."

The girl turns to the microphone on her walkie-talkie. "Costume base … dupatta on its way. ETA is two minutes."

Before Iti can ask anything about anything, the girl has vanished around the corner. Iti's heart is pumping fast. This is going well. She already has a task. She doesn't know what ETA means but she assumes that she has two minutes to find the dupatta. It's a bit like the video games which Surat always plays. She stumbles up the remaining two steps and lands in a hallway full of rooms to the left and to the right. Some of them have labels outside. 'Salman'. *Oh my god! Is this where Salman Khan usually stays!* Iti is tempted to press the door handle, but then, what if he's in there? What would she say? She blushes and quickly retrieves her hand. Just in time.

"Eh madam!" a potbellied man in a black t-shirt is shouting at her from the open room opposite. He has a kettle in his hand which he uses to point at Iti. Hot water spills out. Iti freezes. But he too has a walkie-talkie. So maybe he is also from the film crew? She decides it is better to answer.

"Oh hello. I'm looking for Divya ma'am's room. We (*she can't believe she said 'we'!*) need her yellow dupatta for the shoot."

The man points the nozzle of the kettle to a room with a ferocious looking woman standing outside it.

"This." With a thick Marathi accent he adds, "Ask this *chitkin*."

Iti quickly makes her way to the woman. She breathes in deeply. "Hello, Chitkin, my name is Iti. Can I please have the yellow dupatta for the scene."

"Why the fuck are you being a bitch? Is it funny? I work here, it's my job to see that Divya ma'am is not bothered. Does that give you all the right to be so fucking rude…"

Iti is too taken aback to react.

"What the fuck is going on here?"

The clipboard girl shoots around the corner. "We have been waiting over ten minutes for the shot. What the hell are you doing?"

"I just asked Chitkin here to give me…"

"I have had it. Your entire staff is an asshole behind my back and now they are doing it to my face … this whole production is incompetent!"

The AD turns furiously towards Iti. "What the fuck is wrong with you? Are you stupid?" With a sudden jerk of her head, she takes a step to the side, turns towards the wall and frantically whispers something into her walkie-talkie.

A small, effeminate man prances along the hallway, gesturing wildly with his hands while speaking on the phone and also continuously looking over his shoulder. "Yes, Karishma, you ought to come! This is just no way of working. I tell you! Good luck the designer is not here to see this!"

He turns around, covering the mouthpiece with his hand. "Don't worry, Divya darling, Karishma is just on her way."

Holding her head full of dark red hair high, 'Divya darling' reaches out her alabaster hand with perfectly polished nails and with a pointed wink demands the phone from the little man. "Karishma, I need to focus on my craft and your job is to make that happen!" A pause. "Good." With yet another elegant sleight of hand, she places the phone back into the hand of its owner. He strides ahead, shooing imaginary (the hallway is empty apart from Iti, the serious girl and the angry woman guarding the door) people out of his way. Like an eager courtier would do for his beloved queen of hearts. But instead of 'Heads Off', this queen has more to say: "Why are you all yelling like this?"

Then, addressing the clipboard girl: "Get me a tonic water and call me when the shot is actually ready, I can't just keep waiting there."

She reaches her hand over her shoulder. Another man in a sort of uniform, grey shirt and pants, whom Iti had missed until now places an electric hand fan into the alabaster hand. She eases. Footsteps are heard from the end of the hallway. Taking big strides, a middle-aged man approaches. But Iti hardly notices him.

Her mind still hasn't fully processed the scene which has just taken place, but her face broke into a big smile as soon as Divya had approached. Now that the silver-screen beauty has finished speaking, words blurt out of Iti's mouth: "Oh my god, ma'am. I can't believe I am seeing you on my first day. I'm a huge fan, so is my mother. Can I please get an autograph?"

"Who the hell is this?" The middle-aged man has reached, panting hard.

"Nobody, sir. She's fired."

The clipboard girl gives Iti a death stare and only her glasses, now on her nose, prevent Iti from actually getting killed. She freezes.

"What?"

The girl intensifies her stare.

Meanwhile, the director, actress, make-up artist and junior PA have vanished inside her room and closed the door behind them.

Tears are welling up in Iti's eyes. The assistant director's look turns into exasperation. "Oh please," she rolls her eyes and heads down the staircase. Then, suddenly at the landing, she stops and looks back at Iti. "One tip … find another industry if this already makes you cry."

This is the final blow. Tears are streaming down Iti's cheeks. She slides herself along the wall and sits on the floor – the same wall that Shah Rukh Khan has touched, the same floor that his feet have walked on … *maybe he also sat here hopelessly like this. Right here. Once upon a time* … No, she won't give up. This *is* her industry. No matter what people say. But pep-talking to herself doesn't stop the tears from streaming down.

"Eh Madam."

It's the potbellied man again.

She looks up.

"Sorry."

"What?"

"I did not know that you don't speak Marathi."

Iti does not get it. "Why would I speak Marathi?"

"You come to Mumbai, you should know Marathi."

"Hmm." Iti still doesn't understand. She leans her forehead against her knees, still sobbing but making an effort to compose herself in front of this person.

He comes closer. In his hand a thermos and a stack of paper cups. It smells of chai. He leans down. "*Chitkin* means 'witch'. But not the magical one. In Marathi. Learn some."

As he turns around the corner, she can read the back of his t-shirt. 'Spot'. Is that his name? She shall remember it, in case they ever meet again.

She takes out the little red booklet from the back of her jeans pocket: *Chitkin (Marathi) = witch.*

It is the first of many words she would write and learn.

Iti doesn't really remember how she walked out of YRF. Were people staring at her? Was it obvious that she had cried? Did the guy at the gate pass a comment?

It doesn't matter.

Right now, she is just tired. She has been walking for forty-five minutes and the train station is still not in sight. She takes a break in the shade of a tree and wipes her face. It's burning, from the sweat, the tears and the heat. She sniffs and together with the salt of her tears, the smell of chai enters her nose. At the corner of the street there's a vada pav and masala chai stall. She opens her wallet. A single twenty-rupee note yawns into her face. She thinks for a moment, the growl of her stomach decides for her. She takes vada pav. The vendor hands her ten rupees back and turns towards his kettle, filling two small glasses for the rickshaw drivers standing next to Iti. She looks longingly as he pours the light brown liquid. Iti hands him the ten rupees and takes the chai as well. Her wallet is empty now.

She finally arrives at Andheri station. It is a mess of construction clutter and people. So many people! Iti holds onto the railing – the only thing that keeps her steady in moving against the stream of people coming down the stairs – while heaving herself up the stairs. Iti wonders if she is going up the correct staircase – people seem to be only going down, not up. She glances behind her. No, there are as many people going up as there are going down. Strange. It is as if the staircase has the magical capacity to expand and expand and expand until it can fit all the people on it – much like the magic staircases in Harry Potter which can shift floors at will. Despite the exhaustion, Iti smiles to herself. Mumbai is her Hogwarts. And Harry's first year wasn't easy either!

Slightly disoriented from looking down and behind while simultaneously walking up, Iti concentrates on the announcement. How many trains can leave and arrive in one single suburban station? She tries to listen to find out which platform she has to go to, but as soon as her overwhelmed senses have gathered that this is the English or Hindi announcement, the voice switches to Marathi. Suddenly, Iti feels a hand on her butt, or is it between her legs? That can't be! In the safety of so many human bodies close around which could cushion her fall, she twirls on the step and slaps the hand of the person behind her. She is not sure that this was the perpetrator. But it doesn't matter. The sudden spurt of anger gives her energy. And thankfully she doesn't accidentally start a fight. The slow wave of people continues to heave her up until the landing.

Finally on top, she can make out a pattern in the sea of people: A long line seems to be going straight from the stairs to a row of counters in the very back of the hall. A weirdly orderly glitch in the human mess. Only at one counter, where someone just pulled a shutter down with a faded paper stuck to it reading 'operation timings 3.25-5.40 p.m.', is there a commotion. A fat angry lady is shouting something on top of her lungs which Iti does not understand.

Without thinking, Iti stands in the line straight ahead of her. There is just an inch between the queues on her right and left. On the one side there's a woman in a suit with a lanyard around her neck, on the other two young girls are engrossed in a song on their shared headphones. Iti lets go of her breath which she has been holding since she got onto the staircase. In the safety of fellow females around her, she strains her ears once

more. '*Fast train to Churchgate leaving from platform number two.*'
The line moves forward. Where are all these people going? And
where do they all come from? The ticket counter is approaching
quicker than she expected. She feels her heart skip a beat, the
blue-and-white sign reads '*special window – tickets for Rs 10
only*'. Is this a discount window? Like a reward for standing in
line so patiently and well-behaved? But before she can spin her
dreams of a magical discount counter further, her eyes stop at
the text below – '*operation timings 5.30-5.55 p.m.*' She glances at
the station clock. Only two minutes left. But who even counts
in such minuscule numbers as minutes? Nobody really means
'one' minute when they say it. Or do they, here in Mumbai? She
fiddles with her hand in her pocket. *Shit.* It's empty. And so is
her wallet. But there are anyway so many people…

Now that the thought has entered her mind, it won't leave.
Focusing on her shoes, she quickly makes her way out of the
queue onto the platform. She needs to save the little bit of
energy she has, to get in – and most importantly out – of the
train. At the bottom of the staircase on the platform she takes
a quick right and heads straight to the women's compartment
section. A train has just arrived. She holds her breath once more
and plunges in. Into the sea of saris and suits, fabric clinging to
humid bodies, handbags and elbows poking into her ribcage.
She grabs onto the side handles at the door and lifts herself in.
Made it.

The good thing about being so close to the door is that
the evening breeze cools down her swollen face. Iti wraps her
body around the metal bar in the middle of the door – this way,
the stream of women squeezing in and out at the next station
hardly affects her.

To get down, she has to almost jump. Made it. Again. *See, I
was born for this*, she tells herself, her voice surprisingly coarse.
She feels a tap on her shoulder. Without a word, the woman

in the brown uniform reaches out her hand. Iti's 'cute' survival reflex kicks in: "Ma'am, I have lost the ticket. It was with me. I swear. I think somebody stole it. You should catch them!"

Unimpressed stare.

"Okay, okay, I confess I did not buy the ticket because I did not have any money. Somebody stole my money and probably used it to buy their own ticket. You should catch them!"

The lady towers over Iti like a giant, the big red bindi staring like a bloodthirsty third eye just waiting to feed on little Itis.

"Okay, I admit it was all my fault and I would be happy to pay the fine, but I don't have any money, you can see my wallet."

She shows her wallet. The TT folds her arms and glares at her. Iti sighs.

"Ok, I can go to the ATM and get some money. You wait here, I'll be back I promise."

She makes a move to walk towards the staircase. The TT sticks by her side. Still not uttering a word. Iti is frazzled. Another wave of people rushing down the stairs threatens to crush her. This is her chance. She ducks, runs up the stairs, in between feet and bags and children. At the top she takes a passing glance over her shoulder, the overweight TT is standing in the middle of the staircase, holding onto the railing, panting. She has given up.

Iti rushes out of the station. Yes!

It starts raining. Crap!

The time Iti takes to turn the key in the lock is enough to create a little puddle of water around her feet. Before opening, Iti recites a little prayer – hopefully the landlady is glued to her TV serial and doesn't see her tiptoeing into the house like a wet poodle.

She doesn't.

Exhausted, Iti flings her soaked bag onto the floor, the contents spreading across the room. Jumping on one leg, she peels herself out of her tight jeans and collapses on the bed. Face down.

Chinky, quietly sitting on her bed, as if she was just waiting for Iti to return from her first day of work, picks up the folded call sheet and in not more than a glance makes sense of the wildly arranged columns and scene codes and abbreviations.

"Divya Gupta. Beautiful! So how was it?"

Iti is too tired to lift her face off the pillow. "I just had the worst day. And then I got caught in the rain."

Chinky sits next to her on the bed. She tilts her head to the side, lying down on the mattress. Her face staring at Iti's half-closed eyes, their noses almost touching. Her doe eyes blink. "Come on, there is nothing more romantic than walking in the rain."

Iti opens her eyes and rolls onto her back. Until today this is exactly what she had always told Surat. Rain. Chai. Romance … Isn't this the content of all good Bollywood songs? She lets out a loud sigh. She finds it hard to conjure any such emotions right now.

"Hm. Not really. It's just cold and wet unless you are dancing in it."

"That's because dancing is a choice. Let's alter your last memory right now by overwriting it with a new one."

Chinky reaches out and takes Iti's hand. Iti smiles and holds out her hand, ready to follow wherever Chinky may lead. Chinky stops. Iti turns her head, looking straight into Chinky's eyes.

"What?"

Chinky smiles.

"Your energy lifts fast."

"Just like my body." Iti jumps onto her feet.

"So where are we going?"

"To my favourite place."

"Where is it?"

"Always close…"

Iti is mystified. But whatever its location, she has already decided that it shall be *her* favourite place, too.

29

"The only thing missing to perfection is that we ourselves *become* water!"

Chinky stretches her arms wide, eyes closed, tongue out, and the bottom of her leggings wet.

Just to be safe, Iti has buried her naked feet ankle-deep into the sand. She, too, has turned her face towards the showering sky but her eyes keep anxiously wandering between Chinky and what appears to her as a stormy sea.

"For me this is pretty alright," she shouts bravely.

"There's no need to be scared. I've seen her much angrier."

"Who?" There is no one at the beach except for the two of them.

"The ocean."

Still in a sort of praying position, Chinky wiggles with her left hand for Iti to come closer. She takes her hand.

"Nothing will happen to you. Just let go for a moment. Trust. And listen."

She doesn't know what exactly she should be listening to. The drizzling of the rain on the tin roof of the closed chai stall where Versova beach starts? The gushing of the high waves far out on the ocean? The gurgling of the foam where her toes have just left deep holes in the sand? Clearly Chinky is feeling something that she isn't. She's trying hard to concentrate. Maybe the ocean has something to tell her? But what? This is literally the first time she has ever come this close to the sea. Surat had promised to take her on a 'pre-wedding' trip to Goa. Well, she had kind of persuaded him into promising her. Because taking a trip as a couple before marriage is not the sort of thing either he or her mother would ever think of. But they are a modern couple. And they will anyway get married, so a little 'pre-honeymoon' sounded exciting to him, too.

Without a word, Chinky lets go of Iti's hand. It has stopped raining.

She uses the freed right hand to rub her nose. It had been itching all this while.

"Let's sit."

In silence, Chinky leads her to the weirdly triangular rocks lined up between the shore and the first row of houses. Right now she doesn't know their purpose. But soon enough she will see them being dragged by a big payloader to safeguard the new reclamation walkway in front of her sea-facing apartment from high tide waves … one day, but not today…

The sea has calmed down. The clouds are moving fast to make way for the moonlight. Dawn is still far away, but the beach is becoming brighter.

Iti sits on one of the blocks, looking at the city.

Chinky leans her shoulder onto Iti's. Facing the sea.

The silence is beautiful. Like a concert of quiet notes. Gracefully dancing along the silver horizon, marking the frontier between the ink-blue sky and the equally blue sea… Without trying, this could indeed become Iti's 'happy place'.

"You have a choice, you know. You could go back to Agra. Find a way to revive your father's boutique. Maybe take a loan from the bank. It's not impossible. You don't *have* to be here."

Iti takes a deep breath. "I want to be here. I know it's not easy. It's been over six months and when I finally got a job, I got fired not just on the first day but in the first hour."

Chinky starts laughing. Iti looks at her, then she starts laughing, too.

"I can't believe you called that woman a witch. Don't know why she got offended though ... it's not easy to be a witch. It takes a lot of discipline."

"How was I supposed to know what 'chitkin' means? They didn't even give me a chance to explain. It was crazy – this whole city is crazy, everything that happens here is insane." She smiles as she says this. Then she sighs. "That's why I love it. There is just something about Mumbai. It makes me feel so alive. You know, in school I was the kid who always finished a race last, because I could just not be bothered. That feeling of breathlessness, of listening to my lungs and heart complain that they do not like to work at that pace, threatening to explode in protest if I didn't stop. I cannot understand the people who enjoy it and do it for pleasure, and yet when I ran from that TT, it felt like my feet had wings. My heart was on my side and telling me to go faster. I have never won a race in my life, because I had no idea it could feel so good." Iti laughs. "And even if I had lost, even if I had been caught, I would not have regretted spending my last twenty rupees on that vada pav and chai. I have never tasted anything as satisfying anywhere else. No, Chinky, this is my home, I cannot leave it."

Chinky smiles at her. Iti looks thoughtful.

"Is it strange that I feel this, when I have lived in Agra all my life?"

"One human life does not decide what your soul calls home."

Iti laughs. She spots a transvestite standing on the road, shifting from one foot to another.

"You know, I used to think they were women."

Chinky looks at her. "And you were right."

"But they are not really, are they? I mean not biologically."

"That depends on what you believe came first, the thought or the mind."

Iti grins at Chinky.

"Beauty … and they must have been the first to claim it. Look at her, she is so beautiful isn't she? I wish I was skinny enough to fit into that dress. It's so striking."

Chinky looks at the transgender woman Iti is pointing at. She is indeed beautiful with a perfectly oval face and flawless skin, lit up by the light bouncing off the many sequins on her dress. Her eyes are particularly luminescent.

Chinky's face looks thoughtful, the features almost resembling a frown. She gets up.

"Come on."

She starts walking towards the woman. Iti follows.

The woman sees them coming. She pulls herself up straight and flashes them a pearly white smile.

"Well, normally I don't take female clients … But then again, today is one of those slow-motion nights…" She smirks at both of them appraisingly. "Both together for 750 … I can feel the sex appeal." Slanting her hips side to side she looks Chinky deep in the eye.

"Six hundred," says Iti. A wave of heat flushes her face. "I … my god, I'm so sorry! I don't know why I said that." She is mortified. "I just can't stop myself from negotiating. It's automatic. But it's not what I want…"

"What, you don't want all this?"

Jhansi gestures towards her body. "How have I missed making it perfect? Tell me, I will go speak with a doctor right away."

Jhansi's eyes are teasing, but Iti is too flustered to notice.

"Oh no, you are perfect, absolutely beautiful. I wouldn't change a thing."

"Is it her then? She turns you off?" Jhansi laughs, pointing at Chinky, whose expression is inscrutable.

Chinky touches Iti's hand, then cocks her head at Jhansi.

Iti is absolutely scandalized.

"Chinky, I like you. I mean as a friend, but, like, I have never, I mean…"

Chinky smiles at her, but turns her attention back to Jhansi.

"There's a lot of pain."

"Not if you don't like it. I can be gentle."

"You know that's not what I'm talking about."

Jhansi rolls her eyes, then with a sultry look that fits her voice, she takes Chinky's hand and puts it onto her chest. "For 100 extra I can tell you a really sad story about heartbreak and abandonment. For 200 I will let you hold me while I cry."

Chinky continues looking at her.

Jhansi shrugs. "Trust me, I'm a great storyteller! I can make up any kind of story if you just give me three words."

"Passion, beach, and…"

"Shoes." Chinky interrupts.

"Once upon a time there was a young girl from a small town, who lost her shoes – and found passion instead. At the beach."

"That's more a haiku than a story…" Chinky fakes her disappointment.

"Time is money, babe. And even an artist needs to survive."

She lets go of the hand and shifts her weight, restlessly wiggling her toes.

"True, even an artist in the art of love." Chinky touches Jhansi's chest again. "You are keeping this light, but for all of us there is still the weight of existence to support – and you are not being kind to the part of your body that is keeping you steady."

Unconsciously, Jhansi's gaze moves to her feet.

She sighs. "And you have more brains than the usual mister, sister." She massages the back of her ankle. "From morning till night these darlings are out to kill me."

Iti looks sympathetically at her sandals. They are silver with a plateau and stiletto heel. The enormous bow is still not big enough to hide the fact that Jhansi's toes are protruding completely beyond the front strap. The rhinestones on the back stand out almost by the same amount. *It must be difficult for a transvestite to get these kinds of shoes in a big size*, Iti thinks to herself.

"They are pretty. If you remove the bow in the front and the two diamonds in the back, they could look like straight off the ramp, but maybe you should take them off for a while if they hurt so much."

"Do you want to have them?" Chinky asks as if they were hers. Both Iti and Jhansi look at her in surprise.

"Well, both of you seem to have the same size."

In a mix of disagreement and embarrassment, Iti protests. Her feet are clearly not the same size as this lady's. But, yes, the shoes could possibly fit her.

"So why don't you girls just exchange? Yours may not be as glamorous, but…"

"Oh, my feet would be ecstatic on those, and if the mister has to look at my shoes after I spent so much money on *these*…" (Jhansi points dramatically at her cleavage which is definitely a few sizes bigger than Iti's). She throws her hands up.

Iti can't help but laugh.

Both women bend down and exchange their shoes. Surprisingly Iti's sandals are worn out enough for Jhansi's feet to fit into them.

"At least, all this walking has been good for something!" Chinky utters what had just crossed Iti's mind. She smiles. Her feet look beautiful in her new heels. Maybe she could remove the bow from the front and replace the rhinestones in the back with it. It would give them a cuter look. Her eyes wander up her capris and kurta... "Hmm, but they so don't go with my outfit..." She thinks for a moment, throws a look over her shoulder at the deserted street. No customer in sight... She shrugs, opens the button and takes off her capri. She hands it to Chinky. The kurta is long enough to pass as a mini dress.

Jhansi looks at her appreciatively.

"One second." Iti reaches out her hand for the capri once more. With her pants in her hand and her new shoes on her feet, she wiggles clumsily towards the bus stop next to the streetlight, Jhansi and Chinky trailing behind her in wonderment. "Hmm..." She looks at the light, then sits down on the bench. Inside her right pocket Iti always keeps a little pouch, with basic change, her mom's photograph and most importantly her kit. The light is sufficient for her to do the little adjustment. She threads the white yarn through the needle, and with a quick pull she yanks off the ribbon, handing it to Jhansi and the capri back to Chinky. The fake leather is a bit tough. Halfway through the first shoe, her thumb is swollen and itchy. She proceeds to push the needle through with the force of her front teeth. For five minutes she is fully absorbed in her task, forgetting the world around her, completely focused on the microcosmos of needle holes.

Nobody says a word.

"Done."

Almost surprised to see Chinky and Jhansi standing right next to her, she proudly presents her new design, turning around like Cinderella — only that she is her own fairy godmother.

Jhansi can't help but clap.

"Damn! Now I wish I could take them back. The bow is so much cuter at the back!"

Iti throws her an almost possessive look.

"Maybe some jewels?"

Chinky is already in the process of removing her golden hoop earrings. She hands them to Iti. Encouraged, Iti points to her belt. Chinky hands it to her as well. And as a final stroke of magic, Jhansi, with a quick twist, pulls Iti's hair up into a stylish high ponytail.

Iti laughs. "Great. Only a little bit of make-up and I'm ready to go." She doesn't know where she would go, but instead of an answer, Jhansi plants a firm kiss on her lips. She spreads the transferred lipstick with her fingers and smiles. It is done! Iti is thoroughly scandalized. "She is a woman, right? So I haven't technically cheated on my boyfriend, have I?"

Even though she whispers, Jhansi obviously overhears this and answers on Chinky's behalf. "Only if you preferred my kiss to his."

Iti remembers Surat chastely kissing her on the cheek or forehead or leaving a quick peck on the lips that ended in a second. She doesn't say anything. Instead she turns to Chinky. "Come, let's go somewhere, let's go out! I'm feeling just sexy enough today."

"Of course," says Chinky, before turning to Jhansi: "Join us?"

"No, dear. They won't let me in. Some doors will always remain shut for the likes of us."

"But there are also some doors which will always be open for you."

Chinky pulls out her little dreamcatcher keyring and removes the single key from it.

She puts the key back in her bag and hands Jhansi the keyring. "Hold on to it."

Jhansi looks at it, then nods. She stuffs it down her blouse. "I will."

30

The big banners and boards are calling it *The Latin & Salsa Night*.

"This song ... does it mean 'Oh my Guantana', like 'Oh my Soniya'?"

Chinky halts in the middle of the '8' motion that her hips, shoulders and hands have been doing ever since her ears had caught the unfamiliar sounds of percussion and trumpets – which to Iti's slight embarrassment was on the pavement outside.

Before Chinky can explain to Iti, they are almost knocked over by a sparsely clothed couple twirling across the room like a spinner toy. The woman is wearing a tight white spaghetti dress daringly slit from her knee up until her panty line and the man's shirt, as if mirroring that in some way, has come undone until close to his bellybutton, exposing more hair than even Anil Kapoor could dream of.

Iti has barely finished sizing up the couple when a slightly more clothed man takes her hand, motioning her onto the dance floor. She is pulling back, looking at Chinky, but her friend is lost in her '8', eyes closed. Biting on her teeth – a sharp pain hits her skin every time she leans into the front strap of her new sandals – Iti smiles politely. The man understands that Iti might not be the most fun dance partner and with an elegant bow dances away to find another 'victim'. She is relieved. Another, much younger and admittedly quite handsome boy sets his eyes on her. In panic she turns on the spot, ignoring the open flesh on top of her toes.

She somehow makes it to the bar, holding onto the high table like a toddler learning to walk. Breathing heavily, she closes her eyes, collects her strength and manages to gracefully plant herself halfway on a bar stool.

The handsome boy has changed his target as quickly – or maybe he was in fact the target. Chinky has wrapped her thigh tightly around his hip.

She moves with grace and expertise.

Iti finds herself mesmerized as she watches Chinky. There is something about her face which never for one instant looks the same. It is impossible for the eyes to tire themselves looking at her. Even the light itself seems unable to decide where to land and thus with every little move, turn, shrug, smile, wink, flutter of the eyelids collects someplace different. The first time Iti had seen her, it was Chinky's brilliant smile and the dense blackness of her hair that had caught her eye. But now as Chinky moves, the dim lights of the bar have all collected like tiny dewdrops atop her cheekbones, making them appear as sharp as glass and just as shiny, altering her appearance, slightly feline and very, very exotic. Or perhaps even otherworldly? Her eyes today, or tonight, no just right now, have turned into pools of mesmerizing darkness, repelling the light, hypnotically compelling you to stare into them. The boy certainly seems unable to look or move more than two centimetres away from her. Not just his eyes, his whole body is angled towards hers, like a moth to a flame...

It is a delight watching her, yet Iti suppresses a feeling of shame – this is something for Mills & Boon but not for real life.

"Would you like to order?"

The bartender, as well as everyone else, seems to be oblivious to the scandalizing 'sex with clothes on' taking place right in front of them.

She shakes her head.

"So you're just here for the music then? What do you prefer – bachata, salsa, samba?"

Iti is blank. She tries to cover up.

"Actually, I'm sitting here because you were alone and you looked bored."

The bartender does a semi-bow 'thank you'.

"A free shot then for the pretty lady with a kind heart."

He pours some blue liquid into a shot glass and slides it to her.

Iti is pleased.

"You think I'm pretty?"

"Sure."

Iti grins at him and takes a tentative sip.

"No, no, you have to have it in one go."

Alright. She chugs it. *Gasp.*

"My throat is burning."

Waving her hand in front of her mouth does not do anything. Her eyes are watering. He should have really warned her.

"You forgot to add the cola. Never mind, I'll take it now. Not sure how much it will help, but let's try."

She holds out her hand, like a benevolent queen. He has messed up her 'free' order but she is ready to forgive him if he snaps to it quickly and corrects his mistake.

The bartender gives her a 'you've got to be kidding' look, points her to a jug of water and moves away.

Iti checks the dance floor. Chinky has vanished. The bartender has moved on to giving free shots of some red coloured drink to a few girls and is talking animatedly with them.

She has moved on from being scandalized to being bored. The music has changed into something with an endless guitar solo but Iti is unable to identify anything catchy in it.

To pass time, she gets down from the stool, onto her aching feet and heads for the loo.

The bathroom is surprisingly well designed. The walls and floor are tiled in black, the washbasin looks like it is made of wood and the dim light on top of the dark glass mirror creates quite a mood. Everything about the place is abnormally sensual. The people, the music, the design – even the soundscape in the loo sounds like subdued moaning. *Man, what was this drink?* She splashes some cold water onto her face. The 'soundscape' intensifies. Iti perks her ears – is this Chinky? Without making a sound with her silver stilettos, she steps closer to the cabinet where the noise is coming from. The guy is hardly audible between the lip-smacking and tongue-slurping.

"Gosh, you are so sexy. Hmmm. Your eyes ... And the way you were moving that ... hrrr..." Chinky squeals. "I could've taken you right there ... hmm..." A slap. A growling sound. More slurping. For the second time in one night, Iti suddenly remembers the chaste kisses from Surat – exciting in their rebellion but not much else. The first time he had used his tongue, she had had a little butterfly flutter in her stomach. But the butterfly had died before Surat had even moved his lips away from hers. She had caught hold of his head and urgently pressed her lips against his again, trying to resuscitate it. But it had stayed dead. Not even one tiny wing moved ever again. In fact sometimes it felt like its corpse was getting putrid in her stomach and Surat's kisses made her feel slightly nauseous, especially when there was too much saliva. But she never had the heart to tell him. Still. She had never had to bite her tongue to keep from screaming, she had never had anything that filled her with so much sensation that it had to burst out of her in sound.

She bangs loudly against the door. Startled silence from inside. Iti's heart is racing. She moves her feet back, away from the gap between the loo door and the floor. Still silence. She runs out.

She catches her breath in a quiet spot next to a pillar. Here in the shadow she can while her time away until Chinky is done with her 'business' without anyone harassing her to dance. She feels guilty. Maybe she shouldn't have acted like such a moralist. After all, she's come here because Mumbai is a free city. If she was too scared to get out of her comfort zone, she could've just stayed in Agra. Which is no option. But how was she supposed to know that stepping out of her comfort zone would be so physically and emotionally painful? She looks at her feet. In the dark light of the pillar it is hard to make out, but it looks like the blood from her toes has spread onto the silver strap and left an ugly mark. She is startled. Someone just tapped her on the shoulder. And is not moving their hand away from it. "Seriously, no, I don't feel like dan…"

It's Chinky's face smiling at her.

"I'm sorry. I should not have been so insensitive. Let's go home."

Relieved at the casual sound of her voice, Iti nods. Finally. She is so very ready for bed…

31

The sun is burning through the window onto Iti's face, waking her up to a feeling of guilt. Why? She doesn't know, really. It's just there. Maybe it's because it is already so late in the day – the fact that Mumbai doesn't rise before 11 a.m. is something she will never, even after years of calling the city her home, appreciate. Or maybe it's because she feels like a party pooper. Why couldn't she just enjoy last night? It was like a whole new world. A free world! With men and women dancing to exotic music. Maybe it was just a dream? She looks at her feet. No, the bloody marks on her toes tell her that it wasn't.

Feeling restless, Iti looks around for Chinky, but Chinky has left the bed long ago. She rises with the sun even if she has gone to sleep just minutes before its arrival.

Her eyes fall on the sleeping form of Valarie lying unshapely on the bed. She is sleeping so still, Iti half wonders if she is actually there at all. It would be just like Valarie to leave a couple of pillows under the sheet, fooling the landlady when in fact she hasn't come in the night before.

Resisting the urge to poke at the sheet, Iti gets up and wanders out of the room. Maybe she can fix herself a cup of tea.

The kitchen is occupied by another unshapely lump. The landlady rubs her eyes sleepily as she prepares breakfast for her husband and two sons.

"Mom, make scrambled eggs for me." Iti can hear the younger one shouting.

"But you said fried," the landlady shouts back.

"I meant scrambled."

From the quiet of her corner, Iti can suddenly see the fierce ruler of her den transforming into the tired and vulnerable middle-aged woman she actually is, as she stares helplessly at the two eggs already frying in the pan. Iti feels a twinge of pity as she takes in her dishevelled hair and her faded blue nighty with the big hole on the neck. Even the hem is frayed and half unravelled.

"What do you want?"

Iti feels caught. But hides it well.

"What are you going to do with those?" she asks, looking towards the eggs, the yellow in the centre are as perfectly round as the ones her mother used to make. The smell of them frying is making her mouth water.

The landlady's eyes narrow shrewdly. "If you want breakfast, it will cost extra."

Iti looks pointedly at her nightie. "How about I mend that and anything else you have that needs mending?"

"I don't have so many torn clothes."

"You have two teenage sons. I think you might have more than you like."

Both stare at each other.

Accepting defeat, the landlady shoves the pan with the eggs towards Iti. "You can take two slices of bread with it and I will not take any demands, you will have what I cook."

"Except on Sundays." Iti grins, reaching hungrily towards the pan. Her stomach growls in gratitude.

Valarie is up when Iti returns, her stomach full for what feels like the first time in six months.

"Looks like you danced your feet off, Cinderella."

Valarie is munching on a package of chips. She offers it to Iti.

"Hardly."

"I saw your shoes! Your new job must be paying really well, dude."

Iti had almost forgotten about that. She falls back onto the bed. Exhausted before the day has even begun.

"You are not very talkative today."

"Hmm … What are you doing at home?" Iti hopes that maybe she isn't the only jobless person around. Although, technically Chinky also doesn't have a job. Which makes Valarie with her job the odd one out…

"It's Sunday, dude. Give me a break."

That makes her feel better. It's okay to laze around on a Sunday. In fact one *should* be lazy on Sundays to gather energy for the work week ahead.

"So what's the plan? No shoot today?"

"Nope." She really can't be bothered reliving yesterday's disaster. But then – what *is* the plan? She needs one. Desperately. The restlessness which has been a constant companion since her first day in Mumbai is starting to rise in her again. Her heart races, her blood flows and circulates quicker than normal through her body, pearls of cold sweat build on her forehead under her newly cut fringe – she had used her tailoring scissors just the day before her new job – she has the urge to wiggle her toes… She jumps out of the bed. The blood vessels tingle. Tears shoot into her eyes. Her soles are tender like half-filled water balloons. Iti doesn't care, she keeps standing. Something needs to be done. Her bag is still where she left it after she had come home last evening – before they met Jhansi, before she got her new shoes, before they went clubbing, before she heard Chinky have sex with a random stranger in a half-public place. Wow. How much can happen in one night?

"You know, you should get an umbrella. Or better, a raincoat. I don't know how you folks do it in Agra, but here we try to not get soaking wet every day for three months. It's not healthy."

Valarie is still munching.

"Neither are chips." The munching stops.

"Okayyy." She lifts her hands. Truce. Iti grabs the chips packet.

"Sorry, that was a bit rude."

"It's okay. That's what Mumbai does – it toughens you up. Kicks you around until you're black and blue and your feet are bloody and your bags wet and the only food that you can afford is a pack of chips." She grabs it back from Iti.

"Great."

Valarie laughs. "Don't be so serious. I was just joking. Take a shower, you'll feel better. And I think I forgot to switch off the geyser, so now there's probably enough piping-hot water for an hour of a bath."

A glimmer of light on this humid, rainy day.

Iti grabs her pink towel. It smells freshly washed. A second glimmer of light.

Iti is an only child, which means she has never had to ration her bathroom time. There was even a spare bathroom that she had claimed exclusively as her own. There has never been an irate sibling banging on the door demanding she hurry the hell up with her shower.

A long hot-water bath is a luxury Iti has been sorely missing.

She peeps into the living room. The TV is off. The landlady must have gone out.

So today, Iti takes a shower for one actual blissful hour. And with every droplet of water hitting her skin, the thought manifests in her mind. Yes, she will work as hard and as long as it takes, accepting the bruises and the involuntary diet (which has some positive effect!), so that one day she can take as long as she wants in the bathroom – until the mirror fogs up! For the rest of her life.

When Iti enters her room, she is welcomed with trumpets and drums. Valarie is sitting on her bed playing the 'air saxophone' while Chinky twirls between the beds. She passes by the door and grabs Iti's hand.

"Come, I'm the man and you are the woman – so you just have to follow my lead."

Iti tries hard not to step on Chinky's feet.

"Let go … let yourself go." This instruction has exactly the opposite effect. Iti strains her entire body, trying to keep up with the pace, while avoiding to clash with the furniture and somehow appearing graceful. Valarie has stopped saxophoning.

"Oh my god. You are terrible."

"Don't be so discouraging!" Chinky lets go of Iti's hand, changes the song and gestures her to take her place on the 'stage' between Chinky's and Valarie's bed. The song has changed to something which the trained ear would identify as 'rumba'. Its slow sensuality though seems to be strangely off rhythm. Iti is by no means an expert in Latin music, but she has never heard bells as part of the band. Chinky frowns.

"Oh, the door!" Abruptly, she leaves Iti just where she had put her. Valarie presses 'rewind'. The song starts over.

She stands with her back to Iti. "One, two, chaaa. One, two, chaaa. One, two, chaaa … and so on."

Ok, just three steps – that's not too difficult. In full concentration, she mumbles the rhythm to herself. *One, two, chaa, one, two, chaa, one, two, chaa, one…*

"Hopeless!" Valarie throws her hands up in exasperation. "Your body! It has no rhythm. Leave it, I can't bear to watch."

"I can practise till it gets better."

"It won't. You have no grace."

Iti is annoyed. "I'm not trying to be a professional dancer. I just don't want to be sitting alone at parti…"

Just then, Chinky walks across the room, sits on her bed, folds her hands between her crossed legs and breathes out deeply. She does so a couple of times. At first, Iti thinks that she is going to sit and 'judge' her performance, but nothing like that. Instead, her gaze is fixed somewhere in the distance, moving further and further away. The space between Chinky on her bed and Iti on the 'stage' just in front of her grows increasingly with each exhalation. The room is expanding, but Iti is not moving, only Chinky is travelling back, becoming smaller and smaller. Or is it Iti who is becoming small? She wants her to come 'back' into the room.

"What's happening?"

Chinky seems to become slightly bigger again.

"I'm waiting."

"For what?"

"The universe will be sending me some work."

"Please continue." Valarie breaks the spell.

She is back to her normal size.

"I have decided I want to move from here. I want to manifest something else and the energy here is not right for what I want."

"I'm not staying here without you."

Chinky looks at her, then nods.

"Yes, I think you need to come with me."

Valarie has been listening with interest.

"This is great. One girl who has changed twenty different professions since I've known her and another girl who has earned nothing since she has been here are now going to move into a big new apartment. Who, may I ask, is going to pay for it?"

To this, Chinky and Iti answer in unison: "The universe will manage something."

Iti has not the faintest idea how this thought has entered her mind and left her mouth.

Now conscious, she adds: "I will manage something."

They look at each other and smile.

32

2018

There would be candles flickering in the soft air of the AC just like his lover's heart trembling at his touch. Red wine with the velvety heaviness akin to his lover's sonorous voice. Petit-fours decorated with cherry tomatoes and soft camembert. A bait playfully placed between his fingertips or maybe, as the evening progresses, between his perfectly white teeth.

Abhishek had planned to call his paramour over for a rendezvous. But quickly realized it was rather impossible. His current residence had more random walk-ins than a public park.

Hence he had patiently waited. Seven excruciating days. Until finally Kartik's parents had gone out of town and he had called him over.

Should he be concerned or offended that it is the only invitation for a meeting he has received from Kartik since he has arrived in 'his' town? In addition, his parents have been gone all week and he only bothered to call him now. A week has seven days, so has he already…

'La, la, la, la…" Abhishek tries to drown out the idle, spiteful chatter in his brain and instead focus on feeling happy. He is in Kartik's home. Finally. Just the two of them and the night has just started. If only his brain would shut up. Sometimes he finds his inner voices more disturbing than Chinky's convoluted utterances – and that is really saying something.

"Penny for your thoughts."

I would pay a 100 gold pennies for somebody to take them out of my head and drown them.

Abhishek turns around to face Kartik, who has just come into the room.

"You're 'back'. You looked so lost in thought." Kartik grins.

Abhishek shuts the window he has been staring out of.

"Why do all the houses in Mumbai have such an ugly view? And all this noise. Who can make love to the sound of 'traffic'?"

Kartik snorts, moves towards Abhishek and starts kissing him. "I rely on my technique to make 'em scream louder than the fucking traffic."

Them? How many 'thems' have been 'screaming' in this room?

Abhishek pulls away.

"Did you get the glasses?"

Kartik holds out the two coffee mugs he has in his hands.

Mugs, how classy. Stop it, Abhishek! Nobody likes a prissy little cunt.

"They are coffee mugs. Do you think that you could maybe rustle up something not made of ceramic? What I mean to say is 'glass' glasses – for the really good wine?" He tries making this sound funny. Unsuccessfully.

Kartik pulls a face.

"Don't know why you had to get this fancy…"

He picks up the bottle and tries to read the label…

"*Savage something blank?* We could have just had some beer."

Abhishek looks hurt. He takes the bottle from Kartik's hand and pours the wine.

"You can't have a romantic evening with beer. This is really good French wine, from the land of love."

Kartik rolls his eyes. He takes a sip and pulls a face.

"I don't really like white wine, it tastes too fruity. And if I must taste something 'fruity'…".

He giggles a little and tries to pull Abhishek towards him again.

"Fruity? Why are you being so crass?"

"What? One faggot cannot call another faggot a fruit? What do you want me to call you? My 'queen'?"

He laughs again.

Abhishek, I am begging you, just drink the wine out of the goddam bottle and shut up, don't ruin this.

"What is with all the homophobic jokes? It's a little distasteful, isn't it?"

Kartik holds up his hands.

"Okay, okay, I remember, it's not your sense of humour I find attractive. And okay, I won't mention your desirable butt either in case it's distasteful. Let's start again, *mon cheri.*"

He clinks mugs with Abhishek. Abhishek is a little mollified.

He kisses Kartik on the palm. Kartik pushes him face down on the bed.

A bus honks outside.

"Do you have some music? This traffic is really killing the mood."

Kartik sighs, pulls out his phone and puts on a peppy number.

Abhishek pulls away again.

"Are we in a discotheque? Don't you have something romantic?"

Now it's Kartik's turn to be irritated.

"Can you just shut up so we can do it already?"

Yes, just shut up and do it already, you are pissing him off now.

Abhishek pushes him away. He can't help it, he has dreamt of this moment in so many different ways but not even one version had Kartik asking him to 'just do it already'.

"It's our first time together since I got here. Why are you spoiling it like this? Why can't you be a little more sensitive?"

And let the 'drama' commence. Where is the popcorn?

"Oh my god! What is wrong with you? Do you want to talk about your feelings now? Are we a fucking straight couple or two gay men trying to have some sex?"

Apologize, Abhishek, quick, apologize.

"Is that why I'm here? To have sex with you, just because your parents are out of town?"

A week, they have been gone for a week, but hold your tongue, you have said enough.

Kartik gets up from the bed.

"No, you are here because I thought that was what you wanted, since you send me about ten messages a day begging me to meet you."

He picks up his phone and begins to read Abhishek's messages aloud. His tone is a mocking parody of Abhishek at his whiniest.

Abhishek buttons up his shirt and leaves.

He slams the door shut behind him.

33

Ten minutes later, Abhishek is still pacing. He keeps walking up and down the street, looking up towards Kartik's building, towards his apartment, towards the window he had slammed shut a few minutes ago. It has stayed shut. Nobody is looking out into the relentless traffic, searching for anybody who might be waiting for them to look out, so their eyes could meet and he could rush right back in.

Why did he have to leave? Because Kartik was being impossible. Yes, but has he not heard – you cannot control other people's actions but you can control your reactions, so why could he not have just controlled himself instead of walking? What if this is it? What if he never speaks with him again?

Abhishek can feel his breathing becoming laboured. His vision is blurring. No, no, not again, he does not want to have a panic attack here, in the middle of the road. A memory that he tries to never revisit knocks violently against his mental wall. A couple of bricks fall off, leaving a big gaping hole in the centre. No, no, no ... Abhishek quickly rebricks the structure but not before he has caught a glimpse of himself, in his white-and-blue school uniform, cowering in fright and hurt as the boy who had so lovingly just last night ... but now would rather throw a punch at him in front of his friends ... Quick, the last brick is placed, all memories of heartbreaks, betrayals and unrequited love, locked out of sight once more.

His breathing eases a little. He feels himself relax, his vision clears up, just in time to spot a young boy, holding two bottles of beer, entering Kartik's building.

Beer, that's what he had said. He does not like wine. He likes beer and voila! Here is beer and a non-ugly beer lover in a tight tee to drink it with. Not even ten minutes and Kartik has just picked up a phone and ordered himself a replacement with all his 'favourite' specifications.

Abhishek can feel the bitter taste of bile, mixed with jealousy and resentment bubbling up in his stomach.

The beer boy comes back out, looking pleased with himself. Probably because of the two pretty girls, one hanging on each arm. One of the two bottles of beer is being passed between the three of them. The boy takes the last sip and throws the empty bottle on the street.

Abhishek's legs give way under him. He collapses on the sidewalk, holding his head in his hands, his body heaving with relief and dry sobs.

"I'm pathetic, I'm so fucking pathetic."

A rickshaw pulls up next to him. The driver waits, hoping for a fare. His face looks as ragged as Abhishek's soul feels. Abhishek gives up. He gets inside the rickshaw. He is done with this day. Truth be told, he also feels a little done with life right now. He sinks back in the rickshaw, liberally abusing his fucked-up life, unaware that his life is getting a little fed up with this toxic and abusive relationship, too.

It is a short drive from Kartik's house but Abhishek has not been paying attention and the driver seems to have taken a slightly circuitous route. Why? The obvious answer would be 'to get a bigger fare', but a look at the meter would show the cynic that the driver has not even bothered putting it down. So maybe he likes having company. He certainly keeps turning around to talk to Abhishek.

"What's going on? Why the long face?"

"My face is round."

He looks out, realizing suddenly that the street looks unfamiliar. But that does not have to mean anything. This entire city is unfamiliar to him. Maybe it is the smell. Everything smells of dead fish, except when it smells of rotting garbage. And even when it does not smell, the phantom of it lingers in the smell centre of his brain, always there, attaching itself to everything he sees. The headlight from a passing car illuminates his face and the disgust he feels for everything he is looking at. The rickshaw hits a pothole, his body jerks forward. *Right back at you*, whispers the breeze.

"I know that look," the driver chortles gleefully. "This fucking city is getting to you, too, isn't it?"

Abhishek looks at him, feeling a little validated to have an ally in his disgust but unwilling to engage in conversation. He compromises with a shrug. That's enough validation for the driver. He nods enthusiastically. "I knew it, just one look at your face and I knew your life sucks as bad as mine."

The rickshaw is picking up speed, another pothole and this time Abhishek's body jerks up high enough for his head to smack into the ceiling. The impact shoves him right back onto his seat.

"What the hell, man, slow down."

"Ha ha, slow down? Are you stupid? That's why we both got left behind. Because we slowed down. But as God is my witness, I am never slowing down again."

The rickshaw swerves and honks madly, almost overturning as it squeezes between a speeding bus on the left and the divider on the right.

"Move, you big red bully! This is my turn to win!"

Abhishek screams in fright as the driver swerves to the left, as if aiming to push the bus out of the way.

The bus driver empties his mouth of gutka juice, spraying it liberally all over the rickshaw, the road and Abhishek's shirt. Then he empties his mouth of expletives and cuss words, also sprayed in their direction. The rickshaw driver returns them with equal fervour, "Fuck you, bastard, you don't own the road. I will ram my rickshaw up your ass and your mother's…"

"He is going to beat you up," yells Abhishek.

The bus driver speeds up, then turns the bus to the right, angling it between the rickshaw and the divider, before suddenly applying the brakes. The rickshaw is still hurtling forward, full throttle, right at the bus. Abhishek is too terrified to even scream, he squeezes his eyes shut and braces himself for the crash.

The rickshaw swerves again, there is an almighty bump. His head smacks back into the ceiling. Abhishek can feel a bulge under his styled hair. The rickshaw tilts to the right. Then another bump and they are on their way again. Mad chortles from the driver. More honking. Lots of abusing.

Has it happened? Is he in hell? Complete with the dead fish smell? Splendid – there's no difference between hell and what used to be his life.

Abhishek opens his eyes to take a better look. Instantly blinded ... *by the light at the end of the tunnel?* – no, those are just headlights rushing in their direction. Two boys zip past in a scooter, yelling something. It takes him a second to understand what has happened.

The lunatic driver has jumped over the divider to the other side and is now careering into oncoming traffic, taking him to his actual death, in this ugly metal contraption with pink seats.

"Stop this auto, stop this goddam auto right now, you fool. *You will kill us!*"

A red car zips by, missing them by millimetres.

"Why? Why should I stop? I want to die, you want to die, let's just do it."

"*No, you crazy man, I do not want to die.*"

"Stop lying to yourself. It's written on your face. You are fed up, your life is cursed. Nothing good happened to you when you were young and now even your youth is gone."

"*I am not even thirty!*"

The rickshaw is bouncing up and down as the engine uses all its will to take the speedometer to places no rickshaw speedometer has ever reached before. Speedbumps provide rhythm to the driver's rant: "When you are thirty, you will say you are not even forty, then you will think maybe my luck will change at fifty, these excuses will never end. But your life can. You don't have to live another miserable, pointless day in a one-room chawl with ten people, not even one of whom has ever said one interesting thing. Goodbye, you rubbish, thankless life, we are plunging into the abyss and nothing can stop us."

The speedometer screams in the exhilaration of its victory, or maybe that sound is coming from Abhishek.

The rickshaw shudders to a stop. Abhishek gasps. The car in front of them with its blinking headlights screeches to a halt. He feels nauseous. *Somebody is cooking the dead fish on burnt rubber.* A scooter collides with the car in an almighty crash. Loud yells, honking and cursing all around.

"What happened?" Abhishek whimpers, his legs are trembling so hard, he cannot even step out.

"Goddam CNG finished is what happened. Now I have to roll this useless hunk of metal to the CNG pump and stand in a fucking line..."

The driver from the car, whose headlights are no longer blinking, has stormed out of his vehicle and is yelling at the rickshaw driver.

Abhishek's legs refuse to cooperate. He lowers his body to the floor of the rickshaw and just slides off, clutching at the vehicle to pull himself up.

The driver is already engaged in a scuffle with several people.

A sudden burst of adrenaline floods Abhishek's body.

He starts running. He has no idea where he is going or why he is even running, but now that his legs are in motion he cannot make them stop. He runs and runs and runs.

He runs. His lungs are aching. His nostrils are burning. His eyes are watering. He runs. Runs for his life.

And then. Just like the rickshaw running out of CNG, Abhishek's body, too, runs out of steam. He stops – and throws up his insides on a pair of shiny, green patent leather shoes.

"I'm sorry..."

"It's okay, I stopped feeling them long ago, but it feels wrong to discard something just because you have outgrown it."

Abhishek watches as first one shoe is kicked off, then the other. He is too embarrassed to look up. He knows the owner of that voice and of course who else would wear shoes in this particular shade of green? Two bare feet stand in attention at his eyeline, waiting patiently. They don't look like they are going to be moving away anytime soon.

"What are you doing here, Chinky?" He looks up into the slightly bemused face of his landlady, whose shoes he has just vomited on.

"I was collecting some fallen leaves."

Of course she was.

"No, I mean, why here, why in this part of…" Abhishek stops talking, his eyes have finally taken in the rest of his surroundings. He is in his street, standing right outside his apartment building.

What sorcery is this?

"How did I get here?"

"How does one get anywhere? I guess your feet know where to take you."

He is about to roll his eyes when he notices that she has pulled out a bottle of water from her bag and is pouring it over her shoes.

"What are you doing? Are you trying to plant them and grow more?"

"No, I am cleaning them. For their next person."

Abhishek's eyes roll all the way up into his head, but then he pulls them down. He smiles, it suddenly feels so good to smile over a pair of disgusting green shoes. "You know that is actually just half crazy. I think I almost understand."

Chinky smiles back at him. "You get a lot more than you realize."

She links her arms through his, he lets her. They walk into the building.

"Why were you collecting the leaves?"

"To ask them what the birds said."

Abhishek gently delinks his arm. *So close.*

34

Chinky lets him enter his room without following him inside. She has gone to the kitchen. He can hear the sound of a vessel being filled with water. Abhishek sighs, as he fiddles for the oddly placed light switch in his room. *If only...* It would be so reassuring to hear and be able to believe that all this suffering is part of some elaborate plan by the universe, because he has been chosen for some kind of epic...

He startles in shock. For a second he has had the dizzying feeling that he has stepped over the threshold and entered his room in Delhi. In the sudden brightness of the room, a dreamcatcher comes into focus ... Has he also entered Chinky's room, or has Chinky folded up her room and popped it inside his?

Why is his brain being invaded by a crazy person's thoughts?

He places a palm against the wall and steadies himself, counts to five and looks up again.

The illusion dissolves like a mirage and he is able to see clearly the source of his fright: A poster of Steve Jobs pointing straight at him. Underneath his turtle-necked glory, a mantra in slick white font: 'There's no reason not to follow your heart.'

The technology evangelist preaches his sermon from the wall opposite the door, next to his bed. In exactly the same place as in his bedroom at home.

Right on cue, Chinky appears at the door; alas, her hands hanging uselessly by her side instead of holding a mug of coffee for him.

Nonetheless, she is able to read his thoughts or perhaps his expression. She spreads out her arms towards the poster as if she had actually manifested Steve Jobs in the flesh, crucified with superglue onto the wall of her 'apartment of the bizarre'.

"Do you like it? I saw it in a shop and it seemed like something that would work with the energy of your room."

"I have the same thing in my room at home."

She gives him her smug Chinky smile.

Of course she knows exactly what his room looks like. Maybe she can also tell him where all his lost socks are.

"I don't have a dreamcatcher in my room though." *See you don't know everything.* "And I don't need one here either."

"That's why it's not colourful. It's not for decoration. Don't worry, it will be invisible soon. Just like all the other things you don't 'need' to see when you sleep."

Abhishek lets it go. He is too tired to pick this battle.

He looks again at the poster. Is he imagining it or is there a slight dent on the frame, in exactly the same place as...

"Are you sure you did not go to my room and get it?" A nervous laugh escapes his lips.

Chinky looks at him. "No, when I travel astrally, I cannot touch or move anything. My spirit is not solid, it's not like my body."

Of course, stupid of him to be unaware of that distinction.

She gets up.

35

5.15 p.m.

"So she was into the virtual world?"

Gaikwad perks up. Cybercrime!

Confused, Abhishek does not know how to answer this question. "Pardon?"

"This 'astral' travel. Is it something like this … what's the name, Sahil? 'Other life'? 'Virtual life'?"

Sahil is at a loss.

"You know this thing, where people act like it is reality, but it isn't. It is on the Internet … remember that blackmail case? With the … you know what I mean."

"You mean 'second life', sir."

"Yes! That! Have you ever played this 'astral life' game?"

"It's not a game, sir."

"Yes, it's just some spiritual nonsense."

A ding on Gaikwad's phone. *Your package has been delivered.* Gaikwad exhales in relief. He messages Meenakshi: "*No, I haven't forgotten.*" The sub-inspector pauses for a moment before adding a winky smiley.

"…I wouldn't call it nonsense. She had outstanding experiences doing it, sir. I wish I would dare it…"

"I hope we're not talking about drugs here, Sahil. And how do you know what she has experienced? If you would have known her so well, we wouldn't be sitting here, right?" Notebook still open in front of him, he turns to Abhishek.

"So could these astral travels have something to do with her death?"

"No. I mean, yes. Maybe. But I think she knew what she was doing…"

36

2018

"Are you going to get the coffee?"

Chinky smiles. He catches the approval in her too many teeth and quickly shakes his head. "This does not make me clairvoyant, it's just what you usually do."

"And where does one expect the sameness and comfort of routine but at home?"

Darn, she's good! And unfair ... she hasn't given him any time to think up a fitting reply, just skipped out of the room.

With her no longer perched on the bed, he lies down and stretches out. The poster is right in his eyeline, exactly how it was at home. The familiarity is soothing, but he finds himself feeling glad that the wall it is clinging onto is not quite the same colour. *His room back home doesn't just come with comfort and motivational posters, it also comes with memories of panic and sleepless nights. Just like the dreamcatcher.*

Wait, who said that? Abhishek sits up in bed, his heart pounding fast. *Why is his inner voice sounding like Chinky's?*

Chinky comes in carrying a steaming mug of something that smells like coffee and nutmeg? Chocolate? Something else?

"Did you just say something?"

"Of course, I have not yet achieved total mental silence."

"I mean with your voice, exterior voice, not inner."

"Not with any awareness, no."

Abhishek sighs, he takes the mug from her hand and sniffs. *No, not cinnamon.* "What is it? Have you put something in it?"

He narrows his eyes at her.

Chinky shrugs.

"Just some cocoa I found."

He takes a sip. It tastes delicious.

A yawn.

"Are you sure it's just chocolate? It's making me sleepy."

Chinky smiles at him. "That's not the brew, that's your soul. It needs to detach from your mind and heal itself. Let it. It's had a rough day."

"So have I."

"Once your soul is healed, it will do the same for the rest of you."

Abhishek shuts his eyes, he is already drifting. He can hear someone humming, it's a strangely hypnotic sound. It moves out of the room. He wants to follow, but his body is too heavy, almost paralysed with sleep to move. And yet, he can still hear the humming as clear as if it was being whispered in his ear.

So has he moved then? His eyes feel glued shut to his face or he would have opened them. "I should not speak with Chinky before sleeping," is the last thing Abhishek remembers thinking when he wakes up in the morning.

37

5.25 p.m.

"Do you think she drugged you? Laced your coffee with something that made you see things?"

"I did not actually see anything."

"Yes, but you heard a sound without a source for it. That qualifies as hallucination. What drug would cause that?"

Gaikwad looks towards Sahil.

Sahil bristles, full of importance at Gaikwad finally seeking his opinion.

"Well, sir, I'm sure hashish can do that. But I doubt that Chinky ma'am would do that. She always said her body was a spiritual place of worship. She would not defile it with drugs. Are you sure you didn't have something at your boyfriend's house? What was his full name?"

Sahil looks at Abhishek, his eyes narrowed down to slits.

"I think it was just sleep."

"Never heard of it."

"It's that thing you do when you lie down on a bed and shut your eyes."

The little sarcasm slips out before he can check himself. Abhishek is worried. He does not want to turn the 'good' cop against him.

But Sahil is more disappointed than offended.

"Sleep, Sahil, you know that thing you do before you have that thing called dreams. Or when you're on patrol with Sunder-ji." Gaikwad joins the sarcasm party.

"Are you saying that you were just dreaming?"

Abhishek shrugs.

"I had had a stressful day and my mind was clearly all over the place. And since she was the last person I spoke with before sleeping, well, obviously my subconscious was influenced, contaminated even, by her."

"So nobody was humming?" Sahil looks almost crushed.

"She could have been humming," concedes Abhishek, "right before I fell asleep and my mind supplied the rest."

"I think perhaps the humming put you in a semi-hypnotic state and she used that to guide you. So what happened after you woke up? Were you transformed?"

Sahil is so eager, desperate even, for anything, just a crumb, a shred of evidence that she was special. He leans forward, his elbows back on the table, his expression pleading for confirmation.

Gaikwad makes an impatient gesture. He shares none of Sahil's reverence or hero worship. Nonetheless, his face has become positively animated at the possibility of 'drugs'. *Girl takes drugs, girl dies.* Finally something he can put a hat on and declare it solved.

"You were saying something about astral travel. Was that also with drugs?"

"She did not take drugs." Abhishek and Sahil say, in unison.

"Don't talk as if you were living next door to her," Gaikwad snaps at Sahil.

"But I was and it's true, she was strange but no external substance was responsible for that. It was just her. She was born high." Abhishek shrugs. "I never even saw her have as much as a beer or a glass of wine."

Sahil looks vindicated. "Born on a different plane…"

Gaikwad glares at Abhishek. "Well her bloodwork will tell us that."

38

2012

The night is starless, moonless, dark. What a relief. He knows that his feet are propped up only because the tingling has become slightly less. Or no, actually it has become more intense, the frequency so rapid that his limbs have gone numb, it's almost comfortable now. A weird thing to feel. Just moments ago, which probably was hours ago, his whole being had been in mortal agony. Now, he is floating in limbo. Or rather the bed that he is on. Gravity has stuck his body onto it like a magnet. Every finger joint weighted with a piece of lead. His head is still pounding but otherwise it is almost as if he has transcended the pain. Yet, he is conscious. Hyperconscious. He can hear the parrot on the third palm tree behind the window. How does he know that? He has no idea, he just knows, yes he can almost see it.

A bike comes to a halt at the crossing where the lane meets the road. He stands next to it, he can see how the driver clamps his fingers around the clutch, and kickstarts it. Is this what she means by astral travelling? He wonders if the man can see him. Woosh. The thought has sucked him back into his head. His heart is beating faster. He feels nauseous, but he knows that he has not enough strength to lift himself off the bed. If he has to vomit now, it will suffocate him to death. He shifts his attention to his lungs. Breathing in and out, deeply. Maybe if he opens his eyes, the rollercoaster will stop. He squints. The dimensions of the room elude him. He dares to open his eyes a little wider. Too wide. The pain forces him to close them again. He sees stars. In front of his inner eye. Drawn back into the universe of his own body.

The pressure on his fingers is gone, for a moment he feels lost. He wants to hold onto something, but he has lost his grip. Where is he falling? His body is falling apart. He knows this feeling.

"Shhh."

Cool pressure on his temples. The perspective of his own boundaries returns. At least that of his head. The rest remains in limbo.

He loves this part of it. His head is still pounding but he can feel the end drawing nearer. Only a few more hours, or maybe days, and he can come back into the world.

He relaxes.

Chinky is massaging his feet now. Long, rapid strokes along the soles of his feet. They warm up. The pressure on the balls of his feet is almost divine. He doesn't want her to stop, ever. He is glad that his feet are naturally soft. She moves along the inner side of his right foot, stroking with her knuckles. It is good. It gives him something to concentrate on, instead of the waves of nausea burning in the pit of his stomach.

She senses him surfacing from his state of unconscious hyperconsciousness.

"Do you know that men also have their period?"

"Really?" His immediate reaction is of course sarcastic.

"Yeah, just like women can also ejaculate."

Despite the state he is in, she has piqued his interest. He has seen enough Japanese porn to know this to be true. An image of an underaged schoolgirl comes to his mind. He shakes it off. It makes him want to vomit again. He would much rather concentrate on Chinky's velvety voice.

"It's of course much less hormonal, and also not necessarily connected to the moon ... unless you are in touch with your feminine side."

"So you want me to be more in touch with my feminine side?"

"No, your 'self' wants to be more in touch with that energy ... but you are not allowing that."

He is too weak to respond.

"It comes in waves, cycles, if you will."

A grunt is all he can manage. This is anyway not a conversation. It's a therapy session. But that is something he will only realize later, when it's too late.

"You should be grateful that your body is so in touch with your soul that it can send you such clear signals. All you have to do is follow the signboard – your migraine. And tune in."

This is where he tunes out. Is she telling him to enjoy his pain? He does have his kinks, but SM is not one of them. Still, weirdly enough he wants the malaise to continue, with her cool, soft hands resting on his forehead. Stroking down, helping his eyes close. And yes, maybe this is opening a door … No! A wave of panic rolls over him, he breathes deeper.

"Do not be scared." Chinky's breath smells of eucalyptus. "Trust me."

The scent calms his stomach. No need to hyperventilate. There is enough oxygen in his blood. He can see the bright red fluid flowing through the streams of his body. It's flowing in a regular rhythm, led by a mystical melody on a bed of eucalyptus.

39

8.17 p.m.

"So, let me ask you once more. How would you describe your relationship with the deceased?"

"She was my healer," Vincent wants to say. But he does not. Instead, he stares at the chewing-gum wrapper in the cop's hands.

There's a knock at the window. A crow is pecking at the glass. It must have caught the shimmer of the glass beads.

Vincent slides a couple of earrings towards Gaikwad and Sahil.

"Two hundred and fifty rupees."

"What the hell is this?" Gaikwad can already hear Meenakshi's bitchy laughter if she ever finds out about this. "*Someone tried to bribe you with earrings? Are you such a softie that people think they can just shove cheap handicraft in your face and you will release them? Does anyone even have any respect for you?*"

She still hasn't replied to his message. It seems that his idea did not work.

Vincent shrugs.

"I make these. They are good quality, tell your wife they were made by a real white man, she will love it." How dare he bring his wife…

"No, thank you."

Sahil picks up a pair and looks at it: "These are really good. Where do you sell these?"

"I had a shop. In Auroville. Sold a lot of crap. You take it for *your* wife, I'll even give you a free selfie."

Sahil perks up.

"I wouldn't mind a selfie."

"Sahil!"

Vincent smirks.

The crow lets out an acknowledging caw and flies off.

2013

There's a loud flutter and suddenly the square is empty. Making space for tourists huddling under their selfie sticks.

Chinky is holding a paper shopping bag in both her hands, like a schoolgirl, or rather like a mother patiently waiting for her child to finish his playground banter before taking him home to dinner, while Vincent is ranting at a couple of tourists who have come to him asking to click a selfie with them.

"What the fuck is the problem with you losers? Just because of my skin colour? It's fucking racism. You have put your wife in a burqa so nobody except you can look at her face. What about my face? You think it's ok to put that into your phone and show it off to your friends?" Vincent puts on a fake south Indian accent: "Aah, look at my white friend, his name is John, he from America."

Chinky shifts the bag she is holding to one hand, using the other one to try and calm Vincent. The people who had asked for a selfie have started filming his outburst.

Vincent throws up his hands.

"You want a video? Here, I'll give you a video." He unbuckles his belt, throws his shoes off, and pulls his t-shirt over his head, all in one motion. In no time a crowd has gathered, pulling out their phones as quickly as Vincent is removing his clothes. Chinky looks at him.

Only in his briefs, he holds up his middle finger.

"Fuck this shit."

He turns around, pulling down his underwear to reveal his white hairy ass, pretending to take a dump. And with a yogic-like flexibility turns his middle finger up in the air just above his butt crack. Allowing the skilled social media photographers to get everything in their full glory – his bottom, the raised finger and the red angry face shouting.

Pretending that he's done taking a dump, he puts his clothes back on.

Chinky shakes her head.

"What a wasted opportunity. You were naked, you had their attention, you could have said something more worthwhile, more profound."

She is looking so disappointed. Vincent hugs her, starts laughing.

"What's more worthwhile or profound than 'fuck this shit'?"

"Everything. Love, friendship, art, having this experience of being alive, this sunset. How pink the sky is just now…"

Vincent takes her face in his hands, he looks a little sad.

"Where is this world you live in? I have never seen it…"

Chinky looks up at him. Vincent shakes his head.

"Why do you look at me also like you are seeing something worthwhile…"

He lets go of her abruptly.

"Vincent…"

She is interrupted by somebody asking him for a selfie.

8.50 p.m.

Gaikwad inhales sharply. Blood is dripping from his thumb, leaving a brown stain on the file. Damn, his ass is hurting, his stomach growling and now this paper cut which will remind him of this annoyingly unsuccessful day until the end of the week. Why doesn't this man just admit it? He sucks his thumb. It's strangely pacifying. Well, eventually he gets them all. Just wait for it!

"You know, it does not look good to appear at a police station with a previous conviction."

The moment Vincent had sat down before him earlier this evening, Gaikwad knew that he was on the right track. This man had been at a police station before. Maybe more than once.

"First of all, it's not a conviction, it's an FIR. If you read the file correctly." His voice betrays neither his thoughts nor his emotions. "That's what they should have done with the dude who took unsolicited pictures of me. Just because of my skin colour. That's outright discrimination!"

"Sir, I think you have been discriminating here. A lot of women wear burqas by choice," Sahil responds.

"Yeah? How do you know? I've never met one."

"That is maybe because they chose to not talk to you."

Sahil is stumped. It is left to Gaikwad to bring the conversation back on track.

"Very well. Vincent, I would suggest that you calm down a little. Your foreign nationality won't save you from justice being served."

"But that's what I am saying! There was no justice served!"

"So you prefer to take matters into your own hands when you feel unjustly treated? Like, for example, by your ex-wife?"

"What the fuck? Where is that coming from? She never treated me unjustly. That was the fucking problem!"

Silence. Gaikwad is trying to pick up a thread from what he knows so far in order to corner Vincent.

Sahil interjects with a voice full of deep empathy: "The problem was that she was too nice, wasn't it?"

Gaikwad can't believe it.

"I know how that must have felt. For her. Have you seen her video on 'friendzoning'? It really opened my eyes."

Sahil has unlocked his phone and is scrolling through his starred videos on a WhatsApp group. "*We all have our edges, and we need to keep them, for the other person to have something to hold on to.*" Sahil is engrossed in the screen. Gaikwad taps his fingers on the table impatiently. The younger policeman turns the phone towards Vincent. "*When the sea gets rough, you cannot hold onto a rock that is washed soft and round.*" Chinky leans into the camera. Gaikwad's fingers on the table become more urgent. Chinky's eyes penetrate right into the listener's: "...*meaning the sea is all the people who came before 'the one.'*" She inhales deeply, looks down and then straight into Vincent's eyes: "*And you are the rock. You may think that you need a rock to hold on to, but you will have to be your own rock...*"

The tapping has stopped. Gaikwad locks Sahil's phone and puts it firmly on the table. Unwilling to let Vincent be deprived of his guru's wisdom, Sahil continues: "Chinky Ma'am says that they may have left their marks, but we should never allow them to abrade our soul so much that it becomes smooth and colourless. She also makes a joke here, using the word 'firang'. Did you know that it originally meant 'without colour'?"

Vincent laughs. It sounds louder than expected, more real, less angsty. He's confused, but not tense enough to be disturbed by it. Funny how Chinky still has this effect on him. Even after her death...

"So the learning from this video, Chinky Ma'am says..."

"Said..."

"Said ... is that we should keep our edges because even though our one true love might be hurt about it at times, that is what they love about us. And that is what they can hold on to when they need us most."

"So you left your wife because she had no edges? Did that push you over the edge?"

Gaikwad will not acknowledge it, but he feels Sahil might have just hit the right spot. Gaikwad feels his heartburn coming back. That always happens when he gets excited. Or eats samosa. Or both. He swallows the acid reflux with a loud gulp.

2012

"You know I really like it when you feel all soft and fuzzy."

There's hardly any space. Chinky is standing on the little stool in order to avoid anyone seeing her feet from below the swing door. Her arms are wrapped around Vincent's neck, her nose resting inside the creek of his collarbone. She's taller than him. An unusual feeling. He pulls back and looks at the mirror. He would have never gone near a shirt this shade and fabric. Neither is it the wild hippie print that he usually wears, having bought all his current shirts from a shop at Om Beach for 150 rupees each. Nor is it like the mysteriously taciturn black or white of the t-shirts he has been wearing since he was a teenager.

Nah, he does not want to spend money on this. Or any of the things hanging behind him on the door of the changing room. The mix of colour is already hurting his eyes. He blinks, crinkling his forehead and giant French nose. In the mirror, his eyes meet Chinky's. She looks as if she has just seen an angel. She looks like one too, towering above him, the ceiling LED making a little halo around her head. No, he cannot say no, really. Never had it been so easy for him to make someone so utterly, stupidly happy. Why, it's just a few clothes. And he still looks dashing. Maybe not like himself. Or his 'old' self. But dashing still. He smirks. Chinky jumps down from her stool.

"I'll pay."

9 p.m.

"So, did that push you over the edge?"

Gaikwad repeats his rhetorical question for the second time.

"What's pushing me over the edge is you people not understanding!"

"What I understand is that you did not like someone's behaviour and in an impulsive reaction committed an act of indecent behaviour."

"Being impulsive is a crime now?"

"Indecent behaviour is, sir." Sahil nods gravely. As if he is emotionally on Vincent's side, but needs to remind him of his precarious position.

"You know what's indecent? Wanking out your virtual dick and pretending you are oh so cool … you have white friends. It's stripping me of my dignity. But not like people in this country would understand."

"But you do? By calling a person from the northeast 'Chinky'?"

How fucking predictable.

"Chinky was beyond prejudice. She was beyond a lot of things. Call it enlightened, if you want. She owned up to it. And man, does, I mean, did it make other people uncomfortable to be confronted with their own narrowmindedness. Especially those damn hippies!"

He lets out a condescending laughter.

2012

He almost loses grip of his vantage point. The scene unfolding underneath him is just so bizarre, his body is shaking with laughter.

It all began with Chinky's arrival, naturally. He was about halfway up the trunk when she wrapped her arms around it.

First he thought she was going to come up, too. But she was instead occupied with preparing her bedstead. Like most new arrivals on this beach, she had brought a hammock.

Leaving her to mind her own business, Vincent resumes his. Only to be interrupted by Ram's furious shouting. The scrawny son of a fisherman had never even once shouted at him. During his final lesson, he had called his father to help him explain *loud and clear* how not to cut his own hand when harvesting. But that's about it. Since then, Vincent has been spending his morning hours with this perfect full-body exercise – the satisfying reward of slashing and eating fresh coconuts included – in quietude.

Was Ram shouting at him to not drop the knife? Why would he do that anyway? He wonders, not for the first time, what kind of impression he leaves on people…

"Eeeeeh, Chinky! Yes, you Chinky … eeeeh, are you not listening?!"

No. Definitely not addressing him. He looks down again.

"Yo, show some respect, bro."

A new actor has entered the stage: Sardarji. Pretending that he was still a bouncer in a Delhi club, only that he's now in the avatar of a dreadlocked warrior in harem pants who could be straight out of the Mahabharata.

This is going to be fun. Vincent secures himself with the rope.

"You don't tell me what to do. This is a beach, ain't nobody gonna die here."

"Ey man, why are you insulting her? What has she done to you? She's not gonna curse you – not all people from where she is from are witches."

"But some are," Chinky chimes in.

Vincent did not expect this answer.

"And I'm pretty impressed that you know my name."

Completely ignoring what she just said, Mr Mahabharata steps in between Ram and the girl: "I'd like to apologize for this man."

Ram, as quick on land as he is on the tree, has already begun to untie the hammock. "You know how many people die every year from coconut falling down? You don't put your hammock here. Put it on this tree." He points to a tree next to Vincent's shed.

"That's very thoughtful of you. But, Ram, you cannot call someone 'Chinky', it's not nice." Shaanti, Sardarji's beach-blond yogini girlfriend joins the scene.

"No, no. Call me 'Chinky'. This has been my name ever since I left home, where all of us are technically 'chinky'. Aren't we?" With a glint in her eye, she winks at the hulk. "So here at least I am special!"

Ram steps in-between and breaks the scene, quite literally. He takes a coconut and crushes it against Vincent's tree. Water is gushing out. "I don' care nothing 'bout witchcraft."

With a slurp, he hands the hammock to the new arrival.

It's time for Vincent to step down and save his personal space before this Chinky girl puts up her home there.

40

5.27 p.m.

"So did you wake up a different person?" Gaikwad scans Abhishek's eyes. This man is too well dressed to earn a living from a business of corporate nature alone. And his insatiable taste for caffeine exposes him as a highly functioning addict. Gaikwad feels his hands beginning to sweat – he is onto something! Alas…

"I have woken up many nights since then, I assure you it has always been my own face that I have seen in the mirror."

Gaikwad is not amused.

"I might have felt a little more together the next morning," admits Abhishek hastily.

Although Abhishek's survival strategy has been to say whatever it takes to appease either of the policemen, what he just said is not a complete lie.

41

2018

The morning after, Abhishek wakes up with a completely different reason to panic. He has overslept and it is already 10.30 a.m.

Shit shit shit! He is going to be late for '*we-meet-to-present-awesome-ideas-Monday*'. He has to hurry. His teammates' smugness will be unbearable, almost as bad as all the lame jokes Hassan is most definitely going to crack at his expense.

"*Oh no, Mister Delhi, is the city that never sleeps turning you into the man who never wakes? Ha ha…*" Abhishek can hear this and other similarly tedious but supposedly funny drivel as he quickly brushes his teeth and splashes water on his face. There is no time to take a shower. "*Oh look who came in smelling just like Mumbai? It's Mister Delhi.*"

Abhishek grabs a bottle of cologne from the shelf over the sink and splashes it on, liberally. *Oh damn*, he realizes as the first droplets hit his neck, *who has put this blue bottle where his eau de toilette is usually kept?* Whose smell has he accidentally worn? He sniffs. It is far too masculine to be Chinky, thank goodness. He would hate to reach the office smelling of incense and patchouli. He sniffs again, not quite his style but it does not make him gag. A visual of Satchit's naked body wearing 'nothing but the perfume' floats up into the periphery of his mental vision. Now he wants to gag. *No, no.* Whoever's this is, he has a good taste in fragrances at least.

Abhishek brushes his hair, grabs one of the linen shirts which Chinky had given to him and buttons it up all the way to the top. A different but surprisingly smart-looking Abhishek stares back at him from the tiny shell-framed mirror. Good luck, Chinky kept the shirts ironed and folded. No crinkle.

"Oh, you look sharp," Chinky chimes as she passes by the bathroom door. Despite himself, a small smile hovers over Abhishek's lips. "Like a freshly sharpened colour pencil, ready to paint the sky in blue. How fitting."

Abhishek rushes out.

Abhishek is in the cab, fielding calls. His phone has been in his hand for the last forty-five minutes and yet he hasn't checked his WhatsApp or inbox for a message from Kartik.

There is a particularly irate client he is speaking with right now, as busy as any other Mumbaikar, trying to make his commute count.

"Yes, sir, I'm just speaking with them … yes, yes, they are … just hang on, I have those guys on the other line…"

Abhishek disconnects and takes the call.

"Yes, sir, I mean Hassan, yes I am on my way, of course I have been working on the brief. At it, right now … yes, that is an advantage of travelling by cab … I do understand I wouldn't need that advantage if I had taken the train because I would be in office by now … Ha ha. What should we do? I think we should do something spectacular. Umm, yes exactly some kind of viral idea … Yes, that's what I've been working on too. Yes, I have the presentation. I will be there by then. No, I don't want pizza … No, actually, could you make it pepperoni please… yes, Hassan, I won't share it with them without showing it to you beforehand, obviously. Don't worry, it's almost done."

He disconnects. Cripes!

He starts typing and deleting on his laptop. One delete every five words approximately. *Work, brain! Work!*

A child raps on the window. "Hello, hero, so handsome you look. Buy a crayon?"

Abhishek waves impatiently. "No."

"Bhaiya please, five packets for only hundred."

"Why do I need five packets of crayons?"

"You can colour with five friends."

Abhishek gets back to his laptop, muttering under his breath, "I don't have five friends."

"Then you need the crayons, you can make five friends."

The child pulls out one of the wax crayons and quickly draws five distinct faces on the window of the cab.

The driver notices. "Oye! Oye M.F. Husain. Stop that before I smack you and break your hands."

The child sticks out his tongue and runs away.

The driver pulls over to the side of the road. He takes out a dirty-looking rag from under his seat and gets out of the cab, ranting loudly. "…the fuck is this. If they have so much talent, go draw on walls, no. Make something beautiful there. Why ruin *my* car?"

Abhishek looks at the drawing; it is surprisingly good, with so much detail produced in a few deft lines – there is the fisherwoman with a bun and frown, an old man with a monocle, a young couple all smiles and a cheeky little boy.

Without quite knowing why, Abhishek pulls out his phone and clicks a picture before the drawings become just another red stain on an already filthy piece of cloth.

The presentations are already under way when Abhishek reaches.

Today's presentations – apart from being Hassan's way of teaching social consciousness to his team and educating their clients about their social responsibility – are geared towards making CSR money work. Nothing new of course. They have been doing enough corporate social responsibility in their Delhi office, but Hassan prefers to call it their 'woke' movement. In his head this makes the exercise more spiritual and voluntary. Riyan had informed Abhishek when he had asked why the CSR budget of their clients had been allocated to something called 'WOKE'. Of course, in Abhishek's opinion most companies would be better served if woke meant investing in alarm clocks for their employees to maximize productivity.

Everybody takes a break from listening to the person in the white duckie t-shirt standing next to a slide displaying two green dustbins, to stare at Abhishek as he tries to slide in as unnoticed as possible.

"Look who forgot to wake up on 'woke day,'" chortles Hassan.

From the green dustbins to the predictable woke joke, today seems to be "cliche day" at the office. Abhishek nods towards

Hassan and looks around for an empty chair. There is one next to Riyan who pats it and gestures meaningfully towards Abhishek.

Abhishek notices Hassan looking at him with an equally meaningful smirk on his face. The last thing he wants is for it to become office gossip. Given the juvenile sensibilities of his colleagues, he will probably become the butt of '*Abhishek and Riyan sitting on a tree...*' type of jokes as well. He looks around for another empty chair. Hassan, whose eyes are already fixed on him, seems to read some other kind of message in Abhishek's hesitation in taking a seat.

"Wow, looks like Mister Delhi is dying to go next. Okay, let's hear what he has to say."

Shit.

Fifteen minutes later, Abhishek has exhausted his supply of corporate responsibility tropes and cliches. Looking at the bored expressions on the faces of his colleagues and given what he knows of their imagination and creativity, he is sure that he has just been repeating the same empty phrases which they must have been throwing against the wall of this whitewashed erstwhile colonial meeting room in the two hours prior to his arrival. Using their fancy smart art and diagrams and buzzwords, carefully placed slightly off-centre of an otherwise empty slide – to give it an 'edge' – having spent more time on choosing the colour palette than the actual content.

Thank goodness he missed it. It is slick, it is empty. In his world, ideas are presented like a dish in a fancy restaurant: small, bite-sized portions on a humongous well-designed plate. That's why Abhishek fits right in, he believes in the power of presentation. But this time ... Hassan raises an uninspired eyebrow. Abhishek knows. He knows that he has disappointed. *Mediocrity is the biggest enemy of greatness.* Abhishek is embarrassed at his underwhelming performance. Riyan shoots him an understanding, compassionate look.

It fuels Abhishek's rage at himself. He does not need pity.

Should he just get naked and wing it? No, no, not that, but what else would Chinky do? Why is he thinking of Chinky? Because she always finds something in her little 'bag of tricks'. But he is not Chinky, he does not collect tricks.

Unbidden, the face of the cheeky little kid from the signal flashes into his mind. Why? Why in the middle of embarrassing himself in Hassan's annoyingly cheerful conference room is he thinking about a child selling crayons?

Maybe because that's what he is, just another crayon in a box that is already full of them. Or maybe he is soon going to be the child selling the crayons. Poor and living on the street. *Stop thinking about crayons.* But there is nothing else to think about. He has no tricks, except the one he stole and put in his pocket.

He pulls out his phone, connects it to the projector, shuts off the lights, and accidentally also the AC, but he chooses to ignore it. The room is not completely dark but all colours have changed into shades of grey. The sound of the traffic outside is suddenly louder.

"Imagine this is your world. Grey, stuffy, this relentless traffic..."

The faces of his audience are draped in colour. Up on the white wall the crayon drawing stares back at them. He smiles internally at his intuitiveness in clicking a photo of it before the taxi driver erased it. The concept is forming almost by itself in his mind, words flowing out of his mouth without him consciously processing them. He surrenders himself to the process. *Sometimes his brain does good work while he is doing something else. Hear that, Chinky? I can make up clever-sounding shit too.*

The picture looks even better blown up. He has certainly caught everybody's eyeballs.

"Now let us be the colour in their lives. We have previously sponsored the Delhi street art fair." *Where the hell did he store this information?* "Taking it a notch higher, we now *collaborate* with these street artists. Instead of just donating crayons to kids, we paint *with* them and *for* them." *Wow, he is winging it like an expert.*

Ten minutes later he is happy to see that his audience is now voluntarily captive. In fact, Hassan looks like he desperately needs to go to the bathroom, but would rather embarrass himself by having an 'incident' here than miss a second of Abhishek's brilliant marketing plan.

He deliberately prolongs his 'friend-boss's' agony by throwing in a couple of long-winded tropes about the importance of being 'woke'. But not after long his bladder announces the need of a powder room, too. *Always leave them wanting more*, another mantra from his hall of motivational speakers at home.

"... the possibilities are endless."

He looks up at his colleagues: *Now is when you may applaud.* To his dismay there is no such reaction.

They whisper amongst themselves.

Hassan has a question. "I like the idea. Where do you think you can have them put up the logo?"

Silence. That's the trouble with winging it: a question can suddenly cause the brain to stop 'rolling' and go on a freeze.

"Dustbins, we could use dustbins."

Dustbins? Come, brain, you can do better than that, just because you saw green dustbins, green yes, trees are also green...

"Or trees, we could have them paint trees."

Riyan holds up his hand.

"Why not a slum? We identify one and get the kids to paint the walls, it would be such a huge canvas, we could have lots of graffiti, it would not just beautify the slum but also give the kids a chance to express themselves…"

"Yes, it would look glorious from above. We could paint on the roofs … we can get a drone and even make a documentary on it." This from the ten-smoke-breaks-in-an-hour girl.

Now it's a free for all. Everybody has an opinion. Basically rephrasing his thoughts. Abhishek can no longer distinguish individual words from the babble that has broken out all around him. *Wow, so these meetings actually do lead to real things? Who knew.*

But apart from this baffling observation, Abhishek is not really bothered. He has the physical urge to check his phone. Or is it that he needs to pee? He is unable to locate the exact source of his fidgetiness.

Abhishek scans the room for Hassan. He is not there.

With the boss gone, no need to keep up the stage. He switches on the light and removes his phone from the projector. Careful not to get his bladder crushed on his way out, he dashes into the first empty stall. *Phew.*

He has barely unzipped his pants when Hassan chimes, "You did good today, Mister Delhi."

What? "How did you know it's me?"

"Saw your shoes and also your 'I-gotta-pee' face. It was a level five at least. So I knew you would be bursting in any second."

"I do not have a 'I gotta-pee' face."

"Yes, you do, it's even a bit 'Delhi'. Ha ha. So, anyway, I was thinking the most effective strategy for us would be…"

Abhishek sighs, he cannot go now, not with Hassan talking strategy and budgets in the next stall. He almost smiles as he is reminded of his first night in Chinky's house. He should tell her about this, after he tells her how he nailed the presentation with zero preparation...

He stops himself. *What the devil is he doing? Collecting anecdotes to share with his lunatic landlady? Basking in his colleague's admiration? Getting caught up in this illusion of belonging? That is not why he is here.* This is an uncomfortable part of his journey, not his destination. He needs to uproot these little tendrils which seem to be sprouting out of him slyly. He must pull them out like weed.

"You know, if you were working for me, I would have given you a raise."

Well, nothing wrong in being appreciated, it does not mean that he is settling in.

"How much of a raise?" asks Abhishek. The words are out of his mouth before he can snap his teeth and hold them in.

An amused chuckle and finally the sound of the toilet flushing. "I really think that is a discussion better had in the office. Unless you think toilet papers are good for writing agreements on. I personally think the ink would blot, ha ha."

Abhishek chuckles obligingly in reply.

He can hear Hassan washing his hands.

"So, drop by, Mister Delhi, whenever you feel ready to have this discussion."

I will never. "Yes, sir, I mean Hassan, of course." *Unless Kartik begs him to stay of course.*

Hassan is finally gone. Abhishek exhales in relief.

His phone pings, he pulls it out. It's not Kartik. It's Riyan.

"Where have you vanished? Riya from accounts is telling everybody how she's always had a crush on you, you don't want to miss this."

I should forward a screenshot of this to Kartik.

"Coming right out," he replies, shoving the phone back in his pocket. He leans back on the seat and shuts his eyes. *What is he doing with his life?*

42

2010

The broker's 'office' is a hole in the wall. Literally so. If it were not Iti herself who found his number from one of the clandestine hoardings, she would believe that Chinky just 'manifested' it out of thin air. Maybe once upon a time, Adolf sat right here, on this spot that he stole from a cobbler or a momowala, waiting for the first train of the day to arrive and deposit its daily load of homeless hopefuls. Some of them wandered here and found Adolf, atop his brand-new fake-leather chair, his feet resting on his newly polished table, ready to rent them their first house. And as he rented his second house, then his third and then perhaps his hundredth, the leather on his chair wore thin, his table lost its sheen and four walls appeared to enclose him and mark this forever as his spot. This was when Adolf removed his feet from the table, his bottom from the chair, walked to the door, hung a board and called it a shop. Then he went back, sat again and waited.

It takes just one step to 'reach' from the potholed sidewalk into his air-conditioned 'office', then another to land in the once-upon-a-time dark-brown armchair. And then, there is nowhere else to go. You are trapped. The room is made almost entirely out of glass and one step down from the ground-level which gives you the illusion that you are sitting on the sidewalk. In front of the glass 'wall' is Adolf, safely distanced from his clients by an unnecessarily big wooden desk with nothing on it but three paper cups of tea, very milky, very sweet, just how Iti likes it. On the opposite side, with their backs to 'life outside', Iti and Chinky are occupying two equally imposing armchairs. Sinking deeper into the chair, Iti wonders where the tea in front of her has appeared from. There is no other door...

"Alright, but you still have to tell me your budget."

Trapped.

This is the question Iti has feared since they stepped off the sidewalk. How does one set a budget without money? She has done that once and it landed her in a shady PG for which Surat has been paying the rent. Maybe this is a bad idea, maybe she should first find a job and then a house. Like a sensible person. She looks at Chinky, waiting for her to read her thoughts.

Chinky nods.

"When we find a house we like, we will know our budget."

What?

43

2012

Really how long can one squat on the sandy floor scratching one's ass bitten bloody by armies of ants.

Well, Chinky can. For hours. In this weird position that villagers use to shit in the field. She says it's comfortable. The space between her ass and the floor is just enough for a trail of ants to pass through unharmed.

"Fashion brands use models to show their clothes, so why not us?"

He never looked at his hobby which helps him make ends meet as a 'brand'. Yet, just like the good French *artistes* have their *modèles*, Chinky is his muse and inspiration, wearing his latest creations as if the beach was a catwalk.

On her left ankle she dons a simple beige macrame anklet, on her right a more complex piece in dark green which stretches from her second toe in a neat triangle across the foot. In the same colour, she has tied a thick piece with a rose quartz in the middle of her left upper arm, accentuating her slender arms and sculpted triceps. On the right wrist, to balance off the heavy armband, she has tied a few thin bands in earthy colours wrapped around a mix of colourful semi-precious pebbles. Around her neck are two strings, one black choker-style with a row of small lapis lazulis and a long necklace which reaches until her solar plexus where a bright citrin is held together in a sun-shaped macrame. What makes the look somehow otherworldly are not the bright turquoise earrings, which look like drops stolen from the sea, but the triangular headband. Its purple makes Chinky's skin appear a shade darker than it actually is. Not that she cares, and also, he finds it attractive.

"Amethyst stimulates the third eye." Which is why she takes it off every night, carefully, putting it through a rigorous cleansing process. But his favourite piece is the 'carnelian loop', named such because it loops itself around Chinky's tiny waist, just across the belly button in a row of minuscule fiery orange carnelian pebbles.

That she is attracting the ogling eyes of all three types of beach dwellers – foreigners, Indian middle-class tourists who have anyway come to 'watch hippies' and locals – does not bother her. Her purpose is to attract money, and that she sure does.

The pieces she is wearing are obviously the crème de la crème and too much work to make for anyone else, really. At least Vincent can't be bothered. His free time is worth more than pleasing some Russian oligarch's wife. When asked for a price, Chinky comes up with the most exorbitant numbers, varying the amount of zeros depending on the 'vibe' she catches from the potential customer. Vincent is impressed how she can shift between 800 to 8000 rupees for the same neckpiece within minutes. Without flinching. And neither does her counterpart, ever.

"I'm simply validating their expectations." Her strategy pays off. Once they muster up the courage to speak to this aloof Indian goddess, people cannot help but buy something. They then go for a 'less expensive' piece. Which is still a bomb. Compared to what he charged before Chinky came into the picture. He was apprehensive about the price increase to begin with.

"Why not?"

"Why, because … I'll tell you an example. My parents were young, pretty and in love. And then they thought they could make it even better and, tadaa, they had me. It took them just a few years to break up and everything they believed in was gone. Love, their hippie ideals, my mom's figure, my dad's hair, and the hope to have a loving, spiritually mature son." He flips the leftover joint over the edge of the hammock into the coconut ashtray on the floor.

"I think you are beyond mature, and you know it."

Vincent is unsure what to feel. Pity? Amusement? Irritation? Affection? Whatever. She is fun, sexy, easygoing, weird and wild. And life's good. No money problems for sure. Not that he had any before. How much money does one need in – quite literally – paradise?

Less. He's already started accumulating stuff. A side-effect of the 'bourgeoisie'.

"Why do you treat it like a bad word?"

"Have you read Marx?"

"Yes. But doesn't it just mean 'citizens' in French? And aren't you a citizen?"

"Of what?"

"That's a good question…" Chinky leans against the bamboo wall of his hut and looks up. This argument deflated too easily for Vincent's taste. A need to revive it.

"And Marx was German. I'm more German in this respect."

"Hmm." Chinky has gone. She does that sometimes. Her body is still leaning and staring but her mind has gone off, somewhere on the milky way…

Grumpy, he too tries to doze off, turning his eyes towards the darkness of the hut. If there weren't Richard Gere and Julia Roberts staring back at him from through the glassless window.

"We need an LP player. But we don't even have a plug point."

"It'll come." Chinky's eyes are closed now.

"What? The plug point or the LP player?"

The answer is silence.

44

2010

"Which one is your room?"

Iti has reached the bedroom at the end of the tiny hallway. She throws open the window, or rather slides the glass along the rickety metal frame rail. The air tastes of sea salt. On the street three levels down, she can see a momo stall, a sandwich guy, a cobbler, a cigarettewala and a young girl selling idlis – all within less than 20 feet from the building gate. At the end of the street a dry cleaner and tailor have set up their symbiosis. Later, Iti will discover that behind the dry cleaner's façade, on a makeshift second floor, the tailor also runs a zardozi workshop and she will be one of Zaidi bhai's best customers. Until the pretty corner shop is taken over by a fancy coffee roastery a few years later, leaving tailor and cleaner on the lookout for a new, less gentrified abode. At this very moment, though, the only coffee place is a *Cafe Coffee Day* bang opposite the building gate, facing Chinky's room.

Although it isn't really Chinky's room. Not much more than the other one is Iti's. Nor is the bathroom decorated in sea-themed shells and sand candles like Iti was just describing it to Chinky. And neither chilly nor turmeric have found a home in the empty kitchen cupboards yet.

"If you don't think it is real, it never will be." Picking up on Iti's apprehensive vibes, Chinky goes straight into manifestation mode.

"No, no. I mean it is very real. A bit too real…"

Chinky breaks into a smile. "Right? This feels like home already, doesn't it?" She sits on the floor in a corner between the two windows in 'her' room. She bends her head back. "Hmm, I can't tell."

"What?"

"The sun is too high up…"

"For what?"

"You said you can smell the sea, in which direction do you think it is?"

Adolf, sweating in his shirt and suit pants, points behind Chinky. Iti knows he is losing patience. How long is one supposed to be allowed to take in a potential new home before committing to it? Iti feels anxious. But then again, this is going to cost them a bomb and he will make a nice commission, with no skill required except for being able to identify the right key for the right lock. So if his job is to wait and sweat a little, may it well be so.

"What are you thinking, Chinky?"

"I'm thinking that if the sea is there, this is west. Because the sea is always in the west in Mumbai. And that means that I will put my bed right here." She points to the opposite side of the room where there are no windows. This seems to be the only logical place to put a bed, even to Iti. Why would you want to sleep under a window?

"The architect of this place must be intelligent. For anyone will just instinctively place their bed here, against this wall, looking at the west with their head laid to rest facing east. Especially in a city like Mumbai, this makes perfect sense."

Nothing is making any sense to Iti, but she does not dare ask. She has not yet learnt that Chinky never judges the uninitiated.

Instead, she sits down opposite Chinky, leaning against the wall, looking out of the windows. "Yes, I think it would be lovely to have a nice cup of tea in bed at the end of a workday, watching the sun set behind those buildings. Maybe I'll colour this wall purple or pink so that it can reflect the sunset…"

"Exactly! Wow, you are learning so fast! This is exactly what you have to do: visualize it! Do you feel it? The magnificent tiredness of an accomplished day at your dream job? Don't think about the job itself – let the universe handle that – but about the feeling of satisfaction this job gives you. The happiness … the fulfilment…"

Iti is visualizing it. Her heart is beating faster.

"…the acknowledgement, the creativity…"

She sees herself doing a last-minute stitch on Divya Gupta's gown just before she steps in front of the camera.

"…the money…"

Iti's dream comes to an abrupt halt.

"Chinky."

"Yes?"

She hesitates.

"I love it. I love the area, it's so full of life and people. But it's expensive."

Chinky gets up, leaning on the grey marble windowsill, looking out into the street. A couple is sharing a cigarette. A dog is barking at them. They don't bother.

"It might be nice to have a job that makes more money. I've almost never had anything regular long term, except for that one sales job that lasted three months when I wanted to buy Nitin those gold cufflinks."

"Why did it only last three months?"

"Unfortunately, the cufflinks were not expensive enough for a fourth month. Though I really wanted to stay longer. But three months of a salary was enough to purchase them, and once I got them, the job ended."

"Ended? How?"

"My body alarm stopped working. I woke up at ten the next morning instead of eight-thirty like I was supposed to. I still wanted to go, I liked that place, I had made some friends and the work was so easy, but my energy was no longer aligned with it, so I had to put in my notice. It wouldn't have been correct to continue."

She shrugs and turns to Iti. "But I have sent out some messages."

"Oh, you also applied for jobs? Next time we can go to the cybercafe together. Maybe you can help me with my CV..."

Chinky's phone rings. She shakes her head, then holding her hand on the mouthpiece, she winks at Iti, mouthing a silent 'no'. And motioning a wave with her hand ... 'vibrations'. Then, with a beaming 'hello', as if the person on the other side could see her, she locks herself in the bathroom.

Iti is now alone with the broker.

She wonders why anyone would want to name their child 'Adolf'. What future does one foresee for a child with that name? Certainly not that of a broker, she chuckles to herself. Adolf darts her a look. Funny, how this place has already taken away some of her anxiety. Maybe it is the missing landlady, maybe it is the potential of having her own place, becoming her own woman... She walks around the room, awkwardly. Chinky's call is taking forever. She feels Adolf's eyes on her. There are two options now. Either polite conversation to pass the time. Or flight forward. She looks onto the road for inspiration: The dog has given up and is now sleeping in the shade of a palm tree, its paws crossed like a ballerina. She has never seen a street dog with a collar before. Even the dogs here live the filmy motto 'fake it till you make it'.

That's it!

"So how much did you say?"

"Thirty-five."

He must be joking. Or fleecing her. She wonders what gave away that she is not from Mumbai. Her correct Hindi?

"Thirty-five what?"

The broker cocks his head at her. Is she being funny?

"Thousand, madam, obviously not thirty-five rupees. I am renting you a house, not selling vada pav."

"Good, because I would not buy a vada pav for thirty-five rupees when it costs just ten. So I will ask you again, how much is the real rent?"

Adolf sighs. "It is 35,000, like I said."

"And I would like to believe you, but you just tried to sell me a ten-rupee vada pav for thirty-five, so you can see why I cannot. You more than doubled the price, so by this logic, I think this place is actually worth 17,000."

"It's a 1 BHK in Khar Danda, you will not even get a toilet for 17,000 here."

"It really is a tiny toilet, I would never pay 17,000 for that toilet. I don't understand your pricing at all."

Adolf opens his mouth to reply, then shuts it. "Where are you from?"

"Agra."

He chuckles. "Last time I was there, somebody tried to sell me a model Taj Mahal for 500, I bought it for 100."

"I would not have paid more than twenty-five."

A glimmer of respect in Adolf's eyes.

"What do you say we compromise and take it for seventy-five?"

"Why will I pay fifty more than it is worth?"

"You know it is worth at least sixty, the rest is just to satisfy your ego."

"What you call ego, I call pride. I will compromise at thirty but no more."

Adolf laughs.

He holds out his hand. Iti shakes it. Adolf covers her tiny hand with his big one and looks at her. "Welcome to your Taj Mahal."

Iti grins at him. "Not quite. I plan to live here, not be buried here."

Adolf snorts. He keeps laughing for an inordinately long time. Iti is not sure if she needs to keep laughing as well. Maybe not, she wasn't that funny.

Adolf finally stops and looks at her, a strange expression on his face. "Are you married?"

Iti is surprised. She shakes her head.

"Me, neither."

He shrugs and then shuffles his feet a little.

He is clearly embarrassed to still be single. Iti tries to make him feel better.

"Lots of people get married young but their partners die, at least you escaped that." She smiles her kindest smile at him.

His face betrays that he does not quite understand and this was not quite the reaction he expected. Adolf looks longingly towards the bathroom door. It finally opens, but instead of swapping places with Chinky, he excuses himself into the kitchen. Iti and Chinky can hear the tap running loudly.

"What happened to him?"

"I'll tell you, but first you tell me. Why are you smiling?"

"I just got a monthly job reading tarot cards on TV."

Iti squeals in delight.

"Oh my god, oh my god, this is the best news ever. You are going to be on television. I am going to be living with a celebrity, my mother will go crazy when I tell her. I'm calling her right now."

Chinky looks at her in amusement.

"So that means we are moving in here. My salary will cover the rent."

"And a little more."

"What do you mean?"

"I worked *my* magic."

Chinky hugs Iti. She knows. "You know, it is really lucky that you are not from Mumbai and don't know anything about real estate prices."

"Why?"

They are interrupted before Chinky can respond.

45

2018

Blue, green, red, pink, purple ... all around Abhishek is a swirl of colour. From nowhere shapes and stories are materializing on empty walls. On the wall on the left, a cat with a human body is feeding from a bowl full of money. Abhishek has no idea what this symbolizes. Corporate greed probably? Or maybe the greed of cats? Abhishek sniggers, maybe the painter has a particularly selfish cat that's eating up all his money? A young girl in a pink tulle skirt and matching plastic flower in her hair is painting a blue kangaroo with pink polka dots. Abhishek feels obliged to correct her. Kangaroos are actually brown and they do not have dots. The girl fixes him with a steely eye. "Have you seen all the kangaroos in the world?"

"Of course not, but I know what they look like."

"Do you know what all of them look like?"

Abhishek gives up. Anyway, who says art has to be real? Or for that matter who has seen all the kangaroos in the world? Maybe some of them do look like this. His hands take a picture of it with his smartphone. He captions it. *Have you ever seen a blue kangaroo?* His fingers take it one step further and send the photo to Kartik. Within seconds, his phone beeps. Kartik has replied. With a question mark. Abhishek is disappointed.

"It's going well I think, these kids have so much talent." Hassan looks like a few of the kids used him as a piece of rag to wipe their brushes on.

Abhishek smiles at him.

"So are you the butterfly or the cat woman?"

"What?" Has Hassan finally crossed the line into tasteless homophobic humour? It takes him a second to realize that Hassan is not commenting on his personality, rather he is inquiring what Abhishek has painted. *Fine. But it is still a little homophobic, is it not, to assume that Abhishek would paint a butterfly. He could have also painted the astronaut.*

"Oh, I am just supervising. I can't sketch. I am not an artist."

"Of course you are. Anybody who can appreciate art is an artist and you are the one who first drew our attention to that crayon family. So here." Hassan hands him a brush and two jars of paint, red and blue. "Unleash your inner Picasso and give us your *Mona Lisa* ha ha."

If he wasn't seized with instant panic, Abhishek would have rolled his eyes, just as surely as Picasso and Leonardo are both rolling in their graves right now. He takes the paint and the brush from Hassan.

But the white just won't vanish. After what feels like an eternity, but has only been twenty minutes, Abhishek is still frozen, haplessly staring at that patch of empty wall his boss has assigned to him. Luckily Hassan has been called back to office and the kids are too busy with their own creations to care about what Abhishek is or isn't painting. So here he is, paintbrush in one hand, paint bucket in the other, with no other work to do. Nothing can stop him from creating ... anything! Except for the cold sweat running down his neck, slowly trickling along his spine until he stands in a puddle of fear like a toddler who peed in his pants. If it does not turn out well, he can say that one of the kids did it. Nobody is even watching – so should he not be able to make something?

As the sun goes down, Abhishek goes home, feeling disappointed.

The house smells of coffee, nutmeg and cinnamon. Abhishek inhales deeply, trying to 'smoke out' the acrid stench of his failure. *He couldn't even draw a straight line.*

"She would have loved this blue."

Abhishek looks in surprise at Chinky. She hands him the coffee and takes his hand where the paint that had been refused the joy of fulfilling its purpose has left its mark.

Chinky's eyes are misty as she does what freaks him out so much: She leaves him standing alone with her immobile shell as her lights blink out momentarily. This time her still warm although lifeless hand is holding his in it.

What if she never comes back? Would he then be stuck forever with his hand in hers?

She comes back by the time he has counted to two.

She smiles at him.

"Water is not always blue and fire is not always red."

Abhishek stares at her. He goes absolutely still. This time he is the one who is having the 'out-of-body' experience.

Something is forming ... not a picture, but a feeling, an idea...

He is dimly aware of Chinky taking his hand and leading him somewhere...

The sun has set, paintbrushes have long been put away. The lights are on in a few houses. Are those people speaking or the television? Abhishek is unable to tell, the things people say and the things they watch are both equally unfamiliar to him in this land. In an instant all is white noise, blurry background, and he is lost in his mind. His body finds the still empty spot on the wall, it is just the right size.

Chinky has detected a broken piece of pavement to plant herself on. Her dark skinny legs thrown on a pile of grey and brown gravel with some highlights of plastic, she leans back, merge with the shadow of the colourful house wall just inches behind her. Someone's TV paints erratic patterns on her face.

A soft mournful song sung in an unfamiliar language wafts through the air and reaches his ears. Barely aware of what he is doing, he sings along, mouthing 'meaningless' words. The melody transmits its meaning straight to his hands as they render a bright blue fire climbing up on the wall. The fire is unstoppable, it threatens to consume everything in its path, Abhishek can see it already licking the tail of the greedy cat and burning the toes of the barefooted astronaut. It halts in its path only when a red liquid, falling from a heart with several lacerations wherever it was touched by the fiery tongue, douses its flames and renders them to smoke. The fire is contained, stopped by the very thing it was trying to consume.

The song fades, the last of its notes carried away by the wind.

Exhausted, Abhishek collapses on the floor.

The next day he finds most of his painting obliterated by their client's logo and the rest of it covered with butterflies and a riot of colourful flowers.

"Some kid painted some dark shit," whispers Hassan, "and on your spot, too. I'm so sorry."

Abhishek sighs. He should have taken a picture.

It is as if the city does not care for his presence at all.

"Well, that is mutual," he whispers. *I would have never come if I was not so desperate and I would still not be here if anything changed.*

He looks again at the mess of colour and beauty. Hidden under it is his story, now invisible.

46

2010

"And I can make the whole room pink if that's what I like?"

"Even if you don't like it and it's just you pleasing your inner child who could not get her pink room."

Iti looks at Chinky and laughs.

"You're right I don't actually want a pink room anymore. I've just wanted one for so long, but the last time my father got the house whitewashed I did not have my own room. I was only thirteen. I slept in the same room as my parents. My father showed us a shade card that had five different options for yellow. There was no pink, so I picked a pretty lime yellow. But when the whitewashing was done, it was just the same, almost the white yellow we had before. After a while it also got just as muddy. Sometimes I would wonder if the whitewash had even happened. All the old stains reappeared in exactly the same place…"

There's silence. The kind of wistful, yet happy silence that is born when someone visits memories in the presence of people they love.

"So what colour do you think my first own room is going to be? Look into the future and tell me."

Chinky fills the wistful space with her smile. "It doesn't matter what I see. You already know, but the reason is not what you believe."

Iti looks at her quizzically. She turns towards her bed with the same expression. She had moved it away from the wall to right under the window last Monday. 'Don't fix it if it ain't broken,' her father used to say. A good piece of advice but then empty hands have a way of getting restless, and restless hands are clumsy and clumsy hands break things … maybe just to have something to fix.

She proceeds to push the bed back to its original position, using her knees. Halfway through the room she finally plonks her upper body on the mattress. She spreads her arms out, ready to fall asleep, but just after two seconds her inner restlessness forces her feet to move, pushing her entire body, along with the bed, towards the wall.

"What do you think? Is it perfect?"

Chinky grins. "Let's say I would definitely never curse you with perfection. You might burn the house down."

Iti laughs and collapses on the bed. Exhausted but somewhat pleased. Maybe because she is exhausted? Yes, perfection does make her happy, but for her to feel satisfaction she needs to exert herself physically.

"Do you think we should paste some stars here?" Iti squints up at the ceiling. "Is it too bare?"

Chinky shakes her head. "I don't think stars like to be trapped inside homes."

She lies down next to Iti, playing with her hair, intertwining it with her own.

"I wouldn't worry too much about the ceiling. I don't imagine you spending much time looking at it."

Has Surat shown you the ceiling yet? A crude joke, narrated by a friend in Agra, pops so loudly into Iti's head that Chinky obviously hears it.

"I would imagine you would have your eyes shut," Chinky responds to the unspoken thought as casually as if it had been spoken aloud.

Iti doesn't think much of it at the time. It's Chinky, she finishes people's sentences.

Years later when she has stopped spending all her free time with Chinky but found herself around people who would need to be told when and what she would like to drink, who would disappoint her by never answering her questions unless she spoke them out loud, and who would look at her thoughtful face, gently stroke her bare shoulder and ask her what she was thinking about – *'if you have to ask, you have no right to know the truth'* – she would catch herself wondering if she remembers it incorrectly. Maybe she did recall the joke out loud.

"Blue?"

"Why?"

"Like the water…" Iti's thoughts trail off. If she could, she would will her ears to hear the ocean waves crashing…

"Be careful what you wish for. Water is never free. Wherever it flows it creates a bank, a boundary, and when it is put in a vessel it shapes itself to fit in without question. When I was younger, I would look at how the water would first become a jug and then it would become a glass. I would whisper to it, you don't have to change for them every time, tell the glass to be a jug or the jug to be a glass. But water never listened. It just became whatever was needed."

Iti looks at Chinky.

"What do you think is the real shape of water?"

Before Iti can answer, a car horn toots outside the window, twice. The question is discarded as Chinky sits up, quickly detangling her hair from Iti's.

"I have to go, Nitin is here. Do you want to come?"

Iti shakes her head. Normally she would crave Chinky's company, but right now all she wants is to be in this, her, room, and take it in as it is, completely featureless. She wants to learn the shapes that exist in this emptiness, so that she can see every single change, however subtle, which will eventually overtake the space — and from the difference, she will see herself.

Yet, she is surprised when Chinky rushes out. Lately, she has been spending more time alone with Nitin. And returns less at ease than before, immediately vanishing into the shower, as if trying to wash off something malevolent.

"Probably Nitin's cologne," Valarie had said, with her typical cattiness. Iti had smiled, missing her acerbic tongue.

She had visited last week. Iti, who was alone at the time, had heard the key turning in the lock. Expecting to see Chinky, she had been surprised to see Valarie, who stood there with the door half open, a little dismayed at having run into a person she would have to speak with now. In response to Iti's baffled expression, Valarie had said, "Chinky gave me a key. Nobody has ever given me a key to their house before. I wanted to see what it feels like to just walk into somebody's house unannounced and for no reason." She shrugged. "It is super awkward. Good to know that. When I have a house I am certainly not giving anyone a key. Here, I don't want this anymore."

She had tried handing the key back to Iti who had surprised them both by hugging her. "You are our first guest. Come in, what will you have? Tea or coffee?"

A heavy sigh from Valarie and then another typical Valarie shrug. "Okay, you might as well show me around. Do you have any beer?"

An hour later, Valarie had taken in the house. There wasn't that much to show. But much time was spent in figuring out a place that would deliver the beer. Once Iti had called Just Dial for a number, Valarie had taken her phone and saved it on her speed dial. "What kind of Mumbaikar does not have an alcohol store on speed dial?" Then they had both gone on a bout of some serious day drinking.

It took only a short while for Iti to tell Valarie about Chinky's long showers after meeting Nitin. Valarie's bitchiness had eased her mind a little. It was probably nothing, maybe Chinky just took longer showers because now she could. No use obsessing over the fact that they happened only on those days when she met Nitin.

It had felt so comfortable and homely, sitting here with Valarie reminiscing about their PG days, bitching about the landlady with a kind of proprietary glee. Iti had realized with warmth spreading in her stomach that she already had a home in Mumbai to feel nostalgic about. She was belonging more and more every day.

"You should visit more often," Iti had told Valarie, feeling a surge of affection for her as they watched the sun setting and the city lighting up, as if in perpetual celebration of life. "It was so nice having you here."

Valarie had looked at Iti in surprise and shaken her head. "I doubt. You live too far."

"Far? It's the same city. Hardly forty minutes by rickshaw in traffic."

"Iti, just last week I met this incredible guy. So smart and also so good looking. Do you know how hard it is to find someone intelligent in this city who is good looking in a way that does not scream 'struggling actor'? It is almost impossible."

After sipping the foamy bottom of her bottle, Valarie had continued without waiting for Iti to reply. "I felt such feelings I have not felt in a long time. And yet, I had to tell him, we couldn't do it. Long distance never works."

"But Surat and I…"

Valarie had rolled her eyes, before interrupting.

"Different cities. That does not count. Suresh (even though she had heard his correct name not even two seconds ago) would not expect you to take a train every other day to meet him. Distance works differently in Mumbai. One does not travel more than 500 metres to meet someone."

"Where does he live though?"

"In Kandivali."

"Where's that?"

A theatrical sigh. "Exactly."

Iti wonders now if Valarie would be back. She had forgotten to leave the key behind, so maybe, or maybe not. They had not really been friends as Valarie had reminded her – 'just flatmates' – and now Valarie probably has new flatmates.

Maybe she should visit Valarie. Yes, that's what she would do. One of these days…

As she hears Chinky slam the door shut on her way out, she sits down on the cold floor and caresses it with her hand.

Her eyes trace the walls all the way to the big windows with the grill, so typical for Mumbai. The sight of the window and the knowledge of what lies beyond it makes her smile. She walks over to it and flings it open, breathing in deeply. She takes in a lungful of the city. All around her life is happening. The streets are full of people. Iti wonders how many of them would soon have a key to her house.

"Why do people say Mumbai is a lonely city," wonders Iti aloud to herself. The watchman below looks up at the crazy new tenant. She continues her musing – he anyway doesn't understand her. Might as well already set a reputation as *yedha*, the label will give her space to fill over time. Just like her room … She sighs heavily at the rising moon. "It is cities filled with families which exclude those who don't have any that are actually lonely."

As if in agreement, a beer bottle falls from the French window above her. The lonely people in that house party every night.

She hugs herself, staring at the orange light and dark brown shadows dancing on her inner elbow, as if she is looking at someone else's body. "Tell me, why would anyone settle for a family of two when you can have everyone?"

Her phone rings, breaking her reverie. It is Surat. A wave of glee overcomes her.

"I can hear you smiling from ear to ear."

"Yes, maybe I am."

This is her family: Everyone and Surat, thinks Iti. It's perfect.

As she tells him all about her day and every single thing she is thinking, she holds out her hand as if trying to touch the energy pulsating in the air. She knows already that she will soon be holding out her hand to catch the raindrops as they fall in torrents from the sky.

The guard throws her another dirty look.

She decides it is time to turn back inside and listen to Surat telling her about his day and plans. But staring at the blank wall, a part of her brain trails off. Hearing her lover's voice is as comforting as the sound of raindrops on a tin roof.

She doesn't understand what Chinky had meant – the colour she wants for her room is blue and what is blue except the sea? Except water? So what does she want to be if she doesn't want to be water?

It will be a few years before she realizes that water has never been blue. That it is only a reflection of the sky. Blue is not the colour of water, it is the colour of freedom.

10.10 a.m.

Gaikwad squints at Iti.

"I don't understand. Why are you describing your room? That's not where the decea ... I mean Chinky Ma'am died. Or is it?"

Iti leans back. "I wasn't describing the room. I was telling you about her, without being too on the nose."

She shrugs at Gaikwad's blank expression. "It's a film thing. People understand more when you let them read between the lines, because after all how many lines can one person write? So I write some and you read both what is written and what is implied and then you know even more than me."

No reaction from her audience of one.

"At least more than I know consciously."

Gaikwad shakes his head. "Madam, I think it will be quicker if we stick to the facts."

"But you already have the facts. Chinky is dead, her body is in the morgue. Why do you need to question anyone if not to understand why or how she died."

"Exactly, so maybe you just answer that question."

Iti's eyes cloud over.

She suddenly feels heavy. She wishes Chinky were here. To guide her through this unknown, bizarre, uncomfortable situation. She wouldn't even need to be here physically. It would be enough if she could just text her, into the void, knowing that her phone will ping and she will get an answer one way or the other just at the right time. But now, there was only the void. Without any hope for an answer.

"Maybe I have already or maybe the answer is yet to come. How do you find a lost thing unless you search everywhere, under every nook, in every corner, under all the cushions, all the blankets? What if you only search the corners and what you were hunting was right in the middle of the room? Or maybe some of it was in the corner and the rest…" She shrugs. "I don't know where the rest is, but how will we find it if we don't look everywhere? Inside everyone?"

Gaikwad mops his brow and pours himself a glass of water.

He clears his throat in an attempt to regain some authority. "How was she paying for the new place? How were you? Tell me about her job. Before she got online. I heard there was a scandal."

"Yes, and if you had been paying attention to my description, you would have realized that the events that led to the scandal had already been set in motion. And what happened after that is as important because if any of those things had not happened or happened differently, maybe … or maybe the ending was inevitable, we just would have reached it differently."

2010

The set is magnificent. If you are from Agra.

Iti has been working on her aesthetics. Valarie had pointed out, rightly so, that her taste is very 'small town'. Some people would have been offended, but Iti didn't come to Mumbai to not change. In fact she is soaking up criticism like a sponge, her little red notebook being the sponge. Many years later, she would make a fortune and career exactly because of her 'small town taste' – that's where the majority of Indian cinemagoers still live.

But right now her little red book is filling up with names of the fanciest imported brands of nail polish, hair shampoo and shoes, fabric samples snuck from Manish Market and Saroj under the pretext of 'taking it for approval', cut-outs from international magazines (Chinky has told her boyfriend that she likes reading them, so he has been buying them for her), cool phrases to use (in English, Bambaiya and Marathi), a table of colour combinations divided into 'adore' and 'tasteless', and finally an ever-growing section of 'set lingo'.

She is a fast learner and hence concludes, of course only in her mind, that the set design is 'tacky'. But right now the rest of her ignores the disapproval she is mentally training her eyes to discern. Her whole body is tingling with the sheer frenzy of movement around her. Like in Surat's computer games, every character is forever on the move. Even when they pause for a few seconds, the very ground beneath their feet bounces them back into motion. As if the ground was a spring. Coiled so tightly, Iti is sure that if she placed a finger on the girl standing next to her, she would instantly jump a few feet ahead, and find something that needs to be done urgently wherever she lands.

The tiny buzzing electrons on this set are centred around a flashy purple nucleus: A backdrop covered with various star constellations, mixed with ominous-looking tarot signs – the hanged man, the wizard, the lovers. In the centre of it rests a throne-like chair. Neatly arranged on the small red table in front of it is a stack of tarot cards. And hovering on the throne, like a goddess who has just descended from the heavens, is Chinky, bathed in light from all directions – including a sharp backlight which creates a little halo around her head.

Iti is spotted by a spot boy, who rushes to her side. He grins toothily at her and Iti feels her spirits soar even higher as he uncorks his flask. The smell of over-sweetened tea fills the room and like ants responding to a few grains of sugar dropped on the kitchen floor, other people from the crew materialize by his side. The boy deftly fills seven cups and moves away to give the ones milling at the other side of the room their quarter-hourly shot of elixir.

There is something about having tea on a busy set which makes it even sweeter. The air is suddenly filled with energy. Iti feels the ground beneath her own feet coiling, longing to fling her somewhere in the middle of the frenzy. The brown fuel has done its work. Iti sighs, feeling relaxed and energized all at once. Later, Chinky would tell her that the more her soul relaxes the more her body becomes infused with its latent vibrancy.

This is Iti's fifth visit to Chinky's set. She is an addict, who will keep returning for her 'fix'. It seems that Chinky has just finished giving a take. Yet she remains unmoved, as if waiting for something. Iti watches her, intrigued. Chinky is dressed in a long flowing dress with slightly asymmetrical bell sleeves. Iti doubts that this is deliberate, but who is she to comment on the dress. Though it does nag her to see the sleeve sliding down just a little bit by bit. Maybe they are waiting for someone to fix it.

She notices a good-looking boy in the corner of the set, near the monitors. Or maybe she remembers him as a boy … he must have been already in his early thirties when they met, but she could never think of Kunal as a 'man'. He is watching Chinky. Iti knows that look. She has seen it before. He is hypnotized. They are all hypnotized. Maybe she would be jealous if she wasn't hypnotized, too. Chinky has them all in her thrall.

Chinky is saying something about the activation of the sacral chakra.

"Spontaneous Kundalini rising must be dealt with carefully. Not everyone is ready for the kind of spiritual magnetism it can create in your pelvic area. But I can see in your cards that it will help you find clarity in your professional life. Accept your own attractiveness, your sexual desires. Breathe deep into the Svadhishthana."

Her loud clear voice rings across the set, painting vivid pictures in Iti's mind. Surat and she ... no, she cannot think of Surat like this, he would never ... she and a nameless faceless stranger ... Iti looks down at her feet, embarrassed, not daring to look at anyone.

"Truly explore yourself, let loose, experiment – and I don't mean by making love to whoever is drawn to you, I mean by making love to yourself! The other person is just holding the key to opening your own treasure trove of possibilities."

She feels like her skin has become transparent and her thoughts are printed on her face to be read and understood as clearly as Chinky's words.

"And if you feel ready, focus on your root chakra, your muladhara." Chinky is breathing heavily. "That is where the deep red energy of self-love meets the selfless love of the universe. Once you loosen the tight earth around your roots your entire being will shoot up towards the sky, like a plant. Dig deep into the soil, play with the mud, and the lotus of your Sahasrara will open. You will attract the kind of ideas you have been longing for. Effortlessly." Chinky's hands move along the fabric of her gown, from her waist up until her arms are stretched towards the sky. "Breathe in. Feel the fiery snake!"

Iti feels a stirring, somewhere in the area she is too bashful to even think about and yet Chinky is so matter-of-factly speaking of it.

"But." The tarot reader exhales.

"Be careful. The kundalini is the vehicle for the energy you need. It is a means to the cause, not the aim. Those who get lost in ecstasy are lost forever."

The faceless man vanishes and Iti looks up and around, willing herself to appear nonchalant. Her eyes alight on the stranger's face, fixating on the way his lower lip is jutting out ever so slightly, almost in a pout. She wonders what it would feel like to touch it with the tip of her finger.

Iti tears her eyes away from Kunal's face and lets them wander over to Chinky's left shoulder where the niggling movement has been pricking at her eyelids like an annoying eyelash wedged inside. The strap on the dress's left shoulder is just too loose, maybe the rubber ripped. Iti allows herself to fixate on that.

The resident witch has awoken from her daydream and waves at Iti. Happy that the lights have not blinded her friend yet, she waves back. Kunal catches the motion from the corner of his eyes – she is clearly a friend of the star of this show, and she is standing! He smiles at her and immediately instructs a spot boy. Iti doesn't know what to do, but the man who brought her the red plastic chair insists that she sit down and even asks her what she would like to drink. She perches herself awkwardly, then gets up again, standing even more awkwardly next to the chair. Kunal comes and, arms crossed in front of his chest, stands next to her, oozing an air of comfort.

Iti refuses to look at his face, lest her chakras start stirring again. She looks a little to his left, whispers: "I feel a little guilty sitting down when everybody is rushing around doing something." Unconsciously, her left hand fiddles with the pouch in her pocket…

Kunal whispers back: "Don't let it get to you. Set people are pros at looking busy even if they are actually only rushing around for the tenth smoke break."

Iti grins, her stomach does a little flip-flop. They are going for another take.

"I should go out. I'm getting really edgy sitting here. See, Chinky's strap is falling off from the left side, I keep thinking I should get out my needle and thread and fix it." Her hand closes around the kit.

Kunal is immediately all attention. He yells, "COSTUME! Are you fucking sleeping? Fix the dress."

Iti is embarrassed as the costume girl rushes to the set and sets out to fix the dress.

"Shit! I'm sorry. I didn't mean to cause trouble."

She turns to him. Trying to demystify, normalize their interaction. After all, as Chinky keeps saying, the unknown seduces more than the known.

"What do you do here though? I thought you were an actor."

"Strange … I thought the same about you."

Just the tiniest shiver, making her toes tingle, she keeps it in check.

He holds out his hand. "I'm Kunal. I produce this show — and some other TV shows for digital channels."

"I'm Iti. I work in costumes, or at least I will once I have a job."

Kunal looks at her approvingly.

"How good are you at working 24/7 and having no life other than work?"

"It's what I have been dreaming of for months."

Kunal grins at her. "Well, they do say we are in the business of making dreams come true."

A feeling of warmth floods Iti's body. It's like her activated chakra has 'peaked'. She exhales, not really sure what tipped her over – Kunal or the job he just offered her.

Iti had not told Surat about the new house. She had also not returned the money he had deposited this month. The plan was to give it to Chinky as a small contribution towards the apartment, or in case Chinky did not like her job and they needed a little bit of savings. Now, at the end of her first month in her own house with her (almost) own bathroom, she suddenly finds herself with three sources to pay the rent from: Surat's saved 'loan', Chinky's salary and a decent paycheck – if she can keep this job until the end of the month, that is.

Kunal proves to be a tougher negotiator than Adolf. Still, she manages to get Kunal to agree to a monthly salary. Which, in retrospect, seems quite incredible to her – she would never give a newbie anything but an internship with conveyance. After the disappointment with her first 'job', she has become a bit more cautious, avoiding shouting her good news around town too early. Over the years she will cultivate this habit of calculated pessimism. With the signed contract in her backpack – Kunal was quite taken aback that she insisted on one, but then took it as a sign of a penchant for precision – the time has come to use a little bit of her savings from Surat's money to … call Surat!

"I have a job, I have a job. You don't need to send me money anymore. I'm so happy. I love you so … Oh hello aunty, I didn't realize that Surat gave you the phone. Yes, I have a job, on a TV show … Hello uncle…"

Iti discovers after exactly two days that 24/7 is not just a figure of speech in Kunal's world. He has literally described her working hours.

There is no concept of Sundays or even national holidays – as she finds out after having successfully fished out her phone from under the pillow on 15 August at 9 a.m. The head of costume is demanding to know where the hell she is.

"But it's fifteenth August."

"That's exactly what I am saying, we have a telecast on the sixteenth and you decide to be late on the fifteenth."

"No, I mean it's Independence Day."

A two-second silence on the other side.

Then a condescending sigh, followed by an annoyed, "Are the British still in India or have they left?"

"What? They left, of course."

"Exactly, that job is finished, please get here for the one that still needs to be done."

The caller hangs up, muttering something about entitled rookies expecting holidays for everything.

Iti shoves her phone in her pocket, picks up her bag and rushes out. As she hails a rickshaw, she is already looking forward to starting the day with the kadak set chai.

A few years later, when confronted with the demand of a work-life balance from a newly hired intern, Iti will remember this phone call. She will try to use it to explain her expectations to the girl. But then give up midway – even in 2017 a day still has only twenty-four hours and her time has become too precious to waste.

Except of course for Chinky. Just like her 'budget', even time stretches or contracts to her whims. She alone seems to have an endless supply and never runs out of hours, minutes or even seconds to get it all done. Chinky shoots for twelve hours, bathes for thirty minutes, does an hour of yoga, one hour of dance, goes for walks, paints, sings, meets Nitin, spends time with Iti and never sleeps for a minute less than eight hours a day.

Yet, so many times at the end of the day, Iti comes home to find Chinky already washed and curled up in bed, painting her nails and humming to herself as if trying to get rid of all leftover time. Even Iti's super mathematical mind cannot compute how she can account for at least thirty-six hours of activity in a day that has only twenty-four. She had mentioned this once to Chinky to which she replied that time didn't actually exist outside of clocks.

While that may have been true for Chinky, for Iti, whose mind's very essence is contained like grains of sand in an hourglass, time is something that bends her to its will. So the mind of twenty-three-year-old Iti is never clouded with the thought of protesting that people from the set think nothing of calling her up after midnight, waking her from her sleep without even an apology, to alert her to a change in the brief. "You need to come to the set with a red raincoat instead of a blue one."

Iti sits up. "But I picked up the blue one from Gem dresswala and they won't be open at seven."

"Well, find a way to make it red before you come or don't bother coming at all."

The caller hangs up, leaving Iti sleepless and alert, trying to figure out where to get a red raincoat from in the middle of the night.

Luckily it is the middle of the monsoon, and also luckily Mumbai is a city that never sleeps.

Picking up her umbrella and her bag, and slipping on a pair of old flat shoes, Iti walks over to Bandstand. The rain is falling all around her and yet the city is still throbbing with movement.

Within seconds two cyclewalas are by her side, offering to sell her tea. Iti smiles apologetically at the second one, explaining that the other guy got here first.

"No problem, madam, next time I will be faster." He smiles at her as he peddles away, exchanging a few quick pleasantries with the winning cyclist who is pouring out a cup of tea for Iti.

Iti smiles at them, they are just like her, hustling hard in the city which, she has heard, unfailingly rewards those willing to go that extra mile.

Tea in hand, Iti puts away her umbrella, letting the rain fall on her face. The night is balmy enough for the rain to not make her feel cold. The water washes away the last remnants of fatigue and any attachment she might have been feeling towards her probably still warm and cosy bed.

She exhales, adrenaline flooding her body at the thought of the super busy day ahead. But before that, there is work to be done.

She looks around at the people milling about. At Bandstand especially, there is no dearth of people at any hour. Some are yet to go home, some are just out in the rain, trying to walk away their restless thoughts, others have either finished a late shift or are out for a super early one. For the rest, perhaps this is the optimum time for romance or the only time when two busy work schedules collide.

Iti scans the crowd even as she loses herself in it, feeling one with the sleepless midnight revellers. Such freedom would be unimaginable anywhere else in the country. But she has stopped comparing. Why waste time on an imaginary comparison when it will never match up to the perfection right in front of you?

She spots two red raincoats.

One is a girl, walking hand in hand with a boy. The other, a young man sitting on the parapet with his legs dangling as he gazes into the sea. From his toned body he could possibly be an actor, and being an actor, he will surely understand the vagaries of the film industry and the perfect reasonableness of somebody asking to borrow your raincoat in the middle of a rainy night.

Putting on her friendliest smile, Iti walks over to him.

The sky is gracefully slipping into its powder pink morning robe as Iti reaches the set.

She could have probably gone home to snooze for an hour, but she is too keyed up now. The idea of going in early and maybe getting some last-minute jobs done seems more compelling than going home to a sleep from which she will most certainly not wake up in time. Good that she let some of the rain wash over her, it doesn't seem like she will get another shower today.

The set smells of perfume, incense, clothes and a heady mixture of coffee and tea with a hint of burnt milk. Iti inhales deeply. The scent of the set fills her with a sense of calm. Iti pushes open the door and steps in.

She is surprised to see Kunal already there, standing next to a kettle of water, waiting for it to boil. On the wanky wooden table in front of him is a cup with a bag of green tea placed inside, waiting to be infused with water.

"What are you doing here so early?"

Without even asking her or waiting for a reply, he pulls out another cup from the box under the table and puts a teabag inside that as well.

Iti winces. "Can I just have normal tea?"

"This is better for you. It's loaded with antioxidants."

Iti looks blank.

"It will make you thinner."

But she is not fat.

Kunal catches the indignant look. He holds up his hands, placatingly. "I didn't mean to say you are fat. You are good, Mumbai girls are too thin."

"That still sounds like I am fat, but politely."

He grins sheepishly. "I know, I have a problem, I get nervous around pretty girls and then I start to blabber. That must be why I am still single."

Iti preens. She doesn't answer the casually thrown, disguised as a statement, question. Is she available, too? She cannot answer it because she is not yet sophisticated enough to hear it. All that she has heard is that she is pretty enough to make her producer nervous.

"So should I throw this away and we wait for a spot boy to make tea for you, just like you like it?"

The self-deprecating words, coupled with a rueful, almost boyish smile thrown her way makes Iti's treacherous heart beat a little faster than it normally does.

Maybe she has had enough tea for today. After all, as Valarie says, tea at midnight can keep you awake because it has teein which is like caffeine but in tea. Which means that there is already enough caffeine in her body right now. Why else would her heart be behaving so erratically?

"I will try your green tea, since you are putting so much effort into it."

Both pretend not to be aware that all he would be doing is pour some boiling water into a cup.

"So what are you doing here? Doesn't your shift start at seven?" He repeats his question as he fills both their cups with the boiling water. Iti watches the liquid turn the colour of piss. She grimaces before answering Kunal's question.

"Mitali called, she said we needed red raincoat instead of blue and since it was a bit of a last-second change…"

Kunal quirks an eyebrow at her. "So did you manage to get one?"

"What kind of a costume assistant would I be if I just got one? Obviously I got options." Iti smiles proudly as she pulls out three red raincoats from her cloth bag.

Kunal looks them over. He selects one. Then he smiles at her. "Good work."

He raises his cup of tea to toast her.

She takes a sip and pulls a face. "Are you sure you know how to prepare this tea? Because it tastes just like it looks."

Kunal smiles. "You will get used to it. And now since you are here, take this."

He hands her his iPad. "Find some reference looks for the music video which we are shooting next week. Something sexy but also classy. Expensive looking but in half the budget Mitali is quoting."

Iti reverently takes the iPad. This time she got the not-so-subtle message.

"Let me find the correct designs, we can figure cheaper options with the cloth. With the correct lighting, we can make everything look dazzling. Anyway I will speak with the vendors myself and get the best price. Don't worry about that."

Kunal watches her bent intently over the designs she has so quickly opened up. She is already making notes on a piece of cardboard which was lying around.

"You do this right and maybe we can talk about a raise and a promotion. Though of course a promotion would mean that you might have to sleep in the office."

"But the pillow and mattress cannot come out of my salary, not even with a raise. I have already bought all this for my first home." Iti is earnest. She has no idea why this unleashes a laughing fit from Kunal.

47

2018

Chinky is about to move out of the room, but Abhishek calls her back.

"Will you do my tarot?"

She shakes her head. No.

"Why not?"

"Because you will ask me the wrong questions."

Abhishek is irritated.

"You mean you are so clairvoyant that you already know what I am going to ask you? Why then did you say when we met that it was all going to be all right in the end?"

Chinky proceeds to remove her clothes.

Abhishek is not sure whether he has triggered this or whether she was anyway planning to get naked and is simply ignoring his admittedly desperate pleas. This upsets him even further. *This woman has zero empathy!*

"Oh no, what video are you making now? Is it about me again? And why does it always have to be without clothes? Do you know how many perverts you will be attracting?"

"And what makes you think that perverts don't need help?"

She is already talking to her audience on the other side of the phone camera as she walks out of the room.

"Hello World! Today we are going to be talking about how we continue to stay miserable by telling ourselves that only one result out of a million possibilities can possibly bring us happiness…"

Abhishek shuts the door, cursing his life.

He lies down on the bed, picks up the book with the tea stain and flips it open somewhere in the middle, randomly.

The lady has just entered the dimly lit workshop of a local Venetian artisan … Her thin summer dress is clinging to her skin. Cindy can feel her nipples protruding through the white cotton. A strange kind of heat immediately overtakes her apple cheeks, flushed in embarrassment. She wishes that she had checked with the hotel's laundry service for her bra. Outside, the summer rain is gushing loudly on the cobblestone alley. "Ciao?" No answer. She slides her slender fingers along the glass cabinets full of colourful curiosities – elegant figurines, couples in embrace, masks, a few wooden toys, glittery trinkets. The air is becoming hotter. Sweet sweat mingles with the earthy smell of rain in her hair. She follows the crackling sound, shyly peeping her head around the corner. The water trickling from her blond curls create a little puddle on the ground. There, by the fireplace, half in the shadow, half turned towards the heat, she can discern a figure. The fire paints gorgeous patterns on the naked body. Cindy gasps. Her nipples stiffen ever so slightly, forcing her top button to almost burst open. The man turns around. His sun-kissed torso littered with little drops of water dripping from his thick black hair. He is as perfectly sculpted as his wooden art. A fiery flicker grazes his deep dark eyes. Before Cindy can catch her breath, the owner of the shop has already come close. He hands her his towel. It smells of wood and musk. He gently touches her hair, retrieving a golden autumn leaf, accidentally grazing her cheek. "You are wet." Oh yes, she is. As if in response sparks fly from the crackling wood, her heart is on fire.

Abhishek scoffs. *The heart is not a match or kindling to be set on fire. If the heart actually burned as often as the poets wanted it to, everyone would be walking around with charred lumps of flesh inside their ribcage.*

Yes, his own lump of raw flesh is chafing with every beat, while his eyes are translating the words they read into images in his head.

He keeps the book away and pulls out his phone.

The apology to Kartik is so long that by the end of it, he has run out of words. He deletes the essay. He begins afresh 'You…' *No, don't start with 'you'. Good communication means sending 'I messages'.* He deletes the 'You', replaces it with an 'I'. *No, Abhishek. The world doesn't revolve around you – I, I, I.* He deletes the 'I' and types a 'We' instead. *What 'we' do you mean, dear Mr Ghosh?* The cursor jumps back to the start. 'Hey'. *It is pointless.* Abhishek gives up.

The weight of his life pulls him onto the bed. But sleep won't come. Just moments after his phone has hit the side table, it is woken up by a sharp light hitting its surface.

"I've been thinking."

"Really?" Abhishek doubts that his landlady's brain is capable of doing anything else than dreaming up imaginary professions and, sometimes, in more lucid moments, remember the steps to making coffee.

She switches on the light.

"Get up."

"No. Why? I believe this room was given to me for the purpose of sleeping. So may I please do exactly that?"

"Yes! That's what I am saying."

With surprising vigour, she pulls the bedpost at the bottom end of the bed. Abhishek can see the vertebrae protruding from her malnourished back, it's just a question of moments before one of them is going to snap, leaving her forever paralyzed. He jumps off the bed. The bed instantly leaps a foot into the room.

"What are you trying to do?"

"Moving your bed. It's maybe too easy a fix, but worth trying, don't you think?"

No he doesn't. His brain cannot follow her gibberish.

"See, your insomnia might not entirely be due to your various issues. It may be because of the alignment of your head during your sleep. See, if you sleep facing east, you will wake up brimming with new ideas – which is not something you need. You already have too many ideas, don't you agree?"

He does not. But despite himself signals 'Please continue'.

"While west is the direction of 'contentment'. Of course there is a risk of making people lazy, but it also makes you sleep sounder and deeper. Which is exactly what you need. So all you have to do is sleep the other way round!"

"But then my head will be right under the window."

"That's true. You can look at the moon. It's very soothing."

"No, I will look at the streetlight."

He has not felt this kind of fury in a long time. A burning fire completely takes over his body. With much more force than intended, he shoves Chinky out of the room, banging the door behind her, barely missing her bony fingers from getting crushed in between the chipped wooden doorframe. He feels out of control. Unable to douse the little fires blazing in every joint of his body. He closes his eyes and with a loud scream rams the bed back against the wall. This woman is bringing out 'the Delhi' in him. As if she had torn deep into his primal alpha-male energy which he had spent years plastering with the neat shiny white veneer of the twenty-first century. He feels repulsed.

Silence. A bit of the blue paint quietly falls onto the pillow. He stares at it, for a while. But not for too long. His hands are lifting him back into reality, plucking the little pieces of cement off the linen one by one. He throws them into the dustbin next to the door. *No, he is no uncultured brute.* He peeps through the keyhole. The light in the hallway is still on. He can hear Chinky talking. *Maybe he overreacted? No.* He shakes his head. *Most definitely not. He is paying her to sleep here, so sleep he will now.*

He tucks his bedsheet neatly back under the mattress where Chinky had accidentally pulled it out in her effort to disturb his mental peace. He slips under the tight, cool cover.

Chinky's voice becomes louder. *Is she coming back?* He sits up. *No, she is just walking and talking. Probably making another one of her ridiculous podcasts.*

Abhishek turns towards the poster of his idol. The clarity in his words and eyes releases a wave of cooling calm. Abhishek surrenders, staring into space, then at the poster.

His dreams that night are a wild mélange. Steve Jobs is delivering a keynote speech on a Gondola. Next to him, Abhishek is rowing a boat, trying to catch up with his idol while Kartik, on the shore of the wide river far beyond a thick carpet of water chestnuts, is having a pillow fight with this boy from his office, Riyan. Instead of pillows they are using golden leaves and silver masks which are iPads on the inside. On their screens a video of a naked Chinky is running in loop. Blinded by the glistening of the silver metal, he is trying to ask Steve why he needed to include a naked woman in his presentation – where has the signature Apple aesthetic gone – but Steve is busy carving a strange new device out of wood … is it a dildo? Or his penis? Steve Jobs does not answer. Instead, he reaches out to surrender the phallic artwork to the chimney, sparks fly as if yearning to devour the wooden penis and the wood-panelled boutique inside the gondola in a level below water and suddenly full of people from his office. The water level is rising, tongues of fire smack the lace curtains. Where is Kartik? Abhishek's throat fills with water. In the middle of the fire, he is drowning from the inside. Is he going to die? Alone?

Abhishek wakes up. Soaked in sweat.

On the bright side, he at least woke up on time. Yet, he reaches office at eleven. *A perfectly acceptable time for anyone employed in*

the creative industry in the city of Mumbai. Why is he so scared of embarrassing himself? The campaign is going well. The brand has never seen so much visibility since its inception. The slum on his way to office actually looked a bit happier. Maybe they should also paint the roof so the rich people in the high-rise next to it have a better view too ... they could make a puzzle mural which only makes sense from the twentieth floor and above ... *See you can perfectly justify your presence here in Mumbai. And you are late because you had to inspect the feasibility of this new idea. Good.*

As the lift shutter closes, the panic from last night's nightmare rises. *Was this a premonition? Of what? That Steve Jobs is still alive and actually just moved to Italy? Sharing an island on the Mediterranean with Marilyn, Elvis and Jimmy?* His cynical inner voice quickly deflects this occult thought. Chinky's influence on him is growing. *How does she do it?* Anyway, Kartik finds her amusing, and as absurd as it sounds to himself, Abhishek needs her to continue being so obnoxious; it provides talking material. A light, harmless conversation starter to gently lure his lover out of his shell. Or let him into his shell – whatever is required. All of a sudden Abhishek feels a little sad thinking about his tall, man-bunned beauty. This man needs to let love in. The reason for his constant sexual escapades surely lies in the lack of love he is allowing himself to feel, and Abhishek is ready to fill this void with all his being. He cannot wait to introduce him to the bliss of domestication! Just like Chinky makes an extra cup of coffee for him every morning, he will get up ten minutes before his man, taking a moment to observe his angelic face while he snoozes – maybe stroking his thick black curls – then make coffee and wake him up by gently blowing the aromatic steam towards his sleepy head...

The lift door opens. An office boy enters, confused about the broad smile greeting him from the inside. Abhishek quickly removes his idiotic expression, relieved that it wasn't one of his co-workers. He exits the elevator to an almost empty studio, it seems. *He is impressed. I'm late but still not late enough for these 'creative' people. How do they even get any work done here?* But he is wrong. Some of them are there, just not at their desks but chitchatting in the 'lounge' corner. None of his co-workers notice when he settles his bag down at the far end of the large 'collaboration' table. The 'labor'-ious part of the word being the adequate description. At least for Abhishek who most definitely prefers working alone in a cubicle over wasting his energy on 'spontaneous brainstorming' where his colleagues present their utterly hairbrained ideas which have so far never materialized into anything. *No wonder. How does Hassan allow this lack of hierarchy where every intern can voice their opinion?*

Right now, they are busy huddling over Riyan's screen, giggling and amusing themselves with whatever they are watching. Relieved to have some moments of peace and quiet, Abhishek opens his laptop. He places his phone perpendicular to the edge of the table on one side, and on the other, in the same fashion, his reading glasses. He peels the topmost post-it, the one with coffee cup stain on it, from the stack, and shifts the now clean stack to the upper right corner of his desk. Satisfied, he is almost able to start his workday. In order to complete the arrangement he rises to his feet and heads over to the coffee machine, passing his colleagues who continue to be glued to the video playing on Riyan's laptop. It sounds familiar … *must be one of those 'viral' bandwagons that everyone has to jump on …* Just then, a girl with juvenile pigtails looks up and signals for Abhishek to join them.

"Dude, Riyan is watching *straight* porn!"

"If this is porn for you, I'm sorry for your love life … What I'm listening to here is good sensible advice!"

"That I highly doubt," the retort is barely audible between his gritted teeth. It has just dawned upon Abhishek why he felt like he has heard the content of this video before...

"Why?" asks the pigtail girl in the manner of a four-year-old.

"Because" – he suppresses the urge to put on the tone of a kindergarten teacher – "this is my flatmate. Please, I see enough of this humbug live. I have no need for a video on top of that."

Riyan is elated!

"Oh my god! You must call me to your home, Abhishek. I'm a huge fan."

"Ohoo, I didn't realize that you were a fan of naked girls Riyan." The pigtail girl sniggers. Abhishek can almost hear her chanting, *Riyan and the naked girl sitting on a tree...*

"Maybe I'm a fan of her flatmate."

He winks at Abhishek who looks away.

Another co-worker enters the room, waving enthusiastically to Abhishek.

"Abhi, dude, we just got a whole spread in *The Times*. This thing has exploded."

He shows him the magazine with the centrefold, a big picture of the colourfully painted slums.

"Fucking brilliant. Hassan is stoked. There's going to be a couple of extra slices of pizza for you today I think."

Abhishek takes the magazine and clicks a picture.

He sends it to Kartik with a message: *In case you missed it. I seem to be doing well. Meet me to celebrate my 'brilliance'? Ha ha*

He exhales, looking pleased and completely oblivious to the fact that Riyan has taken the magazine from him, reading it aloud to everyone.

The rest of the day Abhishek struggles to concentrate. By the end of it, all he has managed to do is write two emails and fill his dustbin with eight coffee-stained post-its.

His phone has been on permanent charge since he took that picture of the article. In case Kartik called, he would have enough battery to explain everything in detail to him. Not that he ever called or would engage in an hour-long conversation – not even about Chinky. *Kartik is a man of actions, not empty phrases.* Abhishek appreciates that about him.

The smell of expensive wood fired pizza brings back faint memories of last night's dream. His body shudders involuntarily. But his stomach is growling.

Around him, the office has turned into a bar of sorts. The light in the 'collaboration' section has been switched off to prevent even the most ardent workaholic from missing tonight's celebration. *Out of sight, out of mind. Maybe send a nude? But should not distance make the heart grow fonder? And the 20 kilometres between town and Kartik's house really do feel like they live in separate worlds!* Somebody hands him a coffee mug with black liquid. It does not exude the otherwise so inviting smell of caffeine. Has he had so much of it today that his tastebuds have become immune? He holds it closer to his nose. No steam. The cup is cold as ice. *Rum and coke. How old are we? Sixteen?* He scans the room for the culprit. Pigtail-girl lifts her mug – 'cheers'. He rolls his eyes. And checks his phone once more. Nothing. *Surprise surprise. Is he consciously trying to feel more miserable?*

"Abhishek, dude, I am seriously considering letting you sit in my cabin for the rest of this celebration, if *that* is what will make you happy."

Abhishek forces himself to laugh and tries to be pleasant.

"Oh look, people, I got him to smile, and you all think my jokes are bad."

His colleagues laugh dutifully.

Hassan puts an arm around him.

"I have spoken to Sharma. If you plan to relocate, we can find you a proper position here. How long will you be 'visiting' faculty? Might as well start collecting the Mumbai salary. It's been three months already."

Abhishek looks up as if startled. He is about to say something but then decides to not waste energy and simply shakes his head.

"Think about it."

Yes, think about it, Abhishek, it has been three months already and you only came for one weekend. This is the longest weekend in the history of weekends.

"You have accomplished a lot in this time." Hassan smiles at him. His 'colleagues' chorus their agreement.

Yes, Abhishek, tell them how you have accomplished exactly six meetings in three months.

"You know, your 'friends,'" Hassan gestures towards the people who all have a drink in their hands because of Abhishek, "they might have underestimated you in the beginning, because it looked like you thought that every morning was like, 'your best friend's wedding', ha ha, but I knew after our first meeting that here was a man with initiative and drive who would go after what he wanted without any ego or shame, exactly the way he went after my pizza. Ha ha."

Shame? Oh Hassan, you have no idea, if only you could read how shamelessly I have begged for crumbs of affection and those six meetings in these three months.

Abhishek feels a sudden tightening in his chest. Look at all these people cheering him like he is some kind of hero, like he is somebody who came to their city to do extraordinary things. But all he has come to do is exactly what he used to do at home: Look at his phone and feel disappointed.

"I shall take your leave now, sir ... Hassan."

"What? Why? We were just planning to go out and get some expensive drinks. Well, actually it will be the same drinks but we will go to a bar and pay exorbitantly more for them. Hehe."

Abhishek smiles thinly. He shakes his head again.

"I am tired. I think I will have an early night today."

Hassan looks disappointed, about to say something, too, but realizing the futility of any argument leaves it at a shrug of his shoulders. "Well, next time then."

On the way out he passes Riyan who is pouring wine into two white wine glasses. He is too busy staring at the floor in an effort to sneak out invisibly to see the wistful look in his eyes…

In Delhi going for a walk is the most mundane activity for any city dweller regardless of class, creed or occupation. But here in this accursed capital of sultriness he hasn't been able to walk for more than ten steps since he arrived. Three months without any physical exercise. His body hurts, his head hurts, his heart hurts.

He needs to breathe. His feet know where to take him – to the only open space (if one ignores the hordes of tourists) this city has to offer. It is a weekday, and the sun has already set – not ideal circumstances for a Facebook update. Hence the square in front of the Gateway is empty.

Abhishek, instead of appreciating this lucky moment, plunks himself on a small pillar next to the jetty to Alibaug. There he sits for a moment, before he gets up again, restlessly pacing up and down the sidewalk next to the ocean, looking increasingly miserable with every step. He turns around, returning to his original pillar, looking up at the Taj Gateway.

I am just like this damn hotel. Built the other way round.

He feels like a failure. An accident which was actually supposed to be something else, he does not know what this 'something else' would be, but to be it, he would have to change the structure of his being. Just like this hotel.

He takes out his phone and prepares to write a long message, a rant if you will, to Kartik, detailing everything: Why he came here, what he feels for him, how he is so disappointed that Kartik does not even care when he writes to him, how he never calls, not even to congratulate him on how well he has done here, etc., etc. Whenever he has finished a thought, a new complaint pops up in his head. He knows that Kartik does not appreciate his 'whiney' side, but he has nothing to lose really ... and maybe, he hopes, it is all just a big misunderstanding because Kartik is simply unaware of how Abhishek *really, truly* feels!

He is venting it all out, but before he can finish and send, someone taps him on the shoulder. Abhishek's heart jumps! Is it Kartik, just like last time when he saved him, right here at the Gateway. They are connected by love after all! But instead, it is a man in a disconcertingly thin khadi kurta, denims and expensive Fabindia leather slipper. His chiselled face is framed by thin-rimmed glasses matching his greying temples.

"Jaise chand ke haseen til,
Usi tarah tumhari udaasi is sundar
chehere ko poorn karti hai.
Kyunki kya bhala is shayar ka poornta se,
jab kavitaein hi apurnta par kayam hai."

Abhishek looks up in surprise. The wannabe shayar smiles down at him.

"Misery adds mystery
To this perfect countenance
Your broken heart speaks volumes
I'd like to fix it, if I had the chance."

With a bow, he sits down on the pillar next to him. Propping his chin up between his palms he looks at Abhishek. "I've been watching you for a while … it seems someone might have dared to break this beautiful heart of yours?"

Abhishek has no idea what to reply, he just mumbles.

"Nothing special, no."

"It must be a man, I am sure. No woman could be cruel enough to glaze these gorgeous eyes with sadness."

Abhishek has to smile at his cheesiness.

"Of course it has to be a man. Is our half of the species not the more evil one?"

The poet puts a hand to his heart.

"Ouch, my muse wounds me. I feel ashamed to be a man today."

Abhishek laughs. The poet holds out his hand.

"Will you come with me?"

Abhishek looks at him. The man is quite attractive, in an outlandish, almost enchanting way. He gets to his feet, the poet smirks with an approving glint in his left eye.

They walk. First in silence, along the water. As they wander through the hush of old Bombay's night, the 'poet' points out a sight here and there, at times spiced with a little anecdote.

He makes him peep through a window of one of the old Parsi cafes. Its wallpaper, a yellowed black-and-white medley of plastered articles from the British royal family, the photographs displaying the lifeline of a gradually aging man in glasses.

"A life dedicated to the Queen," the stranger whispers into his ear as if it were a secret.

Abhishek wonders whether he is still alive. Before his eyes search for the obituary, his nocturnal guide gently pulls his hand and leads him to a beautifully lit garden, surrounding a remarkable building.

"Named after a prince once upon a time, it now carries the name of a warrior."

A nostalgic sigh escapes the lungs of the grey-eyed man. But he does not wait for, or expect, an answer from his companion. Soon enough the small uneven cobblestone sidewalk opens to a grand crossing, in its centre another one, in the same colonial gothic style, lit up in the abominable neon colours. They only look at it from afar, almost ignoring it. Their path takes a sharp turn, back to where they came from. But along another alleyway.

"Not long ago the air in this gully was filled with the heavy sweetness of opium. Intoxicating…" The poet twirls on his toes, turning towards Abhishek. "Dangerous…" He looks him deep in the eyes. "Revealing the depths of the universe!" His words echo the cosmos' occult mystery.

After walking in content silence for a while, he points towards a public loo. "Imagine … men used to come and meet here … and," he adds wistfully, "…learn about love."

Abhishek is not sure if he understands what he has just heard. He thinks about it as they keep on wandering aimlessly. The poet does not seem to mind the silence. The night is balmy, and the streets are quiet. There are no cars in this part of town. Maybe they have travelled through a different era, to a time when love was less complicated…

At the corner, the poet slows down. "The stories born out of here…" he moves his finger towards another edifice of similar function, "are all from before the Internet. Before it took away all the mystery of courtship and romance…"

Abhishek's memory flashes a snapshot of Kartik, their eyes meeting across a crowded room at a party. He sighs. "I agree. One doesn't find one's soulmate on the Internet."

The poet looks deeply at him.

"You have loved him intensely, I can see. And he is an idiot who doesn't realize how rare it is to be so loved."

Abhishek feels mollified. He nods, biting his lips.

"Would you imagine … I have come all the way from Delhi to Mumbai. Only for him. Can you conceive anyone doing such a thing these days?"

He stares at the floor, hiding the hot tears of humiliation welling up in his eyes. "Everyone is so selfish … people … just … move on." The last words hold more truth in them than he is ready to admit to himself. Too busy fighting back his tears in order to not embarrass himself in front of a stranger, the words just roll out of his mouth without his brain censoring them. The poet is a patient listener.

Abhishek keeps speaking his thoughts out aloud. "Am I asking for too much? It's not like I have forced him to take me to a five-star restaurant on a date. All I am saying is that when you drink wine it should be served in the right glass! That's all."

The poet looks again at him appreciatively. "You have so much passion in you. The kind of love that poets like Ghalib wrote about."

Abhishek smiles gratefully at him. They have reached the local train station.

The poet gently touches Abhishek on the shoulder. He's taller than him, broader also. In the shadows of Bombay's old colonial buildings, his full stature kind of dwarfed. Abhishek feels weirdly safe, protected.

With an apologizing smile, he moves the poet's hand away. Albeit, something in him would have liked for it to linger longer…

"No, no, I'm not taking the local. It's too crowded."

The poet looks at him in surprise.

"But some of the most beautiful stories have been inspired by train journeys."

He takes Abhishek's hand.

"Come, I will take care of you."

The 'something' in him has melted all resistance. *How bad can it be? The colonial clocktower has struck midnight.*

It is bad. Mumbai local makes no difference between night and day, weekday or weekend, there is always work to be done, a party to be attended, people to be ferried around.

"Like the veins in your body which never lie idle, it is the nature of the train to move. To pick us human souls up at one place and through this quick and intense journey drop us at another, faraway." The poet makes a wide gesture with his arms, eventually creating a buffer zone around Abhishek while pushing him inside the train. Inside, he navigates him into a corner, making way and guarding him with his arms. Abhishek relaxes.

The train starts moving. And stops almost immediately at the next station. They have chosen a 'slow' train, which stops at every junction, and further ahead in the journey at the remote suburbs where migrant workers and daily labourers can afford housing. *This explains the crowd.* And promptly a surge of people pushes into the car. Abhishek can feel them more than see – the poet has built himself up behind him. Abhishek fixes his gaze onto the floor. The flood of people won't stop. The poet is being pushed against him from behind. *Is he?* Suddenly Abhishek feels himself trapped. The man presses against him. *On purpose?* Abhishek tries to wring his neck to look up behind him into the poet's face, but he can't. He is unable to move any part of his body. He can feel something hard press against his butt. *It could be the corner of a briefcase ... don't be stupid! Nobody carries briefcases at this hour.* Cold sweat forms on Abhishek's forehead. *This can't be true. What is he doing?* Abhishek instinctively tightens his butt. He tries to normalize his breathing but panic is rising. An uncontrollable panic of knowing. Knowing what is going to happen. He wants to scream but his vocal chords refuse to work. His entire body has stiffened, like a stone. The poet moves his hand inside Abhishek's pants, he squeezes his butt.

And moves his poky fingernails towards the centre. Abhishek tightens his butt further, but to no avail. He prays for another junction, but the train rattles relentlessly on the tracks. The fingernails dig deeper, track switch, they slip, cut. Abhishek feels a stinging pain. He bites on his lips, wishing he could throw himself out of the moving train onto the tracks. And die. *Please*.

He does not know whether it is sperm or blood running between his legs. He bangs his head against the metal wall of the train. Rhythmically. Hard. *Why am I not fainting?* He bangs harder. *Is he still there?* Never was his wish to disappear, dissolve, vanish, stronger. *Why?* Do his trousers have a hole, are they ripped, just like the bottom of his intestines? *How did I ask for this? What have I done?* He tastes blood. Or is it just the smell of the train wall's metal? He hopes his nose is bleeding, so someone might notice that something happened to him. But not a drop of blood hits the floor. He bangs harder. *Why?!*

Suddenly the banging stops, the train has come to a halt. Abhishek sees the platform appear outside the open door on his side of the train, but before he can move, he is transported out onto the platform by a mass of people descending. He gets pushed against a pole, the wave of human bodies slithering like a snake around him towards the stairs; while he stands, with his back towards the pole, frozen. Waiting for it to pass. For it all to pass. For them all to pass.

"Well, that was amusing, wasn't it? Give me your number, maybe we can try some other place next time." He smelled him before his words reached his ears. Musk and bergamot.

Abhishek runs. The platform is almost empty. *Find people!* He runs towards a chai stall, a conductor is leaning against the bar, sipping his tea. Abhishek fixes his gaze from afar. *Please stay where you are. Please don't go away. Please don't leave me alone.*

The conductor does not move. Abhishek makes it to the chai stall. Chalk white.

"What happened? Are you okay?"

Abhishek looks around wildly. He is gesturing, unable to speak.

"What happened? Did someone steal your wallet?"

Abhishek shakes his head.

He suddenly feels ridiculous. *Did this really happen?* Still standing in front of the conductor, he moves his right hand towards his butt. His trousers are still in order, but he can feel the wetness. He takes out his wallet, removes a twenty-rupee note, hands it to the person behind the stall, asks for a bottle of water, takes it, holds it behind his back and walks towards the staircase. Slowly. With his head down, his eyes scanning the area with every step. Still not in control over his movements, he stops in front of the staircase, takes the shirt out of his trousers, washes his hands with the water and wipes them on the bottom of his shirt. Again washes his hands, this time almost drenching the bottom of his shirt. He uses the wet cloth to wipe his face. No blood.

Thus presumably looking like a harrowed but normal version of himself, he slowly awakens from his zombie state. The voice on the platform announces the next train scheduled for arrival in five minutes. Then it is all quiet again. The conductor at the tea stall has already forgotten about him and turned his back to the staircase.

Abhishek dials Kartik's number. It's a reflex. One that Abhishek almost immediately regrets but now that it is ringing, he is unable to hang up.

The phone keeps on ringing. He waits till the tenth ring. No answer.

Somehow relieved, he types one last message to Kartik: "Thank you for not even caring if I live or die."

5.55 p.m.

Gaikwad and Sahil are looking at Abhishek. Both visibly uncomfortable. Gaikwad mostly because his ass hurts.

"I mean, you should have thought about this a little, no? Going like this at that time of the day with a gay man…"

Before Abhishek can react, Sahil comes to his defence.

"Are you saying he asked for it? This is the reason why people do not report rapes! I'm sorry, sir, but I am disappointed."

"When did I say that it was his fault? I just said that he should have been careful, shouldn't he?"

"Careful about what? About whom? About the neighbour? The father, the brother, what? Should he stop living?"

He smiles sympathetically at Abhishek. "You don't have to tell us what happened next if you don't want to."

Gaikwad looks like he wants to object but shrugs. "Take your time." Then adds, turning to Sahil, "Bring me the cushion from the ledge."

Abhishek smiles a bland smile, bereft of all emotion.

"What happened next was just the aftershock. The earthquake had passed, and I just walked on, without pausing to check the debris for whatever might lie buried under. I couldn't, I didn't want to see the 'dead bodies'."

Gaikwad sighs in relief. He should have kept the yoga cushion on his chair in the morning…

48

2018

Abhishek is trembling but eventually manages to put the key into the rickety lock. One has to pull it slightly to be able to turn the key and open the door. A lot of actions at once for someone who can barely hold himself together...

In a daze of exhaustion he takes off his shoes, switches on the light and ... screams.

The stranger sleeping on the sofa opposite the entrance door jolts up into a sitting position. As if she had been waiting for him. But after a few blinks, her posture relaxes.

"Hi."

Abhishek does not reply.

The girl, small, slim, dressed in one of Chinky's t-shirts looks at him. "Are you okay?"

Abhishek shakes his head.

"No, and who the hell are you? Why are you in this house? Why are there always so many people in this house? I am fed up."

He sits down on the sofa. Iti gets up.

"Don't worry, I won't stay the night."

Abhishek scoffs. The quietness in the house is bone-crushing. The air has changed its state of matter to almost solid. With every inhalation, less oxygen enters his lungs. She is eating up the air. He is suffocating. She needs to leave.

"Can I get you some tea? I only have green with me, but maybe Chinky has something. What does she normally give you when you are sad?"

This calms Abhishek's nerves somewhat. He clenches his butt cheeks. They are sore, but the sensation of his intestines falling out has stopped. A little, at least. The sofa is soft. He does not want to move. Shouting at this girl has cost him his last bit of energy. He just hopes that he won't leave a bloodstain on the sofa. But he will take care of that later. At the moment he is scared to take a shower.

Iti is still waiting for an answer.

"Coffee..." Weirdly, the thought of Chinky and their morning routine makes him calmer. He thinks about the last time they had shared a morning coffee. It seems like a lifetime ago. He tries to recall every moment. Again, his brain is transporting words into the world without him cross-checking them. "Coffee ... with a dash of cinnamon ... and then she gets naked."

Iti looks surprised, then she giggles.

"I see, you must be her muse then. I'm sorry but I'm a little relieved. Her last few videos had me thinking there was some real shit going on again in her life. But I guess she has been talking about you."

Abhishek throws a look at Iti.

"I'm sorry. It's not my business, but listen to Chinky. She knows about these things."

The words settle slowly in Abhishek's head ... *Muse? Real shit? Is the Internet now having pity on his pathetic love life? Great! How dare she use him to amp up her followers! What does she even know? Miss I'm-a-perfect-little-witch feeding on other's misery!*

He is hurting. If he is honest with himself, for a moment, somewhere deep, deep inside he had hoped that she would be at home, awake, maybe in the kitchen preparing midnight coffee for him, knowing that something terrible had happened, and he could release the memory of his defilement immediately ... confide in her. To not find her at home, instead being confronted with this stranger feels like betrayal.

"You want me to take love advice from a girl who just sleeps with anybody. What the FUCK does she know about love?"

What the fuck does she know about anything? The next time she makes a video about his miserable love life, perhaps she will talk about the perils he is putting his heart and his emotions in, and he will watch it, full of contempt, because she does not have the faintest idea of how close to the abyss he has come. He has let his desperation and loneliness put his body, his dignity, even his life in danger. But what does she know? Where is her clairvoyance now that she has left him in yet another awkward situation with one of her million friends, Miss Oh-So-Popular. What right does she have to talk about it? He should be the one getting naked for the next video. Remove all his clothes and let them see his scarred, deformed self. It might even be a relief. She is so clueless. Everybody is so clueless.

Abhishek closes his eyes. Gradually he begins to feel every fibre of his body. He scans himself from his toes to his nose, moving mentally through every joint, every muscle, every bone. It takes an eternity to complete this internal survey of damage. He doesn't care anymore about what the person opposite of him may feel. This is his goddamn house, his living room, his space, his miserable lonely night. *How could he allow him …* He stops his mind from going there, concentrating again on the physical pain, something that can and will heal, eventually. A second layer is added to his internal brick wall, this time he fortifies it with cement.

He senses the girl's presence, but shuts it out and resumes assessing the exact points of pain. He feels the urge to vomit. *Breathe … puking will just make the pain worse.* There is a faint smell of jasmine perfume. *Must be the girl.* He focuses on the scent. *Flowers, white flowers. Why is she still here? Nobody has invited her! Breathe … White … Calm … Whatever, now she just has to deal with sitting here and staring with pity –* or leave. He could not care less. It's weirdly liberating.

Iti clears her throat.

"So?"

"I have never felt this shit in my life."

"Then what are you holding on to? A love for misery? You are not Shah Rukh Khan, nobody is paying shitloads of money to watch you in pain. Stop being so angsty. It's not getting you anything."

She grins at him. This girl is bizarre. But how else would a friend of Chinky's be? *What must she be thinking — that he just had a miserable day in office?* He wipes his eyes and exhales.

"You are right, you know. This *is* crap. You know my office people wanted to throw me a party and I was like, 'No, I just want my boyfriend to message me.' Hell, he is not even my boyfriend."

He barely feels like my friend. I have no friends. A wave of self-pity overcomes him.

"Aah crap. I was going to hit on you. But of course, nobody that cute could be straight."

She laughs, an unexpectedly charming laughter. Abhishek joins in despite himself. The girl is more normal than meets the eye.

The glimmer of a moment of relief is crudely interrupted by a sudden sting of disgust. *Cute enough to get ...* he swallows the bile ... *but not enough to be loved.* His face falls. He can feel it. A dark wave descending on him. He wants to shower, or maybe drown. He wants to pull the cover over his head, or maybe for Kartik to hold him tight. He wants to bang his head against the table until it bleeds, or pour boiling coffee over his hand or maybe even cut his wrists. His eyes are locked onto his hand on the couch table in front of him.

Iti gets up, she takes her bag from the table and reaches out her hand.

"I'm Iti. I have some time till I'm needed again on set. You wanna get a coffee at Starbucks downstairs to celebrate your happy life?"

What?

His phone rings. It's Kartik. Abhishek stares at it, in a daze.

"Don't you wanna take it before it stops ringing?"

His finger moves across the screen, in slow motion.

"It's ... it's *him*. I'm just going to speak with him for a second, you go on, I'll join you."

Iti looks at Abhishek. She smoothens her short green dress, it is a little crumpled after her nap, but luckily, the material she has chosen takes on the wrinkles and adds them to the already crinkly design. Iti likes clothes like this, the kind which are intelligent enough to improve themselves.

"Okay, come soon. Remember you don't need him."

Abhishek nods.

Iti shuts the door behind her.

49

10.45 a.m.

"Have you ever gone back to an old home and met the people who live there now? Noticed how they interact with the house that was once yours? Judge every single change they have made? Resent them for the things they have kept the same? Why should they own your choices? It is the same as meeting an old love, who now belongs to someone else. But even through your jealousy, aren't you somehow still connected to this new person? If who or what we love defines us so much, aren't they just another form of you?"

Iti leans back and closes her eyes briefly, remembering Abhishek and his tortured face as she had shut the door and left him behind it.

"I still think about Chinky's flatmate, though I met him just once. But he had crossed the threshold to my home and as I would want a guest to feel comfortable and happy in my home, I suppose I worried that he wasn't having a good time. I really wanted him to have more fun."

Chinky for sure must have tried her best to help him find his happy space, too, she ponders silently.

"At the time though I didn't even know he was living there. I thought he was just another one of Chinky's troubled strays. I waited for forty-five minutes for him. He never came. I guess he chose not to be happy after all." Iti shrugs.

Gaikwad fills up her cup with hot water from a thermos which the office boy has just brought in. She is befuddled.

"Boss said we can use the same tea bag twice. Green tea is expensive."

Iti nods. The second brew is always gentler, she prefers its less bitter taste.

"What *is* it about this thing called love that just takes over our senses so much that we forget we were once happy before it happened and we can be happy again after it's gone? Why is it so important?"

Gaikwad shakes his head, he doesn't know. But what he does know is that love is more often than not the cause for the unnatural deaths which land up on his desk. No one has ever died of a broken heart naturally – that only happens in Meenakshi's TV serials. A lot of people have killed themselves, and even more have been killed by other people, over broken hearts.

"Did Chinky also have an unhappy love affair?"

"Isn't love by definition an invitation to sadness? What can you expect when you place your happiness in someone else's hands."

Gaikwad disagrees. "I'm happy to be with my wife!"

"And what happens if she leaves you? Or you find out that she was having an affair with someone else?"

Not even questioning the incredibly intrusive nature of this question by this stranger, a witness, a suspect, his answer is as quick as a shot: "Such things don't happen in the society I come from. Husbands and wives stay together. Marriage means something. It's not like in your ... I mean some other people's worlds."

"And what if she dies?"

Gaikwad stares at her.

"Love is always dangerous. Sometimes I wonder, why does the universe work so hard – all those machinations, coincidences, synchronicity ... to what end? Make us meet somebody who will give us no more than five minutes of joy?"

Gaikwad looks as if he suddenly remembers something. He turns towards his phone with a certain amount of concentration. Apparently not finding what he's looking for, he leans back and shouts towards the room in front of his office. "Sahil! What's that app called where you order stuff from that comes immediately?"

50

2010

Routine is supposed to be a romance killer, but the heart is strange. As soon as one enters the chaotic country of new romance, it sets out to search for the nicely signposted highway of predictability, for little hints that this period of stomach-hurting excitement is indeed heading for the land of eventual flatline and stability.

Ecstasy is followed, invariably, by the longing for its end. And soon the excitement of a phone call from a new love is replaced with the mundanity and reliability of the 10 p.m. phone call. At least you no longer have to ask that eternally gut-wrenching question, '*Where is this going?*' It is going where all happiness goes to die: The land of '*So now what?*'

Is the start of every new romance then the quest for its eventual death? If the goal is to turn every Kunal into a Surat, why bother with a Kunal at all?

Iti and Kunal have almost established a routine. Almost every evening, for the last one month and five days, Kunal has dropped her home. 'Almost', however, is not the same as 'every'.

As soon as the clock strikes eight, Iti's stomach starts to clench. Kunal's chivalry has decided on 9 p.m. as cut-off time, when the world suddenly stops being safe for a woman to go home alone from office. Iti has been out before – several times at much later hours – but in the presence of male gallantry, she finds it easy to slip into her 'Damsel in distress aka need of a lift' avatar.

Sometimes, despite trying her best, she can find no reason to stay on till late. Sometimes Kunal leaves, no reason, no explanation, he just pops in and says bye to the staff. Iti feels her heart sink a little when this happens – there will be no quick stop and conversation at the tapri as they lean against Kunal's car and rehash the day over steaming hot chai (not green, one real cup), no accidental brushing of hands in Kunal's car as he changes gears, navigating through traffic. Iti has never loved Mumbai traffic as much as she does then, when Kunal has to change gears every few minutes. Every few minutes a new mini explosion in her stomach, which leaves her wishing that he would do more. Maybe just hold her hand, not accidently, but on purpose.

And then as the ride home ends, a new excitement rises inside her. As if moved by themselves, her feet race up the stairs, knowing that Chinky would be waiting, with a cup of tea that they would share sitting by the window talking about ... things. Anything!

Iti cannot really recall any of those late-evening conversations now, but at that time they felt endless. Sometimes they would go out, or a key would turn in the lock and a party would come to them. There would usually be a walk around midnight, sitting by the sea, even as Iti mentally calculated how many hours of sleep she would get before having to wake up and wondering if she could maybe squeeze in reading a couple of chapters before her head would drop, pulling her to sleep into the pages and to a confused mix of dreams where she lay beneath Surat – but with Kunal's face on his.

Kunal leaving before her always brought a stab of disappointment. An important part of the rest of her day went missing. Sometimes she would recover fast and sometimes she would be moody and restless, demanding Chinky take longer and longer walks with her. Or she would sit at Bandstand, looking into the sea, making glorious plans for her future, carefully including Surat in all of them. Who cared about Kunal? He was just her boss. So what if he couldn't drop her home? She could go by herself.

"It's a little strange though, isn't it?" Jhansi had asked a couple of nights back. She had come in at 1 a.m., just as Iti and Chinky were on their third cup of tea and of course Chinky had made extra, knowing that she would soon be pouring it into Jhansi's yellow cup. Jhansi never questions the fact that tea is always magically ready for her whenever she arrives. And that there is always a little extra cardamom in it (a bit more than Iti prefers).

Like right now, the whiff of the sweet, heavy, oddly refreshing and comforting fragrance hits Iti's nose right at the door. She smiles. The arrival of the woman whose character is so much like her favourite spice announces itself before she herself even knows that she is being expected in Khar Danda tonight. As the aroma of the tea fills the room, Iti's eyes keep darting towards the door. Waiting for the sound of the key being turned in the lock. When Jhansi finally walks in, Iti inhales deeply, her smile almost splitting her face in two. Jhansi's presence permeates the room just as strongly as the lingering smell of 'her' tea.

Within minutes the three of them are sprawled on the floor – because Jhansi needs to stretch out and because they only have two chairs – looking at the city, sipping their tea and talking about whatever Jhansi's eclectic mind is in the mood to discuss. Jhansi minces no words ever, she is as matter of fact describing the sexual depravities of her latest 'jhon' as she is in cussing the battered infrastructure of the city, or swooning over a cute boy's dimples, or in pointing out, "Isn't it a little strange how Kunal feels that he needs to drop Iti home at night because it's not safe and yet on those nights that he does not drop her, he does not call her to check if she has reached safely or not. Why does he worry about your safety only on some days and not others?"

Iti looks towards Chinky for wisdom and insight.

Chinky smiles. "I don't think it's worry that makes him drop her home."

The worm of discontent that had been nestling in Iti's stomach ever since Kunal had left for the day while she was in the bathroom, morphs into a pretty little butterfly and flutters about.

Jhansi looks at Iti, her expression suddenly serious. "Do you tell your 'best friend' everything?"

"My best ... oh you mean Surat? Yes, of course I do."

She plays with her little oddly shaped cup which she recently 'handcrafted'. It's not perfect. But it holds her tea. It's a vessel which keeps her second biggest (after Surat and before work) love warm.

"Well, just don't tell him that things are different now."

Iti is defensive. "There is really nothing to tell. I love Surat. Kunal is just my producer. I like working with him, and it's nice and cheaper to get a drop home. You know how I love every opportunity I can get to save money. Ha ha."

Jhansi raises an eyebrow. "I just meant don't tell him that he is no longer your only best friend. Now you have us." The knowing smirk of a woman who has been in love a thousand times crosses her face. "But what are you so guilty about?"

Iti gapes at Jhansi who is chuckling softly. She throws a cushion at her. "You know that's not what you meant."

The room dissolves into laughter, a bike screeches loudly outside as it takes a sharp turn. "Oh my God, do you think that is Salman Khan? He has this crazy new bike..." Jhansi is hanging practically half out of the window as she tries to identify the bike.

All three are staring out now, wondering what other 'celebrities' have driven down this road since morning. At some point Jhansi is regaling them with a story about a famous millionaire who likes to meet her on Tuesdays, the one day a week he doesn't have any alcohol or non-veg. "Except me," chortles Jhansi. "So much for his piety. This intoxicant," she gestures to her body, "is still sending him to hell."

"Strange how all the roads to hell must go through 'heaven' first," says Chinky.

Somebody points to the moon. It is just one day shy of being full.

"Chinky, should we do a cleansing ritual tomorrow? I have a list of names that I want to burn, customers I never want to see again. I would like them to go broke."

"You think that is the only way you can get rid of them, am I right?"

"I can't say no to all that money they offer. It is beyond tempting."

"Then I think we should do a strengthening ritual. For you. Why do a ritual for people you do not care about? It just intermingles your karma even more with theirs. And I don't want to be part of anything which wishes bad upon people."

Jhansi looks a little guilty.

"I didn't mean it that way."

"I think we can all do with an extra dose of willpower. Let me get the almanac. And I have this source who supplies the most gorgeous poppies harvested under the light of the full moon…"

Iti smiles, letting the sound of voices wash over her. The hour is late, her eyes are having a hard time staying open, in some minutes she will no longer be sure what she is actually hearing and what she is imagining. Does her brain make up the more bizarre parts or does it supply the mundane in-between, the delicious absurdity of her reality?

Iti slips in and out of consciousness.

"Here, this will warm you." Kunal presses a cup of hot tea into Iti's hands, his fingers lingering long enough to warm more than just her palms.

Iti looks questioningly.

"Don't you feel that little nip in the air? I think winter is here."

"This is not winter." Iti laughs. "It's just December. If it was winter, I would be wearing a down jacket."

Kunal's eyes linger on Iti's bare shoulders. Little bumps appear under her skin.

"You are cold." He gently rubs her shoulder. "You have goosebumps."

Iti shivers, but not from the cold, though there is the tiniest sliver of winter in her heart. Surat missed their usual 10 o'clock yesterday. She tried calling. But his phone was out of network. At 10.10 she had called up his mother, who had been excited to hear from her and wouldn't stop asking questions about her work and all the famous people she was meeting. But when Iti had tried to question her about Surat, she had turned suddenly evasive and told her that he was caught up in office with some super urgent work, but he would speak with her tomorrow, at the usual time, not to worry.

Well, she wasn't 'worried' worried, though she had wondered for one panic-stricken second if Surat was ill or had been in an accident and was now at the hospital. Just for a second her imagination had taken over before her logical mind had scoffed away this absurd notion.

Nonetheless, it had rattled her. She couldn't remember the last time they had gone through one whole day without speaking at all.

What if he calls now? As Kunal is rubbing her shoulder and her insides are turning to jelly and all she wants is for him to use his hands to put everything back together, in the right place.

Kunal's face is close enough for his breath to be hot on her neck.

What if Surat calls now? He missed their usual time yesterday so doesn't he have a sort of carte blanche to call at any hour today?

She pulls away a little.

"Should we take a walk?"

Kunal looks at her in surprise.

"You want to walk in the middle of traffic?"

"No, let's go to the beach. Let's take advantage of the sea breeze in winter, before it turns into summer again. We might just have today you know."

Kunal laughs too hard and too long. She wasn't that funny.

Two hours later, Iti's normally straight hair has curled into a mass of frizz all around her shoulders.

As she inhales she can still smell the lingering scent of Kunal's perfume, it seems to be oozing out of every loop of her blush-coloured, thinly knitted 'winter' cardigan. She caresses her arm with her hand, gently stroking the fabric, like he did. It is so thin, her fingertips can feel every unevenness, her little mole on the bend of her left elbow, the slight rising of her left flexor, always tight from her nocturnal stitching sprees, the thin silver bracelet with the "I" on it that Chinky had gifted her for her birthday. Her fingertips wander further, tingling the bare skin of the back of her hand, where his hand had brushed against hers. A pleasuring shiver prickles from behind her ear, down her spine, and even further down, curling inside her like a warm whirlpool created by the gentle sea. Her sensitive palm remembers how it had grazed his stubble as she had run her fingers over his face. Her feet are cold. The tide is coming in.

She is still holding her heels in her hands. A foolish idea of course, to decide to walk on the beach in sandals that were designed to raise you more than two inches off the ground. Those pointed nubs were made to trap you in the sand till a pair of gentle hands reached down to slowly slip them off your feet.

Iti feels her face flush as she remembers.

Holding her sandals with one hand, he had casually used the other to brush an errant lock of hair away from her face, so he could look at it better. And then he was too close to look at it at all.

At 9.59 p.m. Iti had switched off her phone.

It is still off as she turns the key in the lock and flings the door open.

She can smell ginger mixing with tea.

Visions dance in her head of another time, another place, a different her.

She sees him even before his face appears in front of her. She feels him even before he takes her in his arms and holds her tight and long as if frightened that she will turn around and leave the second he lets her go.

Even before all that she knows that Surat is here. She is confused that his arrival has taken her by surprise. She has known him since they were in school, how could she not have seen this coming?

51

9.15 p.m.

"She said, we met when we were kids."

Sahil and Gaikwad stare at him.

"So are you saying that you have known each other since childhood?"

Vincent shakes his head.

"No, *I* am saying that I met her the first time in Gokarna. She says, said, when she heard me yelling at someone that it reminded her of this angry kid she had met on a train once."

1992

"Who do you think you are?" the little straw-haired boy yells at a man with an equally blonde moustache.

"*Dein Vater. Und du setzt dich jetzt hin.*"

But the little boy makes no effort to sit down. "I'm not your slave. Just because you want to gallivant around this shit country before going back to your social money. Selfish ass, no wonder Maman kicked you out. Putain."

"Mind your language, young man! Otherwise I'll put you on the platform at the next station and leave you there." The man has switched from German to English, as if to assure the people around them that he still has some control over his bratty son. The man has turned into a tomato. Whether from embarrassment or from anger is unclear. Chinky has never seen someone turn so red.

"Stop staring at me, you stupid monkey."

The little boy gives her a death stare. Chinky starts to cry.

"I'm so sorry. My son did not mean it. Vinzenz, apologize to the little girl!"

"Why? It's impolite to stare!" He squints his eyes, getting ready to show her the finger, when a small piece of candy falls into his hand.

"*Tumi beya lora tuk mithai kiyo disa?*"

Chinky can't believe what her grandmother has just done.

"Because he is so bitter, he needs it. Poor boy, imagine having a bitter taste inside you all the time." Aita deliberately speaks in English, too.

Chinky now looks sympathetically at the boy who plunks himself onto his berth and pulls the blanket over his head. Time to sleep.

The rhythmic rattling of the train is rocking its freight into a dreamless slumber. Except for the little straw-head. He is tossing and turning in his sleep.

Without making a sound, Chinky appears by his bedside.

"What do you want?"

Chinky puts her hand on top of the bed in front of his face. "Take this, maybe if you have sweeter dreams, you will not wake up so bitter."

As she withdraws her hand, the boy feels something tickle in his nose. He opens his eyes. It's a feather. He blinks. Attached to the feather are some strings and more feathers. He lifts the objects. It's a dreamcatcher. In teal blue. His favourite colour. He turns around, the girl is already climbing to her berth. Before snuggling under her own brown blanket, she throws a candy wrapper into the steel dustbin on the wall.

2012

It's early in the morning, the world is a mix of pink and orange, like the prickling candy you can mix with soda or scoop directly out of the packet with your finger, making your tongue tingle for hours. Vincent is laughing.

"So you are saying you gave me this dreamcatcher?"

Chinky nods. "Yes, I remember it. See how this blue is weaved in with the gold? I have always favoured this combination. It looks like the Andaman Sea."

"How do you know what the Andaman Sea looks like?"

"I don't. But that doesn't mean that it does *not* look like this. There's a chance that it is exactly like this: gold and turquoise."

Vincent shakes his head. "I'm pretty sure my parents gave it to me. Goddam hippies have nothing else to give their kids except for dreamcatchers."

"You were so angry with your father, you were both yelling at each other the whole train ride. I couldn't understand the languages though, it sounded like you were using two."

"If that were us, I was probably telling him that he was a German pig and he must have been telling me that I was the son of a French whore. God bless parents who hate each other so much they ruin two nations for you."

He chuckles bitterly. Chinky gently strokes his hand.

"You don't need to hold on to your parents' hate, you know."

Vincent looks down at her face, looking up so earnestly at his.

"You are quite brown. I can imagine you would have looked like a cute little monkey when you were a kid."

He bends down and kisses her.

Leaving the dreamcatcher dangling in the afternoon sun.

A little later, Chinky is sitting by the sea meditating. Vincent comes after her, zipping up his trousers.

"Why would you leave a man high and dry like this?"

She ignores him. He sighs and sits down next to her, watching her. He digs his fingers into the warm sand. Both his hands are working in unison. The right index finger forms slow curves, at times shallow at times deep, upheaving the dark wet sand, pausing to smoothen the piled-up material, correcting the few hardly visible mistakes with a few trickles of additional grains.

It's quiet. Except for the endless foaming of the waves. Both of them are absorbed in their own 'work'.

She opens her eyes and sees him working hard at it, lost and still, almost completely still. She comes closer and kisses him on the lips.

"Hey, I just 'finished' … give me a minute to get ready again."

Chinky ignores his comment. She takes his hand and holds it. "You are so beautiful when you are still. Try it again, this time be completely still. Close your eyes and think nothing, just be…"

Vincent plays along, he closes his eyes but not even after half a breath, they fly open again.

He wants to impress Chinky, but it is just not possible. Even though his ego wants him to pretend that he is totally zen and shanti and shit, this fucking ocean just won't let him.

Vincent is exasperated. He tries to explain himself: "Every time I think I've got it, a damn wave comes crashing as if wanting to be a tsunami."

Chinky looks at him blankly – nothing to be done about that. Here at the seaside.

"And doesn't the fucking sand get into your ass? Maybe I should go and take a shower."

Everything is sticky, it makes his brains sticky. No monkey mind here. Just a sloth of chewing-gum-like thoughts. He wants to get out of this skin, this position, this moment. And start afresh, not being taken by surprise. How the fuck is he supposed to suddenly be meditative? Isn't that something that one needs to prepare oneself for, mentally? He makes an attempt to get up, but Chinky is already behind him, slowly massaging his back. She sings.

Vincent relaxes. Her voice, the waves, the rustling of the palm trees – it all forms one symphony. He closes his eyes, the leaves of the palm tree sway back and forth in front of the sun, creating an alternating pattern of black and red behind his lids.

He feels Chinky's cool hands on his. A shiver tingles down his spine, but he forces himself to keep his eyes closed. It's easier now. She gently takes his hands and turns them, facing his palms upwards, opening each of his fingers with long strokes, until his palms are completely open, vulnerable, soft.

He can feel her eyes on him. He must look quite beautiful. The rosy sunset, the turquoise water and his golden stubble. Her favourite combination…

She hovers her palms on top of his. He can feel the electric energy between their hands. Without touching him, she moves his hands – as if they are attached to hers through an invisible thread – lifting them up until they are straight in front of his heart, facing her chest. She lets go and slowly leans forward to kiss him.

They make love on the sand. A wave comes and washes away Chinky's image drawn in the sand.

"So where were you going?"

"When?"

"With your father."

"Hmpf!"

Vincent looks at the clouds passing by above their heads. With Chinky by his side he at times feels like he has left his adult body and is back to being a little boy. Excited about the world, unjaded, looking for elephants in the clouds...

"He wanted to take a trip across the country before going back to where he came from."

Chinky doesn't say anything. But he can 'hear' her listening. He adjusts his head, resting on her belly, his arm wrapped around her warm and sandy thigh.

"He wanted to show me around 'my' country. At least that's what he told me. So we went crisscrossing India. I think he wanted to retrace the route he took with my mother when they first came here. I remember some embarrassing 'cool dad' moments when he thought he could teach me something about sex at Khajuraho."

"Oh wow! That's early. I think you must've been like nine?"

"Yeah, but it's not like I needed sex-ed. When you grow up in a place of 'perfect human unity', 'human unity' is quite literally everywhere."

"And where was your mom?"

"She was back in Auroville. When my dad fucked off, she was encouraged to give up the big house for something smaller – or to have people move in with us. We tried living in an apartment for a bit but she said what's the point in living in Auroville if your house is smaller than in a banlieue in Paris. So somehow she got the house back and we just pulled up some extra walls to make it more private and converted it into a guesthouse. That definitely taught me more than my dad's lame trip."

"So where's your dad now?"

"In Germany."

"Where in Germany?"

"Why? Do you know anything about the place?"

"No."

"So then?"

"I like the sound of foreign places. There is something exotic, enchanting about them..."

Vincent stretches his tanned chest towards the sun. "You're a funny monkey. I've never heard anyone calling Germany exotic or enchanting ... But I'll tell you ... the place is called Stuttgart."

"Does that mean anything?" Chinky strokes her fingers through Vincent's hair, the salt water has turned it into golden curls.

He thinks for a moment. "Yes, I think it does originate from Stutengarten, which is two words: mare and garden. I guess there must have been a garden with mares in it once upon a time."

"That *is* enchanting..." Chinky sighs, she closes her eyes. Vincent looks back at the blue sky. A few fluffy clouds are galloping across, only to vanish behind the palm trees...

And that's how they spend their days in paradise.

Every few days they trek through the little forest along the coastline and visit the other beaches – Om beach (because it had the shape of an om, apparently), Half-moon beach (because half-circle is not touristy enough a name), Kudle beach (nothing to do with cuddles) – to sell the trinkets (as Vincent would refer to them) or art (as Chinky would call it) to tourists and guest houses.

Promising that he would stay a couple of months, Vincent had struck a deal of 200 bucks a day for a shack with a built-in shelf so that he can keep the bags of beads, silver strings and threads safe from the moisture. The smell of fungus on fabric grosses him out. He has been reasonably productive so far.

"Making is always easy. Selling is the fuck-all part."

"I think that's because you are better at receiving than at giving." Chinky doesn't look up as she twists a string of silver for the fifth time around the ring mandrel.

"Eh?"

"Selling is giving. A lot of people think it is taking, because you're getting money for it. But what is money compared to the hours of thinking and sweating that you have put into it."

"Right, sometimes I think these ignorant fuckers don't even deserve the things I make. They don't appreciate the amount of work. I should add two zeros to the price, damn." He hands her the ring hammer. She has hit the right spot.

"Exactly my point, see. Unconsciously you know that selling is like giving a piece of you. Which is why you hate doing it so much."

He has to admit that she's got a point there. Very well, so she can do the selling.

"I like this design. It's so different, only with the purple and white beads."

"These are not beads. This is amethyst and this is crystal. Not very high quality, but if we put them out in the sun for a short while, they will be happy."

"Who? The people who will buy this?"

"Yeah, that too. But I meant the stones."

Vincent looks at Chinky. How can she be so serious while saying something like this? It's like she is constantly on acid, but sober. It's endearing. It's more than that. It's magnetic. He can't help but smile.

"Alright, let's take these babies out and make them happy."

9.30 p.m.

"The autopsy revealed no traces of drugs." Gaikwad wets his finger as he goes through the report. There's a look of relief on Sahil's face.

"I could've told you that. She was mostly 'straight edge,'" Vincent says.

"What does that mean?"

"People who like to live fun-deprived lives."

Gaikwad gestures, go on.

"No drugs, no alcohol, no smoking, no smoking up, no excess, no non-veg, mostly even vegan. Like Jains. But with the garlic."

He chuckles, thinking about Chinky eating a whole clove of garlic without flinching.

2012

"It keeps diseases away."

"It certainly keeps me away."

Putting her hands on her hips, she continues to chew. She's wearing a lungi, her wet long hair covering her breasts.

"I haven't been sick a day in my life. And neither has my Aita."

"What is your Aita?"

"My grandmother."

"Oh, where does your grandmother live?"

"I don't know."

"What do you mean, you don't know?"

"I mean, I don't know where she lives now. When I said goodbye to her in Assam, she didn't know where she would be going next."

"That does sound pretty adventurous for a grannie. Maybe I should start eating garlic. Badass."

"Hm, I don't know. Only few people know where and how they will reincarnate next. Even the Dalai Lama doesn't know!" Chinky pops in another clove. She stretches out her hand and offers the last clove to Vincent. He takes it. This is just too much to process. He feels his tear ducts opening.

When he recovers his composure and heads outside, he finds Chinky sitting in a perfect padmasana, her eyes closed, hair behind her ears. Contracting her stomach in weird, absolutely unattractive ways. She is breathing heavily. He is amazed at how nonchalant Chinky is about her looks. Most yoga 'practitioners' he knows are more concerned about their looks and ability to impress onlookers with the sharp angles they can fold their bodies into. Much more than about the spiritual meaning and effect of it all. That's probably why it doesn't have any effect on them no matter how many headstands they Instagram.

With her hands in paschim namaste, Chinky contorts her head like an owl. She smiles. At him? Her eyes are still closed. How...

"I can smell you from ten feet away." Her head back on her neck like it is supposed to be, she opens her eyes and rubs her nose vigorously.

"I forgot to do jalneti before my pranayamas."

Beige and silver sand are all over her chocolate-coloured face. It's adorable. How can she be so wise and such a little girl at the same time?

"I can help you with that."

Before she can react, he picks her up, and runs with a loud scream into the surf. She closes her eyes and holds her nose, but it's too late. They both tumble into the turquoise salty water, losing orientation.

As the wave passes, Vincent gently slides her out of his arms. "I think my sinuses have never been this clean."

"You're welcome."

Vincent smiles.

They paddle further into the sea until their feet lose touch with the ground.

The waves of the Arabian Sea are irregular. Much like the human thoughts, Vincent muses as he lies on his back. Either they rear up, wave after wave, incessantly in unpredictable intervals, or they rest flat. No thought at all. He enjoys this state. Blank. He looks at Chinky who has stretched all her limbs and is now floating like a sea star on the surface of the ocean. He blinks into the sun, closes his eyes, and turns himself into a sea star, too. The ocean gently shimmies him side to side. It's all quiet in the world. In his head. Only white noise…

He is tempted to fall asleep. To just let himself sink to the ocean ground. Forever quiet. His body relaxes further. All it would take is one deep exhalation … He readies himself; breathes in. How easy it is to just vanish from the face of earth. Blissful. A word he could never relate to. Now he is only one moment away from eternal bliss.

"Hold your breath," Chinky's voice yanks him out of his suicidal reverie. Her hair in the curl of the wave is the only thing left of her. He dunks under. The giant wave breaks on top of him, he has to hold onto his shorts before the undercurrent snatches them. The sandy ocean shifts under his knees and lifts his suddenly very heavy body up. Salty water drips into his eyes as he tries to tie his shorts.

"Let me help you with that." Chinky's head pops up right in front of his crotch. She smiles the broadest smile at him. Exposing her perfectly pearl-white teeth. He cannot help but smile back.

He leans back to comb the seawater out of his hair as Chinky twiddles with the laces. The water is gentle pushing against his crotch. It feels nice. A rhythmic back and forth. Soft and warm. He feels his blood rising. His lips parting. Chinky digs her fingernails into his butt cheeks. Wait, what is she doing? He looks down. Chinky throws him a mischievous smile, moving one hand up onto his chest, as she continues to slide his cock rhythmically forth and back between her lips. *God*. He exhales deeply. Please let her not stop. She moves her tongue over the tip of his penis. His balls tighten, he feels the blood leave his body and shoot downwards. She is grabbing onto his chest hair. Her lips tighten their grip. Fuck, he is gonna come. He takes her hand and with one smooth lift places her onto his hips, out of the water. She's wet. He slides in. He can feel her ass tighten. He responds by digging his fingers deeper. She moans, burying her teeth into his neck. They move in unison. Her breath is hot and salty in his ear. All thoughts evaporate. The ocean is calm again.

They make love until Chinky is too breathless. Until Vincent's thigh muscles are shaking. Until the stars peek out to watch them melt into the sea.

Vincent is playing with Chinky's hair which is fanned out all over his bare chest.

"Do you think it will piss that bitch off even more? To know that she might have forced you to run and you ran straight into the arms of a sex god like me?"

Chinky frowns at him. "She's not a bitch. She was in pain, because of me. Anyway, I didn't run from her. I came for my own journey. To find you … again. To make you happy."

"I don't really like being happy. It feels strange."

Chinky looks at him in surprise.

"What's the point of life, if not to be happy?"

"There is no point to life. I feel bad for people who can't accept that."

The sound of music and drums wafts in their direction. A few people have seated themselves on the beach and are playing music. Chinky gives Vincent a soft kiss on his lips. She gets up, slips on her dress and walks towards the music.

Ideally, Vincent would like to remain in the postcoital calmness that he otherwise hardly ever experiences, but he doesn't want to be left out of whatever Chinky is doing.

What a strange realization. He brushes it aside.

Chinky is dancing so near the fire the sparks fly dangerously close to her long white dress. Her big silver bangles shimmer in the moonlight as she raises her hands, turning them towards the sky as if she was conjuring the moon goddess herself.

Vincent watches her. *Taa tata taa | taa tata taa.* With two beers in his hand, he sits down next to the tabla player, a fifty-something hippie from France with long dreadlocks kept together with a bandana.

"*Ça va?*"

No answer. Only rhythmic nodding with his head. Perfect. A no-conversation evening, that's pleasant. *Tatataa tatataa.* A spliff is passed around. He takes a few long drags, keeping the joint between his half-open palms while inhaling. *Tata digg-tataa | tata digg-tataa | tata digg-tataa.* Maal from Manali. He can taste it. Sweet. The drums are synching with his heartbeat. *Taa diggidige taa | taa diggidige taa.* Chinky is still dancing. Vincent finishes his fourth Kingfisher ultra. People are taking a break to smoke, drink, piss, but she just dances on. *Tatatatatatatatataa tatatatatatatatataa tatataa tatataataataa.* The tabla is upping the tempo, as if to match her energy. The sand is flying off around Chinky's feet.

"*C'est différent, son énergie.*"

The tabla player is sticking the tip of his tongue between his teeth, he's giving his all to challenge the girl to dance herself mad. *Taadiggidigtaadiggidigtaa taa taadiggidigtaa.*

"*Quoi?*" Vincent isn't sure he heard correctly.

"*Ben, j'suis sûr qu'elle est une bonne baise.*"

A good fuck? "What the fuck is wrong with you man?" *Dung.*

The music stops. Chinky throws her head back. She lifts the hem of her dress to dab the sweat off her forehead. The guitar player gets up and offers her the joint. She laughs, leaning her hand onto his naked shoulder but doesn't take a drag. After catching her breath, she gestures to him to keep on playing. She doesn't even see Vincent fuming in anger. The topless musician nods towards the tabla. The Frenchman starts playing again. Vincent is so taken aback, he forgets to resume his fight. A crowd has gathered around the fire. All topless men. Where are all the women? Is this a performance? Fuck this shit. He turns towards the shack's makeshift bar. He needs to piss… *Tadiggdigtaa tadiggdigtaa.*

Whizz, the bartender, hands him a tequila on the way to the loo. He grabs it with his right hand and knocks it back while walking. The neon light in the toilet is giving him a headache. He walks to wash his face at the sink outside. But a lanky Indian dude is already occupying the place, neatly arranging a line on the dirty glass shelf above the sink.

This is what he needs. "You wanna share?"

The dude shrugs, hands him the straw.

Haaa, so much better.

His nose is still sore from the swim earlier, but fuck it.

"Try this. If you like it, I can supply more. I own the 'crystal' ice cream parlour." He serves him another line. Vincent sniffs it back. This is different. Fuck this is amazing.

Whizz smiles at him, reaching out the tequila silver. The lemon is bitter. Salt tastes like Chinky's skin. Everything is dipped in silver, like the moonlight on her forehead. She's a goddess. *Taadiggidigtaadiggidigtaa taa taadiggidigtaa Tatatatatatatatataa tatatatatatatatataggadiggitagadiggidagadagadaa.* Vincent feels something | *This is not good* | Blood | In his mouth? | Or is it the brain | His fingernails are slipping off | Intestines fall into his pants | He's trying to breath, but the quicksilver is gushing into his mouth, covering his airways, his limbs are torn apart in an ocean of knives | Black.

Vincent wakes up to see Chinky looking down at him. She is crying. She has his hand pressed against her forehead. *Beep … beep … beep…*

The sound of hospitals.

"Hey, don't worry. This shit keeps happening. But I haven't died yet."

"I told them I'm your wife so they would let me stay."

Vincent looks at her. Then he smiles.

"I'm glad. I've never woken up to anybody's face before."

He takes her hand and kisses her palm.

"Mrs Auerbach does suit you."

He catches her tears with his hand. She does the same.

52

7 p.m.

Sahil is counting the number of empty cups in front of Abhishek. He is fascinated.

"I am understanding a little bit why you couldn't let go of this Kartik guy."

Abhishek looks up at him.

Sahil points towards the four empty cups of coffee. "You have the typical addict's personality."

"So Kartik was my substance abuse?"

"Exactly."

Sahil looks pleased with himself.

Abhishek exhales and looks down. *Nothing as insightful as amateur psychology!*

But he has to concede the point to Sahil. "That theory is not completely without merit. You could be right…"

"I am no psychologist of course." Sahil smiles smugly as he takes a stab at modesty. "But being a policeman you do get to observe a whole variety of character flaws. Of course not all flawed characters are criminals … *but*…" He pauses for dramatic affect. "All criminals are flawed characters."

Abhishek wonders if he is supposed to applaud.

He looks towards Gaikwad for guidance, Sahil, too, is looking towards Gaikwad, probably for approval, but the sub-inspector is ignoring both of them. He is busy on his phone.

"Yes, yes, I know it's late … but what should I do? Leave my case? Tell them it's in my contract that I can't work on my anniversary … what? Of course it's not in my contract, I was being sarcastic … hello hello…"

He sighs. She has hung up.

He looks at his phone and mutters an unintelligible curse.

"Sir, you should not have been sarcastic. You do that with me also sometimes. It's very hurtful."

Gaikwad glares at him.

"I'm sorry, should I get *you* flowers next time?"

"See, you are doing it again."

Gaikwad throws his arms up in exasperation.

"I got married just once and yet it seems like I have two wives. I should have stayed a bachelor."

Abhishek smiles at him, wistfully.

"You are lucky you are married. Your relationship has a stamp. You don't have to worry, *'Does my wife think we are just friends? Does she have other friends?'* You know exactly what you are, and the government has approved it. I think all relationships should start in front of a judge … remove the ambiguity from the beginning."

2018

Dirty, ugly, crunchy and sharp, why would anyone ever want to walk here?

'Let's go for a walk on the beach!' they say, and sell you a picture of yourself, barefoot and carefree, burrowing your toes in the still warm sand. *He* has sold this image to countless clueless idiots so many times. The gentle beige sinks beneath your feet with each unhurried step, and then, your ankles disappear and the beige has turned blue. You relax in the icy coolness of the water which has risen to swirl stealthily, it washes your feet, it gently tickles and teases your toes…

Abhishek pulls up his foot in disgust, another soggy garland of dead flowers, thrown away after somebody's morning prayers, has intertwined itself together with the plastic bag which has wrapped itself in between his toes. He kicks this jellyfish of the twenty-first century away with his other foot, silently controlling his mounting irritation.

"Don't you love walking on the beach and gazing into the sea? I find it so relaxing." To his left, Riyan's face has turned rapturously in his direction.

Is he delusional? Does he think those two grains of sand suffocating under their shroud of plastic are the 'beach'? And what the hell is Riyan referring to as the 'sea'? Oh surely it cannot be that heaving pulsating sheet of grey thrashing and receding restlessly, like a miserable drunk bent over a toilet, trying to puke his guts out. Except, it's his feet that are the toilet, the receptacle for all of the city's vomit.

He tries to step back as the sea retches and spews last night's 'dinner' all over his ankles.

"So you don't like the sea?"

Abhishek frowns at the obvious judgement and incredulity in Riyan's voice.

"I love the sea." He tries to force a smile. "Who doesn't like the sea?" *But where the hell is the sea? All I see is spillage from a sewage factory.*

Riyan sighs. "I don't think you like it here very much."

"Well, I was expecting a little more sand and a little less plastic," confesses Abhishek.

A man jogs past them, sleeveless tank top and bulging muscles. An actor obviously. He does not seem to have any problem stepping on a couple of piles of poop on his journey to 'fitness'. And he is not alone! The beach is crowded with people, couples walking hand in hand, with some notion that gazing into greyish sludge is romantic. A few wannabe acrobats are jumping about manically on the 'sand'. Abhishek steps out of their way. The last thing he needs is to be knocked down, heaven forbid, face first. Already now he is positive that his skin may never recover from that rotting pile of toxins at his meticulously pedicured feet.

"No, I mean I don't think you like Mumbai very much."

"Same reason I guess."

Riyan laughs. "You're funny."

"You also think Hassan is funny, so excuse me if I do not take your compliments too seriously."

He winces as he steps into something gooey.

"Yes, I have noticed. I pay you at least one compliment a day and you are still as sweet and unassuming as the day you walked in, in your pale blue shirt and polka-dot tie, looking down on all of us."

Abhishek grins despite himself. Riyan is bantering with him. He likes it. He likes it even more when Riyan pulls out a bottle of wine and two perfect wine glasses from his bag. "I would have got beer, but I don't think that a guy who wears a tie to office would be down to drinking beer on the beach. But now I see you are not quite a picnic-on-the-beach kind of guy either. So where should we drink this?"

Abhishek takes the bottle from his hand and reads the label. It's an Indian brand. *He has never heard of anybody coming to India in search of good wine so obviously it does not exist.*

"It's not bad actually," Riyan pipes in.

Why do people keep reading his thoughts?

"The liquor store guy said that it's 'dry and tart', I figured you would like that."

Ouch.

"How do you know I wouldn't like it sweet and fruity?"

A pensive look flits across Riyan's face but then he grins. "I haven't seen you reach for any … yet."

"Maybe because all I have been offered is dry and tart. You forgot to mention that sweet and fruity was available, too."

Riyan is not the only one with the smart quips, he can banter, too.

His brown-haired companion pulls out another bottle from his bag. "Maybe if the first one gets you drunk enough to change your taste?"

Are they still just bantering?

Abhishek looks at Riyan. The sun is starting to set. The sky, untouched by the filth on the ground, has turned pink and azure. There's nothing quite as mesmerizing as the colours created by pollution. A feeble ray from the sleepy sun is caught in Riyan's hair and sets it on fire. Another beam escapes into his eyes, turning them into little hazel embers inside a ring of chocolate.

You are beautiful … he catches the words before they escape his lips.

A shadow on Riyan's face tells him that he has noticed Abhishek stepping away from the 'moment'.

"Do you pinch or thread?"

"What?"

"Your eyebrows."

Abhishek raises one of the said frames above his left eye. In all these years scrutinizing his own appearance multiple times a day – basically whenever he passes any surface which is even vaguely reflective – his eyebrows have never struck him as something worth mentioning. Why? Maybe he was too busy trying to fix all his other flaws, such as his round face or, worse, the receding hairline marking the onset of baldness which looms somewhere in his gene pool.

"I'm too scared to even think of doing that," he responds to the flattery with a lukewarm shrug. Why does he not allow himself to accept and enjoy this unexpected compliment?

They look at each other. Riyan shuffles a little. Abhishek can sense his trepidation, it mirrors what he feels around Kartik, but so much less in intensity. Yet the anxiety on Riyan's face is palpable. He wants to reach out and wipe it away. It's irritating. *What gives Riyan the right to remind him that despite all his promises to himself he is still hurting? What gives him the right to be the wrong boy feeling the right things? Why is Riyan handing him all this power when he does not want it from him?*

Riyan's body seems to shudder a little as he looks away from Abhishek. *Which of his uncharitable thoughts has his face given away?*

With the fiery sun in his light-brown hair and hazel eyes, Riyan looks towards the sea. He inhales deeply and turns back to Abhishek. "I know a spot from where you cannot see the garbage, all you can see are the waves in their full beauty and majesty."

"But I will still know that the garbage is there."

Riyan shakes his head. "But it isn't really. Garbage does not come from the sea, it does not belong to the sea. That's why she throws it back at us. The water at its core is everything you dreamed of, it just needs you to stop being distracted and notice it."

Abhishek looks again at the boy. Riyan's eyes are fixed on his face. They are naked and vulnerable. His upturned countenance is soft and beautiful but it carries no threat. He could kiss him and all his heart would feel is a gentle rhythm. A pleasant humming that would blot out all the screaming from his head. There would be no violation of his senses, no violation of his body. The face of the poet with his rictus of a smile bleeding from ear to ear, ramming himself violently against him peeks out from a crack in the still malleable and unfinished concrete wall of his mind. Another face with a man bun climbs onto the poet's kurta-draped shoulders, the grimace looking down at him, cold and expressionless, watching him drown but making no attempt to save him.

Desperately, Abhishek reaches down, Riyan reaches up. But at the last second Abhishek moves to the right. His cheek lightly grazes Riyan's as he deftly takes the sweet and fruity bottle of wine from Riyan's hand. The soft stubble gives him shivers. "Come, let's go meet my flatmate and get drunk with her. She will enjoy meeting a fan."

Abhishek is surprised to find himself actually turning the key in the lock. This is unusual. He typically just has to appear on the threshold and Chinky opens the door. But today her clairvoyance is still buffering or something has distracted her at the precise moment of Abhishek and Riyan's arrival. Abhishek stifles a mental giggle as he imagines Chinky glued to the door, looking out for hours, awaiting his return, so she can open the door at the right time for maximum 'magical' effect. He wonders if he should wait, give her a chance to 'catch up', but too late, the key has already turned. *Ready or not here I come,* he pushes the door open. Strange, it's so dark. *Where the hell is...* "CHINKY?" A loud desperate voice completes his thought, a light comes on, and Abhishek and Riyan are treated to a full frontal view of Satchit's large hairy body, completely nude.

Somebody screams.

Is it Riyan? No, surprisingly it's Satchit.

Such a shrill sound, from such a big body, thinks Abhishek uncharitably. Behind him Riyan is trying to take charge of the situation. "Just turn off the light." *Wow such a strong command from such a puny body,* thinks Abhishek, also uncharitably.

"Good idea." The light goes off. The sound of feet shuffling away. Abhishek exhales. *Never a dull moment around here.* He can feel Riyan burying his face against his arm, trying to stifle his giggle. "He's really hung though," Riyan's breath is hot near his chest as he whispers. Despite himself Abhishek laughs softly. "All I saw was the jungle. I cannot believe that you managed to spot the snake in all that foliage."

Riyan can't hold it back anymore, he bursts out laughing. It's a strangely infectious sound, Abhishek joins him, he cannot help it, the sound is just bursting out of him, when he's not even that amused. *Just two lovelorn faggots, laughing in the dark over a straight man's dick ... It must be Tuesday in Chinky's apartment.*

The light switches on. Satchit is back, with clothes. *This is a first.* Involuntarily Abhishek's eye moves towards his crotch, encased in his too white and too tight shorts. *Hmm, he seems to have liked their recent encounter a lot more than they have.* Abhishek catches Riyan's eye, Riyan's grin tells him that he has noticed, too. He winks at Abhishek, thrilled to have shared a secret, conspiratorial moment with him. Abhishek looks away. Whatever romantic fantasies Riyan is cooking up in his head, he does not want to be accused of encouraging them.

Satchit moves towards the couch and sits down, one leg crossed over the other. Abhishek waits for him to say something because he has absolutely no idea how to make banal small talk in a situation like this. Satchit notices the bottle of wine in Riyan's hand.

"I would not mind a drink."

Abhishek looks apologetically towards Riyan, who does not look put out at all.

"Of course, darling, do you want to bother with glasses or should we just have a go at the bottle?"

"I'll get the glasses." Abhishek moves swiftly towards the kitchen. *He is not sharing any saliva with Satchit. What if excessive hair growth in all the wrong places is contagious?*

In an effort to compose himself, Abhishek rummages for glasses in Chinky's kitchen wishing heartily that she was here. He has no idea what manner of things he is going to find in these drawers and cabinets. *What if he accidentally sets off a hex that ends the world?*

The first drawer is quite tame by Chinky's standards. It's full of cups which are so mismatched that it looks like she has something personal against symmetry.

The one at the back catches his eye. It looks rough and unfinished, as if made by hand. He pulls it out.

It's an ugly thing; the green colour is sloppily painted on, the handle chipped, and there is a large crack at the bottom. How does it hold anything? In fact, it looks like it would dissolve the second it came in contact with any liquid. Why is it still here inside this drawer instead of inside a dustbin? He puts it back before it falls apart in his hand, wondering who made it for her. Nobody would be foolish enough to buy it in a store – unless she saw it with all the other properly made cups and felt 'sorry' for it. Abhishek allows himself a chuckle at his silly fancies, although of course with Chinky this could well be what actually happened.

He reaches in and gives the misshapen mug a comforting little pat. *"Don't worry, little cup, you may be ugly and worn, but she will always love you."*

He opens another cabinet, even though he knows there is no way in hell that she keeps anything as socially normal as wine glasses in her kitchen. *So why then is he still looking? Because it is like hunting for a treasure; exhilarating even, perhaps because this is the closest he will ever get to the kind of place where magic lamps hide in plain sight.* This cabinet is full of smells: honey, lavender, rose, chocolate, forest, mud. Abhishek inhales deeply, feeling suddenly calm yet elated.

"Hey, did you find the glasses yet?" Instinctively, the cabinet slams shut. The smells vanish, leaving not even a lingering after-smell. He turns around to face Riyan, feeling suddenly foolish. *What the hell is he doing here? Like some spellbound, helpless wanderer lured into the witch's lair?* Abhishek shakes his head. "No."

"Did you forget I have two? I already poured Satchit a glass." He hands another glass to Abhishek and slides a hand across his waist. "Would you care to share this with me?"

Abhishek takes an unintentionally large sip.

He has done it. Now all of Riyan's illnesses, dormant and active, are racing down his throat.

Riyan has chosen well with the wine. He has matched it to the colour of his lip balm. Or is the wine tainting his lips that delectable shade of red? Abhishek can practically smell the strawberries on them. This could be imagination, or indeed the subtle scent of whatever he has used to redden his lips ... or it is simply the wine reaching his brain ... whatever the reason, Abhishek has a sudden hankering to taste strawberries.

A sharp indrawn breath from Riyan tells him that he, too, has noticed that Abhishek's appetite is finally whetted. It would be cruel to disengage from yet another moment, thinks Abhishek, and before he can give himself a chance to change his mind, he bends over and devours the strawberries. Never before have strawberries tasted so sweet, but the plight with sweet-tasting strawberries is that one tires of them so fast that if he does not possess the presence of mind to pause before he is satiated, he is forced to stop because his stomach begins to feel uneasy.

Abhishek pulls back. Riyan reluctantly retracts his tongue and lets go, too. His hands however continue clutching at

Abhishek's shirt, his rapturous expression making it clear that he has ended the kiss only physically. Inside his head, they are still intertwined and somebody's mouth has gone a lot further south. Abhishek groans, not entirely from dismay. Riyan's feelings are displayed so clearly on his face, Abhishek can almost watch them. *Is it possible to get turned on by seeing yourself in somebody else's imagination?*

The key turns in the lock. The front door opens and shuts with a resounding bang. The vibration jerks the hastily shut cabinet door open as well. Lavender, vanilla, wine, strawberries, musk, even the memory of that moment will be forever scented. Abhishek inhales deeply and pulls Riyan in. From this moment, the city will never again smell solely of sewage…

It is the middle of the night when Abhishek wakes up with a parched throat, a pounding headache and a warm, pliant and completely naked body pressed against his.

Which one of his bad decisions is he trying to correct by noiselessly rolling off the bed?

He grabs his t-shirt from the bedside and clothes himself before proceeding to the kitchen in search of water. The garment ends just a little above his knees, leaving a good bit of his thighs exposed. *Sexy without being tacky. Good.* In fact, it is just perfect for this time of the night, for it tantalizingly exposes a little more with every step he takes. But who is he trying to arouse in this house? Abhishek looks around for his hastily discarded trousers. Riyan stirs in his sleep, his hand stretches a little forward, towards the still warm depression on the vacant, crumpled sheet. Quickly, Abhishek leaves the room, before his hands leave the bed to find him. He does not wish to be found anymore tonight.

The light in the kitchen is off but Abhishek can smell fresh coffee brewing. Despite himself he smiles, the knot that he did not know he had in his stomach loosens.

"Don't switch on the light."

That's a good idea. Abhishek moves his hands away from the switchboard. He turns in the direction of the voice, his eyes adjusting rapidly to the dark until they finally rest on a pair of white tic-tacs suspended midair. A blink. A pair of eyes blinks itself into existence, throwing their light on the shiny tip of a nose and finally a little white smile. Like Alice looking at the Cheshire cat disappearing one part at a time, she is manifesting one part at a time.

"You have really tiny teeth."

The smile gets wider. "Yes, my grandmother used to call me little mouse."

Chinky is close enough now that he can see her. She takes his hand. He starts to pull it back, his lips already starting to form an objection – he has not come here for a midnight tryst with his landlady. Something warm is thrust into his palm. She wraps his hand around the cup of coffee. "Be careful it's hot." Abhishek smiles, feeling foolish. *What arrogance has Riyan infected him with?* He assumes everybody must desire him.

He takes a sip of coffee laced with cinnamon and hot chocolate. His soul feels suddenly cushioned. Chinky looks at him. It is too dark to be sure but he thinks he detected some movement in the general place where her head is supposed to be. But what is she looking at in this total absence of light? *His energy obviously. Why has he never asked her what colour his halo is?*

"You think Riyan is good for me?" he asks.

"You are closed to his energy, it's for you to know if you are more closed to energies that are bad for you or good for you."

When did it get so complicated to know the difference between good and bad?

Has he asked his question out loud?

He is waiting for an answer. But if there was any, the darkness swallowed it before it could reach his ears.

Does it matter?

What does anything matter? What gives pleasure should be good and what pains should be bad ... but then what about the consequences in the end? And how do we know that we have reached a conclusion? That nothing is leading to anything anymore?

Why is she answering his questions with riddles? Stupid question. What else does she ever do?

She sighs next to him. A deeply reflective sigh.

She is waiting for an answer, but not from him.

He shifts uncomfortably in his spot. The cold tiles have made his buttocks go numb.

In the dark, Chinky reaches out and squeezes his hand. "Sometimes, that you find yourself trapped in darkness is not at all your fault."

"Who said it was?"

"Nobody and that is why you can't explain that it wasn't."

An arm around his shoulder, and maybe she pulls her to him or maybe he gravitates towards her. They are hugging each other. He realizes that he had been trembling only once his body stops shaking. The tremor which has been unsettling every cell in his body ever since that train ride rears up into consciousness. Abhishek exhales, a sharp, violent hissing sound, as something black and nefarious uncurls itself from inside his stomach and leaks out through the cracks between the bricks, through every single crevice in the wall of his mind. He exhales harder, trying to expel it, all of it, let not even a tendril remain.

"Hey, why are you sitting here in the dark?"

The light is switched on.

Abhishek blinks in the sudden brightness, out of breath. *Did he get it all out?*

Satchit is taking up most of the doorframe and, in surprising consideration for Abhishek's sensibilities, has draped a toga-like bedsheet all around himself. Alas, Abhishek finds his eyes fixed on the naked shoulder that has been left uncovered.

He looks away quickly, in time to catch an expression of such naked vulnerability on Chinky's face that it violates his senses much more than Satchit's bare shoulder. But an imperceivable millisecond later her expression is again tender and seductive as she smiles up at Satchit and stretches her arms out to him. Satchit runs to her so eagerly, Abhishek is worried that he will step on his bedsheet and rip it away from his body. He shifts his gaze elsewhere, unwilling to look at Chinky either – in case he catches her more exposed than she has been countless times without her clothes.

Satchit moans in pleasure.

Oh damn. Abhishek gets up, hastily. "Well, I wish you both a goodnight, thank you for the coffee, Chinky." *Bravo! A whole sentence delivered with zero eye contact.*

"You can stay here, Abhishek. I will not have goodbye sex with Satchit on the kitchen floor, he deserves much better than that."

"Huh!" Abhishek and Satchit speak in unison.

An identical expression of surprise on both their faces, with bewilderment and hurt layering up on Satchit's.

"I'm sorry, Satchit, but you should know, it's not your energy, it's mine."

Abhishek snorts with ill-timed laughter, his coffee sprays out of his nose. Fortunately neither is in a state to register the mess at their feet in lieu of the messiness of their abruptly shattered relationship, the shards of which are now metaphorically lying at their feet. Sprinkled with probably more than a few drops of blood from Satchit's freshly stabbed heart.

Some lessons are well learnt in retrospect. Such as the fact that it is unadvisable to have a lover over for the night if one has to journey to the same office in the morning. It is impossible to get rid of them in the morning as they would be expecting the two of you to leave the house together.

It is unfair, thinks Abhishek, *to have to be attractive as soon as you wake up.* The rest of the day is going to be filled with the drudgery of social niceties anyway. A man should be allowed to fart or burp in his own bed without having to worry about appearing uncouth or offensive. *Does a fart in an empty room even stink if there is no one around to call it out?*

Abhishek looks in distaste mixed with unexpected and unwanted desire at Riyan's nude body next to him, enticingly draped in crisp white sheet. The usually heartless, early-morning sun is unusually kind to Riyan. The soft rays create a sparkle in the air, the faint dust swirling above Riyan's toned thigh settles slowly, like sugar-cinnamon powder, making him glisten bronze wherever it touches him. His soft body hair shines almost blond. Abhishek's hands want to move of their own volition and caress wherever the light has touched, even as they itch to push the same body away from this bed that is not meant to be occupied by two – at least not the two of them.

Riyan stirs sleepily. Abhishek's hands compromise, they linger lightly for just that one extra second. *Vanilla, cinnamon and sweet sugar crystals ...* Abhishek's tastebuds experience a memory burst of last night's kisses. Violently shaking his head, Abhishek brushes the thought off – his co-worker has to wake up. He gently shakes his surprisingly muscular shoulder.

"Get up or you won't have time to go home and get a change of clothes before work."

Riyan is absolutely not going to the office with him wearing last evening's clothes. *Riyan and Abhishek sitting on a tree...*

"Ooh that's okay, I'll just wear something of yours."

What? No, that's worse...

Before any objection can escape Abhishek's mouth it is laced with sugar...

"Has anyone ever aroused you as soon as you arose?"

It is probably the cheesiest line he has ever woken up to, but twenty seconds later Abhishek is in no state or mood to protest. *Maybe they can buy Riyan a shirt on the way?*

Another twenty minutes later, Abhishek steps out into the living room having declined Riyan's invitation to 'shower together' to save time. "I will be quick and then you can go right after," he had said, dodging into the bathroom and shutting the door behind him, decisively. He had bolted it for good measure. It would rank among the quickest showers he has ever taken, but has he managed to get the smell off? He has sprayed himself rather liberally with perfume, but what is it they say about applying a scent to an odour? It just makes it stronger and travel further. What if everybody gets to know as soon as he walks into the office?

Chinky looks up when he enters. She is sitting hunched over a deck of tarot cards spread out in front of her. Strange, she is not greeting him with her customary, all-knowing smile. In a complete departure from her usual Chinkiness, she neither offers him a coffee nor any words of wisdom. She does not even rearrange her features into 'pleasantness'. Instead, her brows remain furrowed as she looks at him. Abhishek has the uneasy feeling that she is just 'looking' at him but she is actually seeing something else...

"Hey."

The single syllable breaks her focus on whatever she was beholding. She blinks and that which (or who) was in her eyeline just a second ago, vanishes. She can see him again. Her mouth curves into a smile. He is no expert, but it feels like the light in her eyes remains dimmed.

"I did not know that you could do readings for yourself."

"I usually don't, but I thought maybe I needed an 'unbiased' opinion this time."

Now her smile does reach her eyes ... sort of.

"About Satchit?"

Before Chinky can react to his question, a squeaky clean, sweet-looking and strangely appealing Riyan has stepped in carrying his brightest smile.

"Oh my God. Finally, I get to see you in the 'flesh', well actually in 'not the flesh', ha ha, I am so happy to meet you. I am such a huge fan."

Chinky fixes her eyes on Riyan. "Exactly as I would have imagined."

And she's back, complete with her beatific smile.

Riyan smiles as well in return. He does not seem to find whatever she has said confusing or ambiguous at all. *He is clearly used to her 'style'.*

He walks eagerly ... a little too eager ... and almost skips over her fanned-out tarot cards on the floor. "Oh my God! May I please have a reading?"

Exactly as I would have imagined.

53

11.30 a.m.

She squeezes the cold tea bag between her perfectly manicured index finger and thumb. It's the last sip of the second brew. The water is room temperature now, and bitter. If colours had a taste, the beige-brown patina of the police station would be just like this last sip. First tasteless, then bitter.

"Who was Surat to me now? He was someone of course, he could never be just no one. But, what really is 'someone'. I don't know ... was it always like this or had I changed? But I think if he had not come, Chinky would still be alive."

Gaikwad looks up sharply. His mind has been wandering. He had made an effort to not show any reaction to Iti's last question. But it had left a biting feeling somewhere inside him. Naturally if one is surrounded by death all day, every day, the thought of his wife suddenly dying does cross his mind, if ever so briefly. But today, right now, he has nothing to brush it aside, nothing to distract himself with. Except for listening to this strange woman's failed love story.

"Are you saying you suspect Surat had something to do with her death?"

Iti shakes her head.

"Surat is not even in town right now. But Chinky always said that nothing happens in isolation, one thing always leads to another. Have you heard of the 'butterfly effect'?"

Gaikwad has not. He assumes it must be the victim's version of 'the flowers and the bees'. "Go on." And of course, she does.

"So if Surat had not come to Mumbai ... I would have still been in the house. If I had been in the house I could have protected her ... she would have not run away ... she would not have left her job, she would have not met him … she would not have changed … so yes, I guess I blame Surat."

"Met whom? Gone where?"

Shocked by the honesty of her own answer, Iti's mind drifts off. Yes, she does blame Surat. Human decency and social norms tell her that it's a 'wrong' feeling to have. If someone is to blame, it is her. Her mother still hasn't forgiven her, understandably. It must be tough for her, too, having to stand up to the entire family and her friends with this unexpected reality. But at least she has pictures of her daughter with all the stars and starlets of Bollywood to distract the monthly kitty party and the small-town gossip. Luckily her Nani is too disoriented to be able to keep a track on years and believes Iti every time when she tells her that she has just finished college and is still very, very young.

Which is true, in a way. The Iti who left Agra just six months after graduating had the mind, heart and body of a teenager. Yet, the one sitting now perfectly composed in a police station for interrogation just a little over eight years later feels like she has crossed the magic thirty a while ago. Neither of it is factually correct. But what are facts, really? And what does growing up even mean?

Is it that the facts change: At some point she loved Surat and then she did not love him anymore? Or is it that she had never loved him. She remembers the instant when this fact had hit her. That must have been the moment when the connection started forming. It was painful. Like growing pains when one shoots up in height overnight.

2011

It was in her room in their apartment. She had decorated it with so much love, even now she remembers every single item and its place – the big dresser with its many colourful drawers and porcelain knobs, each one different from one another. Each one, like a visa stamp, a memory of a trip which she had taken to places like Chor Bazaar, Behram Baug, Colaba – where Bombay before partition and Agra of the present seem to meet. Every drawer a gateway to both longing and excitement. The small side table by the window where she used to have her tea before going to bed. In her green ceramic cup which she had made from scratch when Chinky had received two invitations to attend a pottery workshop in an artisan studio in Bandra. She loved the process. How something can turn from an unshapely lump of clay to a shiny vessel reflecting the colour of her favourite green tea and keeping it warm. It was evening and the light of the street lamp right under her room dipped it in a warm orange hue. If she pushed her cane chair with the knitted shawl on it close enough to the window she could read even at night without switching the light on, and save a little electricity. It felt cosy, like a real home should be. She had expected it to feel even more like a home now that Surat had arrived, but it didn't.

And most importantly, Chinky never bought a third chair for Surat. Their home still remains a place for two. Every evening when Iti comes home, she looks anxiously at their sitting area, wondering if today she would see evidence that Surat now 'lived' with them. A few nights later she realizes that they no longer sit there by the window on their two chairs either. Now, she comes home to find Surat in her room, sprawled out on her bed, where she joins him.

A little later Chinky arrives and balances herself on Iti's tiny bedside stool, always bringing to Iti's mind a vision of

Thumbelina, nestled inside the petals of a flower. How is she so little? Iti considers herself slimish now and she has seen some skinny women, but Chinky feels almost wispy and a little elflike as she pulls her feet up to her chest, and balances on a space so minuscule it feels crowded after Iti has put more than one book and her phone onto it. It is as if the stool has made an effort to expand itself in order to accommodate Chinky comfortably in the centre, as well as the book and phone on the side. Or maybe it is Chinky who has shaped herself to fit the space, like water.

If Chinky is at all discomfited or feeling displaced by Surat's presence she never shows it. On the tenth (which is rent day), Iti tries to surreptitiously pay two-third of the rent, dropping her share by their usual spot next to the money plant. In the evening she finds the envelope untouched, with Chinky announcing that she has been paid more money this month, so that she would take care of the whole rent. In that moment, Iti assumes that Chinky indeed sees Surat as a temporary guest but is not churlish enough to take money for his presence.

But now, late at night, as Surat falls asleep next to her, the thought has crept into Iti's mind and lodged itself there, refusing to budge, just inflating and bloating as it hunts and feeds on her worst fears. Does Chinky now consider *her* a temporary guest as well? Unable to sleep, she lies next to Surat's prone body, wondering as she has been doing every night since he had arrived. Should she reach out and touch him? Maybe stroke his back? Kiss him? Something? But then again, had Kunal not said just two days ago that the very definition of insanity was to keep doing the same thing again and again and expect a different result? And yet that's exactly what she kept doing, six times now to be exact. When she could have easily stopped after the first and missed precisely nothing.

Inspired by Chinky, she had coaxed him into being 'open-minded' and have sex with her. She wanted to feel what Chinky feels. The ecstasy, the joy, the self-realization…

Nothing like that happened.

She doesn't even remember their 'first time'. She remembers what she wore – a pink lace thong and fitting bra, both terribly itchy, and she doubts Surat even paid attention. Once he had reluctantly removed her clothes, he had difficulties slowing himself down. So she does actually remember. But she chooses to tell herself that she doesn't.

Oh well maybe it would be lucky seven for her. She reaches out and slips a hand under his shirt, and kisses him…

Another wasted twenty minutes when she could have instead read one of her M&B. At least while reading she could 'imagine' without guilt. The hero's face wasn't sacred – she could replace it with anyone's.

Iti keeps her eyes fixed on Surat's face, not daring to shut them, and endures another twenty excruciating minutes of Surat trying really hard to give her attention, awkwardly attempting to please her, but it is so annoying that she gently pushes him to simply proceed. Which he does and comes and finishes with a smile that lasts its usual couple of seconds before turning into an anxious 'was it ok?'

All his endings were so predictable.

"Yes, you were great." She answers even before he finishes his question.

"I always thought we would wait till marriage … but … well, I guess we are as good as married already, aren't we?"

"I feel like we've been married for years."

Sweet trusting Surat, could never sense the underlying disappointment of these words.

A few minutes later he is breathing deeply, a sound which she has learnt meant that he was fast asleep. She looks at his face, willing her heart to be suffused with tenderness, even as her mind shouts angrily for him to go back to Agra and give her back her space in her own bed. Why was he here? As if scared that her loud thoughts would wake him, Iti quickly tiptoes out of the room.

Exhaling in relief as she shuts the door behind her, Iti stands in the darkened living room, letting its familiarity wash over her. She bumps into nothing as she walks over to her chair and spends the rest of the night curled up on it. At some point she falls asleep with the traffic obligingly tooting out an unlikely lullaby for her.

Now that they were officially 'living together', Surat could not stop planning their wedding. As soon as he found a real job in Mumbai, they would get married.

For now he is making money by working in a call centre, but that is of course temporary. He is an electrical engineer after all, with an MBA to boot. Why wouldn't Mumbai just hand him a job? Eventually?

"I am not leaving Mumbai."

Surat looks hurt. "When have I asked you to leave? I'm just saying once we get married our parents will get us a bigger house."

Iti giggles. "You mean like dowry?"

"Yes, but for both of us. We will also get presents. I really wouldn't mind having a microwave."

Iti laughs. "And what if we get five different types of electric kettles?"

"Then we will sell them and buy a microwave. But it will have to be a small one, this kitchen has no freaking space."

"Do you even like living in Mumbai, Surat?"

"I can live anywhere with you."

He hugs her, shuts his eyes and falls asleep. Iti kisses his forehead. And pulls her arm out from under him.

She walks to the window and throws it open. It's a view of the next building and it's really quiet, except for a lone rickshaw playing the radio from its cheap speakers.

She sighs and shuts it.

She texts Chinky: *What are you doing?*

Chinky texts back: *Just having some tea with Jhansi and Nitin. They both send you kisses.*

Iti responds: *Kisses to them and send me a picture of my street.*

Chinky sends it to her. Iti looks at it, wistfully.

With a sigh, she turns around and lies down on 'her side' of the bed. She pulls out one of her M&B books from the bedside drawer, and starts reading it.

The next day manifests the reality of her feelings...

Iti has worked hard to convince Maria to let her take charge of the costume department for this project. She has learnt more about PowerPoint in the process than in all her years at college. And she loved it. Creating a mood board for each character felt like she was 'writing' their backstories in a way. When she went for her pitch meeting with the director, she felt a bit embarrassed to share her many thoughts on them, but Maria appreciated that she had walked 'the extra mile' and attached fabric samples to each printed slide.

"Where did you find all those fabrics?"

"Manish Market, Natraj Market, Santa Cruz Station, Colaba, Crawford Market and then I also called for some specific kinds from my friend in Lucknow. I mean if we want to make people believe that we are in UP while we are actually in Filmistan, I thought this would make it more real. Not that it wouldn't look real otherwise ... no offence, I'm sure you have a great vision, ma'am, but it's also about the actors feeling like they are really from there, no?"

"No offence taken. I agree with you! I'm not sure if we will have the budget for calling for stuff from Lucknow, but you can sort that out with Kunal. And please call me Maria!"

Of course Kunal agreed. "I wouldn't have shared the script with you if I didn't think that you would be able to pull off something different. And you have." A wink escapes his eyes as they linger on her face. "How did you even carry all of this here?"

"She is stronger than she looks," interjects Iti, wondering with the tiniest pang of guilt if she is coming to Chinky's defence or breaking up the moment Kunal is so desperately trying to have with her.

"The weight of most things depends on how you carry them." Chinky smiles, touching Iti's arm.

It's the gentlest of touches, yet Iti's skin feels bruised from the pressure. Iti turns around and envelops Chinky in a big bearhug. Chinky hugs her back, holding her tight.

"Art!"

Maria means Chinky.

Glued to their spot, Iti and Kunal watch in awe the transformation taking place right in front of them in a matter of minutes. From a cheap veneer foundling the table has turned into a glamorous centrepiece, just correct for the elegant dinner set. The lacey crisp tablecloth is hardly visible under the paraphernalia of shiny silver-looking tableware, candle stands, tiny sugar dishes with even tinier spoons in them, a few sugar cubes casually sprinkled here and there, saucers and flower-patterned cups, plates big and small, butter knives, wine candelabras and water glasses cut in crystal-look. A million things have been affixed to this wooden rectangle with its four wobbly legs, yet all in such perfect balance that not a single piece seems excessive or redundant.

Chinky strokes the tabletop like a pet owner her obedient dog.

"She is a natural. She can make a lot of money working like this in the art department till her acting career takes off."

"She just wants enough money for a new fridge and she will only take on another acting assignment if you no longer pay her enough to cover rent, or maybe she will just go after your job."

Kunal shakes his head. "She can have it. I don't particularly love my job. It was supposed to be temporary, till I got my break as a director." He shakes his head again, looking rueful. "You know I even tried giving myself a break, but the producer in me could tell right away that I needed to be fired."

"Oh."

Iti looks at him, not sure why she is feeling this rush of sympathy for the rich producer who just bought a new car. Maybe it's because of how much she loves her own job. She cannot imagine somebody waking up in the morning, getting into their shiny new car, just to drive to someplace where they will spend the rest of the day doing something they don't burn for passionately, knowing that tomorrow and the day and the day after will also be the same. She hugs herself, feeling incredibly lucky.

Perhaps he has confided more in her than he cared to, or perhaps he does not want to linger anymore on a dream he has given up on. The silence between them is unusually uncomfortable. From the corner of her eye, Iti tries to find Chinky somewhere in the mess of cameras, light stands, flags, gels, people, so many people...

"But you will have to do the bargaining in Lucknow for me. Nobody can beat you at that. Maybe I should have hired you for the production department."

Now, for the first time, she considers it. There is a time for everything. So far she hadn't considered the money but Surat's insistence on a wedding has become increasingly less playful ... and to do something entirely new? To be involved with more than just costumes. She feels just the slightest tingling in the pit of her stomach.

"Your department is really big, I'm so proud of you."

"It's alright. But why would you think that?"

"There are so many girls on this set today. Aren't most girls working in costume?"

"This is an all-women crew, my friend." Apart from his persistence, Kunal owes his success as executive producer to his unique talent of being able to appear out of nowhere at the right moment. "Except for me. Thank you for shoring up the minority." He pats Surat on the shoulder, like an old friend. Surat is way taller than him and Kunal has to stand on his toes to make it look effortless. Iti notices, Surat does not.

"I'm glad I can be of some use!"

"Of course you are!" Iti hugs him sideways. Surprised, Surat reciprocates this rare loving gesture in public. Kunal gets the message and trails off.

The shot is almost ready, and Iti has to excuse herself to check on the main actor's costume. When she comes back, she finds Surat on top of a ladder taking directions from Chinky, much to the delight of a gaggle of girls who are busy ogling

Surat's toned biceps and calves as Chinky makes him move "a little bit right … no a little left…"

Chinky grins at her. "It had to be either him or Kunal and I picked the one we have seen 'less' of, it's more attractive."

"In any case, my Surat is the more handsome of the two." Iti throws a giant flying kiss up the ladder, keeping her eyes fixed on him, possessively, proprietorially. He is hers, he always has been.

"I love your dude. He is such a cutie and so well mannered. Lucky girl." With her boy-cut and baggy trousers, Maria doesn't look as if she would appreciate such qualities in a man – or men at all for that matter. But that is something Iti keeps to herself.

Maria is holding a shot glass in her hand. She chucks it down in one go.

"More?"

"Always!"

"Is poppy milk alright?"

"Just what I need for this scene!"

Iti couldn't agree more, she does not care much for the Bombay 'kadak' chai, her tea needs to have an extra dash of milk. A warm fuzzy feeling of contentment fills her insides – if you share the same taste in tea, what can you possibly disagree on?

"I appreciate it." And with that, Maria goes bottoms up on the second glass, handing it empty back to Chinky.

Iti shakes her head laughing. "I just love her 'zero-fucks-given' attitude." She takes the last sip from her glass, careful to place her lips on the exact same spot as the lipstick mark which her previous two sips have left. "If she would only allow herself to be a little bit more feminine in her dressing style, she could be a very pretty girl with men serenading her from morning till night."

"Why would she want that? There are no men here anyway – apart from 'your' Surat."

Chinky has a point there.

"Yeah, I've heard 'unisex' is the height of fashion here. Maria says girls don't get taken seriously, especially not on a film set."

"Good luck you are not a girl."

Iti is confused. Sarcasm isn't usually Chinky's scene. Or what does she see her as? There is hardly anyone more girly around than her...

"You are a woman!"

"Oh."

Iti smiles, she stands on her toes. "Have I grown taller, too?"

"You were always tall and formidable, but yes, there is more of you in that space now."

"I still feel like a child sometimes."

"That's good, because I have never met a wiser person than a child."

"Yeah? Like this boy? Though I have never felt like he was particularly wise."

She points towards Kunal, who is bouncing an empty chai cup on his foot to the amusement of a group of jobless ADs.

Right on cue, Kunal's loud laughter rings through the set.

For the second time today, again without quite knowing why, Iti feels a surge of pity for Kunal.

"I feel bad for him."

"Bad for whom? Kunal? Are you kidding me?"

Maria has come back looking for more chai. But there is none left. Feeling deprived she settles for scowling in Kunal's direction.

"He has it made. Plays the fool half the time and still everybody goes quiet and listens when he enters a room. Just because he has that magic stick."

Iti looks in surprise, a sudden image of Kunal dressed up in Hogwarts colours flashing through her mind. But Kunal's hands are empty, there is no stick, magic or otherwise that he is holding.

"Between his legs," Maria clarifies exactly a second before Iti gets it. "Everybody loves to worship the penis." She looks at Iti. "Don't you have that constant nagging feeling about whether you have been assertive enough but not too bossy, clear but not mean, inspiring but not over excited? So many rules for women, every action equals a label, and you keep wondering which one will be slapped on you today. A man just has to exist. Unburdened and free, knowing that he has nothing to prove."

Iti stares at Maria. She shakes her head. "I never really gave it any thought. But perhaps I should have ... Do you think I will not be successful enough because I don't have a penis?"

"Probably not," says Maria, "but at least you will know it wasn't you, it was just your anatomy. Hey..." Maria has spotted a spot boy, she runs after him. "Do we have any diet coke?"

Iti looks mournful. And there is not even any tea left in her cup to cheer her up.

Chinky takes Iti's hand. "It's only temporary. A necessary bout of violence."

"What?"

"Male rule."

"I don't know..."

"What are a couple of thousand years compared to the million for which the feminine has determined creation? I mean we create *life*! Let them have fun. And a couple of reincarnations down the line the world will be a gentler place again."

"Camera, are we ready?"

Iti wants to talk more. But they should both be heading to the monitors.

"But why should I care about that? It's not going to happen in my lifetime..."

"Can I have silence please?"

Chinky takes Iti's face in her hands. Her dark sparkly eyes beaming straight into Iti's mind, she whispers: "Don't worry about the world right now. The only person who needs to 'listen' to you is the director."

"Cut. Cut. Cut! Can I have a light beam on the wine goblet please?"

"Your future husband doesn't have anything better to do on a Sunday than hang around his wife's set?"

Iti's train of thought is interrupted. Kunal has taken Chinky's place. She feels caught.

"I'm sorry, Kunal, Sunday is a holiday for corporate types like him. I told him he could hang around a bit; don't worry, it won't affect my work."

Kunal smiles at her, gently touches her back.

"I'm not worried at all. You are one of the most committed people I have worked with."

He gestures towards one of the actresses who is chatting up with Surat.

"I'm worried about him distracting my actor."

Wasn't he just distracting the ADs? Iti feels defensive about Surat. He is standing in the far corner of the set where the girl in the mint-coloured evening gown and crazy hairdo complete with tiny fake birds nesting in it, is waiting for her shot. Iti is quite proud of the ensemble.

The actress giggles at something he has said.

"He's quite the charmer, isn't he?"

"Yes, he does seem to be."

Surat looks towards her, as if he felt her gaze. She gestures him over.

"Do you want to see the designs I have made for next week's shoot?"

"Of course." Surat breaks into the broad smile of a proud husband.

Iti hands him her iPad. Surat flips through the slides.

"Even the presentation is designed so prettily! I'll ask for your help next time I need to present something!"

His eyes linger on hers. It's a gentle, warm gaze.

"Move, move!"

From the scaffolding thirty feet above them a light guy waves his hands frantically. Iti looks up, the HMI hanging on top of Surat sways dangerously, it is about to fall!

In a survival-instinct reflex, Iti quickly snatches the iPad out of Surat's hand and moves a step away. Two of the men catch hold of the light.

Nothing happens.

"Man, be careful! Somebody could have died!"

Surat looks at Iti in surprise.

"What happened?"

Iti is shaken. She looks at him, then at the iPad in her hand. She shakes her head.

"Nothing."

Iti finds herself seated between Surat, who is completely ignorant of the fact that someone – anyone – could not like him, and Kunal, who refuses to respond to his friendly small talk in anything else but monosyllables.

It is hot and stuffy, everything is dipped in red and every time Iti takes a break from eating, her forearm immediately sticks to the plastic table 'cloth' which has been put on the rickety plastic tables, presumably to create some sense of civility. Compared to the cramped tent where the rest of the crew takes their lunch, often in a hurry to free their chair up for another person who is already standing behind them, munching demonstratively into their ear, the HOD tent is well ventilated. It's been set up a little further away and there are comparatively less people who can breathe 'away' the oxygen. Two set fans are rotating at full speed on either side of the table, with the effect of a hot hair dryer rather than an air cooler. It's impossible to hear anything and she isn't in the mood for conversation, really. Where is Chinky?

"Man, this food is so oily, I feel transported right back to Agra."

"Hmm..."

"I thought in Mumbai everyone is so health conscious. I mean look at Iti, she's become so slim, she had to sew all her kurtas four inches in. From both sides!"

She regrets having done that.

"Aha!"

"Thanks, Surat"

"Did you know she stitches 'in her free time'?"

"You have free time?"

"No, no! I mean, yes, if you have more projects ... it's not like I am working 24/7."

"Do you need to work 24/7?"

"Who doesn't..."

"I am happy with nine to five. I love number games ... ha ha."

"I see."

"You must like numbers, too, right? Since producing is all about juggling numbers. Iti told me that."

"Hmh, lots of juggling. And now I'm going to jog back to set. Nice meeting you, Sujay."

Surat pushes his red plastic chair back, about to get up to shake hands, but Kunal gestures that his hands are dirty from the food. Halfway out of the chair, he looks at the buffet counter, then towards Iti: "Would you like some gulab jamun?" Surat has a twinkle in his eyes as he says these words.

Iti smiles back, politely. "No, I think I also have to head back."

"Alright, I'll see you at home then. I don't want to add to the things that you have to manage."

"Thank you, that is sweet of you."

"I know. And since I like sweets and you are not coming home with me, I'll take *two* gulab jamuns before leaving." He laughs and gives Iti a peck on the cheek.

When Iti reaches home way past midnight, Surat is still up.

"Were you waiting for me?"

"Yes, why not? I mean even though this isn't Agra, I'm always a bit worried when you are on your way home alone in the night. I know you are an independent woman, so I don't message you, but that doesn't mean that I don't worry. There are all kinds of people in this city – like other men from cities like Agra!"

Iti can manage a half smile. She had been looking forward to some very quiet alone time after a long quiet shower. Before she has to get up again in four hours...

"You really think the worst of your kind."

Surat shrugs.

She doesn't know what to do now. The realization from earlier today is still haunting her. It feels almost as if she cheated on him, or killed something that is dear to him. But no such thing happened, it is all in her head. Since coming to Mumbai she has been living by following her head and heart. Both seem to have weirdly aligned from the moment her feet touched Victoria Terminal. But now, almost three years later, they have clashed and are diverging into opposite directions at full speed...

"You look exhausted. Let me make you some tea."

Iti sits down on the couch. She feels the fabric. It's new – an expensive statement piece. Her understanding of 'expensive' will change over the years, but right now 22,000 rupees for a sofa feels a little unreasonable to her small-town mind. But how will she attract money if she does not create an environment which makes her feel rich? Surprisingly, Surat, who has been raised on similar values, did not even flinch when she explained this concept to him.

"I've been listening to your stories from Chinky so much, it almost feels like I've been living with her. I have full faith that this visualization thing is worth something, if you believe in it. After all, I visualized that one day I'll get a job in the city you love and poof ... here I am!"

Iti strokes the soft yellow velvet. Such a happy colour...

"Your chai."

It is yellow, too. Surat added turmeric to it. He looks down at her, lovingly, as she inhales the scent and takes her first sip. It's sweet, almost like haldi doodh with chai patti. Everything is fitting so well together. Iti feels the tears welling up inside her. Like the hot beverage has lifted the dam to a well of sadness. Surat looks at her in surprise.

"What's wrong?"

She wraps her arms around his waist. Tightly. She hugs him with all her might. And sobs. She can't control it, not the tears, not the sobbing, not her words, nor her feelings. He has always been her 'home' – and now she feels like running away from it. She feels helpless in her own body. Surat's muscles tense as he hugs her tighter, she lets him, holding onto that last straw of hope, something external that will make it all alright.

Can he fix this for her? Just like how he has been fixing things, her heart, her hopes and aspirations since she can remember? Something in her disengages from her 'self'. 'It' takes a step outside, and stares at her and Surat, frozen in what looks like a warm embrace.

But in this relationship, Surat is the fixer and Iti the destroyer, the beginning and the end...

"I don't love you, Surat. No, I don't mean that, I do love you ... but not enough. I can't be with you. It's not fair."

"You do ... what, what, what did you say, Iti?"

Surat stares at her, his expression genuinely confused. His ears may have heard her words, but his brain is refusing to comprehend them.

Is he going to make her repeat herself? That's not fair.

Iti looks down.

He shakes his head.

She waits.

They stare at each other, wordlessly.

He blinks first.

"I don't get it. You said you love me. So what is not enough? Love doesn't have a scale."

Iti shakes her head.

"Surat, you almost died today. That light was going to fall on you. And what did I do? I snatched my iPad out of your hand. You could have died!"

"Iti, that's stupid. I wasn't going to die. That light didn't even fall. Anyway..."

He tries to be sombre.

"If it bothers you so much, I forgive you. Next time don't let me die."

He moves forward to hug her. Iti backs away, gets up, looking down at her otherwise so tall boyfriend of more than a decade...

"You don't understand. You think it's a joke because nothing really happened. But what if it had? What if the house was on fire and I was saving my ... my shoes instead of you?"

"Iti, this conversation is ridiculous. If there is a fire I will be carrying you out, not letting you be inside looking for shoes."

Iti sits back down on the couch. She takes one of the grey cushions, places it on her lap. She stares at the linen fabric. From the corner of her eye she can see Surat about to reach out his hand towards her. Still, with her gaze fixed, she concentrates on playing with the yellow and silver tassels. They go out of focus – an abstract painting of yellow, silver and golden circles. She distracts herself by intently observing the circles merge and move. There's a small yellow dot on the bottom right, it grows, changing colour to something more ... golden? ... it sparkles, because just now it has merged with the big silver circle in the middle. The circle grows, consuming the little yellow dots on the bottom of her frame of vision, until everything is silver ... grey. The salty water in her eyes overflows, emptying out onto her cheeks. The tassels are back to being bundles of silken strings.

She looks up. And Surat is still Surat.

"You love me, Surat. I know you will always put me first, always be there for me. Hell, you sent me 50 per cent of your salary every month and I spent it buying clothes, partying, buying shoes. Even when I started earning I never even thought of giving anything back. You moved to Mumbai for me, but I would never move back to Agra for you. And this has always been our relationship. You give and I take ... it's not fair."

"But, Iti, that is just you. I don't mind it. I love doing things for you."

"I never even make you a cup of tea. You can do better than me, Surat."

Surat backs away. Now he is angry.

"Or is it because you think YOU can do better than me? Find some cool dude in Mumbai instead of a stupid small-town boy?" He gets up, her teacup in his hand.

"No, I'm not stupid. I know there is no one better in the world than somebody who loves you the way you love me. But you have to love them back and I just don't. And I don't want to do this to you or to myself."

Surat starts to cry. Iti moves towards him, his touch still gives her comfort. Comfort to break up with him. She feels sick to her stomach. Surat shoves her aside.

"No, thank you. I don't need your charity."

She gets up. Pacing. Helpless, she sits on the floor and cries, too. Surat is still standing, with the empty teacup in his hand. Neither makes any move to comfort the other.

Iti does not remember when or how she left. She sleepwalked here. It is all dark. Comfortingly dark, she hesitates to destroy the peace.

Eventually, she switches on the small table lamp next to the entrance – and startles.

The open cupboard is emitting a light, a glow. In front of it, Chinky sits still, like a statue frozen in time. It is eerie. Something pulls her closer. On her toes, Iti crosses the room and sits down next to her.

A bit disappointed, she notices that there is no magical fire, no fairy, no ghost of a dead grandmother. The cupboard is painted white from the inside, with glow-in-the-dark stars stuck all over it.

Iti can hear her own breath, it is that quiet in this house. As if Chinky has left and only the empty shell of her body remains. She has never seen Chinky so sombre. It breaks her already broken heart. She interrupts the sacred silence: "What happened? Where are all your clothes? Are you okay?"

Without asking for permission, scared that Chinky may be too weak to respond and also because this is what she had come for, she hugs her.

Chinky lets her. And, not at all her goddess self but like a fairy whose wings had been clipped in the cruellest way, she sobs on Iti's shoulder. For a long time. Over the years, Chinky has imbibed so much strength into Iti, now the time has come to give some of it back. The silence is palpable, a thick fog of black velvet enveloping the two girls into her coat of darkness. Where there is no light, time is irrelevant. Something inside of Iti remembers the comforting touch of her mother's hand on her hair when she heard about the car crash. She doesn't remember anything else, just the calming strokes of her gentle hand, moving from the top of her head to the middle of her back, in a steady rhythm. Iti always wondered where her mother had found the strength to comfort her in the darkest hour of her life. Now she knows. Giving comfort is perhaps the most comforting action the soul can receive.

When Iti's t-shirt is so wet that it won't dry Chinky's tears anymore, she lifts her head.

"She came, Iti. She was so angry with me. She said I had stolen her husband. But I never stole him, he always went back to her."

Chinky looks genuinely dazed.

"Who came?"

Then it strikes her. "Oh shit, was it Nitin's…"

"Yes, Nitin's wife. She was crying. She was so hurt, Iti, and so angry. But more than angry she was in so much pain. She took all my clothes and threw them out. She said I had used them to seduce her husband. I let her. I thought it would make her feel better. But it didn't help. She was still hurting. She was still hurting so much."

Iti does not know what to say.

Chinky disengages herself.

"Can I do anything for you? I can go and fetch some of my clothes for you."

Chinky shakes her head, tired.

"No, you don't have to go back. And it's still night. Let's just sleep."

"Will you be able to?"

"My body will … Your room is just as you left it, it was missing its resident."

"Four walls without a soul," Iti whispers, to herself.

Chinky smiles. Iti smiles, too.

"I have an early call time tomorrow."

Before Iti leaves, Chinky gives her a long hug. The kind people give as a welcome or a goodbye…

In the darkness of her own room, the brightness of the glow hurts Iti's eyes. She blinks, but no tears come to soothe her eyes. She squints as she types: 'Are you alright?'

Surat texts back: 'NO.'

She texts him again: 'Do you want to talk to me?'

Surat texts back: 'Never.'

She closes her eyes, hot tears streaming down her cheeks. They hurt. Her skin is irritated from the salty tears she has been shedding all day. A yearning for fresh air overwhelms her. She goes to the window and opens it, looking out and breathing in the sights, smells and sounds of Mumbai. A couple is just leaving the coffee shop opposite, dodging the dog at the entrance and lighting a shared cigarette right under her window. The nicotine mixes with the sweet smell of garbage rotting in the humidity of the salty air coming from the relentlessly breaking waves.

There's a hint of ghee and curry leaves in the air, too. Someone has already started making breakfast. Leaving the window open, she gets into bed.

The moonlight is falling on the floor and the edge of her bedside table. Enticing the title letters to reflect its silver light. It's her old M&B, the one she had spilled tea on.

A wry smile forms on Iti's lips as she picks it up and starts reading.

54

2018

The day is sweltering hot. *Thankfully the sun cannot bend its rays around corners.* Abhishek dabs the beads of perspiration on his forehead in relief. He is not sure if there has been any drop in temperature, but the long corridor, which the two genies on the board outside the entrance had referred to as a 'shop', is agreeably dark. The dim light, falling on the dusty, wooden furniture has a cooling effect on his brain, and by consequence his body.

The owner, a gentleman with a deep black scissor-cut beard, dressed in a white kurta pyjama, spots them as soon as they enter. Before Abhishek can even put his handkerchief back into his pocket, he has a glass of water in his hand. He inspects it, checking for spots of dust on the water's surface. The glass looks like it has just been removed from one of the cabinets around him. A sharply cut whiskey glass with an unexpected weight – a sudden fear of dropping the antiquity overcomes Abhishek. But it is promptly whiffed away by a strong wind blowing in his face. An equally old-fashioned fan has been placed right in front of him.

"Sir, your face is so red. Do you want to sit down? Chotu, quickly get a chair."

A couple of customers whose presence had been hidden by the obscurely shaped shadows turn to look in Abhishek's direction.

"I am fine." Abhishek turns his back, embarrassed. It never sits well with him to be the cynosure of so many eyes, unless he is courting their attention by doing something spectacular.

Why has he let Riyan drag him here? Why is he letting Riyan drag him anywhere?

"You look so cute with your hair blowing about in the wind." Riyan giggles. "Now all we need is a chiffon sari to drape you in."

Abhishek catches a glimpse of himself in one of the many mirrors on display. He has to admit, he does look rather 'beautiful', although dressing in a sari (or even joking about it) is where he draws a very strong line.

He turns around. His face is no longer red – and a *beautiful* man in distress cuts an entirely different picture, *more poignant than embarrassing. They may gaze upon him now.*

"Are you looking for anything specific or just looking around?"

A small boy with a giant smartphone hanging from a cord around his neck takes away Abhishek's glass.

"I am looking for a shoe rack," says Riyan. "But not too big, I just have four pairs."

The man's gaze turns south towards Riyan's feet, and at the rather threadbare but still somewhat good-looking moccasins.

"Well, quality over quantity I always say. Steve Madden is my favourite."

Riyan smiles at him. "Wow, you have a good eye."

"Yes, and a taste that is unfortunately a little out of my league." He grins at Riyan. "But luckily I work in a second-hand store. So many beautiful and valuable things find their way here accidentally."

"And I can see you guys take really good care of them."

Both men smile awkwardly at each other.

"I am Aladdin."

Of course you are. And you came here riding on a carpet.

"Riyan."

"Great to meet you, Riyan. It's a lovely name, what does it mean?"

Abhishek clears his throat. *Whose ego does he have to 'rub' to get some attention around here?*

"Salam Alaikum, good man. My name is Abhishek and I have been asked to get a box, by my flatmate, a girl. She would probably like something pretty. Or maybe the ugliest thing in your establishment, something that nobody else wants. I am not really sure. What's more is that she has not even told me what she wants it for, so I am not completely clear on the size. But I am sure you have an awful lot of choice, so could you please show us a few pieces which fit this description?"

Aladdin smiles with all of his twenty-eight very white teeth at Abhishek, not at all surprised by his lack of specificity. "We have all kinds of boxes in that corner. If you don't like anything there, we can make something for you."

"Oh no, she specifically said that she wanted something that has already filled a purpose or two and is ready to move on to the next one. The job she has in mind 'is not for a novice.'"

Now, Aladdin quirks an eyebrow at Abhishek.

"What she means is that she needs something second-hand, but she likes to make things sound more interesting than they are."

"Second-hand things are unique, they are not mass produced. You will never find the same piece again. They are interesting."

"That's exactly what I told him. He wanted me to order online! Look, he said I should get this."

Riyan has pulled out his phone. He shows Aladdin a picture of a perfectly acceptable shoe rack which even comes in two colours.

Aladdin shudders in mock horror.

"These online sites are a scam. You should see the things they keep. Totally disgusting, most of them are not even made of real wood. Like this one, it's just some bhoosa compressed together. Zero resale value, we don't even take it for free. Don't you listen to him."

Abhishek scowls, with every passing second the dislike he feels for this unprofessional salesman with his unsolicited opinions rises like the sand in an oriental hourglass.

"He just wants a shoe rack, not something glorious to store his diamond tiara in. And it does not need resale value, he is not planning to 'auction' it later. It just needs to be big enough to fit six pairs of shoes, pretty enough to blend with the rest of his furniture and cheap enough so that he can throw it away once he is done with it."

"Great attitude."

"I beg your pardon, what did you say?"

"I said, the boxes are over there. Please call me if you need something, I will be helping sir with finding a suitable shoe rack."

"Just take two slabs of wood and hammer them together, that's also a shoe rack," mutters Abhishek, making his way to the pile of boxes stacked on top of an admittedly nicely refurbished teakwood desk.

He is decidedly bad tempered as he stares helplessly at the stack of choice he is confronted with. This always happens: Whenever he tries to do something 'nice' for somebody, he suffers. It is proof that people do not deserve kindness. He should have never agreed to come with Riyan to help him look for a shoe rack. Then he would not have had to accidentally ask Riyan in front of Chinky where they were going to look for it and he would have not have been trapped into agreeing to pick up a box for her, since he was in the shop anyway. And most of all he should not have let Chinky talk Riyan into going to a second-hand shop in Behram Baug instead of doing what all civilized people do: Order a brand-new product online for their own use instead of looking for something to pass down to their grandchildren. *As if Riyan will ever have any grandchildren.*

And now, as a sign of gratitude, he has the displeasure of watching Riyan shamelessly flirt with a man who likes shoes he cannot afford, *how classy*. Sighing deeply, Abhishek pulls out a random box from top of the pile and turns it over in his hands. *Should he get this for Chinky?* It is rectangular, the mahogany nicely polished into a reddish brown. It looks almost new. *Would that be a problem? Does it not look old enough?*

Despite his aversion to dust, he decides to move all the boxes to the side until he has reached the far end of the desk. The last one, hidden from the light of day, is chipped and cracked everywhere. He opens and closes it. It 'works'. Somehow. In the scarce light reflected on one of the blind mirrors he can even make out a very faded, although still ghastly pattern of gold paisley along the etched border. Notwithstanding the craftsmanship this would have required, if it really is antique, it is a rather ugly thing. Everything about its construction and design is just wrong. And sadly it is not one of those things which has come to ugliness in its old age. No, this piece of dead tree has most likely been hideous all its life. He is feeling sorry for the poor box. Which is probably a sign that he should take it. To give it the chance of some purpose at last. Chinky is going to love it. Unless of course she believes that a box which has always been unattractive will not be as sad as a box which once used to be beautiful...

A glimmer in the corner distracts Abhishek's eyes. It is a box fashioned of silver with gold plating. In its heart is a hole covered with an intricate rose woven from a filigree wire with a bluish hue to it. True pity overcomes Abhishek. The gold has faded to a dull yellow and most of the silver is black. The blue rose, which must have once been magnificent in the richness of its colour and the sheer detail of its design, has now lost most of its petals. It is almost tragic in its degeneration. Perhaps a skilled hand could somehow patch it up? Alas, there is no way to replicate its former beauty with 'make-up'.

How can she not love this?

But what if she is looking for something conventionally pretty?

Abhishek has just discarded his twenty-fourth box when his eyes slide and stop at a hole in the wall. But wait, it is not a hole at all, rather the opposite. It has a form and shape, but in such a dark black that it refuses to reflect even the tiniest bit of light, hiding its contours completely. It is the deepest black he has ever seen. *So flawlessly black, it is a manifestation of non-existence.*

He pulls it out from under the boxes he is yet to look at, feeling its shape with his fingers where his eyes refuse to discern any.

It is not a box. It is a table. Well, not quite a table, one could not seat a family around it for a formal dinner, or keep it in the middle of a room as a holder for all the questionable showpieces one has received as presents from uninspired friends – and family. It is too small and its legs are too stubby for it to make a useful side table either. In fact as a table it is about as helpful as a stack of books on the floor, and yet it is perfect. It is the most perfect void he has ever stared into, but unlike a void where things go to die, this one seems to be alive with the ultimate meaninglessness of life. It is not just absorbing the light, it is also absorbing all the darkness into itself.

Of course that is a whole lot of gibberish. It is just a beautiful black table, without a single flaw. Most likely it is very expensive and that is why his mind has been cooking up all these thoughts — he just cannot escape his naturally exquisite taste. Now, what is the resale value on this, carpet boy?

He will figure out a use for it later.

"I'm done." Riyan taps his shoulder.

"Lovely. Where is your rack?"

"Aladdin is packing it up, he will have it delivered to my address."

"Yep, I'll give you a call before I come over."

He taps his phone, where he has just presumably stored Riyan's number and address.

"Did you find your box?"

Abhishek sighs, he stretches his hand out and picks up the first box his fingers touch. "Yes."

Then, bending his knees, he reaches down to lift his table, it feels surprisingly heavy in his arms. *What is it made of? All the darkness in the world. Shut up, Abhishek, real wood is heavy.*

"How much do I have to give you for this?"

Probably not the best way to expect a fair price, but he means it. He will pay what they want.

Aladdin's eyes run over him, taking in his 'worth'.

Of course he does not quote a fair price.

Riyan is sprawled on his bed, a little too comfortably. At least he does not take up much room. Abhishek looks away. Chinky is happily perched atop his new table.

"It is not a chair," Abhishek reminds her. She twirls around on it, kicking her legs up high. The golden fairy lights twinkling over her head make her look like a bronze doll atop a black pedestal in a music box.

Even the table top is blinking black and gold. Strange ... had it not refused to reflect any light when he examined it at the shop? Or maybe it is the effect of the polishing which Aladdin had done before wrapping it up.

"I feel like I'm on the dance floor of an underground cabaret." Chinky stands up on the table and shimmies expertly to the 1980s French music playing on a vinyl in the living room.

Riyan whistles.

Abhishek is aware of his mouth smiling at all the bonhomie happening in his room, even as he feels like a shy guest who has accidentally come to the wrong party. Tempted to go in but too scared to ring the bell, because whatever is happening inside sounds like fun but nothing like the fun he was expecting to have and so he has no idea how to enjoy it.

Nothing about this evening is feeling 'natural'.

For starters, he had been laughing way too much as Riyan and he had carried the table up three flights of stairs, panting.

"I cannot believe that your elevator chose this day to not work."

"Oh, it has been out of commission for about a week."

"Good lord! And you didn't think to tell me that before I agreed to help you carry this up?"

Abhishek had snickered, not feeling in the least bit guilty about his deception, maybe because he knew it wasn't needed. Riyan would have helped him anyway. In fact he had surprised himself by saying as much. It was completely tactless, bordering on shameless and totally unlike him.

Perhaps it was the relief at having finally reached the top of their 'mountain' that had made him so reckless with relief and loose with his words. Not that Riyan had been upset at all. He had exclaimed 'touché' and dropped the table just outside the door with the suggestion that Abhishek carry it the last two steps all by himself. Which he of course did not.

Once inside, both had collapsed on the floor, exhausted and laughing. It had taken Abhishek a few seconds to notice that the living room looked a little different. Nothing specific which he could put his finger on, but it looked like things had been moved about.

There were a few new additions to the decoration, items which were surely not there when he had left for his little excursion with Riyan and some things he had never really noticed before, but could still tell had gone missing.

For example, that flower vase, right in the middle of the settee. It even had flowers in it which look at least a day old and yet he could swear that before he had left the house, something completely different had rested on its spot. But what it was he could no longer say, the memory of it was blotted from his mind by the sheer perfection of the new object. The longer he stared at it, the harder it seemed to remember or imagine anything else in its place.

How does she do this sorcery?

"I've been cleaning," Chinky had said, looking down at them. A broom stick stuck between her legs, she had to use both her hands to put the mess of her hair back into the bandana, revealing big colourful glass earrings in each earlobe. A speck of dirt on her nose and dust cloth stuck under her belt completed her 'look'.

"You look like a gypsy!"

'Witch' would be more appropriate. But he was in a kind mood.

"Are you expecting company?"

"Always." Chinky had laughed, reaching down with her hand to pull them to their feet.

Once on his feet, Abhishek had noticed that a couple of paintings he had previously seen in the storeroom were now hanging on the walls.

"Why have you brought those out?"

"I felt that they might like to have something new to look at."

"You mean 'we' would like to have something new to look at?"

"No, Riyan, she meant what she said."

And Riyan had clapped his hands and exclaimed in delight, "You are so cute!"

Well, that is one way to describe it.

"Did you get the box?"

"Yes, I did."

Abhishek had fished inside his pocket and pulled out the embarrassingly small box.

When he had been at the shop, excited about his new table, it had not looked so tiny and blah. It was a box, just like she wanted, it was also perfectly square, just like a box should be, and to be honest he had not bothered to open it to look inside.

If he had, maybe he would have noticed the completely pointless mirror glued to the inside of its lids. *Why would anyone open a box to look at their face?* Just the mirror alone, with the glue still pointedly visible at the edges would have made this box tacky, and he would have put it back. But the joy over his own find had tainted his vision.

This box was not pretty, neither was it extraordinarily ugly, it was just … nothing. It certainly was not something you took money for and so he had declined her offer to pay, telling her that it was a present from him, which actually on reflection seemed worse – it wasn't something one gives as a present either.

But Chinky had held it in her hands and announced it to be 'perfect'.

"Perfect for what exactly?"

"For whatever its purpose is."

"And what purpose is that?"

"It will let me know."

Of course it will.

"But now, show what you have got hidden under all those newspapers."

As Riyan had helped him unwrap the table, Chinky had discovered a single drawer at the bottom. It had no handle and blended in so neatly with the rest of the table that it should have been quite impossible to spot. But of course Chinky did not need to 'see' things to know they were there. Riyan had shaken the table and declared that he could hear something rattling inside.

"If we find another box you can have it and throw this one in the trash."

"And what about what's inside the box?" Riyan had asked. "What if it's diamonds or scandalous love letters?"

The three of them had made a big production of taking the table to Abhishek's room and talking about how the loot would be divided. Even Chinky. Abhishek could not remember the last time he had seen her act so frivolous. But at the time he had been swept away, it had all happened so fast.

They had opened the drawer and discovered a string of used fairy lights inside.

Did they even have fairy lights in olden times?

"Oh, I guess Aladdin must have stored these here and forgotten about them. He is so absentminded. I can return these when he comes with my shoe rack."

"No, I paid for the whole table and everything inside. These belong to me now. He should not be so careless."

"What are you even going to do with these?"

"I am going to put them up."

Did Riyan wink at Chinky? Had he been subtly manipulated by him into decorating his room?

In any case, it was too late, now that he had committed. Quick as a flash the lights were put up and switched on and the entire room was transformed, the black top of the table serving as the perfect foil to the light bouncing about the walls, like a piece of night in *"The Thousand and One Nights,"* Riyan had cheekily added.

And now he is, in the middle of a fun evening with friends, having a good time and wondering when and how the other shoe is going to drop, because that is the thing with shoes, they always drop.

This lack of anxiety is unsettling. It is not 'normal' for him to go a whole two hours without his stomach clenched in tiny knots as he contemplates the next 'calamity'; a text which will not come, a call which will not be made, a call which will be made, a work meeting which will not go well, more evidence that his parents do not love him, or at the very least an earthquake which will leave him trapped under debris for at least a week as he dies slowly and painfully.

But today, his normally proactive mind is floundering about half-heartedly, like an amateur, with no concrete worry to latch onto and get consumed by. *What is he supposed to do with all this unoccupied mind space? Check Kartik's profile?* His hand inch towards the phone in his pocket...

Chinky nimbly jumps off from his table. "So what are you actually going to use it for?"

"A dance floor for you?"

"A breakfast tray? Or maybe something to keep your laptop on?"

Abhishek looks at Chinky, he grins. "Maybe it can be something new every day."

Chinky smiles at him.

A pleasant humming fills the place where anxiety and excitement used to battle for space.

He flicks the button on his phone to 'silent' and keeps it in his pocket. His now 'free' hands run through Riyan's hair.

At some point Chinky slips out of the room, humming softly to herself.

Abhishek can hear the music playing on the turntable outside. It continues playing long after Riyan has drifted off, snoring softly, and Abhishek lies there 'alone', yet not so alone at all, in his bedroom with his eyes open.

This evening is surprisingly relaxing in a way that's not making sense.

Just then, a thought forms in his mind, something which takes form in the quiet of the dark.

What demons is Chinky trying so hard not to listen to?

55

2011

When Iti wakes up after hardly three hours of slumber, her face puffy and with an itching inside her bones, she can tell that something is wrong. She rubs her dry eyes, the inside of her lids feel like sandpaper, and with every rub, glimpses of yesterday's events surface accompanied by bright white lightning. The iPad, Surat's frozen face sitting miles away across from her on the living-room floor, Chinky crying, an empty cupboard. How much can happen in one single day? No wonder she feels like something is wrong. But even as she brushes her teeth – using her finger and Chinky's ayurvedic clove toothpaste which makes the gums so wonderfully numb – and takes a shower in the seaside-themed bathroom, the feeling of something dark looms over her.

The house is empty. Chinky must have already left for her early shift. Since the time Iti has left to move in with Surat, Chinky's workload and popularity have increased considerably – just in time to make up for the lacking half of Iti's part of the rent. There was no question that Chinky will stay in this house which they had made their home – and the universe agreed.

Chai usually makes things alright, but there is no milk in the house and Iti is disappointed that she can find no comfort in the sombre emptiness of her old home. She misses breakfast with Chinky. The kitchen suddenly looks big and uninhabited. Dead? With no trace of human energy. Spick and span, the only shiny item of solace being the metal kettle on the stove. She switches on the gas and goes back into the dark hole of her slumber, standing. Luckily the kettle is alive and whistles her back to reality, its silver body burning red with anger from the bottom. The water is unnaturally hot. She fills it into the thermos, holding the string of the green teabags on the rim. The water burns her whole hand as it continues boiling and bubbling on the inside of the flask, its fury penetrating through the metal coating. Fully conscious, Iti does not withdraw her hand. She deserves the pain after all the misery she has caused to Surat. The teabags jump here and there, bumping against each other as they bleed their green colour into the boiling liquid. Chinky has taught her that green tea should only brew in a cosy temperature of 80 degrees Celsius, anything else is torture...

Eventually, when she can't stand it anymore, she yanks them out into the sink, closes her eyes and covers them with the paining palms. The kettle continues to whistle softly, letting out the last trail of steam, even though the gas has been switched off already a while ago.

The dark cloud follows Iti even as she sits in the cab, even as she enters the film set, even as she greets the familiar faces of a crew which isn't hers. She is hoping that Chinky will tell her more during her break. More importantly, she will make the cloud go away.

She can tell from the moment she opens the heavy, yet tiny door to the shooting floor that these hopes are going to come crashing down from the 100-foot ceiling like the chandelier in *Om Shanti Om*. The set is a mess. All sets are a mess. But this one seems to be particularly out of order. How...

"Thank goodness you are here! I was calling you."

Kunal doesn't even respond to her casual side hug. Instead, he shoves her back towards the entrance of the floor.

"My phone battery died, what happened?"

Without a word, he manoeuvres Iti into a dark corner, where a lone DIT guy is hiding behind stacks of hard drives, his puffy spectacled face illuminated by the cold blue of his computer screen. He throws them a knowing look.

Ignoring it, Kunal takes out his phone, opens YouTube ... *tarot tv, chinky, naked...*

"What are you searching for?"

He clicks on the first hit. More than fifty thousand views and barely uploaded two hours ago.

"Just see what Chinky did on LIVE TV."

The video shows Chinky in her usual transcendental outfit, on her throne, the trademark halo shining from the back. She is turning several tarot cards, then pauses, and stares into the camera. Iti can't hear properly what she is saying. Chinky gets up. Still staring straight into the camera, she unhooks her robe and lets it fall onto the floor. Then she takes a step towards the camera, pauses; takes another step, closer. Iti is expecting her to walk out of the screen at any moment. She kicks off her shoes, one step at a time.

"I can't read this forecast anymore. My energy feels tainted. Someone came to me yesterday. They were in pain, I could not help them. Their pain made them naked in front of me, while I was protected..."

The camera follows her. On the lowest step, in one swift move, Chinky pulls her black spaghetti top over her head, then her bra. Without a blink. Even closer. The camera has stopped moving. Chinky halts, too. Zoom out.

She has removed her skirt.

"Hiding behind my clothes and my ego. I owe it to them to be equally..."

A yell. The recording stops abruptly.

"Shit. Where is she?"

"I don't know. I reached there as soon as I got the call. But she had left. I don't know where she is. Her phone is switched off."

He throws his hands up helplessly.

"And look, already 50k views. How are so many people watching it? I don't think our show even had so many viewers but a girl gets naked and it's trending."

Iti pulls out her phone and starts calling.

12 p.m.

Gaikwad is alert.

"Do you know the name of this woman? Of the wife? She clearly had a grudge against the de … Miss Chinky."

Iti nods.

"Yes, but she had no *grudge* against Chinky. Chinky met her, she apologized. They met a few times after that. Nitin and she shifted to the US long ago. They were trying to rework their marriage. They seem quite happy. She is Facebook friends with Chinky, look."

Iti shows her phone. There are even some photos of Chinky's YouTube show on the woman's Facebook, with Chinky tagged on them and a comment: '*Listen to this advice. It will change your life.* <3'

Iti shakes her head.

"I could never have done something like this. But Chinky lived by her rules and somehow she convinced others to follow them, too."

"So how did you find her?"

Iti shakes her head.

"I didn't, because it was not for me to find her. She would come back when she found herself."

"Is that what you thought this time, too?"

"What time?"

"Yesterday. Before she died."

"No, I didn't even know she was missing this time. Our relationship wasn't so dependent anymore. No actually it was never dependent, which would imply that both people needed to speak with or be around each other to be happy? But I never felt like Chinky needed anybody outside of herself. Sometimes it felt like there were so many of her living inside her head that she had enough company already."

Iti smiles one of those smiles that one gives without being actually aware of it.

Gaikwad is too occupied with his desire to close this case and open the tiffin which Meenakshi has packed for him to see it.

Instead he pounces at her words.

"You mean she was schizophrenic?"

Iti's smile deepens.

"Oh no, nothing that could be so easily labelled. That was not her, but she wore so many hats and the things she did, I could never predict what she would do next. Like take me, for instance, I have one internal Iti that I listen to and after a point, I kind of know what she is going to say and feel about a certain thing. It is easy, it does not take long to know me. But with Chinky, it was as if she was receiving instruction from multiple Chinkies and I could never tell which one she was listening to at any time. I'm not sure there was even a finite number."

She picks up the photographs of her and Chinky, the background is washed out.

"But the first time she went missing, I felt like somebody had amputated a limb. And not one of those vestigial ones that you have no more use for. It creates this phantom pain so you know when the limb still sends out little stabs of pain to your brain to remind you that it used to exist and makes you miss it even though it no longer serves any purpose. What felt severed then was something as important as my hand. With it gone everything felt different and more difficult. Even buttoning up my dress was complicated and every second I wondered how I was going to negotiate the rest of the day with just one hand? More than anything, I just wanted my hand back. And so to answer your first question again, no I did not find her, but it wasn't because I did not look. I looked so hard, it seemed as if my body with its remaining one hand, two feet and a torso were all completely pointless and useless without the one part that was missing."

2011

It is late at night and dark, except for the light bouncing off the many sequins on Jhansi's dress. Jhansi's isn't the only shiny sparkly dress here either. All around Iti, who is what one can only describe as 'dressed down' in her monochrome grey sweatshirt over faded blue denims, are Jhansi's colleagues who are also family, who are also transvestites and who are also following her trade, the oldest in the world, dressed up in their sexiest best.

Iti is taken aback at the seemingly cheerful atmosphere amongst the prostitutes. And so is Jhansi – for other reasons: "Iti, do you realize you are killing the vibe of the entire street. You are bringing down everybody's price in those ugly grey baggies of yours! If you must stand here, at least dress properly."

"Jhansi!" Iti throws up her hands in exasperation. "How can you make jokes when Chinky is missing?"

Jhansi's trademark eyeroll and wave of hand are the answer to this obviously rhetorical question.

"Do you know that 'grey' isn't even a colour?"

"What?"

An eyebrow is raised.

"Listen, I'm very worried. Now tell me again, are you sure we have checked with all of her friends? Just think, is there any place she could be that we haven't looked?"

Jhansi fixes Iti with a steely eye. "Have you ever thought that maybe you are the one who is missing and she is exactly where she wants to be?"

"Why are you trying to speak like her?"

Jhansi is not the only one annoyed here.

The face with the steely eyes and its mouth move closer to Iti's ears, whispering with a hot breath that despite the warm night breeze sends shivers down Iti's spine. "Maybe because her spirit is communicating with me and trying to tell you to leave her the hell alone."

Iti is not amused, her eyes fill with tears. She blinks them back angrily. Jhansi's expression softens. She wipes away a tear that Iti was trying hard to not shed.

"Ok, baby doll. Do you have 1000 rupees?"

Iti nods.

"Give it and I am yours for the night. We will go home and talk about Chinky."

Iti is annoyed.

"You want to profit off looking for Chinky?"

"Look at me, love, do you think 1000 a night is a profit for this booty? What you are getting is highly subsidized Jhansi, but a working girl must have her principles, so no freebies. Now do you want to or not, or do I get into that car? I bet he will give me at least 10K an hour…"

Hands on her hips, Jhansi gestures towards the opposite side of the road. A big black, expensive-looking sedan has pulled up, the glass rolls down just enough for a hand, heavily bedecked with rings to beckon Jhansi towards its owner. Iti puts an arm around her and yells aggressively, "Fuck off, loser, she is mine for the night."

"Hey, be nice," whispers Jhansi, "I want him to come back tomorrow."

She flies a kiss towards the car as another prostitute walks over to it, swaying her hips and sticking her tongue out cheekily at Jhansi.

Iti pulls out her wallet and gives 5000 to Jhansi. "He won't come back tomorrow. You are mine for the rest of the week. The price is less because I am paying wholesale."

Jhansi laughs, she takes the money and stuffs it down her cleavage. "Happy to see your stingy little self is still well and undistracted. Also happy to see you are getting paid, I have heard such stories about production houses."

Despite herself, Iti smiles, too.

Jhansi takes her hand. "So your place or mine?"

Iti sighs. "I don't know. Where do you think Chinky would be?

"The beach?"

Iti looks at her sharply. "We have already been there, she wasn't."

"I didn't mean this beach, I just think that if she is anywhere it must be some beach somewhere."

"Should we go to Goa and look for her?"

"Don't you have a job?"

Iti looks down. "Yeah … But it doesn't feel the same without her there."

"Did you come here for a job or for Chinky?"

Silence.

"Come, let's go sit on the beach. Maybe she will be able to astrally reach your thick head and tell you to go to work."

The waves are gentle today. It is annoying Iti.

Is she the only one whose heart is in turmoil? Jhansi is sprawled out on the sand, making little sand angels and humming tunelessly to herself. Can nobody understand what she is going through?

With this question in her eyes, she looks towards the water moving leisurely towards her before gently receding without even touching her toes.

She looks at her phone, willing it to ring. It stays silent.

Iti checks the battery, it's over 70 per cent, that's a relief and also the new normal. Iti makes sure to keep her battery at over 50 per cent at all times now. *What if Chinky calls?*

But she never does.

Iti puts her phone away. It rings on cue. Iti immediately whips it in front of her face, even Jhansi sits up, her face hopeful. So she isn't really as flip about this whole thing as she has been pretending to be?

Iti stares at the name flashing on the screen. Surat. Her heart skips a beat. He hasn't spoken with her at all, since … true she hasn't called him either, but he has been on her mind. Of all those sleepless nights she has spent since Chinky has gone missing, her thoughts have strayed again and again to him as well. *If only she could speak with him and tell him how wretched she is feeling about Chinky …* and that is one of the reasons why she has not called him. Why isn't she more devastated about losing him? She just hopes that he is alright. But Surat does not deserve her 'pity'. He deserves to have her call and beg him to take her back. If she can't do that, what right does she have for her name to be flashing on his screen? She misses him, but just not enough. She thinks of him but not all the time. He was her best friend, her lover, her biggest champion and she has already learnt to live with his loss. What kind of an unfeeling monster is she? It takes Iti a second to realize that it is not Surat who is calling, the caller ID is actually flashing Surat's mom. Iti's heart pounds harder, is Surat okay? Why is his mother calling her? She suddenly feels her hands go cold. What if she takes the call and Surat's mother tells her...

"Iti, why are you staring at your phone like that? Who is it?"

Iti starts, her phone has stopped ringing. She has missed the call from Surat's mother. First she dumped her son and now she couldn't even be bothered to answer her call. She is a cold-hearted monster, really. Should she call back? She should. But her hands remain immobile. She can't. What will she say? How will she answer the questions and accusations of the woman who has cared for her since she was fourteen? How will she even begin to apologize for causing so much pain to the boy who always tried to shield her against any?

Tears flow down her cheeks as she hugs Jhansi.

"Where am I? I can't find myself anymore."

Jhansi hugs her back, tightly, she strokes her hair and gently places one palm over her heart.

"Stop searching for things that are not lost. Go back to where she left you, Iti, you will find yourself right there and so will she."

Where did Chinky leave her? Well, technically she was left sleeping on a bed in a house that was no longer hers after she had broken Surat's heart. So had she left her 'sleepless'? No, that's not true. She had actually slept. Slept while Surat had likely spent the night with both eyes wide open, unable to shut them even for a second in case they slip into a dream that no longer existed?

Iti touches that place where she assumes her heart is. It feels heavy and dark. Every day it seems to become fuller with the tears she is supposed to be shedding. But she feels no sadness, only anxiety and this sense of burden.

Has her heart broken, too, without her realizing it, and has the wound begun to fester? Is it the maggots which cause it to weigh so heavily?

Walking on the street, going who knows where, Iti has a sudden urge to lift her shirt and look. She slips in her hand and touches her skin. It feels smooth and soft, completely guilt free.

Out of the corner of her eye, she spots a moustachioed man turning around and staring at her hand that is moving about under her shirt. She quickly pulls it out.

She can't stop herself from checking her fingers for signs of blood. There's not even a drop. Then what is that thing inside that feels so raw and bruised.

Iti wants to sit down on the sidewalk and perhaps ask the people passing by, what is wrong with me?

In Agra, she thinks wryly, that would probably land her in the asylum but here in Mumbai, she might just get an answer.

Iti sits down on the pavement anyway, though she does not ask her question. A few people glance in her direction but most of them ignore her. It's just another troubled girl sitting on the pavement. The city does that to people. Two years later, there would be a boy who would sit there until he would become a man with his hair grown long and matted. He has still not found any answers but it seems like he is still searching, people have often heard him in conversation with himself. They ignore him just like they are ignoring Iti today.

In terms of physical space, calculates Iti, Chinky left her in 'their' house. The house they found together, but she has stayed there every single night waiting for Chinky to return and she hasn't, so that is the wrong place. Where then is the right place? Unless of course the place is not physical at all. Why would it be? When Chinky can access all seven astral planes and their castles made of sparkly stardust, when she can dance inside their swirling blackholes, touch dreams like tangible threads and maybe glide on moonbeams, why then would she settle for coming back to a plain old brick and mortar that anybody with two (or even one) eye can see?

Iti stifles back a sob, half imagining Chinky's body disintegrating into dust itself, sparkling briefly and then winking out of existence. A white feather floats in the distance, carried by a wind that Iti cannot feel. She stares at it, fascinated by its dance. What is it floating on when the day is so still? Not even a leaf or a glade of grass is moving. Iti holds out her hand. Didn't Chinky once say that feathers meant that angels were close? Did Chinky say it or did she read it on somebody's t-shirt? In just a few short years, of course, her mind would be editing the t-shirts to memes, but right now with social media still nascent, the balance of displaying witty quotes is skewed in favour of the tees.

The feather notices her outstretched hand and floats nimbly to the tip of her finger, and, quite naturally, attaches itself to it.

Iti stares at it, up close there is nothing angelic about it. It's just a feather that fell off a bird and is now glued with a sticky substance to her finger. It's even a little bit gross. Iti shakes her hand free, the feather gets the message, it floats off into another direction, perhaps looking for another finger to intercept its flight or fall to the ground. But Iti cannot be bothered to watch. Her sudden indifference to something she was revering just a second ago, before it made her finger feel 'icky', has suddenly snapped something into place for her.

Why does she keep looking for things to fill the spaces that are not empty? A sudden wave of melancholy brushes over her like a hundred feathers, making her shiver in revulsion. Why do all her 'flames' burn so bright only to extinguish so fast? Is that why she has been looking so hard for Chinky. Because she is scared that if she does not find her quickly enough she will learn to live without her too?

Iti gets up, catches her dishevelled reflection on the side of a car that zips past, all red, shiny and new. The gleam of metal and chrome stays in Iti's eyes long after the car has turned the corner. She wants a shiny new car, too. She has wanted one for months. She closes her eyes and imagines herself driving down Bandstand, her shiny new music system blasting (tastefully) the latest hits. No scratch that, old film songs ... "*yeh hai Bombay meri jaan*" ... the drive is at night and the moon is full and beautiful, hanging in the sky, pulled up by a string of stars. Her fingers tap the leather steering wheel, she drives until she reaches an old man selling tea and stops to buy a cup from him.

Iti smiles, momentarily cheered by the vision of a new dream intermingling with an old one.

"Manifest it," Chinky seems to whisper into her ear, and don't worry that it may get jaded – that's the thing with dreamers, they always find a new one to chase when the current one gets old or comes true.

"Isn't that exhausting?" Iti whispers back, to a leaf, a blade of grass, a speck of dust, a feather, whoever is her messenger to Chinky, maybe it is one of them, maybe, it is all of them. "When will I ever be content?"

A girl jogs past, sweating and huffing. Only in Mumbai would people be jogging at 2 p.m. in the middle of a busy street, completely oblivious to the people around, using whatever time they get in their quest for fitness or rather the perfect body. But it is not just the jogger who catches Iti's attention. The message on the black singlet plastered to her body is as loud as the techno music, blasting out from her cheap-quality headphones: *I will sleep when I'm dead.*

Iti laughs, the heavy mass of unshed tears in her chest evaporates a couple of drops. Not many, but enough for a little rainbow of hope to quickly slip into the now empty space. She looks up at the sky and whispers: "Got it, thank you, Chinky."

Iti hails a rickshaw. It is time to get back to work and trust that Chinky will be back. She has to be. And once she is, the two of them will go for a long drive in Iti's brand-new car. Iti can already feel the wind blowing her hair back as she expertly moves the steering. She is going fast, faster than she ever went on her scooty.

She leans back on the seat and shuts her eyes, just for a second.

She sleeps all the way to the production house.

She finds Kunal crying in his office. A sad little 2-BHK in Santacruz, the chipping paint on the fungal walls, so typical for Mumbai, is covered by dozens of posters of films and TV serials.

She passes the kitchenette with its cheap red veneer where two office boys are ogling over one smartphone. Remixes of Chinky's video have become a viral sensation. The door to the last room is half-open and behind the only piece of furniture – a desk which was probably stolen from some TV set by the looks of its cheap paint – Kunal is wailing in misery. Without knocking, she enters and hugs him.

"I can't believe she is just gone, Iti. I loved her, but that was before I met you. Thank goodness you are here."

Without any warning, he plants his lips on hers, tightening his arms around her slender waist. She pushes him away.

"I just broke up with my fiancé, my best friend is missing. I am just about holding myself together. I don't want to start anything with you that will make you feel you can unburden on me. I don't have the time. Please pull your shit together, we have a deadline."

The 'thud' of the file with her printed pitch deck dropping on his table is followed by the 'bang' of his door slammed shut, and the subsequent trickle of chipped paint hitting the floor.

She yanks the iron grill of the lift to close, putting an end to the monotonous operator announcement. Just then, her mother calls.

Iti lets out a sigh. She can hear the anxiety in the way the phone rings.

"Beta, come home for a few days. How will you manage it all alone? Surat … and then your best friend going missing. Work. Take a break."

Iti smiles into the phone.

"I'm fine, Mom, don't worry about me. I can handle myself, I'm a grown woman and … I am home."

12.15 p.m.

Suddenly the room seems brighter. The coconut tree outside is swaying heavily, one moment covering the window fully and then giving away a full view of the blue sky. An illusion. The small window only gives away a tiny portion of the large sky. Iti does not see the purple-grey clouds brooding in the north-west, approaching the city from the Arabian Sea. She only sees the sunlight dipping the room temporarily in a more saturated shade of brown.

It smells of food, she turns around, just in time to catch Gaikwad stuffing a piece of roti wrapped around some bright yellow-coloured cauliflower into his mouth. Feeling her eyes on his back – he's a cop after all – he quickly closes the tiffin box. Accompanied by a heavy sigh of disappointment that he did not have the chance to check the lowest compartment for gulab jamun. He bends down to retrieve the reason why he got up in the first place, before the shiny tiffin tower had distracted him. It is – surprise surprise – a brown box. Iti has a sudden revelation on why police work always takes forever: Things just merge into one big unattractive blob.

"Hmm. So coming back to Miss Chinky's belongings. There is something I want you to see."

Iti is delighted. "I am happy that you have paid attention to the details in my story. The key is always in the details – at least in a well-told story!"

Gaikwad grunts. He opens the box in front of Iti.

A small vial with sand, a plastic ziplock with what looks like hair and a small necklace with a pendant. Iti reaches for the sand.

"Don't touch. This is evidence."

"This?"

That comes out more condescending than intended. This interview is making her tired, she has lost her composure.

Unbeknownst to her, Gaikwad feels the same way. He does not want this lady to doubt the trustworthiness of the Mumbai

Police, but his self-defence mode reacts quicker than his hard-learned diplomacy can kick in.

"The department is shifting buildings – in the middle of monsoon, imagine! We don't have a lot of boxes to keep all the objects and probes."

The look in Iti's eyes tells him that this is not going in the right direction.

"But this case is important. So we keep only evidence of this one case in the box."

Iti stares at him blankly.

"I mean instead of putting different cases into the same box. It can create confusion."

"Yes, I understood that."

"Ah ok. Well fine then…"

"I just really wonder why I even pay taxes…"

The sub-inspector's eyes go blank.

"Never mind." She feels sorry for the man whose taxes get cut from his salary working for a job which is paid by the same taxes and yet it fizzles out somewhere in the process, leaving him poorer and with a job that sucks.

"What do you want to know?"

"Do you recognize this amulet?"

"I'm not sure. It looks like a nice thing to gift though…"

The clouds have reached the window, or maybe it is just the big frame of the overweight sub-inspector covering the only opening to the outside world. The atmosphere turns from its saturated brown into a gloomy grey which swallows all the light. Despite the dustiness of its surroundings, the small silver pendant reflects a ray of light. Where is the gleam coming from? Maybe some reflective surface? But she is unable to focus on the origin of the silver reflection.

"Do you think this could always have been in Miss Chinky's possession…?" Gaikwad consciously lets the sentence fade out.

Iti is mesmerized by the amulet. It is magical, just like Chinky. How does it shine like that without any source of light? Iti continues to stare at it. Lost in thought. The sub-inspector makes a note in his diary. Then decides to break her thoughts.

"Or would you know who has gifted this to her?"

"No idea." She really hasn't. It could be any of her many lovers. A thought that she politely keeps to herself. "Why do you ask?"

Gaikwad's stomach growls in response.

"Madam, I am the one asking questions here!" He speaks louder than necessary to drown out the noise.

"Sure, but I am just trying to understand why of all the things she owned, you are interested in this."

"This was the only thing she wore when she was found."

In horror, Iti pushes her chair back a little – far away from the potential murder weapon.

"What happened? Do you recall someone?"

All blood has left Iti's face. She can feel her lips go numb.

"Did someone strangle her with this?"

The shock in the eyes of the slight lady opposite Gaikwad seems genuine. Still, he wonders why she would have been staring at the amulet for so long. There is definitely something the matter with it. Did she hide a hint in her talkativeness? But to what? A murder? A suicide? A...

"Actually..." Iti fixes her gaze on her hands. "I don't want to know."

Her breath is as thin as her pale lips. "It's tough enough that she is gone, I don't need vivid nightmares to fill the void she left." Even her eyes have become thin slits, bleeding tears. With shaking hands, Iti opens her handbag. She rummages. For a very long time. Unsurprisingly – she is trying to keep it all inside, the pain, the fear, the guilt – her lashes are stopping the salty water from flowing out. Until the pressure of her tears collecting behind her lids becomes unbearable. She gives up. She sobs uncontrollably. Until the world becomes nothing but a blur. A bright orange blur.

"Madam…" Gaikwad is earnestly concerned that she might have a nervous breakdown any moment. "Tissue."

Sniffing her mucus up rather ungracefully, Iti lifts her head and grabs a paper tissue. Even the tissue box is a shade of brown, because orange is nothing more than an overly saturated version of this shitty colour.

Iti composes herself.

"Who could be so cruel?"

"No, no, madam. There are no strangulation marks on her body. She just wore the necklace."

He pulls out his phone, mumbling to himself in disbelief, "She wore *only* this," while swiping a few times. Then, just before turning the screen towards her, he catches something in her eyes, and puts the phone back into his pocket. He can't risk her having a breakdown. She is again staring – at what, he cannot say. He clears his throat, loudly. No reaction. Frozen, like a statue, his suspect does not move. Has she gone into shock? Shock … hmm … He lifts his body out of his chair with a loud screech, allowing the light of the brooding sky to dip the room in a weird shade of dark.

Iti blinks. A frown forms on her forehead – or maybe it's just a shadow … Gaikwad can't tell. He flicks the round black switch next to his tiffin box. The colour temperature of the room changes into tube light white. Iti shifts in her chair.

"Chotu, bring the blood report. And two plates."

The office boy scurries away.

Thunder.

The lightning goes unnoticed in the clinical brightness of the room. Inside the still figure at the table, thoughts are running wild towards the memories of another lightless day a few years ago…

2013

Iti enters the apartment and switches on the table lamp. But she didn't need to. It's not the only light which is on. The door to the bigger room is ajar, light streaming out into the hall. Iti squeals in delight. No, she is not dreaming! Chinky is right there, in the middle of her room, standing as if waiting for her with an unwashed, battered-looking white man by her side.

She runs into Chinky's arms and hugs her. And Chinky actually hugs her back.

"I'm so sorry. I should have said something but I didn't know myself that I was planning to leave, I was going to come home but then I just went to the station and got on the train … I even forgot my phone, somewhere, I don't know…"

12.30 p.m.

Iti blinks again. Several times. Gaikwad does not see it. The sub-inspector is preoccupied with the three savoury compartments on top of his tiffin box – just a few small bites until Chotu comes back.

He is back.

Gaikwad sighs. Defeated, he carefully places two sugar-soaked brown balls onto the paper plates, licks his fingers and takes the small stack of papers from the boy.

His heavy frame covers the window, Iti blinks.

"Madam..." He pushes a plate with one gulab jamun towards her.

Even the sweets are brown. Iti's mouth forms a smile.

"You know, last time ... She was back. Just like that. With him. She looked so happy, she acted so happy ... but if I could sense and talk in energies like her, I think I would have said her light was mixed with somebody else's now. They had exchanged energies and she didn't feel like Chinky anymore."

She tries to think of an image to better illustrate what she means.

"Like two bodies stuck together." By body fluids and sweat, she adds quietly to herself, recalling the exhaustion and dirt on Chinky's and Vincent's faces that night. "But they hadn't become 'one.'" Vincent's body was simply stuck on top of Chinky's by some mystical glue which made it impossible for her to be separate from him. The picture of her first night out dancing with Chinky comes to her mind. Chinky's body wrapped like a flame around that guy...

No, Iti shakes her head. That's not the right image. Because when they went out dancing with Vincent that night after their mysterious return, there were no flames – at least not of passion – and intertwined bodies.

"Vincent had broken the fluidity, the ease. And replaced it with anxiety."

But of course she wasn't able to pass this judgement at that point. It took years of pondering, watching and understanding the complexity of relationships in this city to even be able to identify and articulate such an urban feeling as 'anxiety'.

"My mother still dismisses it as a 'Western' invention." Iti shrugs. "Maybe it *is* an invention, but once something has been invented, it doesn't just go away again back to where it came from. I'm sure, Vincent never went back to where *he* came from..."

Gaikwad raises an eyebrow.

"Yes, maybe you should call him!"

Eager, Gaikwad pushes his notepad along with the pen across the table.

"You can write the full name and phone number here."

Iti takes out her phone, in-between five 'Vikrams' and as many varieties of 'Vineet', Iti finds Vincent's old number.

"Excuse me if I use my own pen." A streak of pink gel hits the crisp white page. She feels a little better.

The sub-inspector rises from his chair a little quicker than usual. "One minute."

Did she just notice a spring in the step of this obese policeman?

Well, of course if everything in life is brown and grey it takes just a tiny dab of colour to spark excitement...

For Vincent it was just the opposite. He couldn't handle the colours.

56

2013

It really was the weirdest night out with Chinky. A strange thing to think, considering that most outings with her roommate were sort of 'weird'.

She was so charged up as if she wanted to show Vincent everything that she loved about this city in just one night! She had come home. And it was obvious that she was craving its energy, its sleeplessness, its people.

Eventually they ended up at one of their favourite clubs. Chinky looked radiant, but also keyed up. She talked a lot that night, mostly asking Iti about what she had been up to. And hardly mentioning a word about who this Vincent was, where she had been, why she had never called and why she had come back. But then again, it's Chinky and Iti was excited at the prospect of finding out all the mysteries one by one over the next few days.

For now, the three of them are at the Mirage, on the dance floor, strobe light zooming past their faces – Chinky's toothy open laughter, her eyes half closed, Iti's hesitant smile, carefully observing the scene and Vincent's grumpy glare; Chinky's eyes open, hips swinging towards her man, Vincent forcing himself to a grin, Chinky twirling, her arms thrown up, Vincent bending down, Chinky giggling in anticipation, he whispers – or rather shouts – something into her ear, she cocks her head, pulling his hands, then lets go. Iti inches towards her, knees bent, faking some tacky belly-dancing moves. Before her disappearance this signature move was usually met by an even bolder, actual belly dance. But Chinky's eyes brush past Iti, she crosses the dance floor to the bar where Vincent lounges, disinterested, on a bar stool with two empty shot glasses in front of him and another one coming. She sees them arguing but can't hear what they are saying.

Iti dances on, moving her body unrhythmically to the blaring of the subwoofer. To the outsider's eye her relationship with dance music hasn't changed since she first set foot into that salsa club with Chinky. But they are wrong. She doesn't care anymore that her body isn't as gracefully merging with the beat; because her spirit is. She doesn't dance *for* anyone, she dances *with* the music. But tonight, her eyes are wide open and on them.

57

9.45 p.m.

The noise makes it impossible to hear one's own words. It's a disturbing concoction of sounds: the fan going on overdrive, the windows frames rattling and above all the gushing of the monsoon rain, horizontally slashing against the windows.

Vincent is looking troubled.

"I don't know why she brought me back with her. Her world was already sorted, what could I add to it? Maybe the amount of happiness in the world is finite, and the more she tried to give me, the more she was losing from herself. But she didn't care, she kept trying to give me everything even though I didn't want to take anything."

Sahil pushes a steel mug with water towards him across the table. He stares at the glass. The whirling fan is reflected on the water's surface.

He closes his eyes. Trying to process what he had just realized himself.

It was an accumulation of moments. The process of Chinky losing herself, and in the process he lost her, too – and his old self.

His head is pounding.

The rhythmic sound takes him right back to one of these dreadful nights. They had gone out dancing.

2013

Dancing without drugs is difficult for him. Dancing without drugs in a nightclub filled with strobe lights is next to impossible.

Dancing to Bollywood songs without drugs in a nightclub filled with strobe lights is just absurd. Chinky though seems to have missed this kind of music. Her slender body is moving rhythmically to the bass beats mixed with some Indian flute. He wonders how her tiny red dress doesn't slip up or down, sheer willpower seems to be keeping it just in place. And Chinky has enormous willpower. She has been trying to make him like this 'music' relentlessly for what felt like at least five hours. But he can't. Just cannot.

"I will sit this one out and just watch you."

"Watch me dance with other men? Are you sure that won't bother you?"

It won't bother him. He is too exhausted. He shakes his head, mustering a lopsided smile.

Chinky lets go of his hand, he plunges onto a bar stool. The AC draft is coming onto his neck. What a relief.

Chinky is dancing near the fog machine. She dances, but not like before. She keeps looking towards Vincent. He raises his waterglass. But after two songs, she comes back.

"You don't like it?" No he doesn't.

She looks him straight in the eye. This wasn't a rhetorical, polite question like he's been used to with his girlfriends in the past. With her he can be honest. She demands honesty.

"The music is a little too loud for me. I will go home, you come later."

Chinky shakes her head. "No way, I would prefer to be with you. Let's go."

"I don't want you to leave. You haven't been able to dance to this music for so long! You are happy here."

"I am happier with you."

Vincent takes her hand and pulls her close.

"Okay, then sit with me for a while, where I can look at you and make this noise and all these other people vanish."

The AC draft has moved onto his face, Chinky smells like wet earth. In a way it is the perfect moment...

58

10 p.m.

His eyes are watering, all the while he had not blinked, staring at the reflection of the fan as if hypnotized. Maybe it was the monsoon rain that triggered the memory.

Sahil puts his hand on Vincent's. "Sir, are you okay?"

The table vibrates.

"Meenakshi" zzt zzt ..."Meenakshi" zzt zzt ..."Meenakshi" ... The hostility emanating from Gaikwad's giant Samsung is palpable.

He clears his throat. "Haan, say." An avalanche of squeaks from the other side.

"And you are thinking of this now? Why is this so important? Yes I can see it's raining."

More squeaking.

"Then put a bucket under it. I'll call the tarp guy tomorrow. What will the landlord do? It's 10 p.m. alright, call him. Sure, call him!" The cop puts the phone down, exhaustion on his face.

"Wife. But you would know what I'm talking about."

"No, actually I don't." Vincent casts a piercing look at Gaikwad, one that is a mix of annoyance and indifference.

"Ah yes, you managed to get divorced." Gaikwad raises one eyebrow, funnelling all his domestic anger at Vincent in response.

Vincent does not react.

Zzt zzt. The gaze-standoff is interrupted by another call. Gaikwad grabs the phone so quickly, Vincent cannot see whether it is "Meenakshi" calling or someone else. The cop leaves the room.

Vincent stares out of the window. On the rusty grill a sad little tulsi plant is tossed back and forth by the thunderstorm.

Chinky had once told Vincent that this plant is divine. He never bothered to ask why. At that time, it hadn't mattered…

59

2013

The house had smelled just like the earth today. Moist, fertile, like summer rain.

There was soil everywhere on the ground. But he couldn't be bothered even thinking about cleaning it. Not after having lifted what felt like ten kilograms of dirt and five bags of various sizes full of clothes up three floors. But building a house requires effort. He had learnt this after his mother had turned their home into a guesthouse. That's why since then he has never harboured any ambition to make a home anywhere. But sitting on the windowsill, rolling a spliff, and watching his girl play with mud wasn't too bad actually. Chinky has taken off her t-shirt and converted it into a headscarf, making her look like a Russian babushka. Dressed only in hot pants and bra, she tiptoes with her muddy feet back and forth between the kitchen and bedroom, navigating in a slalom around a dozen different pots.

"See how happy my babies are in their new beds."

"Hmm…"

"I try to make my bed every morning. It makes me feel like I have accomplished something before the day has really begun. And at night, even if the day was challenging, I can at least look at my bed with the knowledge that I have my life under control. Now you can't of course make a plant's bed every morning – their rhythm is anyway different depending on what plant it is – but at least every few months we human caretakers can make the effort. Every real home needs a plant!"

"Yeah, but you already have so many, why did you have to buy more?"

On this point, Vincent agrees with Chinky's old roommate. Unannounced, she had just appeared out of nowhere to "help" them settle. Before the mud-invasion, Vincent didn't see any need for help to arrange his few belongings in a house that was already furnished.

It turns out, Chinky is excessively social.

But, now that she is here, she can help clean up the mess. And cook. It's her old kitchen after all.

"That's why we only bought one. We should have got a tulsi for your home, too." She arranges the fragrant green herb in a red pot on the window grill just next to Vincent. It wobbles a little on the unsteady iron.

"Did you know that it is considered divine?"

He puffs out a cloud of smoke, there's a twinkle in his eyes. "Yeah."

She smiles. "Yeah."

She kisses him on the lips. Her ex-roomie is obviously uncomfortable but the apartment is so small and with all the pots around there is no way for her to escape this lovey-dovey moment.

Iti picks up one of the paper bags next to Vincent. "You guys went shopping? Cool." She takes out one shirt after the other.

Vincent has used another bag as a backrest, but she doesn't care, she just pulls it out from behind him.

"What did you get for yourself, Chinky?"

"All of this." Vincent's remark is sarcastically pointing towards the piles of shirts now covering the only clean floor space left.

But Chinky is oblivious. "Yes, you did look handsome – just for me." She sits on his lap, wrapping her legs around his waist. "So I got myself all of this." Her finger is moving down his naked chest. She pulls his lip playfully between her teeth.

"Hi!"

Iti, who was still standing next to them, turns towards the door. Vincent pulls away. There's the sound of a key being stuffed inside a handbag. Never a moment alone. "Thank goodness we still had our clothes on." He is irritated.

60

1 p.m.

"He was in my home and he acted like I was the intruder. But I guess I should not have taken it personally. He is the kind of guy who decided from the moment he was born and opened his eyes for the first time that everybody else who breathed the same air as him in a 100-kilometre radius was an intruder. And our apartment ... well, you know how tiny apartments in Mumbai are."

Gaikwad snorts. Does he know?

Meenakshi never stops reminding him that she can hear him snoring all the way to the living room while she is watching TV. Gaikwad finds himself smiling smugly. Miss Iti looks confused. He forces his attention and expression back to the present.

"Sir!" Sahil barges in without a knock. "I have contacted this number," he covers the mouthpiece of his cell phone, "but the person at the other end is saying his name is 'Van Song.'"

Gaikwad does not respond. What is Sahil even saying?

"And when I asked him where Vincent was, he said 'purgatory or limbo' and then he asked me if that's actually the same place. Really strange guy."

Gaikwad glares at Sahil. "Check your phone, Sahil, what number have you called? Did you call up that Chinese restaurant by mistake because you were hungry, again?"

"Sir, that's Wun Jong. And please, sir, you know I feel uncomfortable when you say these racist things."

"Sahil, you feel uncomfortable when I sneeze without covering my mouth."

"It's pronounced Van Saun in French."

Two surprised faces are turned. "Huh?"

"Why?"

Iti shrugs. "It sounds sexier than Vincent. So what if the owner of the name is scraggly, unwashed and bad tempered, at least he can sell a name that sounds attractive. Maybe he wants to be less repulsive, now that Chinky is no longer there to ignore his flaws…"

She falters. Gaikwad takes the phone from Sahil's hand. He looks towards Iti, and decides against having a conversation in front of her.

He gets up and leaves with the phone.

61

Iti shuts her eyes, feeling a little pang of guilt at her unkindness. Even though Vincent got his wish: a world in which only he exists. All traces of beauty and colour that Chinky had forced on him, removed. Iti imagines him physically uprooting every single green plant, letting it wither in his hands before throwing it away, pushing at each tree until it falls and dissolves into the grey earth. All the flowers vanishing one by one until there is nothing for the butterflies to sit on, no reason for the birds to sing. They, too, fall to the ground in despair at the futility of their existence, as he wanders around in the arid desert of his mind, in his single-minded quest for misery.

Iti forces her mind out of the loop it has got into. She crushes the now empty cup of tea with its soggy teabag in a tight fist, until the remnants of the bile green liquid spill over her 35,000-rupee dress making it forever unwearable. She doesn't care. She has closets full of dresses, some with their price tags still on. She has no idea why she has bought most of them any more than she can understand why Vincent had left. She is reminded of a poem by William Blake which Chinky said Vincent liked to quote:

> Every night and every morn,
> some to misery are born.
> Every noon and every night,
> some are born to sweet delight.
> Some are born to sweet delight,
> some are born to 'endless night'.

It's a no-brainer which part of the day Vincent belongs to: it's not the one when the flowers first open their buds or when the dew is still fresh on the ground.

But what about Chinky? Whose endless night was she drawn to? How deep did she get in trying to 'see' the shapes and mysteries she imagined the shadows hid? What invisible wonders was she fooled into thinking she could uncover? Why did she never realize that the dark contained only more dark? Did she get lost searching for a beam of light, a sliver of colour? Or did she finally get seduced by a blackness so thick that...

Iti looks at the black landline phone placed like a relic on Gaikwad's desk. She reaches her hand tentatively, half expecting her fingers to sink into its faded blackness. The phone stays solid, perhaps its dusty cover has robbed it of its power? She rubs at the blackness with her fingers. Is she trying to touch some part of Chinky or is she trying to conjure her out like a genie? She rubs harder. Nothing happens. She does not even charm the phone into ringing. Is it even connected? Maybe she should pick it up and ask whoever lives on the other side of dead telephones to tell her when Chinky first got lost.

Was it when she met Vincent? Or was she already living in the dark while trying to envelop the world in a ring of light? Is that why she burnt out? Because the world was too dark and her light just wasn't enough? Or did everything end and begin that night? That night of Iti's sweet delight but maybe the one where the first star extinguished from Chinky's sky...?

62

2013

Iti is trying to discern whether the sparkle in Chinky's eyes is a sign of approval for how good Iti is looking or whether it is (again) the memory and future expectation of her doing unmentionable things with Vincent?

Chinky's flushed face makes Iti a little uneasy. She looks almost feverish in her excitement. Her face is red as if it's burning hot. Isn't a fever a sign of trying to flush out an infection?

Right on cue, the 'infection' wanders into the room. His eyes take her in. It's like no light bounces from her to enter his eyes. His face twists into a grimace. Maybe he is thinking how it's not bad enough that strangers are in Chinky's house, now they are even inside her clothes. Iti shivers although it is warm in the apartment. She had switched off the fan, so the powder she wanted to dab onto her cleavage wouldn't fly onto Chinky's dress and stain it. But she feels like she has already stained it, just by touching it. Vincent's eyes are blind to most things but can discern like an X-ray when anyone has laid hands upon Chinky's belongings.

Deliberately, Iti turns away as Chinky wraps her arms around Vincent and nuzzles her face into his waist. She looks at herself in the mirror, focusing on her face to avoid looking at what feels like a pantomime performance playing out in the background.

Vincent has his tongue shoved down Chinky's throat. If he is trying to make Iti uncomfortable he has succeeded. Not with the PDA, but with the bliss on Chinky's face as she returns Vincent's frenzied caresses.

It's not safe to love someone so much and to let them see it.

Iti bites her tongue to stop herself from uttering the words, she is frightened for Chinky even as a part of her wonders what it would be like to feel so much, to touch that pinnacle of ecstasy even for a second. To risk being obliterated just to feel so alive. Would she ever know? All her bright burning flames, all her twinkling joys feel as invisible as the million stars which are shamed into hiding by the brilliance of one magnificent sun.

Tears prick at her eyes, pooling into little drops on her bottom eyelid, making them shine. In a split second, she is distracted by the next shiny thing: Herself.

"I look so pretty," she breathes into the mirror.

Chinky disengages from Vincent and looks at Iti. The fever has turned her eyes into little pins, she is on the verge of delirium. Iti is frightened again. But a second later, Chinky seems to be back, she smiles her normal radiant 'Chinky smile' at Iti's reflection.

"I like what you have done with my dress. I would have never thought to wear it the other way round like this."

Iti grins and twirls for Chinky's benefit. "Thanks for letting me wear it. Though it makes sense the invitation is for YOU, so at least your clothes should go." Pleased with her own wittiness and her best friend's approval, she winks at herself in the mirror.

Vincent has wandered out, probably to the kitchen to get another beer, not that he ever pays for any of them, thinks Iti, feeling instantly ashamed of her uncharitable thought. When has Chinky ever begrudged her anything that she resents her boyfriend freeloading a couple of beers so much?

Chinky starts braiding Iti's hair into one thick side plait. It instantly adds years and sophistication to her face. Iti gazes at herself with such love, she is sure that she can actually feel her pupils dilating.

"Are you sure you don't want to come with me, Chinky? Won't those people feel bad?"

Chinky shakes her head.

"I don't even really remember them. I just did a very small part in the film because I needed the money for this bed and the universe sent it…"

She has a smirk on her face, probably thinking of all the things which took place on the said piece of furniture. "It's kind of them to send the invitation but it's not a personal invitation, it's work and network. No, I think it will be okay if you attend the big party instead of me." She smiles. But her eyes drift momentarily towards the door.

"Are you sure it's not because you know Vincent would not like to attend?"

Chinky doesn't reply. She has a question instead.

"Iti, do you think it's unfair to Vincent that I have given so many keys to people? He doesn't seem to resonate well with many energies. I think it upsets him."

Iti exhales. The knot in her stomach is back. Everything is changing. Of course Vincent does not like other energies or other people, why would he? When his own is filling up every corner of this house and Chinky's like a nefarious dark cloud.

Iti has a sudden vision of Chinky getting lost in the swirling smoke and debris that is Vincent. She reaches out and grabs Chinky's hand, holding it tight, assuring herself that she is still there. Is her touch as warm as she remembers? Why does her hand feel so clammy? Iti holds Chinky's hand with both of hers, unwilling to let go, trying to force life and heat back into her friend.

"Chinky, your beer is getting warm."

Chinky's hand goes limp in Iti's. She looks at her, Iti can see she is itching to go. Her eyes are sparkling again with a frantic light.

Iti reluctantly lets go of her hand.

"We will talk about this properly. When I'm back. I'll make some sinfully sweet and milky chai for you."

She runs her hands along the length of the silk fabric. It's sexy, almost as if these were someone else's hands wandering gently along her waist. The high neckline makes her collarbones and shoulders look a bit bony. She likes it. It also adds a few years to her otherwise young round face. Over the years she has learnt how to cover her flaws and highlight her favourite body parts. Lacking sufficient volume to fill up the original waterfall cleavage, she has crossed the thin straps across, letting her bare back take centre stage.

Chinky nods.

"You should keep my dress. It looks great on you."

So she too knows that it is contaminated and Vincent will not touch it again?

Iti's heart is heavy as she leaves the house. What else will Chinky give up for Vincent? He thinks the whole world is contaminated.

63

Where are the paparazzi? Is she at the right place? Iti looks at the blackboard, outside of the tiny, incongruous-looking bar, with the letters 'Train to Dharamshala – Success Party' scribbled on it with chalk. Unless this is the entrance to a secret railway station where there is an actual train leaving *successfully* for Dharamshala, the board seems to indicate that this must be the place where the film's success is being celebrated. But what kind of a film is celebrated without a gaggle of press waiting to click pictures of the guests? Iti checks her watch, it says 10.30 p.m. The party was to start at 9 p.m. For a filmy party that starts at 9 p.m., arriving at 10.30 p.m. should have ensured her arrival with perennially and stylishly late stars, but there is nobody here except a bored doorman who has just glanced in her direction and then looked away.

Should she wait for the famous people to arrive?

An autorickshaw pulls up outside. Two girls in tight black dresses get out. One of them checks her reflection on her phone. Pouts, clicks a selfie, while the other pays the driver. Both walk past Iti, nod at the doorman, who doesn't even bother asking to check the invites. He just opens the door and the girls walk in.

"Hey, check their invitations, they could be crashing the party, I don't recognize them," Iti tries to signal to the doorman. His eyes narrow suspiciously as he looks at her.

A song from the film that Iti has heard on the radio spills out through the open door, along with the sounds of people shouting and singing. A lot of people shouting! The bar doesn't look that big, what if the number of people that are to be allowed in is limited? Perhaps she would be better off waiting inside for the stars.

"Invitation please." The doorman stops Iti as she tries to walk in.

"Now you are doing your job, but don't worry, I have an invite." Iti hands him the invitation card.

The doorman snatches it from her and takes a long, hard look at it. Then he peers at her. "I am also an actor," he declares, handing her back the card.

Iti is confused. "So are you a part of this film? Are you still acting?"

The doorman sneers at her. "No way, have you seen the film? Everybody is so ugly. I have come to be a hero, not 'real people.'"

He emphasizes how strongly he feels about this by using his hands to make elaborate air quotes before ushering Iti in.

The long room is so packed full of bodies, it reminds Iti of her first time travelling by the Mumbai local. A second of panic and then the adrenaline kicks in. Iti knows how to navigate the local. This is what separates the true Mumbaikar from the transients. That magic ability to – no, not to be packed in like sardines in a tin can – what's so special about that, even dead sardines can manage it – follow the tiniest visible ray of light as it skirts around a seemingly impenetrable mass of humanity and finds in-between them, little threads of empty spaces to glide through and claim as its own.

Iti's eyes scan the room, picking out a spot to the left of the bar, where she can stand with a drink. But how to get to the bar? Again Iti's expert vision picks out the temporarily unfilled spaces within the crush of bodies, so tiny they are practically invisible to the naked eye till she maps out a path for moving in and out from one spot to another without stepping on enough toes to warrant an objection. Her feet follow the way lit out by her eyes all the way to the sea of black silhouettes jostling for their complimentary drink at the bar.

"A pint of beer, please," gets her almost instant service from the grateful bartender, who is busy mixing cocktails and straining his ears to hear requests for specific kinds of wines and hard liquor. It's how she had managed to buy the beautiful earrings she is wearing right now, from those gone-in-the-blink-of-an-eye vendors who step in and out of platforms, hawking their wares. You decide what you want before they get to you and be ready to announce your order in that tiny microsecond, that is all the time you get between their appearance and disappearance. There is no time to leisurely look at the wares and make up your mind. Unless you want to make your purchase tomorrow, but who knows what goodies tomorrow will bring.

"Wow, that was efficient. I have been waiting for fifteen minutes for my long island ice tea and you just got here and already have your drink. If only I was a pretty young girl too."

Iti wheels around to find herself staring into the slightly jowly face of a man with a receding hairline. His smile is pleasant enough for her to smile back. And a compliment is a compliment. Iti racks her mind for a witty reply that's clever enough to gain her another compliment.

"If the objective is to get drunk, a beer works as well as a long island ice tea and it's easier for the bartender."

"Oh, you young people. That's like saying, the objective of food is to just fill the stomach. Why then do we have caviar and petit fours."

Honestly she has no idea why. She doesn't even know what caviar or 'petty foor' is but she is not sure she likes being spoken to so condescendingly and having her wit dismissed so summarily. Who is this guy? If she doesn't know him, he is not famous, and if he is not famous, she has no reason to be nice to him.

"Maybe because old and rich people are so bored with life they even need their food to be expensive and entertaining," she replies, arching an eyebrow to emphasize the tartness of her words.

The man throws his head back and laughs. He has a nice laugh, Iti has to concede, albeit grudgingly. Though she has no idea why he would find her rudeness amusing.

"You are hilarious. So what do you do? You are pretty all right but you seem too smart to be an actor."

Iti gapes at him. How is she supposed to reply? Now that she has impressed him, she does not want him to lose his approval. A fan is a fan after all. What would Chinky say? But Chinky is an expert at evading questions about herself, she would say a lot without really saying anything and yet nobody she knows has more fans than Chinky. Iti lightly touches Chinky's dress, willing her leftover essence to enter her fingers and inspire her words. Her mind stays blank.

What would Chinky do?

"If you are asking for my resume, I have already sent over 200. To send number 201 at a party, I need to know where it's going. They charge me by the hour at the cafe."

The man's laughter rings out even louder than the music. His eyes are twinkling their approval as he grins at her. He pulls out his wallet and fishes out a card.

"Actually, I don't care what you do. If it's anything to do with films, anything at all, you come and meet me. I'll be looking for some new people in my crew for my next film, you are definitely hired."

He hands her the card. Iti reads the name. Umesh Chatterjee.

"I directed this film. And believe it or not, for my next one I even have a producer and a budget, so I will be able to pay my crew a token this time."

"Do you normally get people to work for you for free?"

"I don't like it but my talent has been more compelling than my budgets so far. And you know how hungry an artist's soul is. I make sure I feed that well."

Iti smiles at him. Words are no longer eluding her, she has never been shy of asking for her worth.

"I think my tongue deserves to know the taste of caviar eventually, so I will take my fee, not just a token."

"And what is it that you do that warrants a real fee?"

She holds out her hand. "Iti ... I'm a costume stylist."

Now it is Umesh's turn to quirk an eyebrow at her. "You know, I didn't have one in my last film, my actors were wearing their own clothes and that worked out just fine."

"Well, you have a producer now, how are you going to give them a costume budget if you are taking clothes from your actors?"

Umesh looks at her. She smiles, then looks away, focusing all her attention on her drink, while also casting a discreet yet blatant look around to check if there is anybody more interesting to lock her eyes with. It's instinctive. It's what she does when she is negotiating with the street vendors, it's how she lets them know that she doesn't really want what they are selling, but she will take it if they make it worth her while. But don't take too long, her eyes are already wandering. Sometimes they bite, sometimes they don't. It's a game they are both experts at.

But Umesh is either new at it, or he really wants to make this sale, or perhaps, as she will wonder later after she does his next three films and they form an enduring and real friendship, maybe he was the buyer and he already knew he was getting a bargain. After all, after that first time she has never again negotiated with him. She feels like she owes him that much for being the first to take a chance on her and to be fair, he is right about the artistic merit and the content of his films. They continue to feed her soul whose hunger is getting sharper after the hunger in her stomach has long been satiated – although not from fish eggs. He nods at Iti and tells her that he will see her at his office on Monday at 10 a.m. sharp.

"I like punctuality and respect for my time even more than I like presence of mind and wit."

Then he wanders away to speak with someone else. Iti gulps down her beer, her knees are shaking with excitement. She is so keyed up. Should she get another drink?

"Excuse me…" Iti looks into the face of Rahul, a barely recognizable TV actor. He is dithering on the outside of the wall of people circling the bar, asking her for access.

She steps aside, he smiles gratefully at her. "Thank you, senorita."

Iti puts her empty bottle on the bar. Yes, there is no way the night is going to get any better. It's time to go home.

64

She can't sleep. How will she? The lights at the coffee shop across the street are still on and her heart is racing as if she had been its customer all night. She stares out of the window. She is too excited to sleep. Visions are dancing in her head. Already, this house has started feeling too small. The street feels too plebeian. What would Chinky say if she told her that she was thinking that they should get a bigger place? Maybe a place with two toilets. One in each room. And perhaps a terrace. Do houses in Mumbai come with terraces? Obviously some must. A whole city of people could not be living enclosed in four tiny walls. Strange, she had never really minded the lack of space before. Iti feels a pang of disloyalty, this is her room. The first-ever room that was totally hers, doesn't she owe it more than to sit here and dream of another bigger room, somewhere else? Is she cheating on the room? Speaking of bigger things, it's not like she hasn't cheated similarly on Surat, a few times when they were...

Perhaps it's the headiness of the night, combined with the buzz of the hastily gulped beer but for once the memory of her disloyalty to Surat does not make her cringe or fill her with self-loathing. She finds herself chuckling as if sharing a private, slightly off-colour joke with herself. She wonders what Chinky would say if she told her that when it comes to 'cheating' she definitely has a 'type'. A pang nips at the heels of her amusement as habit makes her wonder how Surat would react if she told him the same.

The buzz evaporates a bit, regret jostles to fill the empty space. Will they ever share irreverent jokes again? Iti shoves the regret back before it makes a home in her mind. Maybe not, but as long as she can find things to joke about she will find someone to share them with. She does not doubt that.

But that someone will not be Surat. Regret, however, is really determined to get in. Iti's euphoria wears off a little more. Regret calls loneliness to join the party. Will she ever find a partner again? Finally, Iti's body starts to give in to the fatigue as a wave of sadness takes advantage of her momentarily lowered defences. It washes over her.

A sound, almost like a muted crash, outside her room, startles Iti. All thoughts and emotions are firmly shoved aside, as Iti moves away from the window and walks over to the door to open it. She peeps out into the dark, to see who or what has been moving about. But all is still and quiet now. Iti holds her breath. A few seconds of stillness convince her that there is nobody here. If they did have an intruder, he had left. Or maybe it was just Vincent rummaging around the fridge for more things to freeload. She glances towards Chinky's room, the door is open just a crack, but only a light grey lining hits the dark floor. No sound or movement to indicate somebody sitting in the dark, guzzling a can of beer. Stifling a mental giggle at the thought of Vincent doing just that, Iti slips back inside the room and shuts the door.

As she snuggles in bed and starts to drift away, a thought nags at the corners of her mind. Why would an intruder just leave? If he bothered to come in, wouldn't he take something? Before her consciousness can muster the strength to heave itself against the wave of pleasant dreams clamouring to be left in, the coffee shop's light is switched off. Now, her room is grey, too. Iti drifts away. She will find out in the morning what is gone. Hopefully it wouldn't be anything she would miss.

Maybe she should have hoped it wouldn't be something Chinky would miss either.

65

1.05 p.m.

Gaikwad walks in with a stride. The phone is no longer glued to his ear. He is holding it in his hand. He looks around. "Where is Sahil?"

Iti shrugs. If he is referring to that boyish-looking cop who was here, he must have wandered off.

Gaikwad sighs. "I have to do everything myself around here."

Iti sees him pull up a thick register from a drawer. He flips it open, hesitates, then looks at Iti. "Do you spell it Vincent or…"

"Vincent will do."

Gaikwad looks at the clock, he seems to be calculating something. Then he sighs again. Out of the corner of her eye Iti sees him scribble 8 p.m., next to Vincent's name, which has been misspelled Vinsent.

Vincent would not like that, thinks Iti wryly, in fact he would like none of it. She doesn't care. It's time he learnt that his cherished freedom is nothing more than an illusion he is hanging on to by a thin thread. And what better place to learn that than at a police station? He is welcome. Iti chuckles softly.

66

2013

Chinky bends down, unties her laces, and neatly places her green wedge sandals next to her chair. She then proceeds to take off her bangles, their glitter throwing rainbow-coloured patterns against the wall as they catch the sunlight. From the side table, she removes the tiny Turkish coffee cup and its floral saucer. Is she going to read into the future now? Iti has seen her do it before. You have to flip the empty coffee cup onto the saucer and then wait for the grounds to dry. An arduous wait! Turkish coffee is so strong that the one time when she asked Chinky to read *her* coffee grounds, she didn't manage to come to the point where the future is actually revealed. Her heart was racing uncontrollably. Add to that the excitement of the impending revelation of the future and it becomes impossible to sit still. Luckily the cup didn't break, but the saucer suffered a hairline crack.

Chinky makes no effort to get up and make coffee, instead she places her bangles on the saucer. Inside the tiny coffee cup, she drops her rings and earrings. Iti cannot decide whether to be confused or intrigued. But she does not dare to interrupt Chinky in whatever it is that she is doing. She proceeds to unbutton her blouse with the solemn expression of a nun putting on her veil. She takes off her bra. Iti tries to look elsewhere. It is a different matter to see half-naked people all day when you know that they are just in-between costume changes and can be sure that they will be covered properly again in a matter of seconds. Chinky makes no effort to cover her breasts. Instead, she goes on to unzip her skirt. Iti cannot sit still any longer.

"Why are you removing your clothes?"

"I want to tell the world what I've learnt about love. But I can't do it with clothes. I have to be completely vulnerable if I am to speak the truth … and if they are to trust me."

She can't believe her eyes. But Chinky's expression and a vivid memory of her astrology TV episode leave no doubt that she means it. Completely absorbed in the earnestness of her ritual, Chinky does not notice when Iti slips out of the room. She already has her hand on the door handle, when she pauses to listen to what would be Chinky's first words of her first viral video message.

"Hello world, this is Chinky, your resident witch. Today I have decided that it is time to bewitch myself. But it's a spell that will work for everyone. So follow me to finally find equanimity and self-love. For bliss is at home in a house made of those two. Maybe you think love is at home inside an orgasm and self-love means bubble baths. And that is true. But you know deep down that's not all."

67

11 p.m.

"It's not possible to be in a relationship with someone who loves some superior version of you that doesn't exist. It's like being cheated on constantly, with your own self."

Only with great difficulty does Vincent manage to mask his emotions. This third-rate cop is not going to bring him to his knees. He feels his stare on his face. Vincent keeps his eyes locked to the screen. The minion cop does the same. Are these tears rolling down his cheeks? That's probably how he should have reacted right when they called him. Then he wouldn't have to sit here still. It's almost midnight. How many samosas can this cop eat? This video is a lot to stomach. He feels like calling his doctor, or running straight back to the rehab. Damn just when he thought he could get through with it, all by himself. Is he even capable of doing anything by himself? Will he ever be? Of course, it was he who divorced Chinky, but he knew that he will never truly lose her. But now he had. Or maybe not. This is just too real. He suppresses the urge to touch the screen.

"You need to heal your own broken heart." The naked figure on the display seems to be talking to him, and only him. "So you can once again hold love for the person who broke it. Don't lose this love. They need it." *How did she know this?*

"I saw this a week after I left. She wasn't even angry. She was never angry. She continued to love me. There was no escaping it. I waited and waited to hear at least one message that made it clear that she was done. That she hated me now. So I could be free. Her love had me trapped even when I wasn't there."

Gaikwad raises an eyebrow towards Sahil.

"And now do you feel free?"

Vincent raises an eyebrow right back.

"I used to think one day I would ask her and she would grant me my freedom. Who should I ask now?"

68

2019

The party is loud but for reasons incomprehensible to Abhishek, some people seem to be having fun. He nurses his drink, a bright pink cocktail which somebody handed him as soon as he stepped through the door. One sip was all it took to confirm that it tasted as on the nose 'gay' as it looks. The Delhi slur of *meetha* pops unbidden in his mind. He pushes it away and takes in the ambience of the place: Psychedelic lights dancing everywhere, bouncing off an overabundance of bare skin, lighting it in pink, blue, green.

You would be excused for thinking you had stepped into a girl's college hostel party, thinks Abhishek unkindly, looking around at scantily clad men, dancing to '*Sheila ki Jawani*' with moves that would make the real Sheila leave the dance floor and just watch in awe. Disgust would be a better word for what Abhishek is feeling, though. *This is so not his scene.*

A tiny person, all lit up in blue like a Smurf, gyrates towards Abhishek, swaying suggestively, twirling his fingers with their blue painted nails in a clear invitation to dance.

"I have come with company."

He may be a dwarf, but no reason not to be polite. Unfortunately, the music and the party are both too loud for politeness to be audible. The Smurf who is now puke green has turned his back to Abhishek and is shaking his backside rather aggressively near Abhishek's crotch.

Some might find it sexy, but not Abhishek. He hastily escapes from there and makes a beeline for the closest couch he can find. He scans the room for Riyan who had upon their arrival whispered into his ear, "I've to go to the ladies' room," and then disappeared. He is annoyed at how long Riyan is taking. Even the Sheilas have turned into *Badnam munnis* but Riyan has still not returned. *Maybe he climbed out of the bathroom window to escape this horror show.*

A tall man, with blond-streaked hair – which instead of giving his countenance the desired youthfulness, has a rather unflattering effect on his deeply creased face – stilts over to Abhishek and holds out his hand. *Is he expected to kiss it?*

"Hi, my name is Shamun, I'm the birthday boy, hope you are enjoying my party."

Abhishek is mortified. "I had no idea it was a birthday party! I ought to have brought something."

"Ooh no, I was under the impression, somebody brought 'you.'"

"Hands off, Shamun, I brought a real present."

Abhishek looks at his date. No wonder it took him so long.

It appears that a glitter bomb exploded in the washroom where Riyan selflessly stayed back to evacuate all the survivors, died, and came back a zombie covered in the debris of the explosion. His eyes are lined so black that Abhishek can barely see them at all, even though they should be in sharp contrast to the white paste covering the skin of his face.

Shamun runs an appreciative eye over the impossibly tight and tiny shorts that Riyan has somehow managed to squeeze into.

"Don't worry about it, darling. I was just being polite – what would I do with this one? He even sits like a ... Now, you on the other hand..."

Riyan grins, not at all put off. He gives Shamun a quick peck on the lips – "Just because it's your birthday" – before handing him a brightly coloured box with a big bow on top.

Exclaiming gleefully like a child, Shamun rips off the wrapping paper and pulls out his present.

Abhishek can hear him thanking Riyan, but he does not get to see what the present is. He has been distracted by the sight of another tall man, with a stubble and man bun, walking into the party in a tee so tight Abhishek's breath stops midway in his throat. In fact, he cannot hear anything anymore – anything but his hammering heart.

He has not seen Kartik since he had tried to call him up 'that' night. In a daze, Abhishek had almost considered going to his house. He had even showered, gently, in a lukewarm drizzle, and changed his clothes, into his comfortable black pyjamas. He had even walked out of the building, but then his feet had stopped. He was simply glued to the spot. The city had been full of lights but on 'that' day, all his eyes could seek out and fixate on were the shadows hidden within the creases of the bright lights. Together those shadows had congealed and collected into one dense, impenetrable blob. No, it had been impossible. Abhishek could not leave the safety of his building. He did not want to go out. He had turned around and gone back home and waited for the smell of cinnamon and coffee to fill up the room.

Kartik spots him almost immediately and throws him a I'll-get-back-to-you smile, before speaking with Shamun first. "Look at you, all grown up, how old have you turned today?" Kartik envelops Shamun in a big hug.

Shamun dissolves into giggles and answers archly, "Twenty-six, babe."

"Wow! You are younger than me now, I'll have to find another sugar daddy."

As Shamun chuckles and banters with him, Kartik nudges Abhishek. "How are you doing, Abhi? Haven't seen you in ages."

That gets Shamun's attention.

"Who *is* this mystery man? He seems to know all my favourite boys and looks just like my next one."

He graces Abhishek with an appraising look. Abhishek is ready to walk out of this conversation, but Kartik has put an arm around his shoulder. "He's not your type. He's nice and he has his own money."

Abhishek can feel his insides quivering, a torrent of words bubbling inside his stomach, ready to rush out of his mouth. All he wants to do is to tell Kartik how happy he is to see him. And to apologize for not keeping in touch and to…

"Heyyy, look at you, hottie." Kartik removes his arm from Abhishek's shoulder and walks over to where a woman is dancing with a group of guys.

The girl squeals in delight as she hugs him, practically dragging him into the group.

Abhishek had no idea Kartik could move like that. So graceful, so sexy and so uninhibited. More than a few eyes are turned admiringly in his direction. He loves it, he is putting on a show, dancing for all of them, his adoring public. The whole party seems to be celebrating just him.

All, except one.

Abhishek does not even have to turn around to know that Riyan would not be looking at Kartik – he is looking at him. He can feel his gaze. It is not penetrating, not possessive. What is it like? *Like an elegant, thin veil of genuine affection.* The voice inside Abhishek makes several efforts, in the time that he stands frozen in the middle of this strange room, to tell him just that, but it is drowned out each time by the wild hooting of the crowd.

Kartik gestures impatiently in his direction. "Hey, Abhi, don't stand there gawking like a wallflower, come make some friends."

I do not have any friends.

"That's because you don't even want to be your own friend. You find nothing likeable about yourself."

Again, his inner voice speaking in Chinky's tongue. Chinky's honesty has hurt Abhishek yet again. He is surprised that he still feels anything when she insults him like that, his heart and ego should be numb from the million stings of 'insights' that she pokes into them in a day.

"How do you expect anyone else to like you, if you cannot?"

"What? People like me! Only that in comparison to you, who hands a key to her house and god knows what else, to every Tom, Dick and Harry, my standards for friendship are simply higher."

"Maybe these lofty standards of yours should come down to earth, unless you want to date only dead people."

"Why would I date dead people? That is not even possible."

"Because they reside in heaven. And of course, it is possible! My friend is in a very happy and fulfilling marriage with a dead pirate."

"Exactly my point. I do not wish to have such friends."

"Although thinking about it … a pirate probably does not have very lofty standards either…" And thus, she had waltzed off to make yet another video – or maybe talk to her imaginary friend.

Tearing his eyes away from Kartik, Abhishek takes Riyan's hand and pulls him to the dance floor. He has always found being part of a crowd suffocating and claustrophobic. His eyes keep darting in Kartik's direction but the rest of him stays firmly by Riyan's side, all night.

69

Abhishek is no late-night party person. He is one of the few people who, although voicing his shared outrage at the lack of options for somebody who wants to dance all night like a braindead zombie, is secretly happy that most pubs and clubs in the capital and even in Mumbai have a 1 a.m. cut off time. He is the kind of person who agrees to go for an after-party with his friends and then quietly slips home, pretending to everyone the next day that he was actually there but they were all too drunk to remember.

So even though the party shows no signs of abating even at 2 a.m., Abhishek is well past his bedtime and more than a little buzzed. It is also possible there has been some 'hotboxing' in this poorly ventilated and thick with smoke room, which would explain the lightness in his head and also a complete lack of social restrain as he leaves the living room and wanders brazenly about the house of the host in search of a bedroom to pass out in.

He pushes open a semi-open door. *Eureka, a bed!* The colonial beauty, similar to the one his grandmother breathed her last in, right in the centre. Abhishek sets one foot in front of the other heading as straight as he can towards the goal but alas – it is occupied! And naturally not with someone sleeping. That is annoying. Abhishek is dimly aware of his voice asking the 'occupants' if they can carry on their activities somewhere else, like the floor or the kitchen or even the lawn, maybe? Have people lost all sense of romance? And should not a sleepy person be worthy of the bed?

One of the boys laughs and holds out his hand, asking him if he would like to join.

Abhishek is tempted, the bed is so soft and inviting, maybe he could just slide in there, at that spot in the middle and fall asleep? They could carry on doing their thing around him.

Somebody laughs again. *Has he spoken aloud?*

There is a hand on his shoulder. "Hey Cinderella, come, let's get you home?"

Kartik has come to rescue him again. Although he looks different with his hair cropped short and his cheekbones shiny with glitter. Abhishek reaches out a finger and touches him, it looks sharp enough to cut his skin. Strange how he has never noticed before. It must have been because of the stubble. Why has Kartik shaved it off in the middle of the party? Never mind, he is still beautiful. Abhishek takes Kartik's hand and lets him lead him out of there.

Rain is falling, but not like rain is supposed to fall, with the rhythmic pitter-patter of gentle raindrops. This rain is made up of a million raindrops all fused together, breaking at once over his head like water from a hundred buckets. The chilly Lonavala air hits his face hard, waking him from his stupor long enough to see that his hand is holding onto Riyan's hand.

How did Kartik turn into Riyan?

Abhishek shakes his head violently, trying to make him turn back into Kartik.

"Come," says Riyan gently, "I have managed a lift back to Mumbai."

70

Two hours later, Abhishek is wide awake. The girl who is driving them back, the one who had been dancing earlier with Kartik, does not seem to know how to use the break or maybe that is just yet another part which has gone missing in the vehicle, along with the left taillight.

The ten-year-old blue Chevrolet Spark shakes so violently each time the speedometer crosses 120 that Abhishek is forced to shut his eyes, in anticipation of the car disintegrating, each piece flying off in a different direction all over the highway, commencing with the door next to him.

He can hear Riyan and whoever is sitting next to the girl chatting animatedly, completely unconcerned that they are all obviously hurtling towards death any second now. His eyes and mouth both remain squeezed shut, in abject terror until he hears Riyan say, "Alright, we shall get off here."

Get off here? How? Are they supposed to jump out of this accursed rocket?

"Abhishek?"

Very, very reluctantly, Abhishek opens his eyes and looks around. The ground is still, the car is still moving but everything around him seems to be stationary.

He watches Riyan get out of the car and hold the door open for him. He holds out his hand. Abhishek grabs it like one would hold onto the last straw in the eye of impending death. But the straw is surprisingly strong. He steps out gingerly. His legs are still trembling but at least he is on them now instead of in that metal death trap.

As the girl says bye, puts her car in gear and zips away, Abhishek hugs Riyan in relief. "Goddam! I was so bloody certain that she was going to kill us. Why was she going so fast?"

"She said she needed to go to the loo."

Abhishek collapses into giggles. "I think I might have gone a little in her car."

Now Riyan is giggling too.

They are both still whispering and laughing as Abhishek turns the key in the lock and pushes it open.

Both stop short, Chinky is sitting on the couch, in semi-darkness, so dazed and lost, she does not even register their presence.

The last bit of 'buzz' evaporates from Abhishek as he looks at her.

Riyan immediately rushes to her side and takes her hand. "Are you okay, darling?"

A tall, blonde and rather handsome gold-locked man saunters into the room. He stops. And stares at them with his bright blue eyes.

Abhishek and Riyan stare back.

Some part of Chinky seems to re-enter her body.

"This is Vincent. He is my husband. He has come to ask me for a divorce. Can I get you guys something to eat?"

Yet, she keeps sitting.

Vincent holds out his hand. Abhishek takes it, hoping briefly that he has not actually died and this latest addition to Chinky's stable of craziness is not a part of his own, dressed up as bizarro land, hell.

71

1.15 p.m.

The spongy sweetness trickles down her throat. Damn, she has missed sugar. It's so yum, she is willing to forget its brown colour. Instead, she remembers the sweet innocence of the past when she had sugar all day long and believed in marrying her best friend.

"So why did your friendship decline?"

Hadn't she tried to explain this to him hours ago?

"With Miss Chinky, I mean."

"Oh. But it didn't!" Iti protests. "I just didn't meet her so much after Vincent left. I had to leave on an outstation shoot. I told her I would stay with her but she said no. Said it was her journey and my being there would not let her complete it. So I left and then I left again. I spoke to her sometimes, even met her a couple of times and she seemed happy again, Chinky again ... and finally I took my own place ... I felt I was ready and..." Iti falters a bit. "I love Chinky and I loved living with her, but I finally wanted a place to which only I had the key. Others are welcome to visit of course ... anyway, she never took my key back. I should have visited more often, I should have. I didn't even know that Vincent was back..."

Gaikwad snorts deprecatingly and makes a note.

72

2019

The mirror on the blue wall is reflecting Vincent's face as he speaks to his ex-wife. It's unsettling. To see himself talk. He is vain, admittedly. But watching himself look down at Chinky is like a visual affirmation of what their relationship must have looked like to people outside of it. While in reality he felt exactly the opposite. She is so much grander than him...

"Why should you not stay in your own room, Chinky? I can stay in a hotel."

Vincent picks up his towel and puts it back into his bag. He had intended to just take a shower and then lie down on the mattress in the living room. The only bathroom in the flat is attached to Chinky's room. Just entering this space where they had spent so many wild, and also quiet, nights made him tremble internally. Funny how no one ever assumes that a 'proper' Germanic-looking man can experience internal tremor. No one except for Chinky...

"I want you to stay here ... it will help when you are gone."

Help whom? Him? Or Her? She needs no help! She just needs to let go of him. So that she can be back to her magnificent, frightening, radiating former self. The one he fell in love with.

"Where are you going to go?"

"I don't know. But I just don't want to stay here anymore. Maybe I want to go back to my mother's old hometown, Charleville. To France. Maybe I will find..." He spreads his hands helplessly. "I can't say I will find any peace but maybe I need a new place to be angry with."

"Love is not finite, Vincent, but anger is. One day it will finish."

"Don't wait for me, please. I don't want to know that you are here, waiting. I want to be free."

"But I have never ever been the one to cage you ... or you me."

She kisses him on the forehead. It burns. Or is it cooling? Two sensations so close to each other. Like ecstasy and agony.

Then, Chinky leaves the room.

He can hear her speaking with Abhishek, asking if she can sleep there.

He sits down on the bed, stroking the deep-blue linen bedsheet. His fingers follow the individual threads, each one in a slightly different shade of blue, cobalt, ink, sky, black, grey, hardly noticeable unless one adjusts the eyes to a microscopic vision. On their first night, on and under it, the fabric was still coarse, the way new linen tends to be. Now it is flowing softly through his fingers like a river in the night.

The room's only illumination is a cane lamp. He cannot remember whether they had bought it together. He would like to believe that they did ... but then again, not. That would mean that within the space of these four walls Chinky has kept alive an alternative reality where the possibility of 'them' continues to exist. He resists the urge to lift it from the nail in the wall and put it into his bag. He knows that she would not mind him 'stealing' it. But no, carrying this extra weight, even though cane weighs only as much as the empty spaces between its weaves, will only keep him tied to her.

He sighs deeply. Lost at what to do, for a moment. Sleep is obviously what he came for. But just the thought of placing his head on this, her pillow, his nose touching the places where her hair, her lips, her skin has touched it, breathing in the iridescent symphony of lavender and pepper, is dreadful. He shakes his head and grabs inside his bag. He needs to sleep, if he wakes up too late this won't be his last night in the city. If he puts the towel on top, the smell of his own shower gel will drown out, neutralize, her presence.

It is all entangled. He needs all his force to yank it out.

Plonk.

Something has hit the wall.

He bends down to pick it up, he cannot remember packing this. It is a small wooden box. Absolutely unfamiliar to him. But it's not the first time that this sort of cluelessness descends on him. An after-effect of years of abuse. He has been told to not fret over it. That just makes it worse. Still, a dark cloud is brewing inside his lower abdomen. He takes the box in his right hand and opens it with his left.

The tears well up without any bidding. They wet his pyjamas, wet the wooden box, wet the floor between his legs, as he slides down against the wall. Salt drips from the corners of his lips into his mouth; mingling with the sweet taste of the candy which Chinky has left for him.

He does not even notice his own, red, face staring back at him.

73

There is no sense of dread, no need to stay bonded to his phone screen.

Abhishek has his laptop open, trying to prove or perhaps disprove the myth perpetuated especially by the kind of people who liked to roll dried, crushed leaves into a piece of paper which they light on fire on one end – that being high makes you more creative.

Alas, the regular buzzing of his phone is a distraction. Riyan texts fast and Abhishek sees no reason to delay his replies. It is sexting, not a dance of courtship.

Riyan sends him a picture.

Abhishek shuts his laptop. It's no use. His eyes have wandered to the phone screen for good. Now relieved of the pretext of having to work, they take a leisurely look at the picture, taking in every lovely detail. How has Riyan even managed this angle? He must be really flexible.

'*You should have just stayed back,*' he writes, '*this is not fair.*'

'*You should have made me.*'

Abhishek grins, trying to think up a clever reply about free will and how Riyan should have sensed his, no, not energy, he is not going to use that word, what is another word for something Riyan should have sensed?

There is a tentative knock on his door.

Riyan?

No, it's Chinky.

"Can I sleep here tonight please?"

Abhishek stares at her, feeling suddenly as frightened as a child who has seen his parent cry.

He is not sure if he should comfort her or go hide under the bed to save himself from whatever has made her so scared.

"Yes, sure. Would you like me to sleep on the couch?"

Chinky shakes her head.

"Would you like me to make you some…" Abhishek stops. "What do you like to drink, when…"

Chinky stares at him. It takes her a long moment to gather up the leftover strength somewhere deep down inside to twist her mouth into a wry smile. "I have forgotten, but…" She closes her eyes, a soft, sad little smile plays on her lips. "But my Aita, she used to give me warm milk with turmeric."

"Coming right up then. What's an Aita?"

"She used to be my grandma."

"So, what is she now?"

Chinky shakes her head. "I don't know. I would have to ask her."

More questions will just lead to more riddles, so Abhishek, although reluctantly, leaves Chinky behind to hunt for milk and turmeric in the kitchen.

When he comes back, Chinky is standing next to the window, she is looking out, absolutely still.

She either senses his presence or she has been standing here talking to herself since he left.

"I had a best friend when I was small. But when I told my Aita about her, she said calling one friend 'best' was unfair to other friends. And anyway, all friendships and relationships are temporary. If they were meant to be permanent, our souls would have just one life, one friend, one lover, one love ... but it's not, so attachment to any one thing or person is not normal either."

She pauses. Abhishek takes that as his cue to hand her the sun-yellow milk.

"But what if the soul picks one person for all its journeys? Then is that person also temporary? She didn't tell me that. She forgot to tell me about that."

Chinky takes a sip of her milk. She is a million miles away. Abhishek can feel his stomach tightening into one big lump of dried-up clay again.

"Maybe you should ask her then."

Did he say that? He is not sure. He might have. He remembers he was casting around in his mind for something to fill the silence with. Something to make her come back and be 'normal' (*look what it has come to*) again.

But whatever he had said, it seems to have worked. Chinky looks at him. Little spots of 'expression' are already returning to her big blank face which had taken on the colour of dried leaves.

Abhishek exhales, she is still sad, but she seems to be Chinky again.

"Should we go out dancing tomorrow? You and me and that sweet little boy who came here?"

"What about your husband?"

A look of pain crushes the leafy patina on Chinky's face again.

"He doesn't like to dance. At least not in this incarnation."

74

1.20 p.m.

"Sometimes I wonder, did she even exist? She was there when I needed her and when I didn't, when I was okay, when everyone was okay … she was gone…"

Gaikwad is staring at Miss Iti. This lady has lost it. Miss Iti shakes her head, she smiles.

"I know, I'm talking like her. I seem to be doing that a lot since…" Iti trails off, staring into the distance.

"Look outside. How the light is painting all those leaves different shades of green."

The leaves where the light has decided to concentrate its force look bleached, almost translucence, like pieces of coloured glass. By contrast there are leaves where the light has decided to partner with the shadows or maybe they are vying for the same space, with the light plundering the depths of the darkness as the darkness seeks to trap all of it inside for daring to enter its boundary … those leaves are the deepest emerald, sparkling wherever light finds a way out.

Iti is mesmerized, she is reminded of the time she had gone dancing with Chinky and watched the light play hide and seek with her face.

She shuts her eyes, the insides of her eyelids have turned green, too.

"The correct lighting can make anything look dazzling." Chinky's advice, which has so often come to her advantage, rings in her ears.

Just a few hours ago, her light joined the cosmic sun.

Maybe that is why the otherwise faint monsoon sun has the strength to work its magic on this monochrome police station reality, Iti thinks, as her right eye catches the unexpected shine on the sub-inspector's metal nameplate.

"Do you believe in guardian angels?"

"Madam, we found a body. She was human."

"Hmm."

Gaikwad follows her gaze.

The stormy weather has blackened the sky, turning the window into a mirror. In its reflection, the sub-inspector can see Iti's wheatish face evenly lit by the tube light. Unmoved.

But does he really? If one stares at a mirror long enough it becomes difficult to tell reflection and reality apart. A bristling sound has filled the silence of the room, as the palm tree gently taps against the window. The wind has picked up, bending even the gulmohar's red blossoms into waving a timid greeting. Patterns skirmish across the glass, and Iti's face. Drawing a thick black line across her left eye, then brushing away; a streak of light catches the colour and plants a full happy pink onto her lips; the tree heaves, throwing shadows onto the young woman's shoulders like soft thick locks of hair. Simply by the force of nature, her expression alters. The tube light behind her head remains unmoved, like a halo, ethereal.

75

11.45 p.m.

Vincent is staring straight ahead; his face is expressionless.

"Chinky would never harm herself on purpose."

It's been a long night. He can't remember the last time he had something to eat. He *can't* eat. Why should he? With her gone. He didn't want her to put him in chains. So he removed her from his life. As much as bureaucratic procedures are capable of doing this. But he never wanted her to be separate from his soul…

"She would not do that to me," he interrupts his own thoughts. He's losing his grip. "I would have come back. She knew that. She knew everything all the time, how could she not know that she had changed me?" When he met his mother in Auroville the last time, she told him that he had changed. Become tender. She is right, though she meant 'sweet, nice, gentle' when in reality he feels like an open wound, sore, hurting, sensitive. How funny that we have the same word for virtue and pain. And that's exactly the reason why he never bothered to be virtuous. He still isn't. He is just in pain. And people are too easily satisfied with someone finally conforming that they don't bother to question the facade. If pain has made him a better human, would a noble virtuous society mean that everyone is hurting? That's just cruel. The world is fucking cruel.

Vincent is still sitting on his chair, at the police station, in Versova. Unconsciously he is drawing circles around the highlight that the fluorescent neon-light is creating on the cheaply polished wooden table.

But in his head, he can feel himself descending deeper into the rabbit hole of his own mind. His mother thinks his changed 'self' is the outcome of the year he spent at '*Land*' and the months of travelling that preceded the rehab. He had followed the route his dad had determined thirty years ago. It sounded like the kind of trip anyone would expect of him – lovechild of hippie parents goes backpacking across India. Oooh, exciting. No surprise in the itinerary here. But it wasn't about the itinerary anyway. Though only he knows that. Somewhere, deep inside, he had hoped that he might just wake up in a parallel universe, where he is eight years old again and meets a little monkey girl with an Assamese accent.

And then what? He never thought further. Would he smash the dreamcatcher back into her face? Or ask her for her address and become pen-pals? Either way, if he could turn back time … Chinky would still be alive.

"I was used to the darkness and her light frightened me, but after seeing it, how could the darkness remain comforting either?"

Vincent's words are audible only to the neon reflection on the table in front of him. He caresses the unevenness on the varnish. It wasn't his trip which magically made him realize that he has a substance issue. That thought alone is just ridiculous. Who has ever visited hippie strongholds and come out clean? Aren't they by definition the exact opposite? Yoga by the gloriously Ganga and a spliff afterwards. Suryanamaskar on top of the ruins of Hampi followed by some acid. Or why not combine the two? Enlightenment guaranteed.

No, he didn't need any of this. He had had his glimmer of enlightenment. But he wasn't equipped to deal with it. Neither was Chinky. That's the one thing she was wrong about.

"And finally, I would have had to choose because for the first time I had a choice. But it wasn't really a choice. Going back into oblivion … it just makes no sense … No, she always went to the sea when she was lost and this time, she was so lost. I think she wanted to speak to her Aita and she just went too far, she forgot to come back…"

As these thoughts take shape in his mind, Vincent's voice has again become audible.

Gaikwad looks at Vincent. He is not sure if there's anything he could say that would comfort him. He gently touches the white man on the shoulder.

"I have no more questions. You are free to leave."

Vincent's face twists into a wry smile.

"Freedom is a little overrated, isn't it?"

In this moment, his soul is free. Somewhere between the angry eight-year-old in a train compartment, the broken man dancing in a bar in Gokarna, the vulnerable lover in his goddess' arms, the solitary traveller, the forty-year-old looking for a home...

Vincent gets up, shakes hands with the both of them and leaves the room.

76

12 a.m.

"Sir, what are we going to write in the report?" For the first time today Sahil is speaking in Marathi.

"I think accidental death," Gaikwad replies in his mother tongue.

He looks pensive. He takes out his phone and taps the call directory. He dials the topmost.

"I'm sorry about today. But if you are up to it, let's just go out for a walk ... I don't know. Anywhere. I just feel like walking with you ... maybe holding your hand ... Meena? Okay, okay, I'm sorry. You're right, it's stupid. Okay, you sleep. I will see you in the morning."

Gaikwad sighs.

"Get me a cup of tea, will you? I'm feeling quite drained."

Sahil yells for a cup of tea.

Epilogue

Vincent, Abhishek and Iti are sitting at the cafe. Abhishek had suggested it. It is where Chinky had picked him up.

A blow of hot air. The AC goes on full blast. Jhansi spots them immediately. Iti hugs her. Abhishek shakes her hand. Vincent pulls a chair for her next to him. Jhansi sits down.

"Thanks for not giving the cops my contact, they would have…"

"Just harassed you, we know."

Jhansi looks at the urn on the table.

"Is that…?"

Abhishek nods. "Yes … Chinky. We are thinking what to do with the ashes. I believe that we should take them to Assam, that was her home."

"I think we need to throw it into the sea, she loved the sea." Iti taps gently with her fingers against the urn.

"I am still her husband, I want to take them with me, wherever I go."

This is going to be an ugly argument. Vincent places the urn on the floor. The four of them stare down at it, like grand marshals of a secret cult.

A muffled voice breaks the sacred silence. "Jahaan!"

The ball zooms towards the table quicker than the small boy can run. His mother barges through the glass door. But it's too late. She stops at the threshold. Frozen.

Helplessly, Iti, Abhishek, Vincent and Jhansi first see, then hear the urn topple over.

The ashes splatter across the floor before the thermic of the AC paired with the hot air outside carries them away – out into the winds of the open sky.

Silence.

Jahaan, his mother, Iti, Vincent, Abhishek and Jhansi look up at the ashes flying across the city.

"Well, now she will go where she wants."

"Imagine the view – the whole city…"

"…the beach … the big wide ocean…"

"…floating…"

"…free."

Acknowledgements

To all of you who took the time to read through the unpolished drafts of our manuscript – typos, missing commas, et al. – and gave us your thoughts, feedback and most of all, encouragement. Especially min Älskling K and Matthias Strobel, dank Dir fanden die Zweifel keinen Platz.

Aditi says a big thank you to Brayden Yoder (who found and added a lot of the commas).

We would also like to thank Patricia Galea (love your colourful post-its), Sheba Alexander, Tyler Landa, Iti Agarwal (no relation to the Iti in the book), Ritu Sehgal, and Heike Rümmler.